Praise for THE COLUMBUS AFFAIR

"Berry's imaginative mix of Judaic and Columbus lore as well as Tom's transformation from suicidal flop to heroic everyman should please his many fans."

— *Publishers Weekly*

"A thrill ride—and [Steve Berry's] best book to date."

— *The Daily Herald*

"A page-turning novel that's filled with historical truths."

— *The Huntington News*

Praise for other Steve Berry books

BY STEVE BERRY

NOVELS

The Amber Room
The Romanov Prophecy
The Third Secret
The Templar Legacy
The Alexandria Link
The Venetian Betrayal
The Charlemagne Pursuit
The Paris Vendetta
The Emperor's Tomb
The Jefferson Key
The Columbus Affair

E-BOOKS

"The Balkan Escape"
"The Devil's Gold"
"The Admiral's Mark"

THE COLUMBUS AFFAIR

A NOVEL

STEVE BERRY

BALLANTINE BOOKS • NEW YORK

A Ballantine Books International Edition

Copyright © 2012 by Steve Berry
Map copyright © 2012 by David Lindroth, Inc.
"The Admiral's Mark" copyright © 2012 by Steve Berry
Excerpt from *The King's Deception* copyright © 2012 by Steve Berry

Published by Ballantine Books, an imprint of The Random House Publishing Group, a division of Random House, Inc., New York.

BALLANTINE and colophon are registered trademarks of Random House, Inc.

A hardcover edition has been published in the United States by Ballantine Books, an imprint of The Random House Publishing Group, a division of Random House, Inc.

"The Admiral's Mark" was originally published as an eBook by Ballantine Books, an imprint of The Random House Publishing Group, a division of Random House, Inc.

This book contains an excerpt from *The King's Deception* by Steve Berry. This excerpt has been set for this edition only and may not reflect the final content of the forthcoming hardcover edition.

ISBN 978-345-53835-2
eBook ISBN 978-0-345-52653-3

Cover design: Mark J. Cohen

Printed in the United States of America

www.ballantinebooks.com

9 8 7 6 5 4 3 2 1

For Simon Lipskar, literary agent
Thank you

ACKNOWLEDGMENTS

For the 11th time, thank you Gina Centrello, Libby McQuire, Kim Hovey, Cindy Murray, Quinne Rogers, Debbie Aroff, Carole Lowenstein, Matt Schwartz, and everyone in Promotions and Sales. It doesn't seem like nine years have passed since we were working on *The Amber Room*.

To Mark Tavani, thanks for another great job.

A few special mentions: Johanna Hart who showed us Jamaica; my old friend Mikey Blount in Prague; Rupert Wallace, our expert Jamaican driver; Frank Lumsden, colonel of the Charles Town Maroons who led us on an extraordinary journey into the Blue Mountains; Richard Keene for some appreciated reconnoitering in Vienna; Chuck Watson, for insights on Florida orange groves; Morris Shamah for help with things Sephardim (though any remaining mistakes are mine); Meryl Moss and her extraordinary publicity team for all they do each day; and Jessica Johns and Esther Garver, who keep me out of trouble (which is not an easy task).

And there's my wife, Elizabeth, who's always "in the car."

The antagonist of this book is named Zachariah Simon. That label came from my agent, Simon Lipskar, incorporating his first and middle names. Simon mentioned one day that he'd love to be the bad guy in a book. But nothing more than his name is associated with the character. Simon is smart, savvy, straightforward, and widely regarded as one of the top agents in the business. He also co-heads one of the largest and best literary agencies in the world—Writers House. The birth of this stand-alone came about partly because of his advice.

I'm honored to have him on my side.

Simon, this one's for you.

For 500 years historians have pondered the question:
Who was Christopher Columbus?
The answer is simply another question:
Who do you want him to be?

—ANONYMOUS OBSERVER

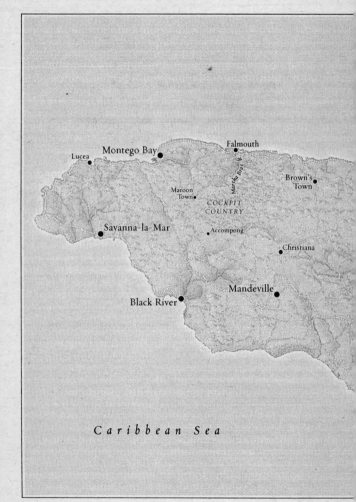

Lucea

Montego Bay

Falmouth

Brown's
Town

Maroon
Town

COCKPIT
COUNTRY

Martha Brae R.

Accompong

Savanna-la-Mar

Christiana

Black River

Mandeville

C a r i b b e a n   S e a

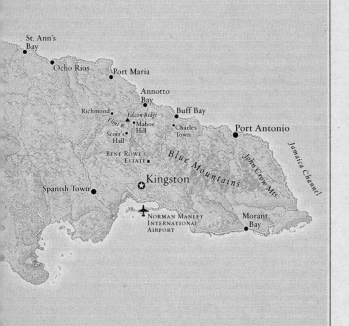

JAMAICA

St. Ann's Bay

Ocho Rios

Port Maria

Annotto Bay

Richmond

Falcon Ridge

Mahoe Hill

Buff Bay

Charles Town

Port Antonio

Flint R.

Scott's Hall

BENE ROWE'S ESTATE

Blue Mountains

John Crow Mts.

Jamaica Channel

Kingston

Spanish Town

NORMAN MANLEY INTERNATIONAL AIRPORT

Morant Bay

JAMAICA

1504 CE

PROLOGUE

CHRISTOPHER COLUMBUS REALIZED THAT THE DE-cisive moment was approaching. His party had trudged south through the lush forest of this tropical land for the past three days, steadily gaining altitude. Of all the islands he'd discovered since that first landfall in October 1492, this was the fairest his eyes had seen. A narrow plain rimmed its rocky coast. Mountains formed a misted spine, rising gradually from the west and culminating here, in the east, at the tortuous chain of peaks now surrounding him. Most of the earth was porous limestone covered by fertile red soil. An incredible array of plants flourished beneath thick stands of old-growth forest, all nourished by constant, moist winds. The natives who lived here called the place Xaymaca, which he'd learned meant "isle of springs"—apt, for water abounded everywhere. Since Castilian substituted a J for X, he'd come to call it Jamaica.

"Admiral."

He stopped and turned to face one of his men.

"It is not far," de Torres said to him, pointing ahead. "Down the ridge to the flat point, then beyond a clearing."

Luis had sailed with him on all three previous voyages, including the one in 1492 when they'd first stepped ashore. They understood and trusted each other.

He could not say the same for the six natives who carted the crates. They were heathens. He pointed at two who toted one of the smaller containers and motioned with his hands for them to be careful. He was surprised that after two years the wood was still intact. No worms had bored through, as they had last year with his ship's hull. One year he'd spent marooned on this island.

But his captivity was now over.

"You chose well," he said to de Torres in Spanish.

None of the natives could speak the language. Three more Spaniards accompanied him and Torres, each specially chosen. The locals had been conscripted, bribed with the promise of more hawk's bells—trinkets, the sound of which seemed to fascinate them—if they would but haul three crates into the mountains.

They'd begun at dawn in a wooded glade adjacent to the north shore, a nearby river pouring sparkling cold water down smooth ledges, forming pool after pool, finally making one last silvery plunge to the sea. A constant chirping of insects and the call of birds had increased in volume, now reaching a boisterous crescendo. The trudge up the wooded slope had taken effort and all of them were winded, their clothes soaked in sweat, grime layering their faces. Now they were headed back down, into a lush valley.

For the first time in a long while, he felt rejuvenated.

He loved this land.

The first voyage in 1492 had been carried out under his personal leadership, against the advice of so-called learned people. Eighty-seven men had ventured into the unknown on the strength of his dream. He'd struggled for decades to obtain the funding, first from the Portuguese, then from the Spanish. The Capitulations of Sante Fé, signed between him and the Spanish Crown, had promised him noble status, 10 percent of all riches, and control of the seas he discovered. An excellent bargain on paper, but Ferdinand and Isabella had not kept their end. For the past twelve years, after he'd established the existence of what all were calling a New World, one Spanish ship after another had sailed westward, each without permission from him as Admiral of the Ocean Sea.

Whores. Liars.

All of them.

"There," de Torres called out.

He stopped his descent and glanced through the trees past thousands of red blossoms the natives called Flame of the Forest. He spotted a clear pool, flat as glass, the roar of more active water leading in and out.

He had first visited Jamaica in May 1494, on his second voyage, and discovered that its northern coast was inhabited by the same natives found on the nearby islands, except those here were more hostile. Perhaps their proximity to the Caribs, who lived on Puerto Rico to the east, accounted for that aggressiveness. Caribs were fierce cannibals who understood only force. Learning from the past, he'd dispatched bloodhounds and bowsmen to initially deal with the Jamaicans, killing a few, savaging others, until they all became anxious to please.

He halted the caravan's advance at the pool.

De Torres approached and whispered, "It is here. The place."

He knew that this would be his last time in his New World. He was fifty-one years old and had managed to accumulate an impressive array of enemies. His experience of the past year was evidence, this fourth voyage cursed from the start. He'd first explored the coast of what he'd come to believe was a continent, its shoreline endless, extending north to south for as far as he'd sailed. After completing that reconnoiter he'd hoped to make landfall in Cuba or Hispaniola, but his worm-eaten vessels only made it as far as Jamaica, where he beached them both and awaited a rescue.

None had come.

The governor of Hispaniola, a sworn enemy, decided to let him, and his 113 men, die.

But that had not occurred.

Instead a few brave souls had rowed a canoe to Hispaniola and brought a ship back.

Yes, he had indeed amassed enemies.

They'd succeeded in negating all of the rights he once possessed from the Capitulations. He'd managed to retain his noble status and title of admiral, but they meant nothing. The colonists in Santo Domingo had even revolted and forced him to sign a humiliating settlement agreement. Four horrible years ago he was returned to Spain in chains and threatened with trial and imprisonment. But the king and queen provided an unexpected reprieve, then granted him funds and permission for a fourth crossing.

He'd wondered about their motivations.

Isabella seemed sincere. She was an adventurous soul. But the king was another matter. Ferdinand had never cared for him, openly saying that any trip across the western ocean seemed a folly.

Of course, that was before he'd succeeded.

Now all Ferdinand wanted was gold and silver.

Whores. Liars.

All of them.

He motioned for the crates to be lowered. His three men helped, as each was heavy.

"We are here," he called out in Spanish.

His men knew what to do.

Swords were drawn and the natives were quickly cut to pieces. Two groaned on the ground, but were silenced with skewers to the chest. Their killing meant nothing to him, they were unworthy to breathe the same air as Europeans. Small, copper brown, naked as the day they were born, they possessed no written language and no fervent beliefs. They lived in seaside villages and, to his observations, accomplished nothing other than growing a few crops. They were led by a man called a *cacique*, whom he'd made friends with during his marooned year. It was the *cacique* who'd granted him six men yesterday when he'd dropped anchor for the final time along the north shore.

"*A simple trek to the mountains,*" he'd told the chieftain. "*A few days' time.*"

He knew enough of their Arawak language to convey his request. The *cacique* had acknowledged that he understood and agreed, motioning toward six who would carry the crates. He'd bowed in gratitude and offered several hawk's bells as gifts. Thanks to heaven that he'd brought a quantity of them with him. In Europe they were tied to the talons of trained birds. Worthless. Here they were hard currency.

The *cacique* had accepted the payment and returned a bow.

He'd dealt with this leader twice before. They'd forged a friendship. An understanding. One he took full advantage of.

When he'd first visited the island in 1494, stopping for a day to caulk leaks in his ship and to replenish the water supply, his men had noticed fine bits of gold in the clear streams. On questioning the *cacique* he'd learned of a place where the golden grains were larger, some the size of beans.

At the place where he now stood.

But unlike the deceitful Spanish monarchy, gold did not interest him.

His purpose rose higher.

His gaze locked on de Torres and his old friend knew what was next. Sword in hand, de Torres pointed the blade at one of the three Spaniards, this man short and stumpy with a grizzly face.

"To your knees," de Torres ordered as he relieved the man of his weapon.

Two other crewmen raised their swords in support.

The prisoner knelt.

Columbus faced him. "Did you think me so stupid?"

"Admiral—"

He raised a hand for silence. "Four years ago they returned me to Spain in chains and stripped me of all that was rightfully mine. Then, just as suddenly, it was restored." He paused. "With but a few words, the king and queen pardoned me for all that I supposedly had done. Did they think me ignorant?" He hesitated again. "They did. And that is the greatest insult of all. Years I begged for funds to sail the ocean. Years, I was refused. Yet with one letter to the Crown, I was granted the money for this fourth voyage. One request, and all was provided. I knew then something was wrong."

Swords continued to be held close. Nowhere for the captive to go.

"You are a spy," Columbus said. "Sent here to report back on what I do."

The sight of this fool disgusted him. The man represented all of the treachery and misery he'd been forced to endure at the hands of Spanish liars.

"Ask the question that your benefactors want to know," Columbus demanded.

The man stayed silent.

"Ask it, I say." His voice rose. "I command you."

"Who are you to command anything?" the spy said. "You are not a man of Christ."

He absorbed the insult with the patience that a hard life had provided. But he saw that his compatriots were not as forgiving.

He pointed to them. "These men are not of Christ, either."

The prisoner spit on the ground.

"Was your mission to report back all that occurred on the voyage? Were these crates we have here today their goal? Or is it simply gold they are after?"

"You have not been truthful."

He laughed. "I have not been truthful?"

"The Holy Mother Church will see your eternal damnation in the fires of hell."

Then he realized. This agent was from the Inquisition.

The greatest enemy of all.

A fire of self-preservation rose within him. He caught the concern in de Torres' eyes. He'd known since they'd left Spain, two years ago, of this problem. But were there more eyes and ears? The Inquisition had burned people by the thousands. He hated all that it represented.

What he was completing here today had been designed solely to thwart that evil.

De Torres had already told him that he would not risk being discovered by any Spanish examiners. He would not be returning to Europe. He intended on settling in Cuba, a much larger island to the north. The other two men holding swords, younger, more eager, had likewise made their decisions to stay. He should, too, but his place was not here, though he wished things could be different.

He glared down.

"The English and Dutch call me Columbus. The French, Columb. The Portuguese, Colom. Spaniards know me as Colón. But none of those is my birth name. Unfortunately, you will never know my true name and you will not be making a report to your benefactors waiting in Spain."

He motioned and de Torres plunged his sword into the man's chest.

The prisoner had no time to react.

The blade was yanked free with a sickening sound and the body hinged forward at the knees, slamming face-first to the ground.

A growing pool of blood stained the earth.

He spit on the corpse, as did the others.

He hoped that would be the last man he would see die. He was tired of killing. Since he would shortly return to his ship and leave this land forever, there would be no repercussions from the *cacique* for the six deaths. Others would pay that price, but that was not his concern. They were all enemies and he wished them nothing but pain.

He turned and finally studied where he stood, catching every detail that had been described.

"You see, Admiral," de Torres said. "It is as if God Himself directed us here."

His old friend was right.

It did seem that way.

Be as courageous as a leopard, as light as an eagle, as fast as a deer, and as strong as a lion to do the will of your Father in heaven.

Wise words.

"Come," he said to the others. "Let us pray that the secret of this day will long stay hidden."

CHAPTER ONE

TOM SAGAN GRIPPED THE GUN. HE'D THOUGHT ABOUT this moment for the past year, debating the pros and cons, finally deciding that one pro outweighed all cons.

He simply did not want to live any longer.

He'd once been an investigative reporter for the *Los Angeles Times,* knocking down a solid six-figure salary, his marquee byline generating one front-page, above-the-fold story after another. He'd worked all over the world—Sarajevo, Beijing, Johannesburg, Belgrade, and Moscow. But the Middle East became his specialty, a place he came to know intimately, where his reputation had been forged. His confidential files were once filled with hundreds of willing sources, people who knew he'd protect them at all costs. He'd proved that when he spent eleven days in a DC jail for failing to reveal his source on a story about a corrupt Pennsylvania congressman.

That man had gone to prison.

Tom had received his third Pulitzer nomination.

There were twenty-one awarded categories. One was for "distinguished investigative reporting by an individual or team, reported as a single newspaper article or a series." Winners received a certificate, $10,000, and the ability to add three precious words—*Pulitzer Prize winner*—to their names.

He won his.

But they took it back.

Which seemed the story of his life.

Everything had been taken back.

His career, his reputation, his credibility, even his self-respect. In the end he became a failure as a son, a father, a husband, a reporter, and a friend. A few weeks ago he'd charted that spiral on a pad, identifying that it all started when he was twenty-five, fresh out of the University of Florida, top third of his class, a journalism degree in hand.

Then his father disowned him.

Abiram Sagan had been unrelenting.

"We all make choices. Good. Bad. Indifferent. You're a grown man, Tom, and have made yours. Now I have to make mine."

And that he had.

On that same pad he'd jotted down the highs and lows. Some from before, as editor of his high school paper and campus reporter at college. Most after. His rise from news assistant, to staff reporter, to senior international correspondent. The awards. Accolades. Respect from his peers. How had one observer described his style? *"Wide-ranging and prescient reporting conducted at great personal risk."*

Then his divorce.

The estrangement from his only child. Poor investment decisions. Even poorer life decisions.

Finally, his firing.

Eight years ago.

And the seemingly nothing life since.

Most of his friends were gone. But that was as much his fault as theirs. As his personal depression had deepened he'd withdrawn into himself. Amazing he hadn't turned to alcohol or drugs, but neither had ever appealed to him.

Self-pity was his intoxicant.

He stared around at the house's interior.

He'd decided to die, here, in his parents' home. Fitting, in some morbid way. Thick layers of dust and a musty smell reminded him that for three years the rooms had sat empty. He'd kept the utilities on, paid the meager taxes, and had the lawn cut just enough so the neighbors wouldn't complain. Earlier, he'd noticed that the sprawling mulberry tree out front needed trimming, the picket fence painting.

He hated it here. Too many ghosts.

He walked the rooms, remembering happier days. In the kitchen he could still see the jars of his mother's jam that once lined the windowsill. The thought of her brought a wave of an unusual joy that quickly faded.

He should write a note and explain himself, blame somebody or something. But to who? Or what? Nobody would believe him if he told them the truth. Unfortunately, just like eight years ago, there was no one to blame but himself.

Would anyone even care he was gone?

Certainly not his daughter. He hadn't spoken to her in two years.

His literary agent? Maybe. She'd made a lot of money off his ghostwriting. He'd been shocked to learn how many so-called bestselling fiction writers could not write a word. What had one critic said at the time of his downfall? *"Journalist Sagan seems to have a promising career ahead of him writing fiction."*

Asshole.

But he'd actually taken that advice.

He wondered—how do you explain taking your own life? It is, by definition, an irrational act. Which, by definition, defies explanation. Hopefully, somebody would bury him. He had plenty of money in the bank, more than enough for a respectable funeral.

What would it be like to be dead?

Were you aware? Could you hear? See? Smell? Or was it simply an eternal blackness. No thoughts. No feeling.

Nothing at all.

He walked back toward the front of the house.

Outside was a glorious March day, the noontime sun bright. Florida was truly blessed with some terrific weather. Like California, without the earthquakes, where he lived before his firing. He'd miss the feel of a warm sun on a pleasant summer's day.

He stopped in the open archway and stared at the parlor. That was what his mother had always called the room. This was where his parents had gathered on Shabbat. Where Abiram read from the Torah. The place where Yom Kippur and Holy Days had been recognized. He recalled the sight of the pewter menorah on the far table burning. His parents had been devout Jews. After his bar mitzvah he, too, had first studied the Torah, standing before the twelve-paned windows, framed out by damask curtains his mother had taken months to sew. She'd been talented with her hands, a lovely woman, universally adored. He missed her. She died six years before Abiram, who'd now been gone three.

Time to end this.

He studied the gun, a pistol bought a few months before at an Orlando gun show, and sat on the sofa. Clouds of dust rose, then settled. He recalled Abiram's lecture about the birds and the bees as he'd sat in the same spot. He'd been, what, twelve?

Thirty-eight years ago.

But it seemed like last week.

As usual, the explanations had been rough and concise.

"*Do you understand?*" Abiram asked him. "*It's important that you do.*"

"*I don't like girls.*"

"*You will. So don't forget what I said.*"

Women. Another failure. He'd had precious few relationships as a young man, marrying Michele, the first girl who'd shown serious interest in him. But the marriage ended after his firing, and there'd been no more women since the downfall. Michele had taken a toll on him.

"Maybe I'll get to see her soon, too," he muttered.

His ex-wife had died two years ago in a car crash.

That was the last time he and his daughter spoke, her words loud and clear. "*Get out. She would not want you here.*"

And he'd left the funeral.

He stared again at the gun, his finger on the trigger. He steeled himself, grabbed a breath, and nestled the barrel to his temple. He was left-handed, like nearly every Sagan. His uncle, a former professional baseball player, had told him as a child that if he could learn to throw a curveball he'd make a fortune in the major leagues. Talented left-handers were rare.

But he'd failed at sports, too.

He brought the barrel to his temple.

The metal touched his skin.

He closed his eyes and tightened his finger on the trigger, imagining how his obituary would start. *Tuesday, March 5, former investigative journalist Tom Sagan took his own life at his parents' home in Mount Dora, Florida.*

A little more pressure and—

Rap. Rap. Rap.

He opened his eyes.

A man stood outside the front window, close enough to the panes for Tom to see the face—older than himself, clean-cut, distinguished—and the man's right hand.

Which held a photograph, pressed to the glass.

He focused on the image of a young woman lying down, arms and feet extended.

As if bound.

He knew the face.

His daughter.

Alle.

CHAPTER TWO

ALLE BECKET LAY ON THE BED, ARMS AND FEET TIED
to the rails. A strip of tape sealed her mouth, which
forced her to breathe rapidly through her nose. The
small room was dark and unnerved her.

Calm down, she told herself.

Her thoughts centered on her father.

Thomas Peter Sagan.

Their last names were different thanks to a marriage she'd tried three years ago, just after her grandfather, Abiram, had died. Bad idea all the way around,
especially when her new husband decided that a ring
on his finger entitled him to carte blanche use of her
credit cards. The marriage had lasted ninety days.
The divorce took another thirty. Paying off those bal-
ances required two years.

But she'd done it.

Her mother taught her that owing people was not
a good thing. She liked to think that her mother had
provided her with character. God knows it had not
come from her father. Her memories of him were
terrible. She was twenty-five years old and could not
remember a single time the man had ever said he
loved her.

"Why did you marry him?"

"We were young, Alle, and in love, and we had many

good years together before the bad ones came. It was a secure life."

Not until her own marriage had she understood the value of security. *Utter turmoil* was a better description for that short union. All she took away was the last name, because anything was better than Sagan. Simply hearing it turned her stomach. If she was going to be reminded of failure, at least let it be of an ex-husband who had, on occasion—especially during those six days in the Turks and Caicos—provided lasting memories.

She tested the restraints holding her arms. Her muscles ached. She worked out the kinks and readjusted herself. An open window allowed cool air inside, but sweat beaded her brow and the back of her shirt was damp against the bare mattress. The few lingering smells were not pleasant, and she wondered who else had lain here before her.

She did not like the feeling of helplessness her predicament provided.

So she forced her mind back to her mother, a loving woman who'd doted on her and made sure she'd earned the grades necessary to make it into Brown University, then graduate school. History had always been a passion, especially post-Columbus America, the time between 1492 and 1800, when Europe forced the Old World onto the New.

Her mother had also personally excelled, recovering from the hurt of the divorce and finding a new husband. He'd been an orthopedic surgeon, a loving man who'd cared for them both, 180 degrees away from her father.

That marriage had been a success.

But two years ago a careless driver with a suspended license ran a stop sign and ended her mother's life.

She missed her terribly.

The funeral remained vivid in her mind, thanks to her father's unexpected appearance.

"Get out. She wouldn't want you here," she told him loudly enough for the mourners to hear.

"I came to say goodbye."

"You did that long ago when you wrote us both off."

"You have no idea what I did."

"You only get one chance to raise your child. To be a husband. A father. You blew yours. Leave."

She recalled his face. The blank expression that revealed little about what lay beneath. As a youngster she'd always wondered what he thought.

Not anymore. What did it matter?

She tugged again at the restraints.

Actually, it might matter a great deal.

CHAPTER THREE

BÉNE ROWE LISTENED FOR HIS DOGS, PRIZED BLOOD-hounds of expensive stock. They were first imported to Jamaica from Cuba three hundred years ago, descendants of hounds ferried across the Atlantic by Columbus. One celebrated story told of how, during Ferdinand and Isabella's successful fight to retake Grenada from the Moors, the great beasts had feasted on Arab children abandoned at the doors of mosques. That supposedly happened barely a month before the bastard Columbus first sailed to America.

And changed everything.

"*Da* dogs are close," he said to his companions, both trusted lieutenants. "Mighty close. Hear the bark. It quickens." He flashed a smile of shiny white teeth, on which he'd spent a lot of money. "*Dem* like it when the end nears."

He mixed his English with patois, knowing that his men were more comfortable with the common dialect—a mutilation of English, African, and Arawak. He preferred proper English, a habit ingrained into him during his school days and insisted upon by his mother. A bit uncommon for him and her since, generally, they liked the old ways.

His two men carried rifles as they trudged the Jamaican high ground into what the Spanish had named the Sierras de Bastidas—fortified mountains. His ancestors, runaway slaves, had used the hills as a fortress against their former masters. They'd called themselves Katawud, Yenkunkun, Chankofi. Some say the Spanish named those fugitives *cimarrons*—untamed, wild—or *marrans,* the label given to hunters of sows and hogs. Others credited the French word *marron,* which meant "runaway slave." No matter the source, the English eventually mangled the word into Maroons.

Which stuck.

Those industrious people built towns named for their founders—Trelawny, Accompong, Scott's Hall, Moore, and Charles. They mated with native Taino women and forged paths through virgin wilderness, fighting pirates who raided Jamaica with regularity.

The mountains became their home, the forests their allies.

"I hear Big Nanny," he told them. "That high yelp. It's her. She be a leader. Always has been."

He'd named her for Grandy Nanny, a Maroon chieftainess of the 18th century who became a great spiritual and military leader. Her likeness now appeared on the Jamaican $500 note, though its image was purely imaginative. No accurate description or portrait of her existed—only legends.

He envisioned the scene half a kilometer away. The dogs—equal to the mastiff in bulk, the bloodhound in agility, and the bulldog in courage—red, tawny, and spotted with bristled coats, running aligned, all four behind Big Nanny. She never allowed any of the males to dart ahead, and, as with her namesake before her, none challenged her authority. One that tried had ended up with a broken neck from her powerful jaws.

He stopped on the edge of a high ridge and surveyed the distant mountainsides covered in trees. Blue mahoe dominated, along with rose apple, mahogany, teak, screw pine, and thick stands of bamboo. He caught sight of a fig tree, tough and stubborn, and recalled what his mother had taught him. *"The fig dominates. It says to those who challenge it, 'My will to power rests in your will to endure.'"*

He admired that strength.

He spotted a group of workers on one of the mountainsides, arranged in a line, swinging picks and hoes, tools flashing in the sun. He imagined himself here three hundred years ago, one of Columbus' misnamed Indians, toiling for the Spanish in slavery. Or a hundred years later, an African subrogated for life to an English plantation owner.

That had been the Maroons—a mixture of the original Tainos and the imported Africans.

Like himself.

"Yu wi go toward 'em?" his chief lieutenant asked.

He knew his man feared the dogs but hated drug dons, too. Jamaica was overwrought with criminal filth. The don presently half a kilometer away, being hunted by a fierce pack of Cuban bloodhounds, thought himself immune to authority. His armed henchmen had turned Kingston into a war zone, killing several innocents in the cross fire. The last straw was when a public hospital and school came under fire, patients forced to cower under their beds, students taking their exams with bullets whizzing outside. So he'd lured the don to a meeting—a summons from Béne Rowe was never ignored—then brought him into the mountains.

"A wa yu a say?" the insolent don asked in patois.

"Speak English."

"You ashamed of who you are, Béne?"

"Ashamed of you."

"What do you plan to do? Hunt me down?"

"A no mi." *Not me.*

He intentionally switched to patois to let this man know that he remembered from where he came. He pointed to the dogs baying in their cages atop the trucks. "Dem *will do* dat *for me.*"

"*And what will you do? Kill me?*"

He shook his head. "Da *dogs will do* dat, *too.*"

He smiled at how much the bastard's eyes had widened, pleased to know that someone who murdered for little or no reason actually knew fear.

"*You're not one of us,*" *the don spit out.* "*You forgot who you are, Béne.*"

He stepped close, stopping a few inches away from an open silk shirt, tailored trousers, and expensive loafers. He supposed the ensemble was intended to impress, but little about this fool did. He was thin as sugarcane, with one bright and one glassy eye, and a mouthful of bad teeth.

"*You're nothing,*" *he told the don.*

"*I'm enough you think I should die.*"

He chuckled. "*That you are. And if I thought you worthy of respect, I would shoot you. But you're an animal, one the dogs will enjoy hunting.*"

"*The government pay you to do this, Béne? They can't do it, so they get you to?*"

"*I do it for me.*"

The police had tried to arrest the no-good twice, but riots in Kingston had broken out each time. So sad that criminals had become heroes, but the dons were smart. As the Jamaican government failed to care for its citizens the dons had stepped in, handing out food, building community centers, providing medical care, ingratiating themselves.

And it worked.

People were willing to riot in order to prevent their benefactors from being jailed.

"You have thirty minutes before I open the cages."

The man had lingered, then realized this was serious and fled.

Just like a slave escaping his master.

He savored a lungful of the clean, mountain air. Rings of azure haze, thick as milk, had settled around the far peaks. Three topped 2,000 meters, one nearly 2,500. They ranged east to west, separating Kingston from the north coast. So prominent had been their foggy halo the English had renamed them the Blue Mountains.

His two men stood beside him, rifles resting on their shoulders.

"The other problem of the day," he said, keeping his gaze outward. "Is he coming?"

"On *da* way. They'll wait at *da* trucks until we ready."

All of the land for kilometers in every direction belonged to him. Most Maroons farmed a few square meters of somebody else's property, paying a yearly stipend for the privilege. Now he owned tens of thousands of acres and allowed them to work it for free.

The dogs continued to bark in the distance.

He checked his watch.

"Big Nanny is gettin' close. She rarely lets the bait run more than an hour."

Fierce, long-legged, and blessed with amazing endurance and strength, his hounds were well trained. They were also skilled climbers, capable of scaling tall trees, as today's target would shortly discover if he foolishly thought high branches would offer him security.

Cuban bloodhounds had been bred long ago for one purpose.

Hunting black fugitives.

His were more progressive and hunted both black

and white. But like their ancestors, they killed only if the prey resisted. Otherwise they confronted, barked, and terrified, holding the target for their master's arrival.

"We'll move toward them," he said.

He led the way back into the forest. No trail existed, just dense and healthy vegetation. One of his men produced a *machet* and hacked a path. With that word he always reverted to patois and left the *e* off the end. Funny how with some things he could not help himself.

A wind snarled its way through the branches.

How easy it would be to hide amid these ferns and orchids. No one would ever find you. Which was why the British had finally imported the hounds to hunt their runaways.

Scent knew no boundaries.

They plunged on in the direction of the dogs. His man with the *machet* advanced, hacking the foliage. Thin slices of bright sunlight found the earth.

"Béne," his other man called out.

A thick carpet of leaves provided a springy softness to every step, which also allowed songbirds to be heard. Rocks and stones beneath the mulch worked his soles, but he'd worn heavy boots. He fought his way through the low-hanging limbs and found his men at a patch of cleared ground. A rose-colored ibis sprang from one of the far trees, its wings flapping as they grabbed air. Orchids colored the clearing beneath a canopy of high limbs.

He spotted rubble scattered among the ground ferns.

The dogs had started to howl.

Signaling success.

They'd cornered the prey.

He stepped close and bent down, examining the

stones, some larger and embedded in the earth, others mere pieces. Lichens and mold infected the surfaces, but the faint outline of what had once been letters could be seen.

He recognized the script.

Hebrew.

"There are more," his men said, as they'd fanned out.

He stood, knowing what they'd found.

Tombstones.

A cemetery they'd not known existed.

He chuckled and smiled. "Oh, it is a good day, my friends. A good day. We have stumbled upon a treasure."

He thought of Zachariah Simon, and knew he would be pleased.

CHAPTER FOUR

ZACHARIAH SIMON STEPPED INSIDE THE HOUSE. TOM Sagan waited, still holding the pistol. Zachariah recalled the background report he'd commissioned, its notation that this man was left-handed.

"Who are you?" Sagan asked.

He introduced himself and offered a handshake, which was refused. Instead he was asked, "What are you doing here?"

"I've been watching you for several days." He motioned toward the gun. "Perhaps it is good I came along."

"That picture. It's my daughter."

He held out the image for them both to see. "She is my prisoner." He watched for a reaction. Seeing none, he asked, "Do you care?"

"Of course I care. And I have a gun."

Sagan brandished the weapon, and Zachariah took stock of his adversary. Tall, with a boyish, unshaven face hardened by dark eyes that seemed quick and observant. Short black hair that he envied, since his own had long ago betrayed him. Little evidence of physical exertion could be seen in the arms or chest, another detail the report had noted with the concise *"doesn't do laps or crunches."* Still, Tom Sagan was remarkably trim for a sedentary man fifty years old.

"Mr. Sagan, there is something I need you to understand. It is vitally important that you believe me when I say this." He paused. "I do not care if you kill yourself. It is your life to do with as you please. But I do require something from you before you do that."

Sagan pointed the gun straight at him. "We're going to the police."

He shrugged. "That is your choice. But I must tell you that nothing will happen except your daughter will experience unimaginable agony." He held the photo of Alle Becket higher for Sagan to see. "You must believe me. If you do not do as I ask, your daughter will suffer."

Sagan stood silent.

"You doubt me. I see it in your eyes. Perhaps as you once doubted a source telling you something that could make for an incredible story. You had to constantly wonder. Was it true? Embellished? Or outright false? Considering what ultimately happened to you, it is understandable you would now doubt me. Here I am, a total stranger, who shows up at this most inopportune moment, making outlandish claims."

He slipped the black Tumi travel bag from his shoulder. Sagan continued to aim the gun. He unsnapped the clasps and found his iPad.

"I need to show you something. After watching, if you still want to involve the police, I will not interfere."

He laid the satchel down on the floor and activated the screen.

———

LIGHT BLINDED ALLE'S EYES. BRIGHT. SINGULAR. Focused on her as she lay tied to the bed. She squinted and allowed her burning pupils to adjust, finally focusing on the now lit room.

She spotted the camera. Just to the right of the flood lamp, supported on a tripod, the lens pointed at her. A tiny red indicator signaled that it was capturing her image. She'd been told that when that happened her father would be watching. She tugged at her restraints with her arms and legs, raising her neck, angling her head toward the lens.

She hated the feeling of confinement. The loss of freedom. A total dependency on someone else. If her nose itched, there'd be no way to scratch it. If her shirt came askew, no way to adjust it. If bad people tried to do bad things to her, no way to stop them.

Two men approached the bed, from beyond the lamp's glow.

One was tall, thick through the waist, with a thin nose and equally thin lips. He appeared to be Italian or Spanish, his oily hair dark and curly. She'd learned that his name was Rócha. The other man was the blackest she'd ever seen. He had a bulbous nose and yellowed teeth, and eyes like drops of crude oil. He never spoke and she only knew him by the nickname Rócha used.

Midnight.

Both men approached the bed, one on either side, the camera and her between them. Rócha bent close, a few inches from her face, and gently caressed her cheek. His fingers smelled of citrus. She shook her head in protest, but he only smiled and continued his stroking. Midnight, too, climbed onto the bed, his right hand cupping her breast through her shirt.

She reacted to the violation, her eyes alight with fear and anger.

Rócha shoved her head back onto the mattress.

A knife appeared in his hand, glistening in the flood lamp.

The camera continued to record every moment of their assault, the red dot signaling that her father could see. Two years they hadn't spoken. For her, she had no father. Her stepfather had always been there for her. She called him Dad and he called her daughter.

An illusion?

Sure.

But one that worked.

Rócha shifted to the foot of the bed and grasped her left shoe. He slipped the knife inside her pant leg and slit the cloth up to her waist.

Midnight chuckled.

She raised her head and glanced down.

The cut ended at her waist.

Bare skin lay exposed.

Rócha plunged a hand into the tear and made his way toward her crotch. She protested, yanking on the restraints, shaking her head. He tossed the knife to Midnight, who brought the blade to her throat and ordered her to lie still.

She decided to comply.

But before doing so, she locked her gaze on the camera, the meaning in her wild eyes unmistakable.

For once in your sorry life, help your daughter.

CHAPTER FIVE

TOM STARED AT THE iPAD, ALLE'S PANICKED GAZE from the feed piercing his soul.

He aimed the gun at Zachariah Simon.

"All that will do," his visitor said, "is speed the rape of your daughter. They will ravage her, and you will be responsible."

He watched on the screen as the black man slit Alle's other pant leg up to the waist.

"You are a troubled man," Simon said to him. "Once a respected journalist, a premier international reporter. Then, total disgrace. A story you fabricated. Nonexistent sources, imaginary documentation. Not a word could be substantiated, and you were revealed to be a fraud."

The muscles in his throat knotted. "Anybody can surf the Internet."

Simon chuckled. "Is that what you think? That I am so shallow? I assure you, Mr. Sagan, I have spent a great deal of energy looking into you. Now you are a purveyor of fiction. You ghostwrite novels for others. Several of which have become bestsellers. How does it feel for someone else to claim your success as their own?"

On the screen both men were taunting Alle. He could see their lips moving though no sound came from the muted speaker.

He trained the gun on Simon, who gestured with the iPad.

"You can shoot me. But what of her?"

"What do you want?"

"First, I need you to believe me when I say that I will harm your daughter. Do you?"

His left hand kept the gun leveled, but his gaze darted back to the screen. Both men were exploring areas that the slits in Alle's pants had made readily accessible.

It had to stop.

"Second," Simon said. "I require a task from you. After that, your daughter will be released and you may finish what I interrupted here this afternoon."

"What task?" he demanded.

"I need your father's body exhumed."

―――――

THE FLOOD LAMP EXTINGUISHED, AS DID THE RED light on the camera. Alle lay back on the bed, freed from the cocoon of illumination.

Another light came on. Less bright, but enough to expose the room.

Rócha sat beside her.

Sweat soaked her brow.

The first communication with her father in two years had ended.

Rócha stared down at her, the knife now back in his hand. Midnight stood beside the camera. Both of her legs could be seen from the slits, but at least their hands were not on her.

"Shall we continue?" Rócha asked, a touch of Portuguese in his voice.

She bore her gaze into him and fought the urge not to shake from fear.

"I guess not," he said, adding a smile.

He cut away the restraints on her arms, then the ones for her legs. She sat up and stripped the tape from her mouth, telling herself to handle these men carefully. "Was all that necessary?"

"You like?" Rócha asked, clearly proud of himself.

She'd told them to be convincing, even suggested using a knife. But she'd never mentioned anything about slitting her clothes and groping her body.

But what did she expect?

These men were undisciplined opportunists, and she'd presented them with a golden opportunity.

She stood and stripped the bindings from her wrists and ankles. She just wanted to leave. "You made the point. We're done."

Midnight said nothing, nor did he act particularly interested. He never did. He was a quiet sort that seemed to do only what he was told.

Rócha was the one in charge.

At least while Zachariah was gone.

She wondered about what was happening in Florida, at her grandfather's house in Mount Dora. The call had come less than an hour ago from Zachariah, saying that her father had driven there from Orlando, a thirty-minute trek east on Interstate 4, one she'd made many times.

Then, another call.

Her father had a gun and seemed about to kill himself. For an instant that had bothered her. No matter what had happened between them, he was still her father. But showing that man compassion was what had gotten her heart broken time after time.

Better to leave the wall up.

She rubbed her sore wrists.

Her nerves were frayed.

She caught both men admiring her bare legs, which protruded from the mutilated pants.

"Why not stay?" Rócha asked. "We can finish the performance. Without the camera."

"I don't think so," she said. "I've had enough acting for one day."

CHAPTER SIX

TOM WAS PERPLEXED. "WHY WOULD YOU WANT THAT body exhumed?"

The video feed from the iPad had stopped, the screen once again black.

"My associates are awaiting a call from me. If that is not received in the next few minutes, then the suffering of your daughter will begin. The video was to make clear the situation." Simon motioned at the gun. "May I have that."

He wondered, what *would* happen if he just let the police handle this?

About as much as what happened eight years ago, when he'd needed them to do their job.

Not a damn thing.

He handed over the weapon.

Interesting how defeatism worked. Back in the days when he roamed the world for the next big story, he never would have been cowed by someone like this. Confidence and audacity had been his trademarks.

But they'd also been his downfall.

He'd been a moment away from ending his life, lying on the floor with a hole in his head. Instead he was staring at a man, neat as a bird, who seemed about fifty years old, his hair a mixture of silver and black. The face contained hints of East European, confirmed by high cheekbones, a ruddy tone, full beard, and deep-set eyes. He knew the look. He'd seen it many times in that part of the world. One trait he'd mastered as a reporter had been the rapid assessment of people. Their looks. Habits. Mannerisms.

This one smiled a lot.

Not to convey amusement, more to help make his point.

He was pleased that some of the skills acquired in his former profession had bubbled back to the surface.

They hadn't appeared in a long while.

"Your father died three years ago," Simon said. "He lived here, in this house, until that day. Did you know that your father was an important man?"

"He was a music teacher."

"And that is not important?"

"You know what I mean."

"Your father taught for most of his adult life. Your grandfather, though, on your mother's side, was a most interesting personality. He was an archaeologist, involved with some of the great digs in Palestine during the early 20th century. I read about him."

So had Tom. Marc Eden Cross, whom he'd called Saki, had worked many digs. He recalled, as a child, listening to stories of those exploits. Not all that exciting, really. Archaeology was nothing like what George Lucas and Steven Spielberg made it out to be. In fact, it was a lot like journalism, where the vast majority of the work was done alone at a desk.

Simon surveyed the parlor, walking around admiring the dusty furnishings. "Why did you preserve this house?"

"Who said I did?"

Simon faced him. "Come now, Mr. Sagan. Is this not a time to be honest? Your father deeded this property to you. In fact, it was all he left you. Everything else he owned went to your daughter. Which was not much. What? A hundred thousand dollars, a car, a few stocks, some life insurance."

"I see you visited the probate court."

Simon smiled again. "There are inventories the law requires to be filed. Your daughter was named the estate's administrator."

Like he wanted to be reminded of that insult. He'd been expressly excluded from the will, all legal responsibility passing a generation. He'd attended the funeral but stayed out of the way, doing nothing expected of a Jewish son. He and Alle had not spoken.

"Your father," Simon said, "transferred title to this house to you five weeks before he died. You and he had not spoken in a long time. Why do you think he did that?"

"Maybe he just wanted me to have it."

"I doubt that."

He wondered how much this stranger actually did know.

"Your father was a devout Jew. He cared for his religion and his heritage."

"How would you know?"

"I have spoken to people who knew him. He was a follower of the Torah, a friend of his synagogue, a supporter of Israel, though he himself never visited the Holy Land. You, on the other hand, are quite familiar with the region."

Yes, he was. The final three years of his career had been spent there. He'd filed hundreds of stories. One of the last exposed a rape committed by a former Israeli president that made headlines around the world and ultimately led to the man's imprisonment. He re-called how, when all of the bad things happened later, the pundits wondered how much of that story had been fabricated.

Pundits. People who made a living finding fault. Didn't matter what, they had an opinion, which was never good. Pundits had reveled in his downfall, con-demning him as a journalist who decided that the news itself wasn't good enough.

Better to make up your own.

He wished it had been that simple.

"Why does my family interest you so much?"

Simon pointed a finger his way. He noticed the per-fect cuticles and manicured nails. "Probing like a journalist again? Hoping to learn something? Not today. All you need to know, Mr. Sagan, is that your daughter is in grave danger."

"What if I don't care?" He thought some bravado might be good for them both.

"Oh, you care. We both know that. Otherwise, you would have pulled the trigger while you still held the gun. You see, that is the thing about children. No matter how much we disappoint them or they us, they are still our children. We *have* to care for them. Like with your father. You and he had barely spoken in twenty years, yet he left you this house. That fasci-nates me."

The man called Simon walked toward the pewter menorah on the far table and lightly stroked the dulled metal. "Your father was a Jew. As was your mother. Both proud of who they were. Unlike you, Mr. Sagan. You care nothing about from where you came."

He resented the condescending attitude. "Comes with a lot of baggage."

"No, it comes with pride. We, as a people, have

endured the greatest of suffering. That means something. At least to me it does."

Had he heard right?

His visitor turned toward him.

"Yes, Mr. Sagan. Me being a Jew is exactly why I am here."

CHAPTER SEVEN

BÉNE STOOD IN WHAT HAD ONCE BEEN A JEWISH CEM-
etery. How long ago? Hard to say. He'd counted fifteen markers cracked to rubble, others lying embedded.
Sunlight fluttered through the thick canopy of trees
casting dancing shadows. One of his men had stayed
with him, and the other, who'd gone in search of the
dogs, now returned through the foliage.

"Big Nanny and her clan did the job," his man
called out. "They cornered him near a bluff, but he
stayed still."

"You shoot him?" he asked his man.

A nod confirmed what a gunshot a few moments
ago had already told him. This time the prey had not
resisted.

"Good riddance," he said. "This island is free of
one more stinkin' parasite."

He'd read with disgust newspaper articles about
drug dons who imagined themselves Robin Hoods,
stealing from the rich, giving to the poor. They were
nothing close to that. Instead, they extorted money
from struggling business owners so they could grow
marijuana and import cocaine. Their soldiers were
the most willing and ignorant they could find, de-
manding little, doing as told. In the slums of West
Kingston, and the bowels of Spanish Town, they ruled

as gods but, here, in the Blue Mountains, they were nothing.

"Do we let *dem* know how he's gone?" one of his men asked.

"Of course. We send a message."

His chief lieutenant understood and gestured to the other man. "Fetch *da* head."

"Yes, indeed," Béne said, with a laugh. "Fetch *da* head. That will make our point. We would not want to waste this opportunity."

A dead drug don no longer concerned him. Instead, his attention was on what he'd accidentally discovered.

He knew some.

At first only Christians were allowed in the New World, but as Spanish Catholics proved inept at colonization the Crown turned to the one group who could produce results.

The Jews.

And they did, coming to Jamaica, becoming merchants and traders, exploiting the island's prime location. By 1600 the native Tainos were nearly wiped out, and most of the Spanish colonists had fled for other islands. What remained were Jews. Béne had attended a private high school in Kingston, started by Jews centuries ago. He'd excelled at languages, math, and history. He became a student of the Caribbean and quickly learned that to understand his home he had to appreciate its past.

The year 1537 changed everything.

Columbus was long dead and his heirs had sued the Spanish Crown, claiming a breach of the Capitulations of Santa Fé, which supposedly granted the family perpetual control over the New World.

A bold move, he'd always thought.

Suing a king.

But he could appreciate such nerve, something akin to kidnapping a drug don and hunting him with dogs.

The lawsuit dragged on for decades until 1537, when the widow of one of Columbus' two sons settled the fight on behalf of her eight-year-old son, the next direct Columbus heir, agreeing to drop all legal actions in return for one thing.

Jamaica.

The Spanish were thrilled. By then the island was deemed a nuisance, since little precious metals had been found. Béne had always admired that widow. She knew exactly what she wanted, and she obtained both the island and something else of even greater importance.

Power over the church.

Catholics in Jamaica would be under the control of the Columbus family, not the king. And for the next century, they kept the Inquisition out.

That's why the Jews came.

Here no one would burn them for being heretics. No one would steal their property. No laws would restrict their lives or their movements.

They were free.

He stared over at his men and called out, "Simon will have to see this. Take some photos."

He watched as one of his men obeyed.

"Oh, Mrs. Columbus," he whispered, thinking again of that widow. "You were one smart *gyal.*"

Of all the lands her father-in-law discovered, and all the riches she and her heirs may have been entitled to receive, she'd insisted on only Jamaica.

And he knew why.

The lost mine.

When forced in 1494, during his fourth voyage, to beach his ship in St. Ann's Bay, on board was a cache in gold. Columbus had just come from Panama where he'd bartered the precious metal from the local population. Unfortunately his worm-eaten caravels could sail no longer, so he ran aground in Jamaica, marooned for a year.

Sometime during that year he hid the gold.

In a place supposedly shown him by the Tainos, its existence kept secret even from the Spanish Crown. Only Columbus' two sons knew the location, and they took that secret with them to their graves.

How stupid.

That was the lot of sons, though. Few ever outshone the father. He liked to think he was the exception. His father died in a Kingston jail, burned to death the day before being extradited to the United States to stand trial for murder. Some said the fire was intentional, set by the police. Others said suicide. Nobody really knew. His father had been tough and brutal, thinking himself invincible. But in the end, nobody really cared whether he lived or died.

Not good.

People would care if Béne Rowe died.

He thought about the Jews lying beneath his feet. They'd been an ambitious people. Eventually, they welcomed England's dominance over Jamaica. In return Cromwell had allowed them to live openly and practice their religion. They'd reciprocated and helped build the island into a thriving British colony. Once thousands of them lived here, their burial grounds scattered near the parish capitals or on the coasts.

Now only about three hundred Jews remained.

But the live ones did not concern him.

His search was for graves.

Or, more particularly, *a* grave.

He watched as his man continued to snap pictures with a smartphone. He'd send one of the images to

Simon. That should grab his attention. Twenty-one documented Jewish cemeteries existed on Jamaica.

Now a twenty-second had been found.

"Béne."

The man with the smartphone was motioning for him. Unlike the drug lords who liked to be called *don,* he preferred his name. One thing his father had taught him was that respect from a title never lasted.

He stepped across to his man, who said to him, "Look at *dat* one there in the ground."

He bent down and studied the markings. The stone lay flat, facing the sky, its etchings nearly gone. But enough remained for him to make out an image.

He brushed away more soil. He had to be sure.

"It's a pitcher," he said.

He wanted to shout with joy. Nowhere in the other twenty-one graveyards had they found the image of a pitcher, held by hands, being poured.

Zachariah Simon had told him to look for this symbol.

Was this *the* grave?

"Fetch a shovel," he ordered, "and dig it out."

CHAPTER EIGHT

ALLE LEFT THE BUILDING FEELING VIOLATED AND dirty. Those men had gone too far. Earlier, they'd discussed the performance and agreed on how to make it compelling, but no one had mentioned anything about groping her. Zachariah must have witnessed what happened from the other end of the transmission. She wondered what he thought. The idea had been to spur her father into action, to make the situation appear dire. Anything less and her father might not do what they wanted. Too much, and the threat would be meaningless.

One thing she could say.

What just happened should be sufficient.

She'd met Zachariah six months ago. He'd appeared in Seville, where she was working in the Biblioteca Columbina, among an extraordinary collection of materials from Christopher Columbus' time. Her doctoral thesis was to be on the great explorer's map, the one he'd used to find his way to the New World. A famed chart, it had disappeared in the 16th century, and much had been made of its fate. Some postulated that it could have been the *mappa mundus*, the so-called original map of the world. Others argued that it contained geographic information supposedly unknown to navigators of the 15th century. Still more thought there might have been connections to the Phoenicians, the Greeks, ancient Egyptians, or even Atlantians.

No one knew anything for sure.

The Spanish government only added to the mystery with its official pronouncement that no such chart was secreted away in its archives, yet they would not allow any independent searches to verify that fact.

On a lark she'd written an article about Columbus for *Minerva,* a British journal on ancient art and archaeology that she'd read for years. To her surprise they'd published it, which pointed Zachariah her way.

He was an extraordinary individual. Self-made in every way, from his modest education to his triumphs in international business and finance. He shied away from the limelight, preferring to live alone, never having married or fathered any children. He employed no publicists, no public relations firm, no cadre of assistants. He was simply a multibillionaire the world knew little about. He lived outside Vienna in a magnificent mansion, but he also owned buildings in town, including the apartment she now occupied. She'd also learned that his philanthropic efforts were extensive, his foundations donating millions to causes with Judaic connections. He spoke of Israel in solemn terms. His religion meant something to him, as it meant something to her.

He was born and raised. She'd converted five years ago, but told no one other than her grandfather, who'd been so pleased. He'd wanted his grandchildren to be Jewish, but her father had seemingly ended that hope. Unlike her mother, Alle never found solace in Christianity. Listening as a child, then as a young adult, she'd decided Judaism was what she held dear. So she quietly underwent the training and made the conversion.

The one secret between her and her mother.

And a regret.

She kept walking, navigating the maze of narrow cobbled streets. Bells echoed in the distance, signaling 8:00 P.M. She should go home and change, but she decided to pray first. Luckily, she'd come to the broadcast wearing her wool coat—Vienna's weather remained on the chilly side—which fell below her knees and shielded her ripped clothes. Here in this ancient city, which once housed 200,000 Jews but now supported a mere 10,000, she felt a connection with the past. Ninety-three synagogues were razed by the Nazis, every scrap of their existence eradicated. Sixty-five thousand Jews were slaughtered. When she thought of such tragedies her mind always drifted to 70 CE, and what her new religion regarded as one of the greatest tragedies of all.

First came Nebuchadnezzar and the Babylonians in 586 BCE. They carried away all of Jerusalem, its officials, warriors, artisans, and thousands of captives. No one remained except the poorest of the land. The invaders destroyed Solomon's First Temple, the holiest of places, and carted away its treasures, hacking to pieces the sacred vessels of gold. The Jews remained in exile for several generations, eventually returning to Palestine and heeding God's command that they build a new sanctuary. Moses had been supplied a precise blueprint for its construction, including how to fashion the sacred vessels. The Second Temple was completed in 516 BCE, but was totally refurbished and enlarged by Herod beginning in 18 BCE. Herod's Temple was what greeted the Romans when they conquered Judea in 6 CE, and it was the same temple that stood when the Jews rose in revolt sixty years later.

A revolt they won.

Joy filled Judea. The Roman yoke had finally been cast off.

But everyone knew the legions would return.

And they did.

Nero dispatched Vespasian from the north and Titus from the south, a father-and-son pair of generals. They attacked Galilee in 67 CE. Two years later Vespasian became emperor and left Titus with 80,000 men to teach the Jews a lesson.

Judea was reconquered. Then, in 70 CE, Jerusalem was laid to siege.

Fighting was fierce on both sides, and conditions within the city became horrific. Hundreds of corpses were flung over the walls daily, hunger and disease becoming powerful Roman allies. Battering rams finally breached the walls and shock troops drove the defenders back into the temple compound, where they barricaded themselves for a final stand.

But six days of pounding caused no damage to the Temple Mount.

Its massive stones held.

Attempts to scale the great wall failed. Finally, the Romans set fire to the gates and burst through.

The Jews also set fires, hoping to check the Romans' advance, but the flames spread too quickly and burned down barriers protecting the sanctuary. The defenders were but a handful fighting against far superior numbers. They met their death willingly, some throwing themselves on Roman swords, some slaying one another, others taking their own lives by leaping into the flames.

None regarded what was happening as a destruction.

Instead, they saw their own demise as a salvation,

and felt happiness at perishing along with their Second Temple.

Through the pall of smoke centurions ran amok, looting and killing. Corpses were piled around the sacred altar. Blood poured down the sanctuary steps, bodies slithering down the risers atop red rivers. Eventually, no one could walk without touching death.

Titus and his entourage managed to gain entrance to the sanctuary before it was destroyed. They had heard of its magnificence, but to stand amid the opulence was another matter. The Holy of Holies, the most sacred part of the Temple, was overlaid with gold, its inner door crafted of Corinthian brass. Suspended above the twelve steps leading to the entrance was a spreading vine of gold, replete with clusters of grapes as tall as a man. A silver-and-gold crown—not the original, but a copy of the one worn by the high priest after the return from Babylonian exile—was prominently displayed.

Then there were the sacred objects.

A golden menorah. The divine table. Silver trumpets.

All had been commissioned by God, on Mount Sinai, for Moses to create. The Romans knew that, by destroying the Second Temple and removing these treasures, the essence of Judaism would also be symbolically extinguished.

Another exile would then occur.

Not physically, though many would die or be enslaved, but certainly spiritually.

There would be no Third Temple.

And for the past 1,940 years that had been the case, Alle thought, as she entered the only Viennese synagogue the Nazis had not destroyed.

The Stadttempel sat among a block of anonymous apartment buildings, hidden away, thanks to Emperor Joseph II who decreed that only Catholic churches could face public streets. Ironically, that insult was what saved the building, as it had proven impossible for the Germans to torch it without burning the whole block to the ground.

The 19th-century sanctuary was oval-shaped, its ceiling supported by gilded beams and a ring of twelve Ionic columns—symbolic, she knew, of Jacob's twelve sons, the progenitors of the tribes of Israel. A star-speckled, sky-blue dome loomed overhead. She'd visited here many times over the past month, the building's shape and elegance making her feel as if she were inside a jeweled egg.

What would it mean for the Jews to have their Third Temple in Jerusalem?

Everything.

And to complete that accomplishment her adopted faith would also require its sacred vessels.

Her gaze drifted around the dimly lit sanctuary and her eyes watered.

She could still feel hands groping her body. Never had anyone touched her like that before.

She started to cry.

What would her mother have thought? She'd been a good woman, who rarely spoke ill of her ex-husband, always encouraging her daughter to forgive him.

But she never could.

What she'd just done to her father should bother her, but thoughts of what lay ahead helped with her rationalizations.

She stemmed the tears and calmed herself.

The Ark of the Covenant would never be found. The Babylonians had seen to that. The golden menorah, the divine table, and the silver trumpets? They could still exist.

The Temple treasure.

Or what was left of it.

Gone for 1,940 years.

But, depending on her father, maybe not for much longer.

CHAPTER NINE

ZACHARIAH WAS PLEASED. THE VIDEO HAD PLAYED out perfectly. Rócha made the point, albeit a bit more forcefully than they'd discussed.

Tom Sagan seemed to have grasped the message.

And this man was even more vulnerable than his daughter had described.

Never had there been any mention of suicide. Alle had simply told him that her father lived a solitary life in a small house in Orlando, among two million people who had no idea he existed. He'd moved back to Florida after losing his job in California. Anonymity had to be a major change for Sagan, considering that he'd stayed on the front page for over a decade. He'd been a regular on cable news, public broadcasting, and the networks. Not only a reporter, but a celebrity. A lot of people had trusted Sagan. The background investigation made that clear. Which probably explained, more than anything else, why so many turned on him so completely.

"You're a Jew?" Sagan asked.

He nodded. "We are both Children of God."

"Speak for yourself."

"You were born a Jew, and that you cannot renounce."

"You sound like the man who once owned this house."

He noticed that Sagan never used the word *father.* Alle had told him of the estrangement, but the divide seemed even greater than she believed. He pointed a finger and said, "Your father was a wise man."

"Let my daughter go and I'll do what you want."

He caught the exasperation in the statement but decided not to concede anything just yet. "I studied what happened to you eight years ago. Quite an experience. I can see how it would bring you to this end point. Life was especially cruel to you."

And he wondered. Could this poor soul even be motivated to act? Was anything important to him any longer? His background work on Sagan ended a few weeks ago, and there'd been no mention of suicidal tendencies. Obviously, some major life decision had been made. He knew that another manuscript had just been completed, written so anonymously that not even the publisher or the "author" knew Sagan's identity. The literary agent had suggested the tactic, since it was doubtful anyone would have consented to Sagan even ghostwriting for them.

That was how complete the downfall had been.

Five of the seven books Sagan had written became top-ten *New York Times* bestsellers. Three had been number ones. Critical praise for the cover authors on all seven had been admirable. Which was why, he supposed, work had continued to flow Sagan's way.

But apparently, it had all taken a toll.

This man was ready to die.

Perhaps he should allow him?

Or maybe—

"Your father was the keeper of a great secret," he said. "A man trusted with information that only a few in history knew."

"That's nonsense."

"I assure you, it is not."

He saw that, despite himself, Sagan was intrigued. Maybe there was enough reporter left inside to motivate him one last time.

So he said, "And it all started with Christopher Columbus."

Columbus stood on the pier. The Niña, Pinta, and Santa María rode at anchor in a branch of the Tinto River, near Palos de la Frontera on Spain's southeastern coast, not far from open ocean. It had taken months to locate, outfit, and man the three vessels, but now all was ready.

It had to be.

Midnight was approaching.

Breaking with custom, Columbus had not waited to board just before the ships sailed. Instead he'd been present all day, personally supervising final preparations.

"Nearly all are here," Luis de Torres said to him.

Eighty-seven crewmen would man the three ships. Contrary to the gossip he'd heard, none was a convict royally pardoned for volunteering. Instead each was fully capable, as no one but true seamen would endure this voyage. There was one Portuguese, one Genoese, a Venetian, and a Calabrian, the rest all Spaniards from in and around Palos. Two representatives of the Crown were included, required by his commission, and he'd already cautioned de Torres to be careful around one of them.

"Luis."

De Torres stepped close.

"We must have all on board before midnight."

He knew de Torres understood. After midnight, when it became August 3, 1492, the police, the militia, and the white-hooded Inquisitors would begin their sweep of houses. Jews had been outlawed from France in 1394 and in England since 1290. The edict expelling them from Spain had been signed by Ferdinand and Isabella on March 31. The church had insisted on the move and the king and queen had agreed. Four months had been given to either leave the country or convert to Christianity.

Time ran out tonight.

"I fear that we might not make it away," he whispered.

Thankfully, it was next to impossible to physically identify a Spanish Jew. Among the Celts, Iberians, Romans, Phoenicians, Basques, Vandals, Visigoths, and Arabs, there'd been a thorough mixing. But that would not deter the Inquisition. Its agents would stop at nothing to apprehend every suspected Jew. Already, thousands had converted, becoming conversos. Outwardly, they attended mass, offered confession, and baptized their children. Inwardly, and at night, they kept their Hebrew names and read from the Torah.

"So much depends on this journey," he said to his friend.

And so much depended on de Torres.

He was the voyage's interpreter, fluent in Hebrew, formerly in the employ of the governor of Murcia, a city that once possessed a large Jewish population. But those people were either gone or converted and the governor had no further need of a Hebrew interpreter. De Torres, like a few others in the crew, had been baptized only a few weeks ago.

"Do you think," de Torres asked, "that we will find what you seek?"

Columbus stared out to the dark water and the ships, lit by torches, where men were busy at work.

The question was a good one.

And there was but one answer.
"We have no choice."

"Are you saying Christopher Columbus was Jewish?" Sagan asked.

"He was a *converso*. That is part of the great secret your father knew. He never told you any of this?"

Sagan shook his head.

"I am not surprised. You are not worthy."

"Who the hell are you to tell me what I'm worthy of?"

"You renounced your entire heritage. How could you possibly understand things such as honor? Tradition? Duty?"

"How do you know I did that?"

"Is it a lie?"

"And you?" Sagan said. "A kidnapper? Things like honor mean something to you?"

"I have staked my fortune and my life to its fulfillment."

Zachariah reached into his jacket pocket and found the folded documents. "I need your signature. These will allow lawyers to petition a judge for an order of exhumation on your behalf. I am told it will not be a problem, provided the closest living relative consents. Your daughter has already signed, as the estate's representative. Of course, she had little choice."

Sagan refused to accept either the papers or the pen he offered.

"There are but a few minutes remaining for me to call and stop those men."

He watched as his ultimatum sank in.

Finally, Sagan snatched the pen and papers and signed.

He retrieved them and started to leave. "I will need

you at the cemetery, in the morning, at 10:00 A.M. An heir must be present. I will have a representative there on my behalf. Do as instructed. Once the exhumation of your father is complete, your daughter will be released."

"How do I know that will happen?"

He stopped, turned, and appraised Sagan with a curious glare. "Because I give you my word."

"I feel better already."

He pointed at Sagan. "See, there still is some wit left in you."

"I need my gun."

He held the weapon up. "You can have it back in the morning."

"I would have pulled the trigger. I'd be dead right now, if you hadn't come along."

He wondered whom Sagan was trying to convince. "Please, do not fret. You will have another opportunity, *after* tomorrow morning."

CHAPTER TEN

BÉNE WAITED AS ONE OF HIS MEN DUG OUT THE grave. His dogs had returned and now lay placid beneath the trees, basking in the broken sunlight, satisfied from the hunt. His animals were thorough, a talent bred into them long ago. His mother had told him about the *chasseurs* from Cuba. Small, swarthy men who'd worn open checked shirts, wide trousers, and light straw hats with shallow crowns and broad rims. But it was their shoes that set them apart. They would skin the thighs and hocks of wild hogs then thrust their feet into the raw hide. The pliant material became a kind of short boot, which fit close, and lasted for weeks. They wore crucifixes around their tanned necks and were armed only with a *machet*, sharpened on one side, the other used to beat the dogs. They first came in 1796, forty of them with their hounds, imported to hunt down the Trelawny Town Maroons.

Which they did.

With no mercy.

Hundreds were slaughtered, and the fear of the dogs was born.

Which he intended to resurrect.

While gangs sought favor with the poorest in Jamaica's cities, he'd always cast his lot here, in the windward mountains and, to the west, in the leeward

Cockpit country, places where Maroons had existed for four hundred years. And though each ran their community through colonels and elected councils, he liked to think of himself as their collective savior, protecting the Maroon way of life. In return, his compatriots provided men and women to staff his many ventures. True, prostitution, gambling, and pornography were covert interests, and they made him millions. But coffee was his passion. All around him, on the slopes for many kilometers, grew shrubs of modest height with glossy, dark green leaves. Every year, sweet-scented, white blossoms sprouted and eventually matured into bright red berries. Once ground and boiled they produced what many said was the finest drink in the world.

Blue Mountain Coffee.

His ancestors had worked the plantations as slaves. He now owned one of the largest and paid their descendants as employees. He also controlled the main distribution network for all of the remaining growers. His father wisely conceived that opportunity, after a devastating hurricane in the 1950s wiped out nearly every grower. A national board was established, with membership limited and criteria for quality, cultivation, and processing decreed. If not grown within sixteen kilometers of the central peak it was Jamaican Prime, not Blue Mountain Coffee. His father had been right—scarcity bred mystique. And through regulation of the product, Blue Mountain Coffee became valued around the world.

And made the Rowe family rich.

His man continued to dig.

Twenty minutes ago his other lieutenant had returned to the trucks to meet more of his men. They now arrived through the trees leading a blindfolded prisoner—late twenties, a mixture of Cuban and African—hands tied behind his back.

He motioned and the younger man was shoved to his knees and the blindfold yanked off.

He squatted close as the man blinked away the afternoon sun.

The man's eyes went wide when he saw Béne.

"Yes, Felipe. It's me. Did you think you could get away with it? I pay you to watch the Simon. And watch you do. Except you take his money, and then watch me, too."

Fear shook the man's head in violent nervous gestures.

"Listen to me, and listen real good, 'cause everything depends on it."

He saw that his warning registered.

"I want to know what the Simon be doing. I want to know everything you've not told me. Tell *wi di trut.*"

This turncoat was of the streets, so patois would be his language.

Tell me the truth.

He'd not heard from Simon in nearly two weeks, but he shouldn't be surprised. Everything he'd learned had only confirmed what he'd long sensed.

Trouble.

The Austrian was enormously wealthy, a philanthropic man obviously interested in Israeli causes. But that did not concern Béne. He had no dog in the fight that was the Middle East. He was interested only in Columbus' lost gold mine—as, supposedly, was Simon.

"I swear to you, Béne," Felipe said. "I know nothin'. He tells me nothin'."

He silenced him with a wave of his hand. "What you take me for? The Simon does not live here. He knows no one in Jamaica. I'm his partner. That's what he says. Yet he hires you to work for him, too. Okay. I come to you and pay you to tell the Simon only what I want him to know and to tell me what he does. Yet you tell me nothin'."

"He calls me up, pays me to do some things. I do them and he pays. That's all, Béne. All."

The words came fast.

"But I pay you to tell me *di trut*. Which you not be doing. You better start talkin' quick."

"He wants records. Papers from the archives."

He motioned and one of his men handed him a pistol. He jammed its muzzle into the man's chest and cocked the hammer. "I give you one more chance. What. Kind. Of. Things."

Shock filled the prisoner's eyes.

"Okay. Okay. Béne. I tell you. I tell you."

He kept the gun firmly against the man's chest.

"Deeds. He wants deeds. Old ones. I found one. Some Jew named Cohen bought land in 1671."

That grabbed his attention. "Speak, man."

"He bought land and all the riverfront property beside it."

"The name."

"Abraham Cohen."

"Why is that so important to the Simon?"

"His brother. His brother was Moses Cohen Henriques."

That name he knew. A 17th-century Jewish pirate. He captured a great Spanish silver fleet in Cuba, then led the Dutch invasion of Brazil. He ended his life on Jamaica, searching for Columbus' lost mine.

"Does the Simon know this?"

He shook his head. "He's out of touch. Gone. Don't know where. I swear, Béne. Don't know. I haven't told him yet."

"And you not tell me, either. This deed you find. Still in the archives?"

A shake of the head. "I stole it. I have it at my place in Spanish Town. Your men know where *dat* is. Go get it. Beside my bed. I swear, Béne. Right beside my bed."

He withdrew the gun.

His man digging in the grave had stopped and was motioning.

He needed time to think so he tossed the weapon to his lieutenant and walked over. In the shallow excavation he spotted a flat chip of stone. On its face was a symbol.

"Fetch it out," he ordered.

His man lifted the fragment and laid it on the ground. He brushed away the dark earth and studied the etching. The Simon had told him to look for a pitcher on a grave marker and a hooked X.

The chip he stared at had once been part of a tombstone. He lifted the chunk and saw that it fit at the bottom right corner of the marker with the pitcher, its rough edges close enough of a match to convince him.

He propped the piece up so the prisoner could see the hooked X.

"You know *wa dis bi*?"

"I saw *dat* on the deed, Béne. On *da* deed in the archives. The one beside my bed. Simon told me to watch for *dat* X thing. I did. I did real good, Béne. It's there. I can still do real good for you, too. I can."

Unfortunately, it didn't work like that. As a child his mother taught him something she'd been taught by her mother, and her mother before that. Maroons wrote little down. The spoken word had been their history book.

> *Speak the truth and speak it ever,*
> *Cost it what it will.*

His mother was always right.

And something else she said.

To hide a sin was to commit another.

Felipe was a minor government official who worked at the national archives in Spanish Town. He was somewhat educated and ambitious, but earned barely enough to survive. His main task had been to search the old records for anything on the lost mine. But, when offered the opportunity to work for someone else, this cheater had decided to bite the hand that first fed him.

Luckily, Felipe had a big mouth.

Which was appreciated, since knowing the situation had allowed Béne to cultivate a spy of his own.

He motioned for his man to bring him a phone. Reception in the mountains was excellent and he pressed one of its memory buttons, the number already programmed. Three rings and the man in Vienna answered.

"What is happening there?" he asked.

"It's becoming . . . complicated."

"Maybe it's time you act."

"I've been thinking the same thing."

"Then do it. All's quiet here."

"Good to hear."

He clicked off.

He'd known for the past few days that the Simon was on the move. Things were happening in both Austria and Florida. As to what, he was not entirely sure, but he knew enough to know that his European partner was double-crossing him. To his great fortune, Béne had found a new cemetery, with both a pitcher and a hooked X. Now he had a deed. All of which helped ease the ache of betrayal, and the anxiety he felt for what had to be done.

His gaze locked on his man with the gun. He held his minion's eyes for a split second, then gave a nod. The weapon was aimed down and a bullet to the head ended Felipe's life.

Speak the truth and speak it ever, cost it what it will.

"Dump him in the grave and refill the hole," he said. "Then go bury the don."

His dogs never ate what they did not kill.

"I'm going to Spanish Town."

CHAPTER ELEVEN

TOM SAT ON THE SOFA. ZACHARIAH SIMON HAD BEEN gone for over an hour. Ever since, he'd thought of Alle. His only child. Who hated him.

What happened to them?

He could not identify one defining moment where the break occurred. Instead, their estrangement had evolved, starting when Alle was in middle school, as she became more aware of the distance between her parents. By high school, their schism was complete.

Had Michele encouraged it? Not that he could see. No, this was all his doing. He'd hurt his ex-wife beyond measure. Even worse, he'd appeared not to care. That was back in the days when he could do no wrong. When he was invincible. Or so he thought. How many affairs had he had? He shook his head. Too many to count, in too many places. Michele never knew anything for certain. She'd only suspected. Intimacy bred a radar capable of detecting even the slightest emotional change, and Michele's had eventually identified his betrayal. Unfortunately, he'd been too self-absorbed to care.

Regrets?

So many that he was ready to die.

"Our time is over, Tom."

"And Alle?"

"I'm afraid if you don't act soon, that relationship will be over, too. You've let that slide far too long. She's seen the pain in my eyes. I can't hide it."

"I'll fix it with her. I swear to you, Michele. I'll fix it."

But he never did.

Alle was seventeen when he was fired, his disgrace reported in every media outlet around the world. Unfortunately, patching up his relationship with his daughter had not seemed a high priority at the time. A mistake? Oh, yeah. Big-time. But that was eight years of hindsight talking and there was no way to jam that toothpaste back in the tube.

He could do something now, though.

He could get her free of Zachariah Simon.

He'd signed the papers. Tomorrow he'd appear at the cemetery and make sure she was okay.

After that?

Finish what he'd started?

He rubbed his tired eyes with shaking hands and glanced at his watch. 2:15 P.M. Outside was quiet. Most of the people who'd lived in his parents' neighborhood while he was growing up were either gone or dead. Trees that had then been saplings now towered over everything. He'd noticed driving in that the block remained in good repair. Time had been kind to this place.

Why had it been so tough on him?

He made a decision.

He wasn't going to die today.

Maybe tomorrow, but not today.

Instead, it was time to do something he should have done long ago.

———

ALLE ENTERED THE CAFÉ RAHOFER, A PLACE SHE'D discovered a couple of weeks ago, not far from her

Viennese apartment. She'd showered and changed, dressed in tan chinos, a sweater, and flat-soled shoes. She was feeling a bit better and wondered what had happened in Florida, but assumed her father had co-operated since Rócha had made no further contact. They were all scheduled to meet again tomorrow, at 4:00 P.M., back where the video had originated, there while the grave was being opened, ready if needed for another show.

She did not like the idea of exhuming her grand-father. He'd been a dear man who'd loved her uncon-ditionally. He was the blood father she'd never had, and his death still affected her. She always hoped her conversion to Judaism compensated, at least a little, for the pain her father had caused him. Despite all that happened, his granddaughter still became a Jew.

"Did your grandfather leave any papers or instruc-tions to you that may have seemed unusual?" Zacha-riah asked her.

She'd never spoken of it before, but it seemed okay, now, after three years, to discuss it with him. "He told me to bury a packet with him."

"Describe it."

She used her hands to outline something about a foot square. "It was one of those sealed vacuum bags sold for storage on television. It was thin and light."

"Could you see anything through the bag?"

She shook her head. "I paid no attention to it. He left written instructions, as his estate representative, to make sure the packet was placed in his coffin. I did that myself, laying it on his chest, just before the lid was closed."

"That had to be difficult."

"I cried the whole time."

She recalled how Zachariah had held her hand and they'd prayed for Abiram Sagan. She adhered to the

Jewish belief that soul and body would eventually be reunited. That meant the body had to be honored. Custom required someone to attend to the deceased, closing the eyes and mouth, covering the face, lighting candles.

And she'd done all that.

A late-blooming cancer had stolen her grandfather quickly. But at least he hadn't suffered. The Torah commanded that a body must not go unburied overnight, and she'd made sure that her grandfather had been interred before sunset. She'd also not embalmed him, dressing him in a simple linen shroud inside a plain wooden coffin. She'd heard him say many times, *"Wealthy or poor, nothing should distinguish us at death."* She'd even kept a window open where she sat with him, awaiting burial, so his soul could easily escape. She'd then followed all four stages of mourning, including *avelut*. Dutifully, she'd abstained from parties, celebrations, and all forms of entertainment for a full twelve months.

Her grandfather would have been proud.

She found a table and sat.

She liked the Café Rahofer, with its marble tabletops, crystal chandeliers, and bentwood chairs. She'd learned this place came with some history, as both Stalin and Trotsky had played chess here. A piano in a far corner entertained a light crowd for after 9:00 P.M. on a Tuesday night. A glass of wine and a plate of schnitzel sounded great. She ordered both with some mineral water and began to relax.

"Are you alone?"

She turned to see a man standing a few feet away. He appeared a little older, maybe thirty, trim, extra fit, with a two-day stubble dusting his chin and neck. The hair that covered his head was thin and closely cropped, like a monk's cap, his blue eyes alert and lively.

"I'm alone," she said, "and prefer to stay that way."

He threw her a smile and sat at her table.

"I told you I wasn't interested," she made clear.

"You will be."

She resented his forwardness. "How about you leave now, before I call someone over."

He leaned in close. "Then you won't get to hear what I have to say about Zachariah Simon."

CHAPTER TWELVE

ZACHARIAH ENTERED THE ROOM AND CLOSED THE door. He'd driven straight back from Mount Dora to Orlando and his west-side hotel. He quickly found his laptop and connected to the Internet, linking with a secured server in Austria, the same one used during the video transmission to Tom Sagan. He'd commissioned the system himself, equipped with an ultra-sophisticated encryption program. He checked in with his personal secretary in Austria, satisfied that nothing required his immediate attention. He then severed the link and ordered food from room service.

Sagan was cooperating. He'd signed the papers and would be at the cemetery in the morning.

He'd accomplished the first phase.

But time was running short.

He'd read the American press reports, lauding the coming summit. Danny Daniels, the president of the United States, in his final year in office, had staked his legacy on securing some sort of lasting Mideast peace. Thankfully, that summit was still four months away.

Plenty of time for him to complete what he'd started.

But what he sought had stayed hidden a long time.

Could it all be myth?

No. It existed. It had to. God would not have allowed anything less.

Alle had confirmed that her grandfather ordered a packet buried with him, contrary to Orthodox tradition, where nothing save the body went into the grave. Even more convincing was the fact that she knew information that no one, short of the Levite, could possibly know.

He was on the right path.

He had to be.

Surely the Levite had been cautious in what he shared with his granddaughter, given the task was exclusively for a male. Abiram Sagan could not pass ultimate responsibility to his granddaughter. So he solved his dilemma by taking the secret with him to his grave.

Thankfully, he had Alle totally under his control. A willing partner with no knowledge of what was truly involved. She was an ideologue, consumed by her passion for her new religion and her grandfather's memory. Her beliefs were sincere. All she required was careful handling.

And that he would provide.

Until she was no longer useful.

Then he would kill Alle Becket.

———

ALLE WAS INTRIGUED, SO SHE ASKED, "WHAT ABOUT Zachariah Simon?"

"He should be a concern of yours," the man sitting across the table said.

She wasn't in the mood for more games. "Do you plan to explain yourself? Or do I leave?"

"You met Simon in Spain. Didn't you find it strange that he found you?"

"I don't even know your name."

He smiled. "Call me Brian."

"Why are you here?"

"I came to speak with you. Privately."

Cautionary flags rose. This stranger was frightening her to the point that she even wished Rócha and Midnight were around.

Brian reached into his pocket and withdrew some folded sheets of glossy paper, which she recognized as her article from *Minerva*.

"I read this," he said. "Fascinating stuff. Let me guess, Simon wanted to know your sources."

It had been one of the first things they'd talked about, along with the fact that they were both Reform Jews. She'd immediately liked that about him. Unlike the Orthodox, Reform Jews believed the Torah, though divinely inspired, was actually written, edited, and revised by man. And while Reform Jews revered the Torah's values and ethics, they were free to follow whatever they believed would enhance their personal relationship with God. Nothing was absolute. Everything was subject to interpretation. Even more important to her, Reform Jews treated the sexes equally.

"You still haven't said what you want."

The waiter returned with her wine.

"No, thank you," Brian said to her. "I wouldn't care for anything."

To spite him, she savored a sip. "You won't be here long."

"Zachariah Simon is not what he claims to be. He's using you."

"For what?"

"To find out what your grandfather knew."

She sipped more of the wine, trying to appreciate the smoky aftertaste. "How do you know this?"

"I know that he's in Florida, where your grandfather is buried. I know that he's made contact with your father. I also know that you just lied to your father in a shameful charade."

"And the reason you've come here to insult me?"

"To try and save your miserable life."

CHAPTER THIRTEEN

Tom STEPPED FROM THE CAR AND ENTERED THE CEMetery beneath a cloudless afternoon. This was a place where the Jews of central Florida had long been laid to rest. Decades ago, Abiram had been instrumental in securing the land and having it consecrated. It sat away from almost everything, among rolling hills, oak hummocks, horse farms, and orange groves.

He hated graveyards.

They were places of the past, and his was best forgotten.

He stared out at the *matsevahs,* the vertical slabs standing in ill-defined rows, most facing east, each a cut rectangle with modest decorative elements—circles, pitched corners, odd shapes. He recalled his training as a boy. Each stone evidenced the eternal essence of the person lying beneath. Since Alle had been in charge of burial and Abiram had been an uncompromising soul, he assumed she'd strictly adhered to ritual.

Which meant the marker would not have been erected until a year after death. During that time Alle would have kept his memory alive with regular visits and studied other graves, deciding carefully what the epitaph should be. Once convinced, she would have commissioned a carver and erected the *matsevah* in a simple ceremony.

None of which had involved him.

All he'd received was the deed to the house with a curt explanation from a lawyer that the property now belonged to him. He'd finally visited here one dismal afternoon, six months after Abiram's death, standing in the rain and remembering their last encounter.

"I'm going to be baptized Christian," he said.

"Why would you do such a thing?"

"Michele is Christian and she wants our children to be Christian."

"That doesn't require you to leave our faith."

He shrugged. "I don't believe in any of this. I never have. Judaism is important to you, not me."

"You were born to Jewish parents. You are a Jew, and always will be."

"I plan to be baptized Episcopalian. That's Michele's church."

Shock flooded Abiram's eyes. "If you do that, you and I will be through."

"You and I were through a long time ago. I'm twenty-five years old, yet you treat me as if I were ten. I'm not one of your students. I'm your son. But if you no longer want me to be that, then that's the way it'll be."

So he'd ceased being a Jew, married, become a Christian, and fathered a child. He and Abiram barely spoke after that. Family gatherings and holidays were the worst. His mother, though devout and respectful of her husband, had not been able to stay away. She'd come to California, but always alone. Never had he and Michele, as a family, visited Florida. Alle stayed with her grandparents for a few weeks every summer, flying back and forth alone. After his mother died those visits became longer. Alle had loved being with her grandfather. Abiram's resentment of Tom had spilled over to Michele, and their relationship had always been strained. The old man was a proud Jew, and only in the past couple of years had Tom come to understand some of that passion. As he lost the drive for nearly everything in life, he remembered more and more what Abiram had taught him in those years before he turned twenty-five.

When they were still speaking.

He stared at the grave.

A lumpkin shrieked in the distance. *The crying bird,* one of his uncles had called them because of their humanlike tone.

The first time he'd come the marker had not been here. Alle had done well with its creation. Tall and substantial, much like the man beneath. He bent down and studied its reliefs, running his fingers across the two elegant letters at the top.

פנ

Po nikbar. Here lies.

He noticed art at the bottom.

A pitcher, tipped, as if pouring.

More of his early training came to mind.

A felled tree marked those who died young. Books evidenced a learned person. A saw and plane meant craftsman.

Pitchers symbolized that the deceased had been a Levite.

He'd never known that about his father.

According to the Bible, Levites were descendants

of the tribe of Levi, the third of Jacob's twelve sons. Both Moses and Aaron had been Levites. They sang psalms at services during the time of the First and Second Temples and physically maintained those sanctuaries. The Torah specifically commanded that Levites should protect the Temple for the people of Israel. Their usefulness, though, essentially ended when the Temples were destroyed. Because one of their assigned duties had been to cleanse the rabbi's hands before the service, the pitcher had evolved into their symbol. He knew that Jews still considered themselves divided into three groups. Cohanim, the priestly caste. Levi'im, the Levites. And the Israelim, everyone else. Observances and laws specific to Cohanim and Levi'im were still practiced. Levites existed in synagogues, though their role was little more than honorific.

Was that why the symbol was here?

A recognition of Abiram's service?

He glanced at his mother's *matsevah*.

He'd attended her funeral, and Abiram had been customarily silent toward him. He'd stood right here a year later when the stone was raised but again played no part in its creation. A menorah adorned hers, symbolic of a righteous woman.

And that she'd been.

He heard a sound and turned.

A car eased to where he'd parked a couple of hundred feet away. A small sedan with tinted windows.

No one emerged.

Had Zachariah Simon followed him here?

The drive from his father's house was only a short few miles, and no one had been behind him.

Yet someone was here.

He faced the intruder and called out, "What do you want?"

No reply.

"I said, what do you want?"

Silence.

With the courage of a man who'd not planned on even being alive at this moment he started forward.

The car wheeled from the graveled lot.

He watched as it drove away.

What in the world?

He turned back to the grave and thought of Alle.

"What in God's name have you done, old man?"

CHAPTER FOURTEEN

BÉNE HATED SPANISH TOWN. THOUGH FOR THREE hundred years it had served as Jamaica's capital, an architectural delight perched on the west bank of the Rio Cobre, it had evolved into a hard-edged, gang-infested urban center of nearly 200,000 impoverished people. He rarely visited since his business interests lay either to the east in Kingston, or into the mountains, or across the north shore. He was born and raised just outside Spanish Town, in a tough neighborhood his family had controlled until his father made the mistake of killing an American drug agent. The United States demanded justice, the Jamaican government finally obliged, but his father had the good sense to die in jail. His mother took his death hard. Since he was an only child—medically, she could have no more—she made him promise that he'd never follow in those footsteps. His mother was a spry seventy-one years old and, to this day, had no idea what Béne's empire entailed. He hated lying to her but, thankfully, he owned a host of legitimate enterprises—coffee, hotels, mining—that he could point to with pride and assure her he was no criminal.

Which, to his way of thinking, he wasn't.

In fact, he hated criminals.

True, he supplied prostitution, gambling, or pornography to a willing buyer. But his customers were grown adults and he made sure none of his products involved children in any way. He once shot a man in Montego Bay who refused to stop supplying young boys to tourists. And he'd shoot a few more if need be.

He might break society's rules.

But he followed his own.

He rode in the rear seat of his Maybach 62 S, two of his men in front, both armed. The car cost him half a million U.S., but was worth every dollar. He loved the high-grade leather and the fact that the backseat reclined to nearly a flat position. He took advantage of that often with naps between destinations. The roof was his favorite. One push of a button and glass panels changed from opaque to clear.

They eased through a conglomeration of neighborhoods, the boundaries clear only to those who lived there.

And to him.

He knew these places.

Life spilled out from the stores and houses onto the streets, forming a sea of dark faces. His father had ruled here, but now a confederation of gangs, led by men who called themselves dons, fought with one another over control.

Why?

Probably because their lives offered little else in the way of satisfaction, which was sad. What he'd heard many times rang true. *"Jamaica has a little of everything but not quite enough of anything."*

They eased through the congestion, the buildings old, two to three stories high, packed so close that even a breath of fresh air would have difficulty squeezing through. When they turned onto a side street, two men appeared in front and signaled with outstretched arms for the car to stop. Both had ropelike hair and wild beards. They flanked the vehicle, one on either side. Shirttails hung out and low—shielding weapons.

Béne shook his head and muttered, *"Buguyagas."*

And that's what he thought.

Nasty tramps.

He wound down the rear window and asked, "You need something?"

He intentionally avoided patois, which he knew would be their preferred way to speak. The man on his side of the car clearly did not know him and was about to speak, but the other one rushed around the hood and grasped his friend's arm, signaling for the driver to go on.

"What is it?" Béne asked. "Neither of you can talk?"

Mumblings passed between them that he could not hear, then the two men ran off.

He shook his head.

What were they going to do? Rob him right here in the street?

"They lucky we don't have time to shoot 'em. Go."

He found the shanty where Felipe lived, its walls a collage of scrap lumber and rusted tin. Four individual rooms were padlocked from the outside. Barrels of rainwater lined the edges, which meant no plumbing, confirmed by a strong scent of urine. Goats roamed the front and sides.

"Bust it open," he ordered, and his men kicked down the makeshift doors.

Inside the largest enclosure was a room about six meters square. There was a bed, television, stove, dresser, and laundry basket. Eighty percent of the people in Spanish Town and Kingston lived like this or worse.

His gaze found the bed and, just as Felipe had said, lying on the filthy floor was a stack of old documents.

One of his men brought them to him. Another stood guard at the door. Guns were drawn. Their two greeters may have alerted the local don that Béne Rowe was in the neighborhood, so they might receive a visit.

A courtesy, for sure.

But still a visit.

"If anyone bothers us," he said, "move them away."

His men nodded.

He found the deed the man had described from 1671, written in Spanish or Portuguese, he wasn't sure, the faded ink difficult to see. There were several other parchments, each sulfur-colored, brown at the edges and brittle, all in the same language. He was able to read a few words, as Spanish had been a language he'd learned.

He heard a commotion outside and turned as a woman with two small girls appeared at the doorway. His men had the good sense to conceal their guns. She was deeply black, wearing a dress of yellow, pink, and green. Her bare feet were stained with road dust.

"Who you?" she demanded.

"A friend."

She stepped into the room, a defiant look on her face. "You broke in?"

"It was necessary." He gestured with the documents he held. "I came for these."

"Where's Felipe?"

He shrugged. "Are you his wife?"

She nodded.

"His children?"

"One of 'em."

That was the thing about killing. Somebody always suffered. But he could not allow anyone to play him for a fool. On this island reputation meant everything, and Felipe sealed his fate when he sold out.

A shame, though, that these three would also pay the price.

He reached into his pocket and found his money clip. He peeled off twenty $100 U.S. bills and tossed them on the bed.

"Wa' that for?" she asked.

"I owe Felipe. His pay."

She appraised him with a mix of anger and dependency, one he'd seen all too many times. This woman would never see Felipe again. The big-eyed child would never know her father. No one would ever know what had happened. Felipe would rot away in an abandoned cemetery high in the Blue Mountains.

But such was the fate of liars.

"We go now," he said. "You take care."

He headed for the door with his documents in hand.

"He not comin' back, is he?" the woman asked, her words laced with worry and fear.

He decided to be honest. "Take the money on the bed. I'll send some more. Be grateful and silent."

Her rough face was drawn, her brown eyes bloodshot. This woman's tough life had just gotten tougher.

"Ev'ry gal look for man to tek care o' her. When she fine him she is woman and she is true." Her voice had turned icy.

He knew what she meant. The men she attracted changed lovers as often as moods. She'd finally avoided that with Felipe.

But there was nothing he could do.

So he left.

CHAPTER FIFTEEN

ALLE KEPT HER COMPOSURE AND SIMPLY STARED BACK at the man who called himself Brian.

"Have you and Simon ever discussed religion?" he asked.

Like she was going to answer him. "I want to eat my dinner. I'd appreciate it if you'd leave."

"He's a devout Orthodox Jew. You're not. How do you get along?"

That comment surprised her. In their many discussions of Judaism, Zachariah had always talked reform. Fundamentalism repelled him. Orthodox Jews claimed to be *authentic,* which was insulting, he'd said, to all of the rest. She agreed. Until the 19th century, the Orthodox dominated. But not anymore. *Thanks to heaven,* Zachariah had told her.

"You don't know what you're talking about."

"Do you know much about the Simons," he asked, "the family history? Zachariah's father and grandfather were great supporters of Israel. They supplied money and political influence that helped form that state. They were ultra-radicals, linked to things that today you'd be prosecuted for. The Simons have been politically connected to every government elected there, always on the conservative side."

"That doesn't make Zachariah a radical," she said, hating herself for even debating the point.

"I'm sure he's tried to convince you that he's some sort of progressive. He probably needs you to believe that in order to get what he's after."

The waiter returned and laid a salad before her.

She reached for her fork.

Brian's hand came across the table and grabbed hers. "What you just did to your father was despicable."

She flushed with anger. "Let go of my hand."

"He's your father. No matter what may have happened between you. To lie to him like you did is unforgivable."

She yanked her hand free and stood from the table. Bad enough she had some regrets, she wasn't going to listen to a stranger berate her.

"Go ahead," he said. "Leave. But know this. You're in way over your head and you're going to end up dead."

No one had ever before used the word *dead* while referring to her. "Why would you say such a thing?"

"You know nothing of who you're dealing with. Simon found you for a specific purpose. He's after something."

He motioned to the *Minerva* pages still on the table.

"And it has something to do with that article."

———

Of all the great explorers, Christopher Columbus is the most enigmatic. His birth, his character, his career, his achievements are all mysteries. No authentic portrait exists. The ones that now grace galleries around the world were painted decades after his death and conflict in the most obvious of

ways. It is known that he married in 1478 and a
son, Diego, was born in 1480. Either his first wife
died or Columbus took Diego and abandoned
her. No one seems to know her true fate. He then
had a tryst with a Castilian woman who bore him
an illegitimate son, Fernando, in 1488. He was
close with both of his sons all of his life. Of
course, Fernando favored a Spanish origin for his
father, while Diego supported an Italian ancestry.
Unfortunately, nothing has survived that attests
to Columbus' birthplace. The man himself spoke
little of his past and wrote nothing about it while
alive. Though the time of his death is certain—
May 20, 1506—the year of his birth is a matter of
great debate. Columbus himself said 1447 one
time, 1453 another. The best guess is somewhere
between August 25 and October 31, 1451. Fernando actually searched for Columbus' relations
in Genoa, Italy, but found none. Of course, Fernando's bias toward his Spanish homeland may
have colored those investigations. History, though,
owes Fernando a great debt of gratitude. At his
home on the banks of the Guadalquivir River, in
Seville, he amassed one of Europe's largest libraries. He also inherited his father's personal papers.
Fernando made provisions in his will to ensure
that the library and papers would survive but, despite this precaution, ownership was contested for
decades until eventually the books and papers
passed into the hands of the cathedral in Seville.
Sadly, many thousands of originals were lost before that transfer happened. What remains, about
7,000 items, is named the Biblioteca Colombina
and still exists in Spain.

History notes that Columbus maintained a daily
account of his first voyage, the *Diario de a bordo,*

the *Onboard Log*. This journal was presented to Queen Isabella on his return, and the queen herself commanded a scribe to prepare an exact copy. But by 1554, both the original and the copy were gone. Fortunately, before they vanished, the copy passed through the hands of Bishop Bartolomé de las Casas who used it to produce *El libro de la primera navegación, The Book of the First Navigation*—or, as it's generally known today, *The Journal of Columbus*. But again, there is no way to know if de las Casas' creation is either complete or accurate. In short, no authentic, firsthand account of Columbus' first voyage exists. Even worse, the chart Columbus used to guide his path has also been lost, that map not seen since the early 16th century.

His youth is also entirely unaccounted for. An Italian lineage does not concur with reality since he always wrote in Castilian, not Italian. He possessed no discernible educational background, yet he was clearly schooled. Fernando wrote a biography stating that his father attended the University of Pavia, but Columbus himself never mentioned that fact. This omission is curious given that he spent the better part of his adult life trying to convince the monarchs of Europe that he was qualified to spend their money on a voyage west, across the unknown sea. The fact that he possessed a university degree would have been an excellent way to raise his prestige with scholars the various crowns appointed to assess his proposal.

Ironically, his entire ocean venture was based on an error—that the western shores of Europe lead to the eastern islands of Asia. The modern belief that people of that time thought the earth was flat is fiction. Since the Greeks all mariners knew the

earth was a sphere. The unknown was what lay beyond the western horizon, out of sight of land,
where nothing but water abounded. In reality, Columbus did not discover America since millions of
people already lived there. He was not the first European to set foot on its soil since the Vikings accomplished that feat centuries earlier. He was,
instead, the first European to place the New World
on the map, though to his way of thinking he actually placed it in Asia.

From an early age I listened to tales of Columbus. Both my grandfather and great-grandfather
were fascinated by him. Many myths are associated with the man, but none more romantic than
the notion that he came to the New World for a
purpose other than profit. His *La Empresa de las
Indias, The Enterprise of the Indies,* was openly
geared toward gain. The idea had been to discover, then to exploit what was found. But some
say Columbus possessed other motives. What
those might have been vary. Much has been made
of the fact that not a single priest accompanied
him on the historic first voyage. Yet he did bring
along a Hebrew translator named Luis de Torres.
History has never been able to supply an ade-
quate explanation for that, but conspiratorialists
have not been as hampered.

Another tale that has gained momentum through
the centuries is one I heard as a child concerning
Columbus' lost gold mine. By 1600 Spain had tri-
pled the amount of European gold that had been
in circulation prior to Columbus' first voyage. A
story developed of how Columbus found a mine on
Jamaica but concealed its location from everyone,
including the Spanish Crown. My grandfather was

fascinated with the story and told me about it, along with introducing me to Columbus' signature.

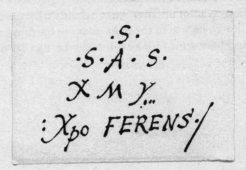

It is unusual, to say the least—a cipher that has never been decoded. Why did he not simply sign his name? Why a triangular-shaped series of letters that could mean almost anything? And why the hooked X's that appear in two locations? My grandfather always alluded to this but never explained the significance. As with so much else, we simply do not know the real story. But it is hard not to become enthralled. I know I did. So much that the subject of Christopher Columbus has formed the basis of my academic life.

Zachariah stopped reading Alle Becket's article. He'd fished it from his satchel to refresh his memory.

Thankfully, he maintained a worldwide watch for any mention of Christopher Columbus. Google Alerts and similar referral services kept him abreast of anything pertaining to that subject.

One day an article in *Minerva* had flagged.

Most of it was nothing new, but two words grabbed his attention.

Hooked X's.

Only a few people in the world knew to use that phrase in conjunction with Christopher Columbus.

So he'd located Alle Becket.

Now he'd found Tom Sagan.

Clearly, he was in the right place.

And tomorrow he'd be inside the Levite's grave.

CHAPTER SIXTEEN

TOM ENTERED HIS HOUSE, THE ONE PLACE LEFT ON the planet where he felt a margin of comfort. He stayed here the majority of his time, behind closed windows and a locked door. He'd tried an apartment and a condo, but had not liked the close proximity of neighbors. He didn't want to know anybody and he sure as hell didn't want anybody knowing him. He liked solitude, and his nondescript rental, located at the end of a long block on Orlando's south side, offered exactly that.

The visit to Abiram's grave still unnerved him.

As had the car that appeared, then disappeared.

On the drive back his thoughts had returned to the deed sent to him for the house. When it arrived in the mail the lawyer had also included one other item.

A short, handwritten note.

He needed to see it again, so he opened the drawer where he'd tossed both it and the deed three years ago.

He unfolded the pages and, for the second time, read.

The house is yours. You were raised there so you should own it. I was born a simple Jew. My faith and religion were important to me. Those were not important for you. I can't say I understand that. Sadly, though we are of the same blood, we're strangers. A lot of life was wasted between us. Things changed. Unfortunately, there is no way to go back. It's all over. If it matters, I know you were not a fraud. Whatever the explanation for what happened, it wasn't that you made up that news story. I want you to know that I felt the pain of your destruction, though I realize I kept that to myself. Son, I kept a great deal to myself. Things that would surprise you. Now I take those secrets with me to my grave. Please understand that I always tried to do the honorable thing. I hope maybe one day you will, too.

No *I'm sorry.* No *I love you.* No *Good luck.* Not even a *Go to hell.*

Just matter-of-fact.

And those last two lines. *The honorable thing.*

Typical Abiram.

On his high horse right to the end.

Three years ago he hadn't really understood *"Now I take those secrets with me to my grave."* He'd thought it more parental dramatics. Now he wasn't so sure. How would Zachariah Simon know anything about what may or may not be inside the grave? The only explanation was that Alle had told him.

What did she know?

He stepped to the window and glanced outside. The street was devoid of traffic, the neighborhood deep in its daily slumber. Not many children lived here. More retirees enjoying Florida's sun and no state income tax.

Why was someone following him?

Simon had what he wanted. So who'd appeared at the cemetery?

Someone else who might know either Abiram's or Simon's business? He was thinking like a reporter again, his inquisitive mind racing with questions. After all, he'd been damn good at what he did. Apparently good enough that someone decided to destroy him.

Who?

He knew enough.

But there was nothing he could do about that.

Then, or now.

Nothing at all.

————

ALLE STARED DOWN AT THE *MINERVA* ARTICLE LYING on the café table. She'd worked on it for weeks, keeping its length within the magazine's submission guidelines, gearing it topically so a wide audience could appreciate her points. They'd paid her €300 and she'd been elated to be published, especially at age twenty-five, fresh out of graduate school. A short bio after the piece had explained who she was, and offered an email contact.

That's how Zachariah found her.

"There's nothing sinister in that article," she said, retaking her seat. "It simply describes the mysteries surrounding Columbus."

"Yet a billionaire recluse goes to all the trouble to find you," Brian said. "Then convinces you to deceive your own father so he can open your grandfather's grave?"

She was curious. "How do you know all this?"

"You never answered me. What you did to your father was wrong."

She didn't like his attitude. He didn't know how Tom Sagan hurt her and her mother. "My relationship with my father is none of your business."

His gaze drifted around the room, then refocused

on her. "You're being used. Simon wants what your grandfather trusted you to keep safe. Doesn't it concern you that his grave is about to be opened?"

More than anyone knew.

Still—

"Your grandfather kept a great secret," Zachariah said to her. "One important to all of us."

"But opening his coffin? Is that the only way?"

"What lies with him is vital, Alle. He was the Levite. Not of the house of Levi, but chosen for a duty and called a Levite. One of only a few men since the time of Columbus who knew the truth."

"What truth?"

She'd listened to what he had to say, and finally agreed that opening the grave was the only way.

"Jews around the world will sing your praise," Zachariah said. *"What has lain hidden for nearly two thousand years will once again see the light of day. Our prophecies will be fulfilled. And all thanks to you."*

She'd never dreamed that she would be in such a unique position. Her new religion, her adopted heritage—those meant something to her, as they had to her grandfather. To help that, in any way, would be important.

"His grave must be opened," she told Brian.

He shook his head. "You're a foolish woman. And you speak of your *father* as a problem. He's an *un*willing participant. You're not."

"And who are you? Why does any of this matter?"

"Unlike you, I actually have a grip on reality. Zachariah Simon is an extremist. And those are a problem to us all."

Her gaze drifted past Brian, toward the café's front door.

Rócha and Midnight burst inside.

Brian caught sight of them, too, and stood from the table. "Time for me to go."

Zachariah's men marched over.

Brian brushed past them.

Rócha grabbed Brian's jacket. Two men at one of the other tables immediately stood, obviously with Brian. Rócha seemed to assess the situation and released his grip.

"Smart move," Brian said to him, and he and his two compatriots left.

"Who was that?" she asked Rócha.

"You tell me. You are the one eating with him."

"He forced himself on me. Called himself Brian."

"You must stay away from him."

That drew her interest. "Why?"

Irritation swept across Rócha's tanned face. "We must go."

"I'm staying."

He grasped her arm. Hard. Lifting her from the chair.

"Get your hand off me or I'll scream."

"We have to go," he said, his voice softening. "It's for your own safety."

He was serious, she could see.

"Who was that guy?" she asked again.

"A problem. One Mr. Simon must know about immediately."

———

TOM LAY ON HIS BED, FULLY CLOTHED. THIS MORNing he'd decided to die. Now, tomorrow, he would see a body.

Quite a reversal.

"He'll come around," Michele said to him. *"He's your father. He loves you. He'll eventually understand*

that you have to make your own choices, even when it comes to religion."

"You don't know Abiram. He's made his choice. It's my call now. I have to make the next move."

"Why do you call him by his first name? He's your father."

"It started in college, when we began to drift apart. It gives me . . . some distance."

"He's still your father."

He shrugged. *"He's only Abiram to me."*

She hugged him. *"I don't agree with how this has evolved, but I love you for doing this. Giving up your faith is a big deal."*

"If this makes you happy, then I'm happy."

She kissed him.

They'd been married for less than a year.

"I have some news," she said.

He stared into her eyes.

"You're going to be a father, too."

Eight months later Alle was born. What a beautiful child. For the first few years of her life she'd meant the world to him, then the world began to mean more. His time away grew longer until he was gone far more than he was there. Temptations started presenting themselves and he'd succumbed. What had he been thinking? That's just it. He hadn't thought.

And Abiram. A Levite?

He remembered Deuteronomy, Moses' blessing to the Israelites.

About Levi, he said of his father and mother, "I have no regard for them." He did not recognize his brothers or acknowledge his own children, but he watched over your word and guarded your covenant. He teaches your precepts to Jacob and your law to Israel. He offers incense before you and whole burnt offerings on your altar.

Amazing he still remembered the words, but Abiram had been relentless in his teachings. He also recalled that, after the sin of the Golden Calf, when the Israelites wrongly worshiped a false idol, Levites, who'd abstained from that act, were chosen to serve the Temple.

But how did any of that relate to Abiram?

Never had anyone in his family ever mentioned that their Jewish roots came from the Levites.

Until Tom reached high school he and Abiram had been close. Being an only child came with the advantage—and disadvantage—of constant parental attention. During his teenage years they began to drift apart. The gap widened in college. Meeting Michele and falling in love finally confirmed what he already knew.

He was not a Jew.

No matter his birth, heritage, custom, or duty.

None of it meant anything to him.

His mother had tried to persuade him otherwise. Perhaps she knew what her husband would do. But Tom had not been convinced. So he renounced his birthright and, to please his new wife, became a Christian. For a few years he, Michele, and Alle attended Episcopal services. That happened less and less as he traveled more and more. Eventually, he realized Christianity meant nothing to him, either. He just wasn't spiritual.

Chalk that up as another failure.

"Patch things up with your father," Michele said to him.

"It's too late for that."

"I'm out of the picture. We're divorced. He should be happy with that."

"It's not that simple with Abiram."

"He never cared for me, Tom. We both know that.

He resented that you were baptized and blamed me.
He only cares for Alle. That's all."

Maybe not, he thought.

He may have cared for something no one ever realized.

Son, I kept a great deal to myself.

Things that would surprise you.

Now I take those secrets with me to my grave.

CHAPTER SEVENTEEN

ZACHARIAH WAS READY FOR REST. TOMORROW COULD be the day he'd been waiting for all of his life. Had he found the Levite? The keeper of the secret? Finally, after five hundred years?

Columbus had been a clever one, that he'd give him.

In 1504 the admiral returned to Spain from his fourth and final voyage, spending the next two years trying to force Ferdinand and Isabella to honor their promises. In 1506 he died and his sons assumed the cause. When they died, it remained for one of their widows to finally make a deal with the Crown, one that gave the Columbus family total control over Jamaica for the next 150 years.

Luis de Torres, Columbus' Hebrew interpreter on the first voyage, never returned to Europe.

He stayed.

And for good reason.

De Torres' birth name had been Yosef Ben Ha Levy Haivri—Joseph, the son of Levi the Hebrew—making him the first person of Jewish origin to settle in the New World. He'd been forced to convert to Christianity in order to be eligible for the voyage but, like so many other *conversos*, he remained a Jew all of his life. History liked to downplay the fact that de Torres was, most likely, the first person ashore that day on

Hispaniola in October 1492. Since he was the expedition's interpreter, he would have been the one who initially confronted the natives. What a thought. The first words spoken in the New World were probably Hebrew.

Some historians claimed de Torres died in 1493 on Hispaniola, one of 39 left there by Columbus at the end of the maiden voyage, part of the settlement called La Navidad. All of those men were slaughtered by natives before Columbus could return months later on the second voyage.

But de Torres had not died.

Instead he'd guarded three crates that had crossed the Atlantic with Columbus on the first voyage and had been deposited on land for safekeeping.

The first person, called the Levite, charged with that duty.

And there'd been a succession of others ever since. Each guarding their secret, remaining in obscurity.

Until Abiram Sagan.

Finally, a mistake.

Sagan had told his granddaughter things. Meaningless to her and 99 percent of the rest of the world.

But not to a Simon.

Where the Levites went to great lengths to keep their secret, the Simons had gone to even greater lengths to expose them. His father and grandfather had both searched, learning bits and pieces from old documents, especially ones found in a forgotten archive. They'd wanted to provide the new state of Israel a magnificent gift—restoring the Temple treasure. But they'd both failed. History mattered, his father would many times say. Thank heaven for the Internet. That resource had not been available before his generation. From there he'd been able to discover Abiram Sagan's mistake.

Now he would capitalize on that error.

He climbed into bed.

His phone buzzed and he checked the display. Rócha.

"What is it?"

He listened as his acolyte told him about Alle Becket and what had happened at a Viennese café.

"It was him," Rócha said. "Brian Jamison. He is here."

That meant trouble.

He'd spent the past few months coddling Alle Becket, listening to her progressive garbage, all the while thinking that she embodied everything wrong with the current state of Judaism. She was naïve to the point of stupidity. But this unexpected contact directly with her signaled a problem.

He could not afford any mistakes of his own.

"Where is she now?" he asked Rócha.

"Back at the apartment. She went home. I am having it watched."

"What did she say happened?"

"He appeared. Pressed her about you. She told him to leave a couple of times, then we showed up."

"She revealed nothing?"

"She said no."

But he wondered.

Brian Jamison worked for Béne Rowe. He was to Rowe as Rócha was to him. Jamison being in Vienna and connecting with Alle was a clear message that his Jamaican partner was both well informed and perturbed.

He'd been ignoring Rowe.

But Rowe had not been ignoring him.

Luckily, he and Rócha had discussed contingencies before he'd left Austria for Florida. One of those dealt with what would happen when Alle Becket was no longer useful. "Handle things with her, as we agreed. With nothing to find."

"She may not cooperate."

He knew what Rócha meant. *With what happened on the video.*

"I will make sure she does. Give me an hour. And, one thing. After that stunt you pulled today, don't do this yourself. She will go nowhere willingly with you. Use someone else."

And he ended the call.

———

ALLE WAS BOTH ANGRY AND CONFUSED. RÓCHA HAD followed her back to her apartment with Midnight leading the way. The man who called himself Brian was gone, but his warning lingered in her mind. Rócha had quizzed her on what had happened, and she'd told him the truth.

For the most part.

"Zachariah Simon is an extremist.

"And those are a problem to us all."

But how could that be? Zachariah seemed so genuine. They'd spent a great deal of time together. Thirty years separated them in age, but she found him both charming and interesting. Apart from some glowing compliments, which also seemed sincere, he'd remained the perfect gentleman and confined his attention to business. Not that she would not have minded an advance or two. He'd been nothing but open and honest in their discussions, never a hint of deceit, and he seemed to genuinely care about their religion.

She sat alone in her three-room flat, the windows open to a cool night. Vienna was enchanting after dark, and the angle afforded her an impressive view of the brightly lit and ornately patterned glazed tile roof of St. Stephen's Cathedral.

She thought of Mount Dora, remembering all the summers she spent with her grandparents. Such a picturesque place, with its tree-lined lanes, Victorian streetlamps, parks, shops, and galleries. Later in life, she came to see how much the town resembled New England. It occupied rolling terrain that appeared downright mountainous for central Florida. Numbered avenues ran east to west and rolled steeply down to Lake Dora—both the town and water named for Dora Ann Drawdy, the first permanent homesteader. Alle had always been fascinated with Drawdy, reading about her, listening to the tales from locals.

Fiercely independent women interested her.

She considered herself one of those, as her mother had been.

Her laptop dinged, signaling an incoming email. She stepped over to the desk and saw a message from Zachariah.

> All is well here, but I need your assistance. We will be traveling extensively for the next week so could you pack all of your things? Rócha will arrange for you to be driven to the airport. I imagine you are upset over what happened during the video. I am, too, and I will personally deal with Rócha. Your flight leaves in three hours with a connection through New York. I will be at the Orlando airport waiting on your arrival tomorrow afternoon. I apologize for the short notice, but will explain once you are here. Take care.

She wondered about the urgency, but she actually preferred leaving. Rócha had gone too far. Not to mention Brian, who'd appeared from nowhere. She'd feel safer being with Zachariah. Still, she wanted to know something, so she replied.

I was contacted today by a man named Brian. Rócha advised me he was a threat of some kind, but wouldn't elaborate. What's going on?

The reply came back quickly.

He informed me. There are people who would like to stop what we are trying to achieve. There have always been such people. For your safety, it is better if you are here with me. I will explain it all once you arrive.

She decided not to press and started to pack.

She'd arrived here a month ago from Spain with only a few clothes, not expecting to stay long. Her summer wardrobe was not exactly Austrian-friendly, so Zachariah had taken her shopping. She'd felt a little uncomfortable at his generosity, but he'd assured her that it was the least he could do.

"Consider it compensation for all your hard work," he said.

"I haven't done anything."

"That's where you are wrong. You have done a great deal."

That day with Zachariah in Vienna had reminded her of another, years ago, when she was only eleven. Her father, for once, had been home and took her to the mall. School was starting in a couple of weeks and he'd wanted to be there as she picked out some new clothes. They'd wandered the stores, searching the racks and tables, trying on items. In the end, they'd left with several bags full.

One of those magical days she would never forget.

Father–daughter.

What had happened to them?

How could something so natural turn so ugly?

She didn't necessarily want to hate him, but she'd come to believe that she had to. It was her way to avoid being hurt, because there were more bad memories than good.

And she simply did not *like* or trust her father.

Zachariah?

Not only did she like him, she had no reason to doubt him, either.

So she kept packing.

CHAPTER EIGHTEEN

BÉNE REMAINED UNSETTLED AFTER HIS CONFRON-
tation with Felipe's widow. Her stare—distant yet
piercing—was one he would not forget. But Felipe
had sold him out and almost compromised everything.
And if Béne had relied solely on that one double agent
to supply him accurate information, he would know
next to nothing as to what the Simon was now doing.
Thankfully, he'd not made that mistake. He'd learned
long ago the value of a spy, particularly one in a position to witness everything. Still, he wasn't exactly
sure what the Simon was after.

Supposedly, it was Columbus' lost mine.

But he wondered.

The papers he'd obtained from Felipe's house might
help answer his questions. To get them deciphered
he'd called on a man he actually trusted, and there
weren't many of those in the world.

His men drove him a few kilometers east from Spanish Town, through horrendous Kingston traffic, to the
University of the West Indies, Jamaica's premier college. He'd graduated from it almost twenty years ago,
and he recalled his time on campus with fondness.
While many of his friends joined gangs or languished
in unemployment, he'd craved an education. He
wasn't the greatest student but he was devoted, which

had pleased his mother. He especially liked history. He realized early on that he would never be a political leader—his father's reputation was too much of a hindrance—but that didn't mean he couldn't make a difference. He currently owned or controlled nearly a quarter of the national Parliament and a majority of the cabinet ministers. His money was appreciated, as was his congenial attitude. Jamaica was divided into fourteen parishes, and he was influential in all those that counted for his businesses. He'd become a person respected by both rich and poor. He was also feared, which was not necessarily a bad thing.

The guard at the university's entrance waved his car through with a smile.

The man he'd come to see waited for him near the rugby field where students were hard into an intersquad match. He loved the game and had played it when he was here. The current team topped the island's intercollegiate league standings. He was a big financial supporter of the university, both scholastic and athletic.

Professor Tre Halliburton headed the Department of History and Archaeology. He was a blond-haired, square-faced man with tight lips and clever eyes. Not native to the island, but he'd adopted Jamaica as his home. Béne met him at a university gathering a few years ago and they began a friendship. Halliburton knew Béne's reputation, as did most of the school's administration, but he'd never been arrested, much less convicted of anything. Rumors were just that— rumors. Reality was that the university liked Rowe's money, and Béne liked giving it to them.

He stepped from the car into the late afternoon. One thing about Jamaica—weather always stayed the same, winter or summer. Either warm or hot, not

much else. It was approaching 6:00 P.M., the sun beginning its retreat behind the Blue Mountains north
of Kingston. He needed to head that way soon, as he
was due at the estate for dinner.

"Béne, you been in the jungle today," Halliburton
said to him.

His clothes were soaked with sweat and grime and
he still smelled of Felipe's stinking house. "I've been
busy, my friend." He held up the documents in his
hand. "I need you to take a look at these."

He kept his words to proper English. No patois here.

The professor shuffled through the parchments in a
quick perusal.

"Quite a find, Béne. These are Spanish originals.
Where did you get them?"

"Don't ask." And he added a smile.

"The Spanish ruled this island for 150 years," Tre
said. "When they left in 1655 they buried most of
their documents, thinking they'd be back. Of course,
they never came back, which is why we have so few
written accounts from that time."

He caught the message, but could not have cared
less.

"I assume you want me to tell you what they say?"
Tre said.

"It would help. It looks like Spanish, but I can't
read most of it."

He watched while the academician studied the writings, angling them to the sun for better illumination
of the faint print. "It's Castilian. That language has
changed a great deal since the 16th century. You
realize these parchments should not be in bright
light."

But he wasn't concerned about preservation, either.
"What are they?"

Tre knew all about his interest in the lost mine.

They'd talked about it in detail many times.

"It's amazing, Béne, but you may actually have something here."

Extremists on Both Sides, Out of Control
By Tom Sagan, *Los Angeles Times*

HEBRON, West Bank—Ben Segev lives in an unassuming house on the outskirts of town with his wife and two children. Segev is an American, from Chicago, once an investment banker. Now he's a self-proclaimed warrior.

"We will drive these Arab whores from the land of Israel," Segev says. "If the government won't get rid of the garbage, then we will."

The house is an arsenal. Automatic weapons. Ammunition. Explosives. On this day, Segev takes eight of his compatriots into the hills, where they practice for the coming fight.

"It only takes a tiny spark to light a big fire here," one of the settlers proclaims. "This city is cursed."

Hebron is an ancient town, disputed for millennia, thought to be the burial place of the prophet Abraham. At present, 450 right-wing Jews live among 120,000 Palestinians. For centuries Arabs and Jews lived here peacefully, but a 1929 riot resulted in the deaths of more than 60 Jews. The British, who governed what was then Palestine, resettled the remaining Jews elsewhere. In 1967, after Israel captured the West Bank, Jews returned. But those who came were the most ideologically extreme. Even worse, government policies at the time encouraged them to move into the West Bank. The Israelis then claimed a biblical right to the city and demanded Arabs leave.

Then in 1997 the Israeli Army withdrew from 80% of the city and ceded control to the Palestinian Authority. The remaining 20% was left for the settlers. Many, like Segev and his colleagues, are now preparing to strike.

"This is a recipe for disaster," Segev says. "And no one, in any position of authority, seems willing to help."

In the hills, away from town, under clear skies, they practice loading and unloading the automatic rifles. How to maximize every round is explained, the goal being to kill as many as possible with the least amount of bullets.

"Aim for the center mass," Segev teaches. "That's the biggest target with less chance of missing. Keep firing until they're down. Then move to the next one. No mercy. None at all. This is a war and they are the enemy."

Segev's fears are not wholly unjustified. Almost daily for the past year there have been shots fired into his settlement by Palestinian snipers. Violence on the Jewish settlers is a common occurrence. At least 30 have been killed by Palestinian gunmen. Little to nothing is done by the Arab governing authorities to stop the attacks. Finally, in response, Israel ordered 30,000 Palestinians, whose homes surround the settlement, under a 24-hour curfew. The ban prohibits the Palestinians from leaving their homes, even to go to a doctor or attend school, and jails them if they do. Twice a week the curfew is lifted for a few hours to allow residents time to shop.

"That worked," Segev says. "For a little while."

Then hundreds of Israeli troops, backed by dozens of tanks and bulldozers, swept into Hebron and destroyed buildings that had been identified as being used by Palestinian snipers. But the attacks started again a few days later.

Segev and his men continue to ready themselves.

"We feel abandoned by Israel's government," an unnamed settler says. "We are determined to rid the West Bank of Arabs."

None of them consider themselves vigilantes. Israeli and Palestinian officials confirm the extremist problem exists on both sides. Jewish extremism has happened before. In 1994 U.S. settler Baruch Goldstein gunned down 29 Arabs in a mosque. In 1995 a radical right-wing fanatic assassinated Prime Minister Yitzhak Rabin. But the latest wave has greater frequency, an Israeli official confirmed, and Hebron has become the epicenter for that violence. But how widespread is the problem?

"Not as bad as you think," say analysts at Tel Aviv University. They estimate that only 10% of the 177,000 settlers in the West Bank and Gaza are extremists. "But that minority sees themselves as guardians of Hebron, considered by many to be Judaism's second holiest city, after Jerusalem. And though several thousand Israeli soldiers and police are there to protect them, they don't see that as enough."

Segev and his men complete their work. He and his friends scoff at human rights groups who say that the settlers often provoke violence. But Palestinian officials tell a different story. Unlike the Palestinians, settlers are free to leave their homes at will. There are reports that the extremists regularly attack Palestinian shops while the Palestinians, who are forced to stay indoors because of the curfew, can only watch. Mahmoud Azam, 67, is a Palestinian. His kiosk has been ransacked three times. He's also been beaten in the back with a brick and punched repeatedly. His shop is now closed and he survives on handouts of food and money.

"If I could," Azam says. "I'd fight them back. They must not be allowed to drive us from our homes."

But the settlers disagree. "We want Israel to regain control of this area," Segev says as he tosses the guns into his car. "It needs to reoccupy all of Hebron. Until that happens, we will take preemptive actions to stop the Palestinian gunfire." The passion in Segev's declaration is clear. "People here are extremely upset by the daily shootings, killings, and harassment by Palestinians. People here feel abandoned by the government. If we don't fight, we will die."

Tom laid the article down. He'd kept the clipping in his wallet for the past eight years.

A reminder of the end.

"What was your source for this article?" his boss asked him. *"Please tell me there's more to this than what has been uncovered."*

Robin Stubbs had not only been his editor, she was his friend. As the allegations against him gradually unfolded, she'd stuck by him. When a committee of former LA Times *editors and reporters had been assembled to investigate the charge against him, he'd welcomed their action. He had nothing to hide.*

But the proof had betrayed him.

"I can only say that what the committee found is wrong. Everything in this article is true."

"That's not going to do, Tom. Your source, Segev, doesn't exist. The Israelis have searched. We searched. The Palestinian, Azam, had been dead for over a year before you supposedly interviewed him. That's a fact. Come on. What's going on here?"

The committee had reviewed all 1,458 stories he'd filed for the Los Angeles Times *during his nineteen-year tenure. Nothing had raised a red flag except one.*

EXTREMISTS ON BOTH SIDES, OUT OF CONTROL

"I approved the use of your 'unnamed settler,' and other unidentified sources," Robin said. "I stretched policy to the max on those. Now it's my ass on the line here, too, Tom. This story is a lie. Nothing about it is true. There are no settlers preparing to attack. No mass conspiracy. Sure, there's violence in the area, but not to the extent you reported."

He'd personally conducted all of the interviews, face-to-face. His expense reports verified that he had indeed been physically present at the specified locations.

But that wasn't enough.

"I'm telling you, Robin. I talked to Azam two months ago."

"He was dead, Tom."

A photo of Mahmoud Azam, shown to him, matched the man he recalled from their hour or so together in Hebron.

But that man had not been Azam.

"I told you years ago to audio-record things," Robin said.

But he hated tape recorders. Sources were far more forthcoming without a machine there, and the ones who insisted on being recorded were usually suspect.

"You have my notes," he said, as if that was good enough.

"They're fake, too."

No, they weren't. They accurately detailed exactly what he'd been told. But that didn't matter if nobody believed him.

His credibility as a reporter had given the explosive story legs, which explained why news organizations around the world ran it. The result had been a disruption of a new round of peace talks, ones that had been making progress. The Palestinian government, in a rare move, opened its files and allowed Israel to verify that the person supposedly quoted—Mahmoud Azam—had long been dead. Israel likewise cooperated and allowed Palestinian officials to be present as they searched for Ben Segev, who could never be found.

The conclusions were inevitable.

The reporter apparently made the whole thing up.

"Tom," Robin said, her voice low. "You're not the only one who will be hurt by this."

She'd worked for the Times *over two decades, rising to editor of the international desk. She was respected in the industry, and her name had been mentioned for promotion to managing editor or publisher. She'd always watched his back.*

Trusted him.

He knew that.

"The committee has verified, beyond all doubt, that the story is a fabrication. Can you prove them wrong?"

Her question carried a plea.

No, he could not.

He stared at her.

Husband number two had left a while back. No children. Only two dogs, a cat, and her career with the Times.

Which was over.

A month after he was fired, Robin resigned.

He hadn't tried to contact her. What would he say? *I'm sorry? It's all wrong? I didn't do it?*

Who would believe that?

His four Pulitzer nominations and one win were

revoked, his name stricken from the official records. All of his other journalism awards, whether won or nominated, were withdrawn. In its online archive the *Times* flagged every one of his stories with a warning, ensuring that though he'd filed 1,458 stories, 1,457 of which had been dead-on, the one in question would be his legacy. Other newspapers continued their investigations even after the *Times* stopped, attacking both him and his editors for their lackadaisical policies and sloppy management.

Especially Robin.

God help her.

She took a beating. Amazingly, she found work at a small community newspaper chain, but her name would forever be linked to his scandal. He often wondered how she was doing.

Would she have grieved at his death?

He stared at the bedroom ceiling. Outside, daylight faded. He should sleep, but a lot of ghosts had come to visit this day. More than he'd ever anticipated. His daughter. Abiram. His former boss. The past.

But only one questioned mattered.

When his gun was returned tomorrow, and after he made sure Alle was okay, should he finish what he started?

———

ALLE TOTED HER SUITCASE OUT OF THE APARTMENT building to a waiting car.

"Sure you would not like to stay?" Rócha asked, adding a nauseating smile. "We barely have spoken to each other."

She slid her bag into the open trunk and wanted to know something. "Were you following me tonight? How did you know where I was?"

"I was doing my job. Which was to protect you."

"Protect me from what?"

He wagged a finger at her. "You're a most clever woman. You think you ask me enough questions, then I will answer. Mr. Simon told me he would speak with you about all of this once you are in Florida. My job is to safely deliver you to the airport, not to answer your questions." Rócha opened the rear door for her to climb inside. "This man will drive you."

She spotted Midnight behind the wheel and cringed.

"There's nobody else who can drive me?" she asked.

"What? Still upset? He was playacting, like you. That's all. Now you must hurry. Your flight leaves in two and a half hours. Please claim your ticket at the Lufthansa check-in counter."

She brushed past him into the rear seat and he closed the door.

"A little kiss before you go?" Rócha asked through the open window.

She mustered the courage to display a single finger.

"I guess not. Do travel safe."

The car eased down the narrow street, finding the avenue at the far end. There, Midnight turned left and they sped toward the airport.

CHAPTER NINETEEN

ZACHARIAH COULD NO LONGER SLEEP. THE SITUA-
tion with Alle Becket had raised too many concerns.
Béne Rowe was far more ingenious than he'd ever
imagined. Thankfully, as with Tom Sagan, he'd
checked out the Jamaican.

Quite a character.

His mother was part Taino, part African, her roots
extending back to the slaves imported to work the
plantations. His father was African, as pure as a Jamaican slave descendant could get considering the
amount of blood mixing that had occurred. Both of
Rowe's parents were Maroons, their ancestors runaway slaves who organized in the mountains and
waged enough war on plantation owners that the
British finally decided to make peace.

He'd studied the Maroons, trying to gain an understanding. The first slaves were brought to Jamaica by the Spanish in 1517 to supplement the
native Tainos, who were dying out. The Africans
became herdsmen, hunters, and farmers with a
semi-free existence. They learned the land, becoming familiar with the dense, thickly wooded terrain.
The Spanish and English fought for years, and the
Africans allied with the Spanish. In 1660 the Spanish left the island forever, but the Africans remained,

becoming the first Maroons. The English governor at the time predicted that they would one day become a great problem.

He was right.

They controlled Jamaica's interior. Any colonist who dared to venture far from the coast paid a price.

More slaves came as sugarcane thrived. Revolts were common and many Africans escaped to the hills to join others already there. British farmers wanted the Maroons wiped out. There'd been a First Maroon War in 1731, and a second in 1795, which ended with several hundred tricked into deportation. Only a few families survived that purge, keeping to their mountain villages.

The Rowes were one of those.

Béne meant "Tuesday" in Maroon, the day of the week upon which he was born, per the naming tradition. Rowe came from a British plantation owner. Again, not uncommon, his background report had noted. Rowe hated his last name, a daily reminder of all his ancestors had endured. Though slavery ended on Jamaica in 1834, its memory still haunted. The island had been the last stop on the traders' route from Africa, which began in South America, then headed north to the lower Caribbean, and finally west, to Jamaica. All of the best and most docile Africans were bought and gone by the time slavers docked in Kingston harbor. The result became a population of aggressive Negroes, some of whom were bold enough to both flee and war on their former masters. Nowhere else in the Western world had that successfully happened.

Béne Rowe was a direct by-product of that rebellious stock. His father had been a gangster, but smart enough to involve his family heavily in Blue Mountain Coffee. Béne was an astute businessman, too.

He owned resorts throughout the Caribbean and controlled leases for several Jamaican bauxite mines, which American companies paid him millions per year to exploit. He held the title to a massive working estate in the Blue Mountains that employed nearly a thousand people. He was a man possessed of few vices. Which was surprising, given that he peddled so many of them. He despised drugs and drank only modest amounts of rum and wine. He did not smoke, nor were there any women in his life, beyond his mother. No children, either, not even the illegitimate kind.

His one obsession seemed Columbus' lost mine.

Which was what had brought them together.

On his first voyage across the Atlantic, Columbus commanded three ships loaded with enough food and water for a year. He also brought navigational equipment, trinkets for trade, ships' stores, and three unmarked wooden crates. Room had to be made in the hold of the *Santa María* to accommodate them. They were loaded aboard by several of the crew who were *conversos*—Jews at heart, forced into a Christian baptism by the Inquisition. Unfortunately, the *Santa María* ran aground off the coast of Hispaniola on Christmas Day, 1492. Every effort was made at salvage, but the ship was lost, her cargo off-loaded to the island. The three crates were buried, at night, by the admiral and his interpreter, Luis de Torres. That much was known for certain because, decades ago, his father had found documents, preserved in a private cache, that told the tale.

After that the story blurred.

The three crates disappeared.

And the legend of Columbus' lost mine was born.

BÉNE WAITED FOR HALLIBURTON TO EXPLAIN, THOUGH he liked the smile filling his friend's tanned face.

"I hope these parchments aren't now missing from the national archives," Tre said to him.

"They'll be kept safe. Tell me what they say."

"This one that looks like a deed grant with a wax seal is just that. For 420 acres. The land description is vague, they all were back then, but I think we can place it. Several rivers are mentioned as boundaries and those still exist."

Eastern Jamaica was striped with hundreds of waterways that drained the nearly constant rain from the higher elevations to the sea.

"Can you actually locate the parcel?"

Halliburton nodded. "I think we might be able to. But that tract will look nothing like it did three hundred years ago. Most of it then was dense forest and jungle. A lot of clearing has occurred since."

He was encouraged. Jamaica comprised nearly 11,000 square kilometers. The highest mountains in the Caribbean rose from its surface, and thousands of caves dotted its porous ground. He'd long believed that any lost mine would have to be in the Blue or Jim Crow mountains, which consumed the eastern half of the island. Today some of that land was privately held—he himself was one of those owners—but most of it had become a wilderness national park controlled by the government.

"This is important to you, isn't it?" Tre asked him.

"It's important to Maroons."

"It can't be the possibility of wealth. You're a multimillionaire."

He chuckled. "Which we don't need to advertise."

"I don't think it's a secret."

"This is not about money. If that cursed Italian found

a mine, he was shown it by the Tainos. It was theirs. He had no right to it. I want to give it back."

"The Tainos are gone, Béne."

"We Maroons are the closest thing left."

"You might actually have a chance to do that," Tre said, motioning with the documents. "This one is unique."

He listened as Halliburton explained about Abraham Cohen and his brother, Moses Cohen Henriques. In May 1675 the two apparently sued each other. The document Felipe stole from the archives was a settlement of that suit in which Abraham agreed to give Moses forty farm animals in return for watching over his Jamaican property during his absence.

"What makes this interesting," Halliburton said, "is that no lower court handled the case. Instead, the island's chief justice, its governor at the time, Thomas Modyford, recorded the decision."

"Too small a deal for him to be the judge?"

"Exactly. Unless there was more involved. If I recall correctly, by 1675 the Cohens would have been in their seventies."

Tre explained how the brothers helped settle Jamaica. Abraham Cohen was expelled from the island in 1640, yet he apparently returned in 1670, purchasing 420 acres that his brother cared for until 1675, when they disagreed over payment for that care.

"I see it in your eyes," he said to Halliburton. "There's more. What is it, my friend?"

"In the settlement, Moses offered to drop his lawsuit if Abraham would provide some information. The mine, Béne. That was what these two old men were really fighting about."

ALLE SAT IN THE REAR SEAT, FEELING BETTER TO BE ON her way out of Austria. The airport lay twelve miles southeast of the city in a place called Schwechat. She did not know the way but noted that the signs they were following to that locale included the European symbol of a jet airplane, marking the route to an airport. Traffic was light on the four-laned highway—understandable given it was approaching midnight. She was tired and hoped to sleep on the plane. She'd flown many times during the night and this flight should not be a problem. She'd rest and be ready for whatever Zachariah would need tomorrow.

She was on her own again.

Why had men so disappointed her? First her father. Then a succession of failed relationships. Then a disastrous marriage. Nothing had ever gone right when it came to them. Zachariah, though, seemed different. Was he a father figure? What she'd always craved? Or something else?

Hard to say.

She knew only that she respected him and, since her grandfather died, she hadn't been able to say that about any other man.

Being in the car with Midnight unnerved her. She felt dirty just knowing he was only a foot away. A few more minutes, she told herself, and she'd be gone, never to return.

A part of her felt bad about what she'd done to her father. She wouldn't want any child of hers doing such a thing. But it had to be done. Hopefully, things had worked out and her father cooperated. Her being summoned meant something significant had happened. Which, hopefully, did not involve any face-to-face encounter with her father.

She'd said about all she wanted to say to him.

The car veered onto an exit ramp, one that contained no reference to Schwechat or the airport.

Odd.

"What are you doing?" she asked.

Midnight did not reply.

They turned left onto a two-laned highway that wove a path into what appeared to be black woods on either side. No lights shone either behind them or in the opposite lane.

Speed increased.

"Where are we going?" she asked again, becoming anxious.

Midnight slowed and turned a second time, into more black trees, the headlamps illuminating a bumpy dirt lane.

"Why are you doing this? Where are we going?"

A consuming panic gripped her. She tried to open the door, but child locks engaged. She pushed the button to lower the window. Locked. Ahead, she spotted something coming into view. A car. Parked at a point where the dirt lane emptied into an open area, nothing but darkness all around.

A man stepped from the far side of the vehicle.

In the uneven wash of light she caught a face.

Terror swept over her.

Brian.

CHAPTER TWENTY

TOM BOLTED OUT OF HIS SLEEP. THE BEDSIDE CLOCK read 6:30 P.M. His brow was moist with sweat, his breathing labored. He tried to recall the dream, but couldn't. It had something to do with Robin Stubbs. Since he'd been thinking about her earlier, he was not surprised she'd remained on his mind. A few months ago he spent $125 for an Internet search and discovered that she still worked in Ohio for the same regional newspaper chain that had hired her eight years ago. It had been amazing that she'd found work, but he recalled how some pundits came to her defense. The story he'd been accused of falsifying, on its face, seemed legitimate. It was only when it was carefully investigated that the flaws became evident. And no editors engaged in such detailed analysis. Instead they trusted the people who worked for them.

"*How did all this start?*" he asked Robin. "*How in God's name did one story of mine come to your attention?*"

"*An anonymous note was sent to me. It told me that the story was false and showed me where to look.*"

"*And you believed that?*"

"*No, Tom. I didn't.*" Anger entered her tone. "*But I'm your editor, so I had to look.*"

"Which only goes to prove that I was set up. An anonymous note? Come on, Robin. If that plant was any more obvious you'd have to water it."

"All I know is everything that note said proved true, and everything you wrote proved false. I've asked you repeatedly if you can offer anything in rebuttal. Anything at all. You can't, Tom."

He saw the concern in her eyes.

"I've been here a long time," he said. "I've worked hard. I didn't do this."

"Unfortunately, the facts say different."

That was the last time they spoke.

She'd left his office and he was fired an hour later.

She quit a month after that.

And never knew the truth.

———

BÉNE COULD NOT BELIEVE WHAT HE WAS HEARING. "What does that document say? Tell me, Tre."

The sun had faded behind the blunted peaks and he caught the tang of salt on the southerly breeze from the nearby ocean. He was feeling better from his trek into the mountains. This day turning into something extraordinary.

"Did you steal this from the archives?" Halliburton asked.

"Somebody else did."

"That's the problem, Béne. Too much stealing from a place that matters."

"We can put it back, after we find out what it says."

"You're not the only one cleaning out that archive. There's almost nothing left from the Spanish time. It's all gone. I'm amazed these were still there."

His attention drifted for a moment to the rugby

field as the players formed into a scrum. He recalled how it felt, being bound together in the rows, arms interlocked, muscles pushing and pulling against other muscles. You had to be careful. He'd heard bones break during a scrum. But what fun. He loved the game. Intense. Fast-paced. Risky as hell.

Just like life.

"I have to know, Tre. What do these documents reveal?"

———

TOM WAS STARTLED BY THE MAN.

He'd been roaming the history section at Barnes & Noble, whiling away another Saturday afternoon. He found he spent a lot of time in bookstores. Never the same one, though, driving all over Orlando, varying where he went in time and place. Part of the self-consciousness that had yet to pass after a year of unemployment. It was hard to get fired. Even harder when the whole world watched.

The man who now stood before him was middle-aged and short-haired. He wore corduroy pants and a light jacket, nothing unusual given that it was actually cool outside for December in central Florida. What raised an alarm was the stare.

One of recognition.

"I came to speak with you," the man said.

"You must have me confused with someone else."

"You're Thomas Sagan."

He hadn't heard anyone speak his name directly to him in over a year. While he thought everyone knew who he was, the reality was that no one knew him. His face had once been a staple on television, but his last appearance had been over a year ago. And the public's memory faded fast.

"*What do you want?*" he asked.

"*To tell you something.*"

He noticed the voice. A near whisper. And he did not like the wary look. Was this someone ready to tell him how much he resented him lying? Just after his firing he'd received hundreds of vile emails. He'd read only a few then deleted the rest and canceled the account.

"*I don't think so,*" *he said, turning to retreat down the aisle and out the front door.*

"*I know who set you up.*"

He stopped.

Never had he heard anyone even hint that he'd been set up, much less voice the words.

He turned.

The man stepped closer.

"*When it was done, we decided not to tell you until enough time had passed that there would be nothing you could do.*"

Tremors shook his arms, but he steadied himself. "Who are you?"

"*We watched your destruction. It came fast, didn't it? But then, we're good at what we do.*"

"*Who is we?*"

The man came even closer. Tom did not move.

"*Did you ever stop to consider the consequences of what you wrote? Did you know people died because of what you wrote? You were told to stop, but you refused to listen.*"

Told to stop? He racked his brain. By whom?

Then it hit him.

The West Bank. Two years ago. A Palestinian official who'd consented to an interview, then promptly walked out of it, but not before saying, "You need to stop, Mr. Sagan. Before it's too late."

"*That's right,*" the man said. "*You do remember.*"

He now knew who they were.

"*First off, this has nothing to do with any government. We're an independent body. We work outside the law. Do the jobs that either can't be done or won't be done. You happen to fit into both categories.*"

"*So you destroyed me?*"

"*We silenced you. It's not always necessary to kill people. Sometimes it's even better not to do something that drastic. In your case, we killed your credibility and that was enough.*"

He thought back to the story that cost him everything. "*You fed that to me. You made sure I went to the Israeli and Palestinian sources you created. You handed it to me, let me run it, then erased it all.*"

The man nodded. "*It took several months to make it happen. You were a pro. Good at what you did. We had to be careful. But you eventually took the bait. It was just too good, wasn't it?*"

Yes, it was.

EXTREMISTS ON BOTH SIDES, OUT OF CONTROL

"*You pissed off some important people,*" the man said. "*They'd had enough. So they hired us to take care of the problem. We're telling you this now so that if you even think about trying for a comeback, we'll be there, ready to take you down again.*"

"*You're saying the Palestinians and the Israelis got together to destroy me as a reporter?*"

"*In a sense. We approached them both, separately, pitched the idea, and they both paid us to do the job. Neither knew the other was involved. They just wanted you out of the way for their own particular reasons.*"

"*I won't be that stupid next time.*"

"Really? How would you ever know? You had no idea then. I told you we're good at what we do. Think about that if you decide on a comeback. Every source you talk to, you'll question in your mind. Every lead that comes your way, you'll wonder. Is it real? Are they back? Is it going to happen again?"

The sorry SOB was right. He would always wonder. Everything that happened—it had destroyed his life, but it also destroyed something else.

His edge.

"You screwed with the wrong people," the man said. "I came to tell you, so you'd know. Listen to this message and keep doing what you're doing. Ghostwriting. That's perfect for you, so long as you stay a ghost."

And the man walked off.

———

BÉNE LISTENED AS HALLIBURTON ANSWERED HIS question.

"Moses Cohen was a pirate. One of the best. He ravaged Spanish shipping. His brother, Abraham, was an entrepreneur. The brothers were never close. They attended separate synagogues and there's little in the records I've seen to link them. That's what makes this document you have so interesting. By all accounts they didn't care for each other, and here we have proof of that with Moses suing Abraham. Brother against brother."

"Why is it important? Seems trivial."

"Not at all. In fact, it could be critical."

Oliver Cromwell died in 1658 and, as one diarist commented, "None but dogs cried." His brand of Puritanism had left the people little to do except contemplate their sins and wail for forgiveness. Having had enough of misery, England looked to its exiled heir, Charles II. In 1660 Charles returned to a magnificent homecoming, one he interestingly compared to "the return of the Jews from Babylonian captivity."

He was restored to the throne with but one problem.

The Crown was broke.

And so was England.

The Lord Protector Cromwell had bankrupted the nation.

To solve that problem, Charles turned to the Jews.

Edward I had expelled them 370 years earlier, and they remained virtually nonexistent until 1492, when Spain and Portugal issued their edicts of expulsion. Eventually, Jews found refuge in England and a protector in Cromwell, who allowed them to stay. With the king's return, many English merchants sought re-banishment. But Charles, too, was tolerant and championed an act of Parliament that protected them.

The king was smarter than many believed. He realized that expelling the Jews would grant English merchants complete control over trade, which meant they could set prices as they saw fit. The presence of Jewish merchants countered that power. Also, by being tolerant, Charles acquired a group of friends with money and resources.

Abraham Cohen was in Holland when Charles regained the throne. He watched with great interest as the king's Jewish policy was established. Jamaica was by then under British control, the Spaniards gone, so Abraham decided the time was right to approach the king. On March 5, 1662, Cohen and two other wealthy Dutch Jews—Abraham and Isaac Israel, a father and son—met with Charles.

The senior Israel told the king how he learned of Columbus' lost mine from Jews on Jamaica when he was imprisoned there. This was shortly before the British invaded the island in 1655. He was about to be released from custody, so his fellow captives confided to him their dire situation.

The Columbus family's hold on the island was gone. The Spanish had regained control and the Inquisition would shortly arrive. No longer would anyone protect Jamaican Jews. Thankfully, the community had taken precautions, secreting away its wealth in a location known only to a man identified as the Levite.

"It's the great Admiral's mine," one captive Jew told Israel.

Columbus himself had found the location, and their wealth would stay hidden there until the Spanish were gone. The Jews then in custody encouraged Israel to promote a foreign invasion of Jamaica, seeing it as their only hope.

Which happened.

England claimed the island in 1655.

"You know where this mine is located?" the king asked.

"We think so," Cohen said. "But Jamaica is a vast place."

Charles was hooked. Reposing trust and confidence in Cohen's abilities, he granted the man full power and authority to "search for, discover, dig, and raise a mine of gold, whether the same be opened or not opened." Two-thirds of the find would go to Charles, one-third to his Jewish partners. Cohen also smartly secured English citizenship and a trade monopoly in

*brazilwood and pimiento spice, Jamaica's two major
exports at the time.*

*Cohen returned to Jamaica in 1663 with the Is-
raels, ready to search. But after a year, with no mine
found, they were accused of fraud and banished from
the island.*

"Cohen dazzled Charles II with dreams of gold," Tre
said. "What he was really after were those trade mo-
nopolies. That entire year, when they should have been
searching for the mine, he spent making money off
wood and spice."

"All this is in that parchment?" Béne asked.

"The story of Abraham Cohen and how he manipulated Charles II is historic fact. Here, in these documents, we learn that Moses forced Abraham to reveal
things about the mine during the lawsuit. That explains the governor's involvement."

"You said we might have something."

His friend smiled. "For what he did to Charles II,
Abraham Cohen was banished from Jamaica in 1664.
If found here he would have been jailed." Tre mo-
tioned with one of the parchments. "Yet he's back in
1670, taking title to a tract of land. A tract his brother,
Moses the pirate, thinks is vitally important."

He saw the point. "You think Abraham actually
found something during that year he was making
money and came back to claim it?"

"It's entirely possible."

He liked Halliburton. They always seemed at ease
with each other, and for Béne there were few people on
the island who fell into that category. So he was not
self-conscious about showing his intense interest.

"Can you search the archives?" he asked. "Find
more?"

"It's a mess, but I'll give it a try."

He clasped Tre on the shoulder. "Tonight. Please. This is important. It's the closest I've ever come."

"I know this is important to you, Béne."

More than this man knew.

Much more.

CHAPTER TWENTY-ONE

ALLE WATCHED AS MIDNIGHT STOPPED THE CAR AND Brian walked around to her side.

"Get out," he said.

She shook her head.

Midnight shut off the engine and emerged into the Austrian night, leaving the headlights on.

Brian opened her door.

She cowered back across the rear seat. "Please. Leave me alone. I'll scream. Come near me and I'll scream."

Brian stayed outside and crouched so she could see his face. "I'm not your enemy."

Midnight bent down, too.

"Tell her," Brian said to the other man.

"I was told to kill you."

She'd been in Vienna nearly a month and had seen this black man almost every day. But that was the first time she'd ever heard his voice.

"By who?" she asked.

"Simon gave the order to Rócha. They want you to disappear. There's no plane to Florida, at least not one for you."

They both stared at her with looks of concern.

"I told you," Brian said, "that you were in way over your head. Simon's done with you. Whatever he needed from your father, he's apparently got. You're not part of his plan anymore."

"I don't believe you."

He shook his head. "Look, I'm taking a huge chance revealing to you that I have eyes and ears inside Simon's camp. This man here is staking his life to save yours. The least you could be is grateful."

"Why are you doing this?"

She held her ground across the seat, three feet from the open door, realizing there was little she could do. The door at her back would probably not open. She was alone, in the woods, at their mercy.

"Alle," Brian said. "Listen to me. You'd be dead, right now, but for me. I had you brought here. Midnight—"

"Is that really your name?" she asked. "I thought it was just what Rócha called you."

He shrugged. "I got the tag when I was a kid."

"You fondled me." She hadn't forgotten.

"And if I hadn't, Rócha would have been pissed. He told me to do it, so I played the part. Just like you, missy."

Then she knew. "You told Brian about all that's been happening."

Midnight nodded. "Yes, ma'am. That's my job."

"Get out," Brian said again.

She shook her head and did not move.

He exhaled, shook his head, and stood. His hand reached beneath his jacket and a gun appeared. "Get your sorry ass out of that car. Now. If you don't, we're going to drag you out." To make his point he thrust the weapon inside. "I'm not in the mood for this."

Her brain seemed frozen, her body paralyzed.

Never had she faced the barrel of a gun.

She slid herself across the seat to the open door.

"It's late," he said. "I'm tired, and we have a drive ahead of us."

"Where are we going?"

"Someplace where you can be dead, at least as far as Simon is concerned. Midnight has to go back and report that you're no longer breathing."

"Why does Zachariah want me dead?"

"Because, little lady," Midnight said. "That man has been playing you for weeks. He tells you what you want to hear, and you believe every word. He's got what he wants. Now you're in the way."

"What is it he wants?"

"Your father on a leash," Brian said. "Whatever your grandfather has in that coffin, Simon wants it bad. And you just helped him get it."

She still wasn't prepared to concede that Zachariah would harm her.

"Why do you care what happens to me?" she asked, still sitting inside the car at the door.

Brian stepped close, the gun still in his hand. "I got news for you. I don't. I only care about what you know. But unlike your great benefactor, I actually saved your life."

"And that's supposed to make me grateful?"

He shook his head and again pointed the gun straight at her. "Do you have any idea how much trouble you've caused?"

She tried hard to master the stabs of panic in her chest. She wanted to retreat inside the car but realized that would be useless.

"Are you going to cooperate?" Brian asked, a look of hope in his watchful eyes.

"I don't seem to have much choice."

Brian turned to his compatriot. "Get back to town and tell them she's dead. Then keep your eyes and ears open. I've got a feeling a lot is about to happen on your end."

Midnight nodded and reached for the front-door handle.

"You're going to have to get out," Brian said to her.

She stepped to the ground.

The trunk popped open and Brian retrieved her bag, tossing it to the roadbed. Midnight climbed into the car and left, taking all illumination with him. She and Brian stood in the chilly dark. Not a sound could be heard from the woods around them.

"Time for us to go," he said.

And he walked toward his car, pointedly ignoring her bag.

She lifted it and followed.

CHAPTER TWENTY-TWO

TOM AWOKE AROUND 7:00 A.M., AFTER HAVING SLEPT for nearly six hours. A record for him of late. Usually he was lucky if he grabbed three hours' rest, anxiety a powerful stimulant, enough to have deprived him of a good night's sleep for the past eight years. He once thought the malady might fade, or at least diminish, but it had seemed to only grow worse. His last thoughts before dozing off had been of that day in the bookstore when he'd found out who and why.

Which had only worsened his dilemma.

The messenger had been right. There was nothing he could do. Nobody would believe him without proof. And finding that would be next to impossible. If he did manage to talk someone into hiring him, there was nothing to stop his enemies from doing it to him again.

And he would never see it coming.

He possessed no options.

None at all.

He was through.

But maybe not entirely.

He showered and dressed in jeans, a crew neck T-shirt, and tennis shoes, then ate a couple of pieces of dry white toast. Food was another pleasure he'd long ago lost interest in. The drive east to Mount

Dora, then to the cemetery, took less time than he'd envisioned. Traffic was a nightmare in Orlando, but he was headed out of town, not in, against the Wednesday-morning flow, which made the trip its usual thirty minutes.

He arrived just before ten and spotted a work crew inside the low brick wall, among the *matsevahs,* at his father's grave. Bright sunshine flooded the sacred ground, the humid air rich with the scent of turned earth. He made his way to the site, where the headstone had been removed, and peered down into the hole.

No coffin.

Apparently, Zachariah Simon had obtained his order and was in a hurry.

He walked toward the ceremonial hall. It was single-storied, wood-sided, and steeply roofed. Black shutters framed its many windows. He could recall as a kid being inside during several funerals—his mother's and uncles' most notably. Abiram had been laid out inside, too. Now he was making a return engagement.

A woman stepped from its half-open doorway into the sunshine. She was short, stout, and dressed like a lawyer, which he assumed she was. Simon's lawyer. Smart of him not to be around. Less witnesses to see his face and to overhear their conversations.

He approached and she introduced herself. She offered a hand to shake, which he accepted, forcing a grin and saying, "Let's get this over with."

"The law requires an heir be present. You can, of course, satisfy that by simply waiting outside, so long as the medical examiner knows you're here. He's inside waiting on your arrival."

"I can handle it."

He wasn't exactly sure that was the case, but he knew he wasn't going to wait out here. He'd been thinking on the drive over. Simon had gone to a lot of trouble to obtain whatever was in that coffin. Once he had it, there was no guarantee he would release Alle. In fact, why would he? She could just go straight to the police and be a witness against him. Of course, the same could be said about himself. But he assumed Simon wasn't concerned with that threat. The last person on earth the police would believe was a disgraced reporter.

Besides, he may kill himself before the day was out anyway.

Or maybe not.

Still debating that point.

He entered the building and stepped down a short hall that led to an open door. The décor inside the room had not changed much. Same drab carpet, bland walls, and musty smell.

An unplaned pine coffin lay on a stout oak table, the same table that had been there for decades. The box's exterior was reasonably intact, considering it had rested in moist Florida earth for three years. A man in a blue jumpsuit that identified him as MEDICAL EXAMINER introduced himself and asked for identification that confirmed he was Tom Sagan. He produced his driver's license, even as his eyes stayed on the coffin. Did he want to see the decomposing corpse? Not really. But he had to know what Zachariah Simon wanted. Alle was depending on him. So he steeled himself and gave the okay to open the lid.

It took a few minutes to pry off. Long nails had been used, which was appropriate. Abiram would have kept things traditional. Tom listened as each one squeaked its way free. The lawyer stood beside him, unemotional, as if she opened coffins every day.

The final nail was removed.

The medical examiner stepped aside: Now was the time for the heir to do whatever it was that had compelled the exhumation. Since he was that person, all eyes locked on him.

But Ms. Lawyer started toward the table.

He grabbed her arm. "I'll handle it."

"I think it would be better if I did." Her eyes conveyed an even more emphatic message. *Stay out of this.*

But she wasn't the man in Barnes & Noble. "I'm his son. The petitioner. I'll handle it."

She held her ground and his eyes conveyed their own message.

Don't screw with me.

She caught his drift and backed off.

"All right," she said. "Handle it."

————

ZACHARIAH CHECKED HIS WATCH.

10:20 A.M.

The lawyer he'd hired to both obtain the court order and be on-site had called twenty minutes ago to say Sagan had arrived. They should be inside by now, and things should be over shortly. The report from Vienna was good. Alle Becket was a problem no more. Nothing would be learned by anyone from her. Rócha sat beside him in the car, just off an overnight flight from Austria to Orlando, via Miami. He'd taken the flight Alle had thought would be hers.

Tom Sagan required handling.

With no daughter to produce once the exhumation was complete, the only course was to eliminate the last remaining witness.

They'd actually be doing Sagan a favor.

He wanted to die.

So Rócha would oblige him.

————

TOM CAUGHT THE BITING SMELL OF DECAY. THE MED-
ical examiner advised him to move quickly as things
would only get worse.

He stepped close and peered into the coffin.

Not much remained. Alle had apparently kept to
tradition and not embalmed. The corpse was wrapped
in a white shroud, most of which had disintegrated,
exposing what little was left of a face. Empty eye
sockets looked like black caves—the querulous,
sometimes hostile gaze he remembered was gone.
Flesh and muscle had collapsed. A fold of skin, like
the wattle of a lizard, sagged from the neck. He tried
to recall the last time he'd seen that face alive.

Five years ago?

No, closer to nine. Before the fall. At his mother's
funeral.

Had it been that long?

Not once in the intervening years had Abiram
tried to contact him. No note, letter, card, email,
nothing. While the press and pundits destroyed him,
his only surviving parent remained silent. Only after
dying, in his final note, sent with the deed to the
house, had some consolation been offered—*"I felt
the pain of your destruction"*—but that was nowhere near enough. True, Tom could have called,
but he never did, either. They were both at fault.
Neither willing to give.

And they'd both lost.

He struggled with waves of fear, apathy, resentment, and resignation. But he drew himself up and
regained a measure of poise.

A sealed packet lay embedded in what had once been Abiram's chest. It appeared vacuum-sealed, airtight creases evidencing that fact. He reached for it, but the medical examiner removed it for him.

"Better that way," the man said, displaying gloved hands. "Bacteria is everywhere on a corpse."

The packet was paper-thin, about a foot square, and appeared light. The medical examiner asked if there was anything else. He saw nothing else unusual inside so he shook his head.

The lid was replaced.

A sink adorned one wall—used, he remembered, for cleansing. The medical examiner rinsed the package off and brought it over to him.

Ms. Lawyer stepped forward. "I'll take that."

"Like hell you will," Tom said. "Last I looked, I'm the petitioner here."

Anger fortified him.

"And by the way," he said. "Do you have something for me?"

She seemed to understand and retreated to a satchel that lay on the floor. From within she removed a small FedEx box and handed it to him. She then turned back to the medical examiner and asked for the packet again.

But he grabbed it first. "That's mine."

"Mr. Sagan," the lawyer said. "That was to be given to me."

He was not in the mood to argue. "I'm going to assume that you have no idea what's really going on here. Let's just say that you don't want to know. So how about you shut up and stay out of my way."

He'd decided that whatever may have been in the grave was his only bargaining power, and he wasn't about to give that away. He had to make sure Alle was okay. Never had he believed in a heaven, or an afterlife, or anything more than when you died, just like Abiram, you turned to mush, then dust. But on the off chance that his parents and Michele would be waiting on him after he finally did blow his brains out, he wanted to be able to say that he'd done the right thing.

He backed toward the door.

The lawyer advanced.

He asked, "I assume you know what's in this FedEx box?"

She stopped. Apparently she did. And she also seemed not to want to have too much of a conversation in front of the medical examiner.

"Tell your client that I'll be in touch about a trade. He'll know what I mean."

"How will you find him?"

"Through you. What firm are you with?"

She told him.

And he left.

CHAPTER TWENTY-THREE

ALLE WATCHED THE VIDEO FEED. SHE SAT WITH BRIAN in a house across the Austrian border in the Czech Republic. They'd driven here last night from Vienna. She was still unsure about any of this and had spent the day in her room, her mind simmering with anxiety. Now, watching the images from Florida, new worries lunged at her.

She recognized the place where her grandfather lay buried. The pictures they were receiving were being shot through a car windshield, from a distance, and elevated. The cemetery was located in Lake County, which had the distinction of having some of Florida's highest terrain. There were actually hills there, along with over a thousand lakes. Brian's man had chosen a hillock near the cemetery as his vantage point. She recalled it. A wooded mound of scrub oak, pines, and palms. She'd watched an hour ago while workers exhumed her grandfather, hauling the coffin into the burial house, the same wood-sided building where she'd kept vigil over him after he died. The camera offered a clear view of its front door.

"Why are you filming this?" she asked.

"To try and find out what the hell is in that coffin."

"What are you going to do? Steal it?"

"I'm not sure what I'm going to do, but if I can get it I will."

Matsevahs dotted the foreground, a portion of the waist-high brick wall enclosing the grounds visible. During summer visits with her grandparents she'd often visited the cemetery, helping her grandmother tend the graves.

She'd yet to see Zachariah and commented on that.

"He gets others to take all the risks," Brian said. "It's his way. But he's out there. Watching."

Her father and another woman had disappeared inside the building about twenty minutes ago.

"You don't know anything about my family," she had to say to Brian.

"I only know your father didn't deserve that crap yesterday. He thinks you're in danger. Every decision he's about to make is based on that lie."

"All we wanted him to do was sign papers. He would have never done that by me simply asking."

"What's the *we* crap? You're part of whatever it is Simon is doing?"

"You speak like it's a crime."

"I assure you, this is not about signing some papers. Simon wanted you dead. He's going to want your father dead, too. That's why I have a man there."

This was all so hard to believe.

"Doesn't it bother you," Brian asked, "that your father was about to kill himself last night?"

"Of course it does. What I did stopped him."

Brian looked incredulous. "And that's how you justify it? You had no idea what he was about to do. You just wanted to help Simon any way you could."

She resented his tone and accusations.

Her father appeared on the screen, rushing outside, holding what appeared to be a blue-and-white box in his right hand and a packet in his left, which she recognized. The same one she'd placed in the coffin.

"You see that," a voice said through the computer.

"Oh, yeah," Brian said. "Get ready to move."

———

ZACHARIAH HAD WAITED LONG ENOUGH. THIRTY minutes was plenty of time. What was taking so long? He and Rócha were parked a kilometer away, far enough that no one would know they were there, but close enough to act. He'd instructed the lawyer that once she held the packet she was to provide Sagan with a telephone number for a disposable phone he'd bought yesterday that would allow a call to lure the former journalist to where Rócha could deal with him.

Hopefully, Sagan would save them all the trouble and kill himself. That was why he'd returned the gun. A suicide would make things so much easier. He should have kept Alle Becket alive at least until today, but with Brian Jamison in Vienna, no chances could be taken. The last thing he needed was for Béne Rowe to know any more of his business. He'd told the Jamaican only what had been absolutely necessary, and he had to keep it that way. He'd not come this far to have everything snatched away. Especially by a Caribbean hood only interested in some mythical gold.

His phone rang.

"Sagan took the packet and left," the female voice said.

"And you allowed him?"

"How was I to stop him?"

Useless. "Did you give him the phone number?"

"There was no time. He said he would contact you through me."

"When he does, give him the number."

He ended the call and faced Rócha.

"Seems Mr. Sagan has decided to grow a backbone. He should be along here shortly. Take care of him before he drives too far."

———

ALLE WATCHED AS HER FATHER RAN TOWARD A CAR parked in the graveled lot just beyond the outer brick wall.

"Tell me the layout there," Brian said.

She stared at him.

"The layout," he said, voice rising. "The road in and out. Where does it go? What's on it?"

She searched her memory. "The cemetery sits about three miles off the highway. There's a paved road to it that passes farms and orange trees. A few lakes parallel the road for a while."

"Houses?"

She shook her head. "Not many. Pretty lonely out there. That's why the cemetery is there."

"You get all that?" Brian asked to the computer.

"I'm on it."

Her father was in his car, backing out and leaving. The woman from earlier appeared at the doorway with a cell phone in hand.

"You know who she's calling," Brian said to the computer. "Follow him."

Movement on the screen confirmed that the car with the camera was leaving its position.

"What's happening?" she asked.

"Your father is trying to save your hide. He probably figures that keeping whatever he was holding made more sense than just turning it over. And he's right. But he has a problem. Rócha's there."

Her heart pounded.

Which surprised her.

"He took your flight last night. Your father's in a whole lot of crap."

———————

TOM SPED AWAY FROM THE CEMETERY.

He'd made his escape.

"Now I take those secrets with me to my grave."

His father had meant that literally and what lay on the passenger's seat was apparently those secrets. He wanted to pierce the vacuum bag and see for himself, but not now. He had to get out of here. He wheeled the car away from the cemetery and caught sight of the lawyer leaving the building.

Making a call.

To Simon?

Who else.

He'd wait an hour or so, then make contact through the lawyer. He didn't own a cell phone. No need for one. Who'd call him? So he'd find a phone somewhere. Going back to his house was not an option since Simon surely knew where he lived.

He sped down the drive between groves of live oaks. Palmetto scrubs hugged the shoulder. The putrid smell of death lingered in his nostrils. At the highway he turned left and headed for Mount Dora, the asphalt winding a path through orange country. Most central Florida orchards were gone, growers long ago switching to squash, cabbage, lettuce, or strawberries.

Here, though, citrus remained.

In his rearview mirror he saw a car.

Coming fast.

ZACHARIAH SAT IN THE PASSENGER'S SEAT AS RÓCHA drove. They were closing in on Tom Sagan. What an unexpected irritation. He'd not anticipated resistance. The exchange should have been made, Sagan accepting that there was little he could do but cooperate. Instead, this fool had decided to change the rules.

"We must stop him before he finds the next highway," he told Rócha.

They were less than five hundred meters away.

"Force him from the road into the fields."

CHAPTER TWENTY-FOUR

Béne stepped from his truck and walked toward the museum's entrance. He'd come alone. He never brought men or guns here. No need. The tiny village of Charles Town sat in the Buff Bay River valley, a peaceful notch a few kilometers south from Jamaica's north shore. After the Maroons Windward sect, led by Captain Quao, defeated the British in 1793, a signed peace treaty between former slaves and masters granted 1,000 acres of land to the Charles Town Maroons, tax-free, in perpetuity. About 1,200 Maroons still lived on that land, in the shadows of the mountains, beside the river, struggling with high unemployment and continual impoverishment. Farming remained their main source of income, tiny mountainside tracts leased from absentee owners that produced coffee, nutmeg, and charcoal. But there was also a block-making and furniture shop, a school, and a few rum bars.

He knew all of the prominent families. Dean, Duncan, Irving, Hartley, Shackleford. Most sat on the Council of Elders. Frank Clarke served as the Maroon colonel, elected three years ago to be in charge of the community.

Béne liked the colonel, an educated man full of expertise and caution. A graduate of the University of the West Indies, born nearby, Clarke worked in the United States for three decades as a stockbroker before rediscovering himself and returning home to Charles Town. He now championed causes island-wide, becoming as close to a national spokesperson as the Maroons ever had.

"Ah, Béne, *yuh noh dead yet?*" Clarke called out.

He smiled at the patois way of asking *how have you been?*

"Not dead yet, my friend. But not for the lack of trying."

Frank grinned. He was pushing seventy, but with only a dusting of gray in his short brown locks. Little fat adorned his lanky frame. He wore thick glasses with round metal-rimmed lenses that provided a singularly intense look to his dark eyes. He was dressed in jeans shredded at both knees and a dirty black shirt that hung shirttail out. One hand held a rusted *machet.*

"You working today?" Béne asked, pointing to the old clothes.

"Taking some people up the mountain. To the ruins. Going to teach them the old ways."

Frank Clarke was passionate about Maroon history. He'd been taught by a great-grandaunt who'd been a local chieftain. Last year Clarke had brought life to that heritage by starting the Charles Town Maroon Museum. Béne had helped with money for the construction of a building, erected in the old style of hewn timber pilings, tin sides, and a thatched roof.

"How's all this doing?" he asked.

He'd not visited in a few months.

"We get people. Not many, but some. The tour guides bring 'em. Slow and steady. Every dollar we make helps keep the place open."

Colonels headed the various Maroon communities

islandwide. He knew they all met at least once a month in a loose form of Parliament. Maroon land was not subject to Jamaican taxation or much regulation. They governed themselves, treaties from long ago assuring that independence.

He liked coming here, discussing the old ways, and he'd learned many things about the lost mine from Frank Clarke.

A Taino legend told the story of two caves. One called Amayauna, meaning "of no importance." The other, Cacibajagua, "of great importance." Neither had ever been found. Part of the tale, which Maroons adopted as their own, included how the Tainos showed Columbus a place in the mountains, a cave, where veins of gold ran two inches wide. But after 500 years of searching no trace of any mine had ever been found. A myth? Maybe not. Something Tre Halliburton mentioned yesterday had tugged at his brain all night.

"The Columbus family's hold on the island was gone. The Spanish had regained control, and the Inquisition would shortly arrive. No longer would anyone protect Jamaican Jews. Thankfully, the community had taken precautions, secreting away its wealth in a location known only to a man identified as the Levite."

So he'd driven across the mountains from his estate on the south slope to here, on the north, to see a man with knowledge.

"I need to know more about the mine," he said to Clarke.

"You still lookin'? Can't shake it?"

"Not now."

Frank once told him about another legend. A cave supposedly guarded by an iron gate that no Maroon had ever been able to penetrate. They called it Cacibajagua, place of importance, same as the Tainos. Many had tried to pass through the gate, all had failed. He realized Maroons, like the Tainos, lived by their stories. The more fantastical the better. Jamaicans liked to say how proud they were of Maroons, but few knew anything about them. Even stranger, Maroons knew little about themselves. Like the Tainos, Maroons left no written history, no edifices, nothing to remember them by except songs, proverbs, place-names, and trails in the forest. His hope was that this old story might be grounded in some fact.

So he asked, "The Jews. How were they with the Maroons?"

This was a subject they'd never broached, but now he wanted to know.

"The Jews were different," Frank said. "Not really Spanish or English. Not African. Not Taino. But they were persecuted, as we were. Sure, they owned most of the businesses and made money, but they weren't equals with the Spanish or English. They were beat down. Many laws were passed against them. Did you know that Jews could only own two slaves, no more. Unless they owned a plantation, and that was rare. And they could only have other Jews as indentured servants."

No, he'd not known that.

"No laws, though, stopped Jews from doing business with slaves," Frank said. "They sold goods to 'em and white people hated that. They said it encouraged slaves to steal from masters, since Jews gave 'em a place to spend the money. That led to a lot of bad feeling toward them. Jews also sold Maroons ammunition. That was the one thing we could never make on our own. Guns we stole off dead British soldiers, ammunition had to be bought."

"You never told me any of this before."

"Béne, there's a lot you've never asked about."

"Where is this place of the iron gate?"

Frank smiled. "There are things I can't speak of."

"I'm Maroon."

"That you are. So you should know that there are things we don't speak of."

"Then tell me more about the Jews."

The colonel appraised him with a skeptical eye. "Like I said, they sold Maroons powder and shot when we fought the English. But they also sold to the English. Bad feelings came from that on both sides. Colored people acquired full rights here in 1830. After that, the Jews were the only free men without the right to vote. That didn't come until years later, and it was the freed colored who fought against Jewish equality for so long." He paused. "Always thought that strange. But the Jews can't be faulted. They were businesspeople. They feared the English would lose tolerance and seize their property, expelling them. So they played both sides."

He relieved Clarke of his *machet* and used the blade to sketch in the dirt.

"What is that?" Béne asked his friend.

Only bird twitters and humming insects disturbed the peaceful morning.

"Where did you see this?"

The words came thin, rasping, and harsh.

"What is it?"

Frank stared at him.

"The key to the iron gate."

CHAPTER TWENTY-FIVE

ALLE STARED AT THE VIDEO MONITOR AS THE CAR SPED down a familiar highway. Orange groves stretched for miles on either side, between horse farms and treed hillocks.

"What is your man going to do?" she said.

"Good question," Brian said.

"There's a car on Sagan's tail," the voice from the computer said. "Closing fast."

"Where are you?"

"Behind that car. But back."

"There's no need to be subtle anymore. Help him. You know who's on his tail."

Brian's eyes confirmed what she already knew.

Zachariah and Rócha.

A lump formed in her throat that she found hard to swallow. Never had she considered the possibility that her father might be harmed.

Yet here it was.

The resolution on the dashboard camera was not good enough for them to see far ahead and road vibrations caused the image to constantly shift.

What was her father doing? Just give them what they want.

This wasn't supposed to be happening.

"Simon is on him," the voice from the computer said.

ZACHARIAH ROLLED DOWN HIS WINDOW AS RÓCHA brought the car parallel to Sagan's, in the opposite lane. No cars were coming their way. Sagan's hands were tight on the wheel, face tense. At first he ignored them, then he finally glanced over.

"Stop the car," Zachariah yelled.

Sagan shook his head.

TOM HAD NEVER DRIVEN A CAR THIS FAST BEFORE. HE was pushing ninety. Thankfully, this road was a straight shot with few curves. His gaze darted left and right and all he could see was orange trees, their verdant leaves thick with spring blossoms. As a kid he'd worked the Lake County fields during the summer and fall, earning extra money. Back then several local families, all friends, owned the largest orchards. He knew where he was and what lay around him. One rule any good reporter quickly mastered was to learn the lay of the land.

The car behind him veered left in the opposite lane and sped up beside him.

Simon.

Telling him to pull over.

There was no evading the directness of his gaze, the eyes the same—cold and confident—so he reached across to the other seat, grabbed the box with his gun, and laid it on his lap.

Simon was motioning again for him to stop.

His hands grabbed the box and ripped it open.

He regripped the wheel as his left hand found the gun and swung it out the window.

————

"SLOW DOWN," ZACHARIAH SCREAMED.

Sagan was pointing a gun directly at him.

Rócha slammed on the brakes, decelerating enough for Sagan's car to race away.

The damn fool had wanted to shoot him.

"Go," he ordered. "Force him off the highway."

————

TOM WAS GLAD HE HADN'T BEEN REQUIRED TO PULL the trigger. He'd never actually fired a gun, and shooting one while driving ninety miles an hour had not seemed the best way to start.

But he'd been prepared to do it.

He'd deal with Zachariah Simon, but on his own terms. What did he have to lose? He doubted Simon would hurt Alle, not until he had what he was after. And Tom could not care less about himself. He should already be dead, so any additional time he spent breathing was simply a bonus. Strange, though, how, in the heat of this chase, he hadn't thought about dying. All he wanted to know was that Alle would be okay. And the sealed package lying on the passenger's seat should ensure that would happen.

Something slammed into his bumper, jarring the steering wheel.

He regained control and held the front tires straight. He was about to run out of highway, as this county road would dead-end into another more heavily traveled state route.

Another pop to the bumper.

Simon was slamming into him from behind, staying away from any bullets. He watched in his rearview mirror as Simon's vehicle dropped back, then sped toward him, this time veering left into the other lane and crashing into his car's side. He struggled to hold the vehicle on the road, then decided *What the hell. Go for it.* One turn to the right and the front tires leaped from the pavement, his acceleration sending him across a narrow drainage ditch that paralleled the road and into an orange grove.

The front end pounded the earth, then rebounded, the rear tires driving him ahead. He jammed his right foot onto the brake, slowed, then spun onto a dirt lane between a long row of trees.

And raced ahead.

Simon was impressed.

Quite a maneuver.

Tom Sagan was proving a challenge.

Rócha stopped the car, wheeled around, and back-tracked to where Sagan had jumped.

"Do it," he ordered.

Rócha reversed and bought himself more roadway, then accelerated, skipping the ditch, landing hard on the other side. He worked the wheel left, then right, and they found the same lane between the trees Sagan had used, a dust cloud ahead obscuring their view.

They'd have to move slower.

But they would move.

Béne waited for Frank Clarke to explain him-self.

The key to the iron gate?

He knew Maroons were zealous about secrets. The entire society had been born in crisis, nurtured through strife, and existed for four centuries almost totally hidden away. They'd been brilliant warriors with a high morale, their entire existence resting on the memory of their greatest deeds, the tales passed from one generation to the next.

An iron gate?

He wasn't interested in stories.

He wanted retribution.

And the colonel should, too.

"Frank, you have to help me. I'm trying to find that mine. It's out there, around us, somewhere, in these mountains. You know it is. It's not a legend. That place, its wealth, belongs to Maroons. It's ours."

He was speaking straight, using perfect English, making clear that this was going to be a modern solution to an old problem.

"I'm not so sure about that, Béne."

"The Spanish stole it from the Tainos. We're the closest thing left to them. Think what we could do if the legend is true."

His friend said nothing.

"Why is that symbol there in the ground so important?"

Frank motioned for them to walk inside the museum.

The structure cast the appearance of a shanty, similar to where Felipe lived. It was authentic Maroon except that cut lumber had been substituted for hewn logs. The floor was old-style, a mixture of clay and ash hammered to the consistency of concrete. He'd used the concoction himself on his estate in the barns, work sheds, and coffee-processing facilities. Artifacts lined the outer walls of the barnlike rectangle, all excavated from the nearby mountains. Placards explained their significance. Nothing fancy, just plain and simple. Much like the people being remembered.

They passed wooden tables displaying bowls and utensils. *Junges* stood upright, the spear's rusted blades sharp. An *abeng* occupied a place of prominence, as it should. He'd learned as a boy how to blow the cow's horn—once the Maroon's version of the Internet—creating specific notes that translated into messages over long distances. There were also drums, bird traps, cauldrons, even a replica of a healing hut used by each community's Scientist to treat the sick.

"I haven't been here in a while," he said. "You have more on display than before."

Frank faced him. "You should come more often. Like you say, you are Maroon."

Which was all a matter of birth. If a parent was Maroon, then so were the children.

"You don't need me around," he said.

"Not true, Béne. Nobody here cares that you make money off gambling or whores. We all know, so don't be ashamed. We're not. Look where we came from. Who we are."

They stopped at a wooden stage that occupied a rear corner, upon which sat three drums. He knew music was a big part of the museum's allure. Some of the local drummers were the best on the island. Shows were a regular occurrence here, drawing both Maroons and tourists. He even owned one of the drums, carved from a stout piece of timber found in the mountains. Frank bent down and slid out a topless wooden crate from beneath the stage. Inside lay a stone, about a third of a meter square, upon which was the same symbol he'd traced outside.

He stared at his friend. "You know of this?"

"Two lines, angled, crossing each other, one with a hook on top. It's been found in several sacred spots."

He studied the carving, nearly identical in size and shape to the one from the grave yesterday.

"Would you like to see another?" Frank asked. "In the mountains."

"Thought you had visitors coming."

"Someone else will take them. You and I have need to talk."

CHAPTER TWENTY-SIX

TOM KEPT THE CAR RACING THROUGH THE ORCHARD, the path ahead clear for a good half mile. If Simon decided to follow it would not be as easy since his tires were stirring up a dust cloud in his wake. At least his instincts had proven correct. Simon was not a man to be trusted. And one other thing. When he'd glanced across into the other car he caught the face of the driver—full of flat planes and angular bones, dark hair curly and coiled—one of the men who'd assaulted Alle.

The lawyer's job had been to retrieve what had been in the coffin. What was the driver here to do? And did that mean Alle was being held nearby? Given the possibilities of the Internet, there was no way to know where she was a prisoner. But one of her captors being here meant that she could be close. Which made sense. Simon would have had to, at some point, produce her. Or had he thought his target was so weak, so beat down, so defeated, that he would have done whatever he was told, few questions asked?

Maybe so.

And that infuriated him.

Right now, he held the cards. His blood flowed. His

nerves tingled. He felt like he had years ago, on the scent of a story.

And he liked it.

Ahead, a makeshift bridge of blackened railroad ties spanned an irrigation canal. He knew orange groves were lined with canals to drain rainwater. In the old days they'd supplied the pumps. He'd spent many a summer day cleaning wet ditches of grass and debris.

An idea came to him.

He slowed, crossed the bridge designed for tractors and picking equipment, and stopped on the other side.

He popped open the door and ran back.

The ditch was a good twenty feet across, the ties extralong and supported by a center post. They sat side by side, designed, he knew, to be movable, other center posts spaced along the canal. He'd also spent time moving ties from one location to another.

Dust from the road on the other side of the ditch began to clear.

He heard the growl of an engine.

Coming closer.

The ties, about four inches thick, were arranged two together, four feet apart, just enough width to accommodate tires on either side of a chassis. He ran onto the bridge and dislodged one long pair from their rails, shoving them down into the ditch.

Then the other pair.

His muscles creaked under the strain.

He retreated to his side of the bank and slid two more from their perch.

Twenty feet of air now separated him from Simon.

Dust on the other side cleared.

He saw the car.

SIMON KEPT A CLOSE WATCH AHEAD.

Rócha was speeding down the lane between the trees as fast as they could go thanks to the limited visibility. But luckily, it appeared the fog was dissipating.

Then he saw.

Tom Sagan stood on a far bank before a wide ditch. A bare post rose from its center. Rócha had seen it, too, slamming the brakes, tires grabbing the earth. The car slid to a stop, his seat belt holding him in place.

Rócha cursed.

He stared out the windshield.

"Shut off the engine."

———

TOM RETREATED TO HIS CAR AND FOUND THE GUN. He kept the driver's-side door open, both it and the car between him and Simon. Sure, one of them could wade across the ditch, but he'd shoot them dead before they made it to the other side.

Standoff.

Just what he wanted.

A warm breeze flayed his skin, raising gooseflesh across his neck and chest.

"All right," Simon called out to him. "What do you want?"

"My daughter."

He stayed low, staring out through the open window frame.

"I realize you have your gun, and you chose your place to take a stand with care. We will not challenge you."

The other man stood beside Simon and never moved.

"I should shoot your friend," Tom yelled. "He touched my daughter."

Neither of them moved.

"He was doing his job," Simon said. "What I pay him to do. My lawyer failed to do hers."

"I want Alle, then you can have what I have."

"She's not here."

"How did that son of a bitch you pay get here?"

"He flew all last night."

He was listening.

"She is in Vienna. If you want her, that is where you will have to go."

Austria?

"That is where I live. But maybe you already know that. After all, you were a reporter."

"Go screw yourself."

Simon chuckled. "I assure you, I can still cause your daughter immeasurable pain. And I might just do that, simply for the trouble you have put me to."

This guy was bluffing and where yesterday Tom might have hesitated, not today. He was Tom Sagan, Pulitzer Prize–winning investigative journalist, no matter what anybody said.

"Then you can kiss what I have goodbye."

Silence from the other side.

"What do you propose?" Simon finally asked.

"We trade."

More silence, then Simon said, "I cannot bring her here."

"How did you plan to release her—if you planned to do it at all?"

"I was hoping electronically would work, with a video of it happening, perhaps a tearful reunion afterward on your own time."

"That won't work."

"Obviously not. What do you propose?"

"We trade in Vienna."

———

HAD ZACHARIAH HEARD RIGHT?

"You are coming there?" he called out.

"And you, too."

This might work out. He had a serious problem, considering that Alle Becket was dead. But he might be able to accomplish his objective after all.

"All right. When?"

"Tomorrow afternoon, 5:00. St. Stephen's Cathedral."

———

TOM MADE HIS CHOICE CAREFULLY. HE'D VISITED VIenna several times, staying there once for nearly a month while covering the war in Sarajevo. He was familiar with the place. He knew the Gothic cathedral, which sat at the heart of the city. Public. Lots of people. A good locale for a switch. He should be safe there. The only trick would be getting away before Simon could make a move.

But he'd figure that out later.

"Five o'clock tomorrow," he yelled.

"I will be there."

Simon and the other man retreated to their car and left, a swirl of dust obscuring the view.

He stepped from behind the door and lowered the gun. Great patches of sweat soaked his shirt. His insides boiled like lava and air fled his lungs in harsh gasps. For the first time he noticed the scent of orange blossoms, the trees all around him dotted with white blossoms.

A smell familiar from his childhood.

Such a long time ago.

He raked a hand across the three-day stubble on his face.

None of his misgivings had vanished, but for a guy who was supposed to be dead he felt awfully alive.

———

SIMON WAS PLEASED.

"Find a way out of here," he told Rócha. "Then straight to the airport."

He'd call ahead and have his jet ready. He'd come here on a private charter and would return to Austria the same way. He should be leaving with the Levite's secret, but he'd have it soon enough.

Sagan probably thought himself clever picking St. Stephen's. True, a public locale should assure both sides an equal footing. Not a bad place to trade a daughter for a packet.

Unless.

He grinned with triumph as his mind played with an idea and the strength of his plan dawned on him.

Tom Sagan had just made a fatal mistake.

And the fact that Alle Becket was dead would not matter.

Her father would soon be joining her.

CHAPTER TWENTY-SEVEN

TOM FOUND HIS WAY OUT OF THE ORCHARD THEN onto Interstate 4 and west toward Orlando. The weariness that had once made his head heavy and his thoughts sluggish had vanished. Unfortunately, as the adrenaline faded, all he could visualize was the decayed mass that had once been Abiram Sagan. Children should never see their parents that way. He'd been a bull of a man. Tough. Unrelenting. Respected in his community. Honored by his temple. Loved by his granddaughter—

And his son?

He wasn't ready to go there yet.

Too much had passed between them.

And all because of religion.

Why had it mattered if he wanted to be a Jew or not? Why had that decision led to a disowning? He'd many times wondered about the answers to both questions. Maybe they were lying to his right in the sealed packet?

He wasn't going to wait any longer.

He exited the highway, found a gas station, and parked. He grabbed the packet and plunged the car key into its exterior, ripping the thick plastic enough that he could peel it away.

Air rushed inside.

Three things were there.

A small plastic envelope sealed with packing tape, a map, and a black leather bag about eight inches tall.

He massaged its exterior.

Whatever lay inside was light, thin, and metallic.

He loosened the straps and removed the object.

A key.

About six inches long, one end decorated with three joined Stars of David. A skeleton key. Named, he knew, for reduction to only its essential parts—mainly a few notches at its end which would operate tumblers for a corresponding lock. You didn't see many of these anymore. From his childhood he recalled a similar one used to ceremonially open the synagogue. That key had been made of iron. This one was brass. Not a speck of tarnish marred its patina.

He turned his attention to the envelope, opening the car door for some air. Stiff fingers worked the clear tape until he pried an end loose.

Inside lay a tri-folded piece of paper. Typed. Single-spaced.

```
If you are reading this, son, then you have
opened my grave. I am the last of the Le-
vites. Not born of that house, but chosen.
The first, Yosef Ben Ha Levy Haivri, Joseph,
the son of Levi the Hebrew, was picked by
Christopher Columbus. Yosef was known to
others of his time as Luis de Torres. He
was the first Jew to live in the New World.
From de Torres the line has gone unbroken,
each Levite selected by the one before. I
was named by your Saki. He was chosen by
his father. It was my wish that you suc-
ceed me. I worked hard when you were a boy
to train you in our ways. I wanted you to
```

become someone to whom this secret may be
entrusted. When you told me of your decision to leave our faith I was devastated. I
was about to reveal to you all that I knew,
but your decision made that impossible. You
thought me strong and unbending, but really
I was fragile and weak. Even worse, pride
would not allow me to repair the damage we
did to each other. We mourned your baptism
as if you had died, which, in a real way to
me, you had. I wanted you to be like me,
the Levite, but you had no such desire.
There are so few Jews, son. We cannot afford to lose any. Alle is now one of us.
You may or may not know that. Her conversion pleased me, though I can see how it
would have upset her mother. She discovered
our faith on her own and freely chose to
convert. I never pressured her in any way.
She is sincere and devout. But the Levite
must be male and I failed to find anyone
capable. So I took the secret entrusted to
me to the grave. I'm assuming that only you
or Alle could ever open my coffin. So now I
pass to you what your Saki gave to me.

3. 74. 5. 86. 19.

What this means I have no idea. Deci-
phering is not a Levite's function. We
are simply the keeper. Until your grandfather's time the Levite also held another item. But that was hidden away after
the Second World War. The key that is included with this note was given to me by
Marc, but he never explained its signifi-

cance. He lived during a time when Nazis
threatened everything Jews hold dear. He
told me that he made sure that the secret
would never be breached. What we protect,
son, is the location of the Jews' Temple
treasure: the golden menorah, the divine
table, and the silver trumpets. They
were brought to the New World by Columbus, who was a Jew, and hidden away by
him. Marc lived when Jews were slaughtered by the millions. Part of a Levite's
duty is to adapt, so he chose to make
changes to what had existed before him.
He told me little about those changes,
saying that it was better that way—only
that the golem now protects our secret in
a place long sacred to Jews. He also gave
me a name. Rabbi Berlinger. Your Saki was
a tough man to know. You probably say the
same thing about me. But he chose me to
keep what remained of the secret and I
never questioned him. Son, do the same.
Carry on the duty. Keep the line unbroken. You may ask, what does it matter
anymore? That is not for the Levite to
decide. Our duty is simply to keep the
faith of all those who came before us. It
is the least we can do considering their
sacrifice. Jews have suffered so much for
so long. And with what erupts by the day
in the Middle East, perhaps your Saki was
right in making those changes and keeping
them to himself. Know one other thing,
son. I meant what I wrote to you in the
note with the deed to the house. I never
once believed you did anything wrong. I

```
don't know what happened, but I know it
wasn't that you were a fraud. I'm sorry
I could not say it while alive, but I
love you.
```

He read the last line again.

That was the first time he could recall, since he was a little boy, that Abiram had said he loved him.

And the reference to his grandfather, Marc Eden Cross.

Saki.

A mangling of Hebrew. *Sabba,* grandfather. *Savta,* grandmother. As a toddler he started calling his grandfather *saki,* and the name stuck to the day the old man died.

He examined the third item, a Michelin road map of Jamaica. He carefully opened its folds and saw the distinct outline of the island with all its topography and roadways. He noticed the copyright. 1952. Then he caught the writing that appeared across the face in faded blue ink. Individual numbers. He did a quick count. Maybe a hundred or more written from one coast to another.

He stared at everything from the packet.

The Temple treasure?

How could that be?

————

ALLE SAT WITH BRIAN. THE VIDEO FEED WAS OVER. They'd watched as the man on the other end had jumped a ditch and entered an orchard, driving down a rough lane between blooming orange trees. He'd then left the car, gone for about fifteen minutes before returning to report what happened.

He'd been about fifty yards away, but was able to

hear Simon and Tom Sagan yell at each other. Sagan wanted his daughter and Simon made clear she was in Vienna.

"But I'm dead to him," she said to Brian. "He's bluffing?"

"A good play because there's no way your father can know the truth."

She'd listened while the eyes and ears in Florida reported the meeting place for tomorrow—5:00 P.M., inside St. Stephen's.

"Your father thinks he'll be safe there," Brian said.

She'd visited the cathedral a couple of weeks ago. "There're a lot of people there."

"But you said it. You're dead to Simon. He knows he can't make a trade."

Yet Zachariah had agreed to the exchange.

Her eyes betrayed her thoughts of concern.

"That's right," Brian said. "Your father's going exactly where Simon wants him to go. The question is, do you give a damn?"

CHAPTER TWENTY-EIGHT

BÉNE FOLLOWED FRANK CLARKE UP THE RUGGED trail through a carpet of ground ferns and across pebbles greased with mud. Luckily, he'd dressed for his trek to Charles Town, wearing old jeans and boots. The colonel was armed with a *machet,* which he used to hack low-lying limbs that blocked their way. The raucous call of a parrot drifted through the high forest, as did the incessant tapping of woodpeckers. No fear of poisonous snakes. Mongooses imported from India centuries ago to deal with rats had eliminated all of those.

He was three years shy of forty and in good shape, but this climb taxed him. His face was streaked in sweat, rivulets soaked his shirt. The colonel was thirty years his senior, yet the inclined trail seemed no problem, the older man's steps slow and cautious, his breathing shallow. Every time he trekked into the mountains Béne thought of his ancestors. Eboes from the Bight of Benin. Mandingoes from Sierra Leone. Papaws stolen from the Congo and Angola. Coromantees captured on the Gold Coast.

They'd been the toughest.

Nearly all of the great Maroon leaders had been Coromantees, including his great-great-great-grandfather.

His mother had many times told him about the

African's tortuous path to the New World. First had come capture, then confinement at a fort or trade post. Next was a clustering with other captives, most strangers, some enemies. The fourth turmoil involved being packed onto overcrowded ships and sailed across the Atlantic. Many had not survived that trip, their corpses tossed overboard. Those who did formed bonds that would last for generations— shipbrothers and -sisters was what they would forever call one another. The fifth trauma happened on arrival when they were prepared like cattle, then sold. The final ordeal, known as seasoning, was when others, already there and accustomed to a yoke, taught them how to survive.

The Dutch, English, and Portuguese were all guilty.

And though the physical shackles were long gone, a form of mental slavery remained where some Jamaicans refused to embrace their African past.

Maroons were not in that category.

They'd not forgotten.

And never would.

They kept climbing. A rush of water could be heard ahead. Good. He was thirsty. The trees were ablaze with the Flame of the Forest. He'd learned about the red flowers as a child, his mother telling him how their stinky juice was good for eye infections. As a boy he'd imagined what it must have been like to be a Maroon warrior, wading up streams to mask his scent. Walking backward to create tracks to nowhere. Luring British soldiers to precipices from which there was no escape, or herding them into narrow passages and pelting them with boulders, logs, and arrows. Goats were used to test water supplies which the enemy liked to poison, but the animals were never allowed into settlements since baying would betray their location. Warriors were masters of ambush, wrapping their bodies from head to toe in cacoon vines. Not even the eyes were exposed. Even their lance, the *jonga*, was concealed under a dense blanket of leaves. Which made them totally invisible in the forest. A huge advantage. One never spoken about, one of those secrets that Maroons kept to themselves.

After a battle they would slaughter every opposing soldier but one or two, whom they released so they could report both the defeat and an unspoken challenge.

Send more.

Please.

"The ol' ones are with us today," Frank said.

"You hear duppies, Frank?"

"Not the bad spirits. Only the ol' people. They wander the woods and look after us."

He'd heard tales of duppies. Spirits that spoke in high nasal voices and were repelled by salt. If they were nearby, your head would seem full, your skin hot. They could even make you sick, which was why his mother had always asked when he was little— after he'd hurt himself—*duppy box you there?*

He smiled when he thought of her.

Such a gentle woman, married to such a violent man. But her only child was also violent. Just yesterday he'd killed two men. He wondered if their duppies now wandered through the trees, searching for him.

"Strike the match," his mother said.

He did as she told him.

"Now, blow it out, say 'one,' and throw it down."

He followed her instructions. They were in the mountain forest high above Kingston. They both liked it here, far away from the frenetic pace of the city. Here, she would tell him about the Tainos, the Africans, and the Maroons.

Tonight it was duppies.

"Do it again," she said. "And say 'two.'"

He struck the match, blew it out, uttered the word, and tossed it away.

"With the third match," she said, "blow it out, say the word, but keep it. What happens is the duppy is fooled. It spends the night searching for the third match while you run away."

"It's there," Frank said, bringing his thoughts back to the present. "Careful on the rocks. You slip, you slide."

He spotted a slit in a shallow cliff, just beneath a massive fig tree, its roots blocking the entrance like bars.

"That cave leads through the ridge to the other side," Frank said. "Maroons once used it for escape. We would attack the English, do what damage we could, then retreat. Soldiers would follow, but we'd be gone through the rock. Good for us the English were not fond of caves."

Jamaica was like a sponge with thousands of passages interconnected by a highway of tunnels, rivers disappearing underground in one parish, rising in another. Knowing their way around beneath the surface had proven the Maroons' salvation.

Frank led him to the entrance and he saw how cut boards had been fashioned as a makeshift door, blocking the way about two feet inside.

"Keeps bats out."

They removed the wood. He spotted three flashlights.

"Easier to keep 'em here."

They each grabbed a light and entered, the narrow duct requiring them to crouch. He was careful of the ceiling, which was sharp, scalloped limestone, the floor moist clay. At least it didn't stink with guano.

A few meters inside, they stopped. Frank trained his light on the wall and Béne saw what was carved into the stone.

A hooked X.

"It's Taino?" he asked.

"Let's go farther."

The passage finally hollowed out into a tall chamber, the dark air chilly. As they trained their lights across the walls, he counted four openings that led out.

Then he saw the pictographs.

Maize, birds, fish, frogs, turtles, insects, dogs, and what appeared to be a native chief in full dress.

"Tainos believed," Frank said, "that their first ancestors' spirits lived in caves and only came out at night to eat the *jobos*. One night the plums tasted extra good and they were still eating 'em when the sun rose, which turned them all human."

Béne had heard that same story of creation from his mother.

"Caves were their refuges," Frank said. "Taino were not buried. They were laid out in dark places. It's said their ashes still cover the cave floors."

He felt honored to be here, the place as serene as a chapel.

"The Tainos hated the Spanish. To avoid slavery they'd hide in caves like this and starve themselves to death. Some went quick, drinking the *cassava* poison. Others lingered a long while."

The colonel went silent.

"Columbus called them Indians. People today wrongly call them Arawaks. Tainos was what they were. They came here 7,000 years before the Spanish, paddling over in canoes from the Yucatán. This was their home. Yet Europeans destroyed them in only a hundred years. Sixty thousand people slaughtered."

He heard the contempt, which he echoed.

"That hooked X is not Taino," Frank said. "It's never been found in any cave they painted. It's Spanish, and marks an important place. Maroons have known that symbol for a long time, but we don't speak of it. Those who search for the lost mine also search for that symbol."

Which was exactly what Zachariah Simon had told him, without an explanation.

"So the mine is real? I've never heard you speak like that before."

"The whole tale makes no sense. Tainos did not prize gold. They placed more importance on *guanín*."

He knew of the alloy, a mixture of copper, silver, and gold. He'd seen artifacts made from the reddish purple metal.

"They loved the smell when the oil from their skin reacted with the *guanín*," Frank said. "Pure gold was yellow-white, odorless, and unappealing. *Guanín* was different. It became special to 'em, especially since they couldn't smelt it themselves. They had to be taught by people from South America, who made their way northward. To them gold merely came from streams, *guanín* was from heaven."

"So you're saying they would not have a gold mine?"

"I don't know, Béne. They definitely used gold. So a source of it might have been important. What I do know is that two hundred tons of gold were shipped to Spain from the New World in the hundred years after Columbus. Some of that came from Jamaica, and tens of thousands of Tainos died because of it."

Clarke went silent and stared at the drawings revealed by the lights.

Béne was drawn toward them, too.

"They would dip sticks into charcoal mixed with

fat and bat droppings." Frank's voice had gone low. "So simple, yet see how the work lasted."

"Who knows of this place?"

"No one outside our community. Maroons have come to this place for a long time."

He, too, felt a special closeness here.

Frank turned and handed him a scrap of paper. Before they'd started up the mountain, the colonel had disappeared briefly inside the museum.

He'd wondered why.

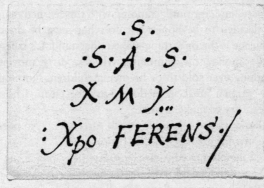

"That's Columbus' signature." Frank shone his light on the writing. "It's a complicated mess that says much about the man. What's important are the X's."

He'd already noticed. Both hooked. Just like the one from the grave, in the Spanish documents, the museum, and on the wall outside.

He stared at Clarke. "You never told me any of this before."

"We be doomed, Béne. Like two hundred years ago, Maroons fight among themselves too much. We become our own enemy. The government knows that and, like the English long ago, they keep us bickering.

That way they don't have to listen to our complaints. I try, but the other colonels are hard to please."

He knew all of that was true.

"You, Béne, are a man the colonels respect. But they also fear you. They know what else you do. They accept your money, but they know you kill people."

"Only when there is no choice."

"That's how Maroons have justified it since we first fled to the mountains. Every runaway slave said the same thing. 'Only when there be no choice.' Yet we have killed so many."

Here, underground, standing with this learned man, he decided to be honest. "I do what must be done. Violence is the only thing some understand. It's true, I make money off gambling, whores, dirty movies. Nothing ever sold to or involving children. Nothing. My women must see a doctor and be clean. I have rules. I try to make it right."

Clarke raised a hand in mock surrender. "No need to convince me, Béne. I don't care."

But he felt a need to justify himself.

Were the duppies working on him?

"Be who you are, Béne. It's all we can do."

Normally he would never question himself, but this place was definitely affecting him.

"I believe that the hooked X is the mark of Columbus," Frank said. "A sign to an important place. Perhaps even to the lost mine itself."

"In this cave?"

The colonel shook his head. "This was not it. They marked here for a reason. What? Who knows. The real place is unknown."

Simon had talked of Columbus, the lost mine, and the Levite, supposedly revealing all that he knew. But never had he mentioned Columbus' signature, or anything else that Frank Clarke had just said.

Because he did not know?

No way.

Simon knew a lot. Enough to be in Florida doing something with some man and his daughter. A woman who wrote a magazine article about Columbus, which he'd not read.

Time to correct that mistake.

"Everyone wants to preserve us," Frank said. "They talk of Maroon culture, and of us, as if we're gone. But we're still here."

He agreed.

"If you find the lost mine, Béne, perhaps you're right. That wealth can be used to change our situation. Money is always power, and we have neither. Unlike other Maroons, I never blamed the Jews for profiting from us. We needed supplies and ammunition. They provided it. The British needed the same and they provided. That's the way of the world. Those Jews are gone, but we're still here."

He thought back to what Tre had told him about the Cohen brothers and the Jews' hidden wealth from the time of the Spanish.

And the Levite.

Who knew it all.

"You think the Jews may have hid their wealth in the mine, too?"

Frank shrugged. "It's possible. All the legends seemed to have merged. That's the thing, Béne. Nobody knows anything."

He was glad he'd come.

Finally. Answers.

And what Clarke said was true. Money was indeed power. He was deeply connected with the left and the People's National Party, but he preferred the ruling center-right Labor Party. Never were his phone calls to government officials ignored. His requests shoved aside. He rarely asked for anything from any minister but, when he did, the answer was always yes.

Something the Maroons believed came to mind.

Di innocent an di fool could pass fi twin.

He was neither.

"I'll find the mine," he told both his friend and the ancestors.

CHAPTER TWENTY-NINE

ALLE RESENTED BRIAN JAMISON'S HOLIER-THAN-thou attitude. Two hours had gone by since the video from Florida ended, and Brian had stayed on the phone in another room with the door closed the entire time. She sat in the house's small kitchen and nursed a cup of coffee. The scene outside the windows was rural and wooded, no roads or other houses in sight. It was after 7:00 P.M. Czech time, which meant early afternoon in Florida. Her father was apparently coming to Vienna to make a deal for her release.

Which still surprised her.

A door opened and footsteps pounded the wooden floor. Brian walked into the room, still wearing a shoulder holster holding a weapon. He poured himself a cup from the coffeemaker.

"This is changing fast," he said to her.

"I don't like you."

He laughed. "Like I care. If it were up to me, I would have let Simon kill you."

His bravado was beginning to wear thin. "What happens now?"

"Aren't you the least bit concerned about your father? He's put his ass on the line for you. What do we do about that?"

She said nothing.

"He's walking into a trap at that cathedral."

"So stop him. Have your man in Florida tell him what's going on."

"How do you suggest I do that? We have no idea how he plans to get to Vienna. My man lost him after the orchard. He surely isn't going to fly out of Orlando. I'm betting he drives to Tampa, or Jacksonville, or Miami. And he's not a dumb-ass, contrary to what you might think, he won't fly straight to Vienna. He'll come in another way. So there's no way to deal with him until he gets to the cathedral."

"You don't give a damn about my father. You just want what he has."

"Sure I do. But I still have the problem of him in Vienna. And so we're clear, he's not *my* father so, no, I don't give a damn."

"My father was one of the best reporters in the world," she said. "He knows what he's doing."

She'd never said any of those words before.

"Is that how you convince yourself to feel better? I assure you, your father has never dealt with a man like Zachariah Simon." He sipped his coffee. "I want to know what this is about. The least you can do is tell me what's going on here."

"I don't know."

"Then tell me what you told Simon."

In 71 CE, after crushing the rebellious Jews and destroying Jerusalem, Titus returned to Rome. His father, Vespasian, was now emperor and welcomed his son back with the greatest celebration Rome had ever seen. Over one million had died in Judea, and now all of Rome came out to pay homage. Eight years later, after Titus himself rose to be emperor, he immortalized the day with a stone relief that showed him, as conqueror, parading the streets by chariot, the Jews' Temple treasure—the golden Table of Divine Presence, the silver trumpets, and a seven-branched menorah—carted ahead of him.

For 380 years those treasures stayed in Rome. Then in 455 CE Vandals sacked the city. A Byzantine historiographer wrote that the Vandal leader, "with no one to stop him entered Rome and taking all the money and the ornaments of the city, he loaded them on his ships, among them the solid gold and bejeweled treasures of the Church and the Jewish vessels which Vespasian's son Titus had brought to Rome after the capture of Jerusalem."

The Temple treasure was taken south to the African city of Carthage, and there it remained from 455 to 533 CE until the Byzantines conquered the Vandals. Another chronicler described the victor's triumphant return to Constantinople in 534. "And there was also silver weighing many thousands of talents and all of the royal treasure and among these were the treasures of the Jews, which Titus, the son of Vespasian, had brought to Rome after the capture of Jerusalem."

The Emperor Justinian displayed the Jewish treasure at various sites around the city. Though one of the greatest Byzantine leaders, Justinian was extremely unpopular, and that discontent finally fermented into open revolt. A contemporary from the time reported, "And one of the Jews, seeing these things, approached one of those known to the emperor and said, 'These Temple treasures, I think it inexpedient to carry them into the palace in Byzantium. Indeed, it is not possible for them to be elsewhere than in the place where Solomon, the king of the Jews, formerly placed them. For it is because of these that the Vandals captured the palace of the Romans and how we captured the Vandals.' When this had been brought to the ears of the

*emperor, Justinian became afraid and quickly sent
everything to the sanctuaries of the Christians in Jerusalem."*

"Justinian was superstitious and paranoid," Alle
said to Brian. "He allowed an anonymous Jewish
courtier to spook him with the fact that all of the civi-
lizations that had possessed the Temple treasure since
70 CE had crumbled. First the Jews, then Rome, then
the Vandals. Would he be next? So sometime between
535 and 554 CE he ordered the Temple treasure returned to the Holy Land."

Brian cast a doubtful look. "Simon is after the Temple treasure?"

She nodded. "The three holiest objects in all of
Judaism. They never made it to the Holy Land. History lost track of all three when they left Constantinople. Zachariah said my grandfather knew where
they were hidden. That he was the Levite, the only
person alive who knew the location. He said whatever I buried with him would lead us there."

"For what? Not its worth. He's a billionaire."

"He wants to restore it to the Jews."

"And you believed him?"

She wanted to know something. "What's *your* interest?"

"Tell me the rest. How do *you* fit into this?"

*After Rome sacked Jerusalem in 70 CE and the
Second Temple was razed, over 80,000 Jews were
deported from Judea to the Iberian peninsula—
which, at that time, lay at the extreme western
reaches of the Roman Empire. More Jews immigrated there over time, until a thriving community
formed that came to be known as Sephardim.
Life for Jews there was tolerable since the emerg-*

ing Catholic Church had difficulty establishing itself so far west. The Visigoths, who ruled the land, did not convert until 587 CE. This began what became a recurring phenomenon in Iberian policy—Jews were ordered to either become Christians or be expelled. Many did convert, becoming the first conversos, maintaining their Jewish identity in secret while openly professing to be something else. Tens of thousands either left or were expelled. Periods of tolerance and intolerance followed. Property seizures occurred frequently, especially when Jewish assets were needed by monarchs. When the Moors invaded Iberia in 711, Jews welcomed them as liberators. Life under Moorish rule became the Golden Age for Sephardi Jews. Their numbers grew, as more immigrated.

But the Reconquista changed everything.

Christians slowly reclaimed Iberia and forced conversions, engaging in pogroms. By 1400 Jews had become a focus of Spanish hatred. To avoid death or persecution thousands more converted to Christianity, creating a new wave of conversos. Laws that restricted Jewish industry eventually brought commerce to a standstill. Soil was left uncultivated, finances were disturbed. Entire communities were destroyed, many more reduced to poverty. In order to restore the Spanish economy the Crown tried to draw Jews back to the country by offering them privileges.

Which worked, but it also bred resentment from Christians.

When Ferdinand and Isabella ascended the throne and completed the Reconquista in 1492, expelling the last of the Moors from Spanish soil, they issued an edict that all Jews must either convert or leave Spain.

They also reinstituted the Inquisition to root out false conversos.

165,000 Jews chose to leave.
Many stayed and kept their secret.
Many more were slaughtered.

"How much of that is you and how much came from Simon?" Brian asked.

"I'm not ignorant of Jewish history," she made clear. "It's what I've studied."

"I didn't say that you were. I just need to know what that crazy man is trying to do."

"He told me a story. I don't know if it's true. But it was quite amazing. About the Jews in Spain, at the time Columbus sailed."

"Tell me."

"Why should I?"

"Because your father's life depends on it."

CHAPTER THIRTY

TOM DROVE INTO ORLANDO AND FOLLOWED A roundabout path to his house. He needed to retrieve his passport. He'd already stopped at a local library and used one of their computers to book a flight out of New York that would eventually land him in Bratislava, Slovakia. The overnight leg across the Atlantic departed New York at 8:00 P.M. To get there he would have to take a plane from Jacksonville. He thought that safer than using the Orlando airport, which Simon might be watching. The drive north was all interstate highway, about two and a half hours. He'd have to change planes again in London, but should be on the ground in Slovakia in plenty of time. From there he would rent a car and drive across the Austrian border to Vienna, about forty miles away.

He parked a block over and approached his house from the rear. He kept an eye out for anything that might cause alarm, but the neighborhood was quiet. He entered through the back door and realized that the measure of comfort he'd always felt here was gone. This place now reeked of insecurity and all he wanted to do was leave. He quickly changed clothes, found his passport and a jacket, grabbed the few hundred dollars he always kept on hand, and left. He'd buy along the way whatever was necessary. It felt like the old days when he was chasing leads, piecing tendrils, hoping the dots would eventually connect into a story. He'd handled things right today, anticipating his adversary's move, staying one step ahead. His daughter was counting on him and this time he was not going to let her down.

He also seemed privy to something extraordinary—a secret his family had apparently been part of for a long while.

Which, despite everything, excited him.

He stepped out the door and headed back toward his car.

One thing bothered him, though.

Zachariah Simon agreed to the terms far too easily.

Sources too cooperative had always made him nervous.

He wondered.

Had he made a mistake?

———

ZACHARIAH BOARDED THE CHARTERED JET. HE DID not own a plane. Waste of money. Far cheaper to rent. This one had been waiting for him at Orlando's Sanford International Airport, a smaller facility north of the city. He wondered from where Tom Sagan would leave America. Surely not from Orlando. The man was certainly smarter than that. But he didn't care. He wanted the former reporter in Vienna, and he would do nothing to interfere with that journey.

He sat in one of the plush seats and fastened his seat belt. The jet's engines were already humming. Cool air rushed from the overhead vents. Rócha, after stowing their bags, joined him.

"It's too bad she's dead," he said, referring to Alle. "I may have been hasty there."

Rócha shrugged. "Jamison knew right where to look."

Which was a problem that required attention. A spy in his midst? Without question. He also had to talk with Béne Rowe and find out why the Jamaican was stalking him. He'd underestimated Rowe's desire to find Columbus' lost mine. He'd volunteered only enough information to prove that he knew what he was talking about.

But maybe not enough.

"It's a grave I am looking for," he said to Rowe. *"That's what we must find. The grave of the Levite."*

"What does that do?"

"The Levite is the person who guarded the secret of the mine. He alone knew its location. He would pass that information on to someone else before he died. But it's possible that may not have occurred. My father once found a clue in a Levite's grave. Look for a pitcher carved into the tombstone. That was the symbol of the Levite. And a hooked X. That has to be there, too."

He could not care less about any lost mine of Christopher Columbus. What he sought was far more valuable. But if thoughts of finding that mine would spur Béne Rowe into action, then why not use it? When he first approached Rowe, what he sought was a lead to the Levite. But his initial conversations with Rowe occurred long before he found Alle Becket and learned that the current Levite lived not on Jamaica but in central Florida.

And he'd been right.

The secret had been taken to the grave.

He'd actually forgotten about Rowe. They'd teamed up over a year ago, the result of him trying to find someone in Jamaica who shared his passion and would search. He'd met Brian Jamison early on. Rowe's man. Smart, resourceful, American.

The jet taxied toward the runway.

Unfortunately, he could not ignore Rowe any longer.

———

BÉNE SAT ON THE VERANDA AND SURVEYED HIS ES-
tate. Storm clouds were rolling in from the north across the Blue Mountains, distant thunder announcing their arrival. It rained a lot here, which was good for the coffee beans.

The great house, a Georgian mansion cast in a Creole style, sat on the crest of a gentle slope. It had been built between 1771 and 1804 by a British plantation owner. White stone walls still stood in stark contrast with lush green woodlands. That Brit had been one of the first to grow coffee. The beans were initially imported in 1728 and quickly flourished. Though it took longer for coffee to ripen in the cooler air, the result was a fuller quality. Today only 9,000 acres in all of Jamaica lay above the minimum 600 meters required by national standards to qualify as Blue Mountain Coffee. His father had set those standards, knowing that all of the Rowe acreage lay high enough. Once, pulperies sat beside the fields so beans could be processed quickly. Modern transports now made that unnecessary. But what came out of the pulperies continued to be dried, graded, then sorted only after six weeks of curing. No other coffee in the world did that. He was proud of his land and the estate, especially the house, which he'd spent millions refurbishing. No more slaves worked here. Most were Maroons whom he paid an above-average wage.

The stone from the Levite's grave sat on a table before him. He'd cleaned it, carefully washing away the dark earth, exposing the hooked X. His drive back across the mountains from Charles Town had been troubling. Frank Clarke told him things he'd never known. He was irritated that his friend had held out on him so long, but he should not be surprised. He wondered—was there a connection between the Taino myth of the cave of importance, the Maroon legend of a place with an iron gate, the Jews' supposed hidden wealth, and Columbus' lost mine?

Four tales.

Similar, yet different.

Separating one from the other might prove difficult. Could the deed that Felipe found point the way? He hoped Tre Halliburton had been successful in the archives. He'd not heard from his friend.

His fingers caressed the stone.

Such a strange symbol.

What was its significance?

His cell phone vibrated. Few possessed the number, mainly his lieutenants. He studied the display and saw that the call was from Zachariah Simon. He allowed it to ring four times. Let him wait. After the seventh he answered.

"I realize that I have treated you poorly," Simon said.

"You lied to me."

"I simply failed to tell you what I was doing outside Jamaica. But actually, that is none of your business."

"If it concerns that lost mine, then it is my business. And what you're doing in Florida definitely concerns the mine."

"I am aware," Simon said, "that you know of my activities."

"You lied to me," he said again.

"There is more at stake here than simply finding lost gold."

"Not for me."

"I appreciate what you did when I was in Jamaica. The information you provided was interesting, but not anything I did not already know. I felt that I was offering far more than you could in return."

He stared out at the mountains and the coming storm. "I wouldn't underestimate what I can offer."

Simon chuckled through the phone. "Come now, Béne, let us not be unrealistic. This quest is more far reaching than your island. It is a secret, guarded for five hundred years. Maybe some of the clues lie there, but the answer is definitely elsewhere."

"Vienna?"

Jamison had already called and informed him of what had happened in a Florida orange grove. He assumed Simon had driven from that grove to an airport and was now aboard a plane.

"You *are* well informed," Simon said. "What is it you want, Béne?"

"To be told the truth. To be treated as an equal. To be respected."

"And what do you offer in return?"

"Something you may be in great need of."

"And what might that be?"

"Alle Becket."

CHAPTER THIRTY-ONE

IN THE MIDDLE OF THE 6TH CENTURY THE BYZANTINE EM-
peror Justinian ordered the Jews' Temple treasure
removed from Constantinople. He believed it cursed
and wanted the sacred objects sent back to the Holy
Land. Simply melting the gold and silver down and
reusing the precious metals would not, to his way of
thinking, remove the curse. Only their banishment
would suffice. The emperor entrusted the task to
subordinates, who contracted with local merchants
to transport the treasure by boat to the south. All
three objects—the golden menorah, the Table of Divine Presence, and the silver trumpets—were loaded
on board.

But once out of sight of land, the captain and crew—
all Jews—turned west and sailed around the boot of
Italy, then north toward Iberia. There the three treasures were brought ashore and entrusted to the Sephardim. Many were distant descendants of those
forced into exile by the Romans when the Second Temple was destroyed. Finally, after 470 years, their Temple treasures had been returned.

And these men would not risk losing them again.

The treasures were secreted away in the mountains,
where they stayed for nearly a thousand years,
guarded by more descendants of those same Sephardi.

That millennium was a turbulent one. For a while Jews flourished in safety, but by the 4th century, when Christianity finally consumed the Roman Empire, Jews were again persecuted. Many, though, had acquired prominent positions in the trades and crafts serving as tax collectors, financial ministers, treasurers, bankers, and astronomers. Kings relied on them. The Catholic Church came to resent their influence and began a campaign to destroy them. Pogroms regularly occurred, the worst in the 14th century when tens of thousands were massacred, their wealth and property confiscated. Ferdinand and Isabella finally expelled all Jews, forcing them to sell their homes, lands, shops, and cattle at low prices. No gold or silver was allowed to be taken from the country, so they were compelled to exchange hard wealth for goods. One hundred and twenty thousand fled to Portugal on an agreement with its king, who eventually reneged on his promise of safety and enslaved them. Others went to North Africa, but found no refuge from the Moors. Even more tried Italy and Turkey, but only pain and sorrow followed. By August 3, 1492, the day Columbus sailed from Spain on his first voyage, the situation for the Sephardi Jews seemed hopeless.

"So they tried something desperate," Alle said. "The only thing they thought might work."

Brian was clearly listening.

"Their world had crumbled. They had no where to go. Europe. Africa. Nobody wanted them. So they hoped that there might be a better place across the ocean in Asia. Where Columbus was headed."

"You're saying that Christopher Columbus was looking for a Jewish homeland?"

"That's exactly what I'm saying. There were tales at

the time of a place to the east where Jews lived free. Was it real? Nobody knew. But myths were all these people had. There had to be something better than where they were. Do you know who actually financed Columbus' first voyage? It wasn't Isabella selling her jewels, as the story is told. The Spanish monarchy was broke. There was no money for foolish ventures, and that's what they thought of Columbus' idea. Instead, it was the Jews who financed that voyage."

Brian was visibly surprised.

"Luis de Santangel was a *converso,* a Jew from Aragon, who converted to keep what he'd worked his life to obtain. His family served in government, and when Ferdinand needed money, he went to the de Santangels. Unfortunately, they were among the first targets of the Inquisition and Luis was brought to trial. Ferdinand himself finally intervened on his behalf. Luis knew the king's deepest secrets. He took care of the most difficult state business. Ferdinand needed him, so he was spared. It was de Santangel who convinced the king and queen to support Columbus. But they agreed only after de Santangel staked 17,000 ducats of his own money on the venture. Three other *conversos* added their money. The Spanish Crown had nothing to lose."

"Why have I never heard of this before?" Brian asked.

"Because no one wants to acknowledge that Columbus could have been a Jew, and that Jews paid for his discovery of the New World. But it's true. I've seen the originals of de Santangel's account books in the archives at Simancas. They clearly show the money being advanced, and what it was advanced for."

This was what she'd spent the past two years of her life studying. What her grandfather had sparked inside her long ago. What Zachariah Simon had seemed so interested in understanding.

"The Jews discovered America," Brian said, shaking his head. "Now, that would change things up some."

"On Columbus' first voyage to the New World," she said, "there were 87 men on those three ships. Contrary to Hollywood's version, not a single priest was included. Not one. But there was a Hebrew translator on board. A man named de Torres, who was probably the first person ashore that day in 1492. Columbus brought a Hebrew translator for a reason. He thought he was sailing to India and Asia, to a place where Jews lived in safety. So he had to be able to communicate with them. Also, in the hold of the *Santa María* were three crates that held the Temple treasure. When de Santangel financed the voyage, he also set a secret condition with Columbus. 'Take our treasures with you and hide them away. Spain is no longer safe.' "

"So that treasure is somewhere in the Caribbean?" Brian said.

"Most likely on Jamaica. The Columbus family controlled that island for 150 years. Zachariah said his family has searched for generations and learned as much as they could. But the Levite knows it all, and my grandfather was that man."

Brian stood silent for a few moments, clearly thinking.

She wondered. Was he friend? Or foe?

Hard to say.

"Do you want to help your father?"

"I don't want to see him hurt."

She meant that.

"What can I do?"

"Maybe a whole lot."

CHAPTER THIRTY-TWO

TOM RECLINED THE SEAT AS FAR AS IT WOULD GO, trying to find comfort in hopes of a little sleep. He'd made it to New York and boarded the overnight flight to London without a problem. They'd left the gate right at 8:00 P.M. and would arrive, according to the pilot, about half an hour early. That would help with his connection to Bratislava, which was tight. Every seat in coach was full, the cabin lights dimmed, the plane settling down after the meal service. Some were watching movies or listening to music, others reading.

He was thinking.

On the way to the Jacksonville airport he'd passed a branch of the city library system. He had time, so he'd made use of one of their computers, surfing the Internet for thirty minutes, learning what he could about Zachariah Simon.

The man was sixty years old, born to old money. A bachelor who lived a secluded life. Little was known about him except for the philanthropic efforts of his several foundations. The family had always been a huge supporter of Israel, and archived newspaper articles described how Simon's father contributed money to the formation of a Jewish state. Nothing existed to say that Zachariah Simon had ever involved himself in Middle Eastern politics, and he could not recall the name ever being mentioned during his time there. Simon owned an estate in Austria, outside Vienna, that hosted a Zionist gathering each year to raise money for his foundations. Nothing political, more a social event. The man clearly kept things close to his vest, perhaps recognizing that the world had changed. So much could be learned about someone now with just a few clicks of a mouse or some taps on a screen. If you didn't want anyone to know your business, then you had to stay out of cyber-friendly media.

Which Simon did.

The note from Abiram's grave, the Jamaican map, and the key lay on the tray table before him, all illuminated by the overhead lamp like a spotlight on a stage. He lifted the key and studied the three Stars of David that formed one end. What did it open? He twirled it around, the brass catching the light with sharp reflections. He hadn't examined it closely in the car, and now something on the stem caught his eye. Tiny. Engraved. He brought the metal closer and studied what was there.

He recognized the first two markings. Hebrew letters. *Po nikbar.* Here lies.

פנ

The same as on his father's tombstone. But those letters adorned many Hebrew graves. The third marking he did not know. An X, one stem hooked. He shook his head. What did it all mean?

The woman next to him had dozed off beneath a blanket. More people around him were heading to sleep.

He should, too.

He'd made a few precautionary preparations while in the library, a printer available for a fee. But there would have to be more. What would he do tomorrow at St. Stephen's?

Good question.

He needed an answer.

And fast.

———

BÉNE CHECKED HIS WATCH. 9:30 P.M. IN JAMAICA meant 3:30 A.M. tomorrow in Vienna.

"I had no choice," he told Brian through the phone. "She had to be bartered." He'd just informed Jamison about the conversation with Zachariah Simon in which he'd revealed that Alle Becket was still alive.

"You compromised your man inside," Brian said from Vienna.

"I've already told him to disappear. Simon and his guard dog are on a plane headed home. My man is gone from the residence."

"Do you have any idea what you've done," Brian said, his voice rising. "We worked with you because *you did* have a man inside Simon's business."

And that was true.

Brian Jamison had appeared at his estate, nearly a year ago, unannounced. He was an American intelligence agent, working for a unit called the Magellan Billet, come to ask questions about what Zachariah Simon was doing in Jamaica. Béne had offered him coffee and cake and told him nothing. Jamison returned three days later, this time with a thick file that contained more information on Béne's illegal activities than he thought could be amassed in so short a time.

"*Actually, this was all done before I came the first time,*" Brian said. "*My superior wanted to give you a chance to work with us on your own.*"

He chuckled. "Like I would."

Brian pointed a finger at him and joined in the laughter. "*That's exactly what I told her. But she's the boss, so I had to do what she said. Thankfully, you said no, so now we get to do this my way.*"

Jamison then made clear that there was more than enough evidence in the file to support a variety of felonies that Jamaica, the United States, several South American nations, or most of the Caribbean could prosecute. Nearly all of those jurisdictions also allowed civil forfeiture of property upon conviction, which meant all of the Rowe wealth could be seized. Of course, that unpleasantness might be avoided if Béne was willing to do one simple thing.

Work with them.

"*Would you have anything to offer?*" Brian asked him.

"*How about a source directly inside Simon's camp.*"

Jamison had been introduced to Simon as Béne's chief lieutenant, and a point was made to underscore their close relationship. Brian had even interacted with Simon and his people twice in Jamaica, including Simon's own lieutenant, Rócha. His appearance in Vienna had certainly spooked the Simon. Enough that Alle Becket's death had been ordered. Béne knew that when he revealed that the young woman was still alive, the Americans would not like it. But what did he care? Liking things was never part of their bargain.

"If I had not told the Simon about her," he made clear, "this would be over. He has no further use of me."

The silent pause signaled that Jamison knew that to

be true. Finally, Brian asked, "What do you want me to do?"

"Make her available tomorrow for the trade. He still thinks you work for me. I didn't sell *you* out."

"Béne, you have no idea who you're dealing with. Simon is a dangerous man, into things way beyond finding some lost gold mine. I've come to realize that there's something big happening here."

"I don't suppose you'd share those thoughts?"

"Get real."

He chuckled. "I didn't think so. But know this. Finding that lost mine is still important to him. I heard it in his voice. Lucky for you he still needs me. Or, better yet, he needs that woman."

"I could have you arrested."

"But you won't. What I did kept this alive. And you know it."

"I'm going to have to run this by people above my pay grade."

"You do that. But I suggest you be at that church tomorrow with the daughter. The Simon is expecting her."

"You know that he wants to kill both her and her father, and probably me, too."

He laughed again. "Your problem."

"I don't buy all this, Béne. Simon could have told you to go to hell. He doesn't need the woman that bad. There has to be more you offered than just her."

"Oh, yes. You're so right. I definitely have something else he wants. So be a good agent and do your job. Have her there. See what happens. Then know that the Simon will be coming back my way."

He paused.

"And that will allow us both to find what we are after."

TOM DOZED IN AND OUT. HE'D ALWAYS BEEN ABLE TO sleep on planes. That had been his time to rest, moving from one place to the next, readying himself for what lay ahead. But he was eight years out of practice. He'd been thinking about Michele and what a mess he made of both their lives.

"*You're a cheater, Tom. Women are your weakness.*"

"*Am I also a fraud?*"

She'd never told him her thoughts about what happened to him.

"*That one I don't know. It's certainly in you, since cheaters always cheat. But I have to say, I was shocked by all that.*"

Her voice was calm, her words clear. The anger that had stayed between them had faded in the year since the divorce.

"*I've met somebody,*" *she told him.* "*I'm going to get married.*"

He was not surprised. Other men would quickly discover her.

"*I'm happy for you.*"

"*It's Alle you have to deal with. I've told you before, don't wait until it's too late.*"

"*I know. I know.*"

"*I have to go now, Tom. And I was wrong a moment ago. You're a lousy husband and an even worse father, but you were a good reporter.*"

He recalled how her affirmation of his innocence had hurt him even more.

All that he'd done to her.

Yet she still believed in him.

That was the last time they ever spoke.

He spent the next seven years wallowing in self-pity,

living alone. She remarried but lost her life far too early.

And his daughter had not even allowed him to attend the funeral.

He grabbed hold of himself.

And wondered.

What would he say to Alle once she was free?

CHAPTER THIRTY-THREE

ZACHARIAH SETTLED DOWN BEFORE THE COMPUTER. He'd arrived back in Vienna four hours ago and Rócha had driven him straight to the estate. He'd dozed in and out for a couple of hours during the transatlantic flight, anxious.

Today was the day.

The Levite had left something in his grave, just as Zachariah's grandfather and father had predicted might happen, and he'd found it. Tom Sagan's stunt in Florida had actually worked to his advantage since disposing of two bodies, once this day was over, would prove far easier here than in America. He'd even made a deal with Béne Rowe. No choice, really. Having Alle Becket to show Sagan would make things much easier. But there was still the matter of the spy within his household. He employed thirty-two people at the estate, including Rócha. The traitor's identity was obvious, and he'd learned on returning that the man called Midnight was gone.

As he should be.

Part of Rowe's bargain was that his asset not be harmed.

Ordinarily, he might not have honored such a request, but Rowe had tantalized him with what had been found at another Levite's grave in Jamaica. A hooked X. And documents that might point the way to the lost mine. Keeping every avenue open seemed important.

At least for now.

The computer came to life and a man's face appeared.

He was middle-aged and bearded, with long sideburns.

"How are things today in Israel, my friend," he said to the screen.

"Another day of negotiations. We are making progress, finally, toward a true peace."

And he knew how. "What are we giving away?"

"Such an attitude, Zachariah. There is nothing wrong with talking to your adversary."

"Provided you do not concede."

"Now, that I cannot promise. As of yesterday, the Knesset was considering more concessions. The United States is pressuring. More so than ever. They want movement on our part. Significant movement. We stall but, in the end, there is a feeling that perhaps we should concede."

This man headed one of six minor Israeli parties. They varied in slant from Ultra-Reform to Orthodoxy. His was more moderate, centrist, which was why Zachariah kept the line of communication open. Ordinarily, all six's presence would be ignored, but the Israeli Parliament was severely divided, coalitions forming and dissolving by the hour. Every vote counted.

"Billions in aid comes from America," the man said. "You can ignore them for a while, but not forever. It is reality. There is even talk of leveling the separation fence. Many think it is time."

A 760-kilometer-long physical barrier defined the border between Israel and Palestine. Most was three layers of barbed wire. Sections that passed through urban centers were concrete wall. Periodic observation posts and gates controlled access from one side to the other. The idea had been to define the border and prevent terrorist attacks and, on both counts, the barrier had worked. To remove it seemed unthinkable.

"Why would such a thing be considered?"

"Because to get you have to give."

No, you did not.

"This government is at an end point. Parliamentary elections are coming soon. Everyone knows there is going to be a change. What that will be remains to be seen. Nobody knows, Zachariah. Uncertainty breeds compromise."

He hated the world interfering with Israel. One world leader after another, American presidents especially, wanted to be its peacemaker. But Jews and Arabs had remained in conflict a long time. Their divisions were impenetrable. No one, other than the participants, could possibly understand the depth of their disagreements.

He did.

And he planned to do something about it.

Which did not involve concessions.

"Our enemies are not interested in peace," he made clear. "They never have been. They are only interested in what we are willing to give away to get it."

"That kind of thinking is exactly why we are in the position we currently are in."

Not at all. Men like the man on the screen, and others in Israel, who actually thought they could negotiate an end to 5,000 years of conflict were the reason.

Idiots.

All of them.

Jews must be *made* to see.

And so they would.

TOM HUSTLED ACROSS THE PLAZA BEFORE ST. STE-
phen's Cathedral. His watch read 12:25 P.M. He'd
made it to Vienna in plenty of time. The drive west
from Bratislava was an easy forty minutes, his rental
car parked in a public lot a few blocks away. He
glanced up at the massive cathedral, its steeple rising
like a jagged arrow to an azure sky. After Simon had
so readily agreed to the swap, he'd decided that he
might need some help. So while surfing the Internet at
the library in Jacksonville he'd caught a break. Someone he knew still worked at *Der Kurier,* one of Vienna's main newspapers. Back in his day the paper had
only been in print. Now it was a mixture of electronic
and print, and he'd noticed the name of one of its
online managing editors.

Inna Tretyakova.

He veered from the square and found a narrow passageway that led to a series of backstreets. He still
remembered the location after ten years. It was a talent that had always come in handy. He was bad with
names, but he never forgot a face or a place. The café
he sought was once one of his favorites, frequented
by the local and foreign press. He entered through a
glass door, his gaze noticing the same fine trompe
l'oeil ceiling fresco. Not much else had changed, either. He also recognized a face in the sparse crowd.

"Inna, you're as lovely as ever," he said in English,
walking over.

"And you are still a man with charm."

She was midforties, with stark blond hair that fell
in broad curls to just above her shoulders. Her face
contained not a blemish, her eyes a pale shade of
blue. Time had been kind, her figure remained thin
and petite, the curves he recalled still there. They'd

never ventured beyond business in their relationship, as she was married, but they'd been friends. He'd called her from Bratislava, and though they hadn't spoken in a long time, she immediately agreed to meet him.

"I need a favor, Inna. I'm in a mess and a hurry, but I'm hoping you can help."

"You always were in a hurry, Thomas." She was one of the few who called him that.

"My daughter is in trouble here, in Vienna, and I have to help her. To do that, I need your help."

"How have you been?"

He allowed her to shift the topic, as she seemed to genuinely want to know. "Not good, Inna. But I made it."

"You were the best reporter I ever knew," she said. "I wanted to tell you that, after everything happened, but I had no way to find you."

"I kind of disappeared. Kept to myself."

"Which, I imagine, was not good. You have friends, Thomas. People who respected you. People who never believed what was said."

He appreciated her loyalty. But few of those friends came to his defense when he needed them.

"Thomas Sagan was never dishonest around me."

He smiled. He hadn't heard a compliment in a long while.

"I push my people now," she said. "Just like you pushed me on the stories we did together. I remember what you taught me."

A decade ago she'd worked the foreign desk for *Der Kurier* and they'd teamed several times in the Middle East. She was good with organization, even better with conciseness, and he'd always thought she'd make a fine editor.

"Is your daughter in bad trouble?" she asked.

"I'm afraid so. She and I are not close, but I have to help her."

"Of course you do, she is your daughter."

"Are your children okay?" Two, if he recalled correctly.

"Both are growing up. One might even be a reporter one day herself."

They were as comfortable together as they had been years ago. Maybe he'd been wrong to lump all of his former friends together in one stinking pile.

He'd made the right call contacting her.

She leaned over the table. "Tell me, Thomas, what can I do to help your daughter."

CHAPTER THIRTY-FOUR

ALLE LISTENED AS THE BELLS ABOVE ST. STEPHEN'S CA-
thedral announced 5:00 P.M. She and Brian had approached the church from the west, positioned at the
edge of the expansive plaza that stretched out from
the main portal.

"Simon's not our problem right now," Brian said.
"He needs you inside to show your father. It's after he
gets what he wants that the trouble starts."

She was anxious about all of this, not pleased with
being bait.

"I have to get you and your father out of here before Simon makes a move," Brian said. "He will act.
The question is where and when."

People hustled in all directions. This was the heart
of Vienna, the cathedral's size accentuated by rows of
low-slung, compact buildings. Two of the city's most
exclusive streets radiated from the plaza, home to
countless stores and shops. Her gaze focused on one
of the many open-air restaurants and a string quartet
playing Brahms. She caught the waft of chicken fry-
ing somewhere nearby. Everything was alive with
sound and movement. Impossible to know where a
threat might lie.

"You have help here?" she asked.

"I work alone."

"You had help in the café when we first met."

He glanced at her. "I needed them then."

"You realize that you could be wrong about Zachariah."

"Then you won't have a problem going in there alone."

She was surprised.

"I can't go with you," he said. "It would only complicate things. This is among the three of you. You're what your father's come for. Simon knows we have you. He also knows you're coming."

"You told him?"

He shook his head. "Not me. But others did."

She wanted to know about those *others.*

Who did this man work for?

She watched as Brian studied the busy plaza. Her gaze drifted up the cathedral's south tower, which surged skyward like a jet of water in an unbroken ascent, tapering steadily from base to finial. The main roof, which the steeple seemed to pierce, glistened with its trademark glazed yellow and black tiles. A familiar sight, which she'd seen many times from her apartment, not far away. The church's north tower had never been completed, which gave the building its distinctive unfinished look. Something Goethe had said came to mind. *"Architecture is frozen music."*

Brian produced a cell phone and hit one of its buttons. He spoke Hebrew to the person on the other side, most of which she understood. She'd studied it in both college and graduate school. She decided not to let him know she knew that he apparently had a man atop the cathedral's south tower, which could be climbed for a fee. She'd done it herself, the view affording a wide angle. Interesting how he wanted her to believe that Zachariah was a danger, yet he could not, or would not, be straight with her.

And Hebrew?

Who was this guy?

He ended the call.

"Time for you to go inside."

———

ZACHARIAH ADMIRED THE CATHEDRAL'S INTERIOR.
Long, triangular rays of late-afternoon sun slanted
through a forest of towering pillars toward the far
altar. Golden bits of dust flickered in the glow, dancing to the strains of an organ. Sculptures stood everywhere, like sentinels keeping watch. Stained glass
blazed with color in the tall windows. Christians did
know how to embellish their churches, that he would
give them. Synagogues were decorated, but not with
human images—that was akin to idolatry. He'd often
thought about the contrast between such simplicity
and the Jews' two Temples, both of which would
have rivaled anything in Christendom.

But they were gone, the buildings razed.

Their treasures carted off.

Seeing something like St. Stephen's sickened him.
First built eight hundred years ago, nearly reduced to
rubble during the final days of World War II, rebuilt
in just seven years.

And that reality only strengthened his resolve.

He'd come inside alone. Rócha was waiting outside
where he could follow Sagan and his daughter once
they left. Neither one of them would leave Vienna
alive. Time for this phase of the operation to end, and
the next to begin.

Tour groups loitered about. The day was waning but
the church stayed open until 10:00 P.M. Maybe that's
why Sagan chose it. But how would he have known?

The man had done little but wallow in shame for the past eight years. He was beaten and broken.

Yet he'd reacted in Florida.

But who could blame him?

His only child was supposedly in danger.

Yet he wondered.

How would Sagan react if he knew the truth?

———

TOM WAITED OUTSIDE WHAT A PLACARD IDENTI-fied as the Chapel of St. Katherine, which jutted from the cathedral's south tower. From here he could see the west portal entrance, the entire nave, and the main altar.

He spotted Zachariah Simon as he walked past the ornate pulpit and strolled toward the altar. Thanks to Inna he'd gained entrance through a little-used door on the north side not open to the public. As he'd sus-pected, she had connections and made a call from the café to the diocese's public relations director. The story was simple. She had a friend in town from America, a reclusive celebrity writer, who wanted to visit St. Ste-phen's unnoticed. Would it be possible to gain access without passing through the main entrance? Her con-nection had been more than happy to help, which al-lowed him to arrive early and stay out of sight.

A quick survey and he estimated about a hundred people were present with cameras flashing, voices occasionally raised over the organ music. The cathe-dral was impressive. Its Romanesque walls were of red and purple-black stone, mottled and striated in bold strokes like some hanging tapestry. He mar-veled at the time and energy it had taken to craft something so grand, and envied such patience. His world had always been hurry-up, no time for much of anything except meeting the next deadline.

He missed that frenetic pace.

He used one of the massive pillars holding up the vaulted roof as cover, glancing around its edge, watching Simon. His gaze darted across the transept to the far side and an open iron grille manned by a single employee.

The catacombs' entrance.

He already knew that it closed for the day at 5:00. The attendant, an older woman, checked tickets, since a visit below required a charge. Inna had provided him with a guidebook and he'd read about the catacombs, deciding they would provide him the opportunity needed.

He'd done his homework and readied himself.

Simon stopped before the main altar.

Tom turned toward the main entrance.

Alle entered the church.

CHAPTER THIRTY-FIVE

BÉNE MANEUVERED AROUND ONE TURN AFTER AN-
other following the tortuous road. It had first clawed
its way up the stunted mountain peak, now it was
winding back down to a forested valley that lay about
thirty kilometers northwest of his estate. At its crest
he'd caught sight of Jamaica's north shore with its
sparkling blue water and glittering outer surf. A mid-
day sun burned overhead, the rays' intensity sharpened by the altitude.

The call finally came two hours ago from Tre Halliburton, and they'd decided to meet on-site—or
where Tre thought the site might be. He realized
things were happening in Vienna, but those were out
of his control. Brian Jamison was surely trying to salvage what he could from disaster, but he could not
care less. All he wanted was the Simon's cooperation,
and that would come only from what he could provide in return. He'd not liked being forced to work
with the Americans, resenting their intrusion, hating
their arrogance. But he'd cooperated. So what they
weren't happy? They should go about their business
and leave him alone.

Ahead, he spotted Halliburton, already out of his
vehicle, holding a briefcase. He wheeled to a stop and
joined him. They were still high enough to enjoy an

excellent panorama of dense jungle for many kilometers. In the far distance he saw the sea, long rollers of the Caribbean breaking on the reef that protected the north shore.

"That deed you found, Béne, was a gold mine all by itself. It led me places."

He liked what he was hearing.

Tre had sounded excited on the phone and seemed equally so now. He pointed toward the distant sea. "During his fourth voyage, in 1504, Columbus was stranded here for nearly a year. His ship fell apart and he beached it somewhere on the north shore. He had a tough time during that year. No rescue ships were sent. The local Spanish governor on Hispaniola hated Columbus, so he decided to leave him here to die. There was a mutiny among his crew, and then the Tainos turned hostile, withholding food. Do you know how Columbus solved that problem?"

Not really.

"He had on board a Regiomontanus *Ephemerides* printed in Nuremberg around 1490 that contained predictions of eclipses for thirty years ahead. He discovered that a total eclipse was going to occur in three days' time, February 29, 1504. So he summoned the local chiefs and told them that his God in heaven was angry with them for withholding food. He told them the moon would rise bloody and inflamed that night—which, of course, it did thanks to the eclipse. Then, he told them, the moon would vanish. Of course, that's also what happened. The Tainos panicked and begged Columbus to make it stop."

Béne listened as Tre explained how Columbus retired to his cabin supposedly to pray to his God for their forgiveness. But what he really did was use his half-hour glass to measure the eclipse's duration so that he could calculate Jamaica's longitude.

"He came back out just as the eclipse was ending and told the Tainos that his God had forgiven them and the moon would be restored, provided they kept supplying food. The moon reappeared and there were no more problems with the locals. And that calculation of longitude was only off by half a degree, which was remarkable for the time."

Béne wondered about the point of the story. He hated anything and everything to do with the Spanish.

"Columbus," Halliburton said, "understood navigation. He was good with the stars and knew their relationship to time and geography. Last night I went back into the archives and discovered some things your thief missed."

Tre opened the briefcase and removed a pad of paper.

"I found this written on another sheet that went with the first one concerning the lawsuit settlement between the Cohen brothers."

Enter at an open land near a 01: 94:01: a. 01. on the coast of 01 . aa . 94 .66 a of right against the Island a a .01 . 94 . 61. 01 . 94 66.13 .01 The prime formula which are to be called upon by word 24. 19. p.p. 000. nl pp. pp. 66. pp are the 11 . 61 94 .61.91 1 or 22. 4. 85. or the Portugals will show you there .61 . 61. 01 . 60. nl 85.

"This is what Abraham Cohen had to provide to his brother, Moses, as part of the settlement. The governor conducting the trial recorded this information in a report he made to Spain about the dispute. It seems there was a lot of interest among the Spanish about anything pertaining to the lost mine."

Béne had already told Halliburton about the hooked

X in the cave Frank Clarke had shown him, and about Columbus' signature.

Tre pointed back toward the sea and said, "Columbus hiked inland from somewhere along the shore and found the mine. To mark his way he used navigational points. That's what those numbers are on the pad. But we have no way of knowing what they refer to. It's a code. What we do know, Béne, is that the 420 acres Abraham Cohen bought in 1670 is down there, below us, in that valley. I found plenty of geographic landmarks on maps. If it exists, the mine is there."

He stared out at the palms, ferns, and luxuriant vegetation several hundred feet below, which extended all the way to the sea. No houses, towns, or farms were in sight.

"The good thing," Tre said, "is that it's uncultivated Maroon land."

Which meant there'd been little outside interference. Maroons guarded their land with a known ferocity. Permission was needed to explore.

"What now?" he asked.

"I'm getting a list of caves for this area. The Geological Society of Jamaica has most of them mapped. I want to see what's here."

That was sound thinking. "But it couldn't be in any known cave, could it?"

"It's a starting point."

"You don't think I'm so crazy anymore, do you?" he asked.

"All I know, Béne, is that this island wasn't noted for gold. There was a little here and there in the streams, but Jamaica's worth was its soil and location. We sat right in the middle of the trade routes, and this dirt can grow just about anything. The Spanish never recognized that, and Ferdinand never believed in any lost mine. That's why he gave the island to the Columbus heirs. He considered this place worthless. The legend came later. Ceding Jamaica was the easy way to get the Columbus family off his back. He was done with them. Finally."

"I have men who can scour that valley," Béne said.

"Not yet. Let's see if we can narrow things down. I've checked the deed you found. The rivers and streams mentioned are by their Spanish names, but we know what those translate to today. I think I can limit the search area."

He heard something else in Halliburton's voice. "What is it?"

"There's another source of documents, Béne. From the Spanish time. The curator in the archives last night reminded me about them. Few have ever seen them, but they could prove helpful. It's held privately."

"Where?"

"Cuba."

CHAPTER THIRTY-SIX

ALLE ENTERED ST. STEPHEN'S AND IMMEDIATELY spotted Zachariah standing a couple of hundred feet away, at the far end of the nave.

She walked toward him.

He was dressed impeccably, as always, standing tall and straight, not a hint of concern on his bearded face. He stood in the center of the transept. She came to within a few feet and stopped.

"Are you all right?" he immediately asked.

"Why did you want me dead?"

"Is that what they told you? *I* wanted you dead."

"Your man took me off into the woods with orders to kill me."

He shook his head. "Alle, he was not working for me. He worked for Brian Jamison. That man disappeared yesterday from my estate. He was Jamison's spy."

She knew that to be true, but wondered how he knew.

"I am here," Zachariah said, "because of your father. He did not keep his end of the deal in Florida and insisted we meet. Jamison's employer contacted me yesterday and told me they had you. They wanted to get to me through you. So they took you, and lied about me."

"Who does Brian work for?"

"A man named Béne Rowe, whom I should have never dealt with, if only for the reason that he placed you in jeopardy."

"Where's Rócha?"

"I know you are upset about the video. I am dealing with Rócha on that. It will not go unpunished. But it did cause your father to act."

Which was true.

"I tried to tell you several times that there are people who will want to stop our quest. Béne Rowe and Jamison are two of those. They are interfering in what we were doing—"

"I saw what happened in Florida when you went after my father."

"You saw?"

"A camera was there."

"There was no choice. I had to confront him. But when he asked for a meeting *here* to make the trade, I agreed."

"Where is he?" she asked.

"Right here."

She turned, as did Zachariah.

Her father stood a few feet away.

———

TOM STUDIED HIS DAUGHTER. HER DARK HAIR HUNG longer than a few years ago, but was still wavy. Her swarthy skin and compact frame came from him, as did her blunt nose, high cheeks, and rounded jaw. The brown eyes were her mother's. Like him, she wore no eyeglasses or other jewelry. She was dressed in jeans, a pullover shirt, and flat-soled boots. Watching her, he instantly thought of Michele. Truly her mother's daughter.

"Mr. Sagan," Simon said. "Here she is, as promised. Now, can I have what is mine?"

He faced Alle. "You all right?"

She nodded but offered nothing more. What bothered him was the fact that she and Simon had arrived separately and spoken calmly, as if they were familiar with each other.

"Mr. Sagan," Simon said. "I want what you have."

"And what are you going to do if I don't give it to you?"

"Your daughter is here, as I promised. Can not our business be concluded?"

Something wasn't right. Alle displayed none of the emotion he would have expected from someone who'd been tied to a bed and molested by strangers. He searched her eyes, looking for anything that might explain his misgivings, but she offered nothing.

"Give him what he wants," she finally said to him.

"Your grandfather would not want me to do that."

"How would you know?"

"I read what he left in his grave."

He saw she was curious, but he did not elaborate. Instead, he removed a folded piece of paper from his pocket and handed it to Simon. "This is it. A note to me."

As Simon read he watched Alle, who clearly seemed uncomfortable.

"This is all?" Simon asked.

"Abiram was a man of few words. That was actually a long conversation for him. I think the note makes clear that I had no idea he was some kind of Levite. Now that task is supposedly mine."

"As I told you in Florida, you are not worthy even to say that word."

"Are we done?"

Simon nodded. "Our business is concluded. Perhaps

you can now finish what you started at your father's house."

He resisted the urge to slug the SOB. "Or maybe I'll shoot you."

Simon frowned. "There is one other matter you might care about. Something I doubt your daughter will tell you. She was not kidnapped. At least not by me. She willingly participated in the charade you witnessed."

He told himself to stay calm.

"Tell him," Simon said to Alle. "The truth is always best."

Alle said nothing, but she was clearly surprised by Simon's admission.

"I mention this because she actually was kidnapped yesterday by others, released today thanks to me."

"I was told *you* were going to kill me," Alle said.

"I assure you, the danger was from them, not me." Simon faced Tom. "Her kidnappers work for a business associate of mine who decided to change our relationship. I intervened and made a deal for her release. I mention this because the man who took her prisoner just entered the church."

ALLE WHIRLED AND SAW BRIAN, STANDING AT THE opposite end of the nave. He'd said he was going to wait outside.

Another lie.

"He is no friend of mine," Zachariah said, "or yours. I wish you well."

"I'm going with you," she said.

"Your father would never allow it. Talk to him. Work through whatever needs to be said between the two of you."

An unnatural fear filled her. One she'd never felt before. "Why did you sell me out?"

"The truth is never a bad thing, is it, Mr. Sagan?"

"I guess you'll find out."

———

ZACHARIAH LEFT AND WALKED ACROSS THE CHECKerboard tiles to where Brian Jamison waited. Casually, he slipped the paper Sagan had given him into his trouser pocket. He stopped a few feet away.

"Get what you wanted?" Jamison asked.

"That's between me and your boss."

"So you're just going to walk right out of here? Let them go? Let me have them?"

He turned back toward where Alle and Tom Sagan stood.

"Not exactly."

———

TOM WATCHED THE SCENE A HUNDRED FEET AWAY, then asked Alle, "Is what he said true?"

She did not answer him, but he saw uncertainty and fear in her face, both of which caused him alarm.

"That man there," she said. "His name is Brian Jamison and he did take me prisoner yesterday. What Zachariah said about him could be true."

The man started their way as Simon left the church. Thank goodness he was ready.

"Let's go."

"Where?"

"Out of here."

He led her across the transept to the iron gate with the attendant. No more tickets for the catacombs were being checked. Inna had arranged for him to have a private tour after the underground area closed for the day. He'd talked with the attendant earlier and she was expecting him, waving them both through. A quick glance back and he saw the man called Brian heading straight for the entrance. Tom stepped to where the tile floor stopped and the stone risers started their descent. He passed through the gate, then grabbed the iron bars and slammed them shut, the lock clicking into place. When he'd arrived a couple of hours ago he'd noticed that the doorway would take a key to reopen. The surprised attendant surely held that key, but the minute or two that would buy them would be critical to their escape.

He'd thought Simon would be his enemy.

Now there was a new threat.

"Follow me," he told Alle.

And they raced down the stairs into the crypt.

———

ZACHARIAH HESITATED AT THE MAIN DOORS AND watched as Alle and her father entered the catacombs. Sagan had apparently closed the iron gate, which stopped Jamison's advance, the cathedral attendant now trying to reopen the lock. He'd wondered what Rowe would do next. Apparently he still wanted Alle Becket—and now her father. He'd compromised Alle because he wanted her to go with her father. That way Rócha could deal with them both. Of course, he assumed they would leave through the main doors.

But that was not the case.

And what Sagan had said to him about the truth.

"I guess you'll find out."

Something was wrong.

He stepped outside and immediately spotted Rócha.

He gestured and his man trotted over and said, "I saw Jamison go in."

"They are all headed down into the catacombs."

He wondered if this might be an opportunity.

"Come."

And he and Rócha reentered the church.

CHAPTER THIRTY-SEVEN

TOM HUSTLED DOWN THE STAIRS WITH ALLE CLOSE behind.

They found the bottom.

Before them stretched a maze of passageways, all hewn from bedrock centuries ago. Now it was an elaborate, Baroque necropolis where bishops and provosts lay buried. He'd studied the cathedral guidebook while waiting and had learned the layout, knowing where he had to go. When he'd met with Inna, one favor had been to get him inside the cathedral unnoticed.

The other had been to get him out.

"That way," he pointed.

———

ZACHARIAH HALTED HIS AND RÓCHA'S ADVANCE AND they sought cover behind one of the pillars. Brian Jamison hurried the attendant, who was still trying to reopen the gate. The commotion had drawn some attention from visitors, but not much. He'd toured the catacombs before. Lots of tombs, crypts, and bones. But he wondered. Was there another way out?

The older woman fumbled with her keys and finally inserted the right one into the lock.

Jamison disappeared, descending stairs.

He and Rócha rushed forward just as the woman was beginning to relock the gate. He was careful to keep his face angled away from her.

"Entschuldigen sie bitte," he said as they slipped past.

The older woman opened her mouth to speak, but Rócha slammed the gate shut behind them.

———

ALLE WAS CONFUSED AND SHAKEN. SHE'D HAD NO choice but to go with her father. Zachariah had sold her out. He seemed irritated. But how could she blame him? She'd accused him of trying to kill her. Had he in fact saved her? And was it Brian, not Zachariah, lying to her?

She had no idea.

She knew about the catacombs, though. A series of vaulted subterranean rooms. Lots of clergy were buried here, along with the bodies, hearts, and viscera of the Hapsburgs who, for centuries, ruled much of Europe. There were also the bones of over 11,000 people moved from the cemeteries above after an outbreak of plague in the mid-18th century. Their remains lay in massive piles, the display a bit macabre for her tastes. She recalled from her tour that the subterranean rooms flowed one into the other, each lit from the amber glow of incandescent fixtures. Her father seemed to know exactly where he was going, bypassing the main visitor areas that lay straight from the stairs, leading them left toward the bone rooms. Along the way they passed several notable tomb monuments with elaborate copper coffins.

She stopped. "Where are we going?"

He turned. "Out of here."

"How do you know there's a way out?"

She caught the irritation on his face.

"Contrary to what you may think, I'm not stupid. I thought ahead."

"Why are you doing this?"

"Maybe because I got to watch while my daughter was groped by two men, tied to a bed. You think that might motivate someone? Now I'm told the whole thing was an act. Was it, Alle?"

She hadn't seen anger from her father in a long while and its presence unnerved her. But lying seemed useless. "He was right. It was an act."

He stepped closer to her. "And you have the nerve to judge me."

She knew what he meant. All those times she'd told him what a lousy husband and father he'd been, calling him a liar, a fraud, culminating at her mother's funeral when she demanded he leave.

"Nothing to say?" he asked.

"I wanted you to open the grave. I knew you wouldn't do it if I simply asked."

"I wouldn't have. But you still should have asked."

They stood at a junction where the main passage continued ahead and another disappeared left. A placard indicated that the bone rooms lay that way. Movement to her right caught her eye.

Fifty feet away Brian appeared.

Her father saw him, too.

Their pursuer reached beneath his jacket. She knew what he kept there.

The shoulder holster.

A gun appeared.

———

TOM REACTED TO THE SIGHT OF THE WEAPON, DECIDING instantly that they could not flee straight ahead, as this man would have a clear shot at them. Earlier, when he'd reconnoitered the catacombs, Inna had shown him the shortest way out—which, unfortunately, waited where they could not go.

No choice.

He grabbed Alle's hand and they raced down the connecting passage toward the bone rooms.

———

ZACHARIAH DESCENDED THE STAIRS THAT LED INTO the catacombs. Light from below illuminated the flooring, and he caught the faint movement of a shadow disappearing to his left.

He grabbed Rócha's arm and signaled for them to slow down.

He also gestured with his head and Rócha found his weapon, a sound suppressor already attached to the automatic's short barrel. He was hoping for a few undisturbed minutes down here. The problem of Brian Jamison irked him, as did something else.

Had Sagan provided him everything?

They ended at the bottom of the stairs in a long room with pews. Some kind of underchurch. A Baroque crucifix hung above an altar. Carefully, he peered around the edge of the wall. A corridor led out. Jamison stood fifty feet away, a gun in hand, turning left around another corner.

He and Rócha followed.

———

TOM WAS CONCERNED. THIS WAS NOT GOING AS planned. He should have entered the catacombs with Alle, the iron gate locking behind them to keep Zachariah Simon at bay. He hadn't expected a third party in the mix and certainly had not expected his own daughter to be in collusion with the other side. From the catacombs diagram in the guidebook, he knew that the route they now were following would eventually lead to the exit he'd planned on utilizing, just in a longer and more roundabout path.

Inna was waiting there, at the top of another stairway beyond the church's east façade, the exit opening into a side alley, there for centuries, rarely used. A metal door, which could be opened only from the inside, protected that entrance, but Inna had managed to convince her contact at the diocese to allow her reclusive American visitor to leave from there once his private tour of the catacombs had ended. Inna herself assumed the responsibility to make sure the door was closed after they left. The diocese's PR person had been more than willing to accommodate, knowing he was accumulating a favor from the press that might come in handy.

Tom understood that currency.

Once he'd been a world-class trader in it.

They came to the end of the corridor and turned.

Niches opened to their right and left, each blocked by iron bars. Beyond the bars, illuminated by more incandescent fixtures, bones were stacked eight feet high. Some in precise piles, others in a bewildering mix, as if tossed there. The sight was troubling and surreal. So much death packed so tight. Who were these people? How had they lived? What was their story?

He noticed Alle's gaze was drawn toward them, too.

He just wanted to get out of here. But the corridor that bisected the bone rooms was long and straight. Maybe sixty feet from end to end with stone arches and iron bars lining both sides. Little cover. Not good.

"Stop right there," a voice said behind him.

He and Alle halted and turned.

Their pursuer stood twenty feet away.

A gun pointed straight at them.

CHAPTER THIRTY-EIGHT

BÉNE SAT IN THE CABIN OF THE KING AIR C90B, a small turboprop that he chartered whenever he traveled anywhere in the Caribbean. Luckily, the plane had been available on short notice and he and Tre Halliburton had climbed on board in Montego Bay. Tre had said there might be more information in Cuba, so he'd made a call and gained them access to the country. He regularly did business with the Cubans. They knew him and had been eager to cooperate. The plane could accommodate up to seven passengers, but with just the two of them on board there was plenty of room. What he liked about this particular charter was the service. The galley was always stocked with fine foods, the bar top-shelf liquors. Not that it mattered much to him, he drank precious little, but it did matter to his guests. Tre was enjoying a rum and cola.

"This archive is privately owned," Tre said. "I've always wanted to take a look but could not get into Cuba."

"Why do you think it would be helpful?"

"Some of what I found last night. There were constant references to Cuba in the Spanish documents left in Jamaica. The archivist and I have talked about this Cuban cache before. He's actually seen it. He said that there are more documents there from the Spanish time than anywhere he knows of."

"He doesn't know what you were after, does he?"

"No, Béne. I know better. I assume we can get a car once on the ground?"

"It's waiting on us."

"Apparently you've been here before."

"The Cubans, for all their faults, are easy to work with."

"When I was in the archives last night," Tre said, "one of the clerks told me about another clerk who'd gone missing. His name is Felipe. Is he the man who stole those documents for you?"

"Not for me. Someone else."

"He's dead, isn't he?"

He wasn't going to admit to that. Not to anyone. Ever. "Why would you ask me?"

"The clerk told me that he's never missed work. Young man. Bright. Now he's gone."

"Big leap from there to me."

"Why do you do it, Béne? Why not just go legitimate?"

He'd often asked himself the same thing. Maybe it was his father's genes swirling inside him. Unfortunately, the lure of easy money and the power it brought was impossible to ignore, though he wished sometimes that he could.

"Should we be having this conversation?" he asked.

"It's just you and me here, Béne. I'm your friend."

Maybe so, but he wasn't a fool. "I do nothing that harms anyone. Nothing at all. I grow my coffee, and I try to stay to myself."

"That man. Felipe. He might disagree with that."

He could still feel the glare of the wife's eyes as he tossed the money on the bed. He'd destroyed her life. Why? For pride? Anger? No. It simply had to be done. Jamaica was a tough place, the gangs many and strong. True, he was not a formal part of that system—he'd like to think that he'd risen above it—but to maintain that status he had to manage fear. Killing that drug don had been part of that. Felipe? Not so much, since no one would ever really know what happened, except the men who worked for him. But that had been the point. If someone like a minor clerk could lie to him with no consequences, what would *they* do?

Now they knew the price for that mistake.

"It's unfortunate that the man is missing," he finally said.

"I read about your father," Tre said. "He was quite a man. He may have single-handedly created the entire Blue Mountain Coffee industry."

He was young when his father died, but he remembered some and his mother had told him more. She seemed to remember only the good. His father saw a need to regulate Jamaica's most valuable export. Of course, the Rowe family benefited. But what was wrong with that?

"My father wanted to find this mine, too," he told Halliburton. "He was the one who first told me about it."

He wanted the subject changed. This trip was about the mine, not his family or his business. But he liked Halliburton enough not to become angry at the intrusion.

"And what will you do if the place really exists?" Tre asked.

A gale of turbulence rattled the plane. They were twenty thousand feet over the Caribbean Sea, headed northeast toward Santiago de Cuba, a populous city on the southeast shore. The flight was short and they'd be landing soon.

"Does it exist?" he asked.

"Two days ago I would have said no. Now I'm not so sure."

"It is there," Zachariah Simon said to him. "My family has searched for this mine a long time."

"Why is it important to you?"

"It is important to my religion."

That surprised him. "How?"

"Christopher Columbus was a Jew. He converted to Christianity on threat of force. But he remained a Jew at heart."

He'd never heard that before.

"His real name was Christoval Arnoldo de Ysassi."

He made no effort to hide his disbelief.

"It is true," Simon said. "His family took the name Colón after converting."

"Why does that matter?" He truly wanted to know.

"To my family it matters a great deal. To the Jews, even more. Do you know the story of Columbus' death?"

"How did Columbus die?" he asked Halliburton.

"Where'd that come from?"

"Something I was thinking about. How did it happen?"

"He died in Spain in May 1506 after a long illness. Nobody knows what killed him. It wasn't so much his death but what happened after that's really interesting."

He listened as Halliburton explained how Columbus was first buried in a convent at Valladolid. Then in 1513, his daughter-in-law requested that the remains be brought to the Seville cathedral. In 1537 the family was granted permission to bring the body back to the New World, and Columbus was interred inside a newly built church in Santo Domingo.

1537.

He knew the significance of that year.

That was when the same daughter-in-law—the widow of one of Columbus' sons—acquired control of Jamaica from the Spanish Crown.

Columbus stayed on Hispaniola until 1795. When Spain lost control of the island to the French, the remains were transferred to Havana. In the early 20th century, at the end of the Spanish-American War, when Cuba gained independence, the bones were brought back to Seville, where they have remained.

"With just one problem," Tre said. "They might not be Columbus. Toward the end of the 19th century, some workers digging in the church at Santo Domingo found a lead box full of bones. On the outside was written, RENOWNED MAN DON CRISTOBAL COLON. That made everyone believe that the Spanish might have dug up the wrong grave back in 1795."

"I've been to the church in Santo Domingo," he said. "There's a monument to Columbus and a tomb."

"That contains those bones from the lead box. The government did all that in 1992 to celebrate the five hundredth anniversary of the first voyage. But there's also a magnificent tomb in Seville. They've run several DNA tests, but nothing has ever been solved. Those bones were moved so much, scattered around, he could be in all of those places. Or none of them."

"My family is searching for Columbus' grave," Simon told him. *"We think that the bones were secretly transported to Jamaica and hidden in his lost*

mine. That location was apparently one the family trusted, since the Admiral himself located it."

But he'd not believed the Simon then, and still did not now. This wasn't about finding some grave. No way. Simon was after something else entirely, something important enough to draw the attention of American intelligence agents. He could not care less about the bones of Columbus. That man had been an invader. A destroyer. His arrival meant the deaths of tens of thousands of Tainos, and eventually led to slavery, which wrought even more pain and suffering. Maroons had rebelled against all of that, becoming the first Africans to win their freedom in the New World. If there was a lost mine, it definitely belonged to them.

"What is it, Béne?"

The engine's angry chorus waned and they began their descent. Out the window he spotted Cuba and the green bastion of mountains that skirted the coast. La Sierra Maestra. He knew that slaves had used its harsh terrain for cover as they escaped the cane plantations. They'd not acquired a name like Maroons, but they were the same nonetheless.

Halliburton was glancing out a window, too. "That's where the Cuban revolution started. Castro and his men hid in those mountains."

He knew coffee was grown there. A strong blend that only mildly competed with his prized beans.

"I want to find that mine," he said, his voice low. "If there be nothing there, fine. But I want to find it. I need you to help me do that." He faced Tre and asked, "Will you?"

"Sure, Béne. I can do that."

He saw that his friend sensed the urgency. He also saw something else. Apprehension. He'd never seen that in Halliburton's eyes before. He hated that his friend might be afraid of him, but he did nothing to ease that feeling.

He would tolerate no more lies, no more mistakes. Not from foe or friend.

CHAPTER THIRTY-NINE

Tom stared at the gun and asked, "What do you want?"

The man Alle said was named Brian marched toward them.

"I knew you were the problem," Alle said.

"Your daughter tell you what a great actress she is?"

He kept his gaze on the weapon. Strange. Two days ago he hadn't feared death. Today was a little different. Not that he definitely wanted to live, it was just that, at the moment, he didn't particularly want to die. Abiram's two messages and Alle's betrayal both raised questions.

And he hadn't been curious for a long time.

"What's your involvement here?" he asked.

"He works for a man trying to stop Zachariah," Alle said.

Brian faced him. "You and I need to talk."

———

Zachariah led the way as he and Rócha crept down the passageway, past centuries-old tombs of cardinals and priests. They came to the junction where Brian had fled and he spotted a corridor, maybe ten meters long and hewn from rock that ended at another right angle. One fixture illuminated the passage closer to his end than the other. He heard voices from around the far corner and signaled for quiet as they eased to a point where he could peer around. He was counting on the fact that Sagan, Alle, and Brian would not expect him.

"You and I need to talk."

Jamison's voice.

Before that he'd heard both Sagan and Alle. Her reference to him sounded almost like a defense. Maybe he'd confused her enough by his revelations about Jamison to have a second chance. He risked a quick look and saw Brian, fifteen meters away, back to him, holding a gun, facing toward where Sagan and Alle stood.

He and Rócha retreated.

He motioned to his left and whispered, "I have been here before. That passage where they are standing will intersect with this one. There are several turns, but it is a big circle. I am going down here to wait."

Rócha nodded in understanding.

Then he explained what else he wanted done.

———

ALLE KNEW ONLY ONE THING. SHE HAD TO GET AWAY from both her father and Brian. They both seemed to believe that Zachariah was the enemy, but the only person to so far place her in danger was standing right beside her, holding a gun.

"What are you going to do?" she asked Jamison.

"We're getting out of here. Mr. Sagan, I assume you came down here for a reason?"

She watched as her father remained silent. Finally, she said, "He has a way out."

"I thought as much. That's why I followed. Let's take it, then I'll explain everything."

Her father seemed unconvinced and even more irritated with her.

"I suggest we go," Brian said. "People upstairs may be coming this way."

"No. They won't," Sagan said. "I took care of that. The gate is locked for the night."

"Then let's get out of here. I assure you, what I have to say is important."

Her father stepped in front of her and faced Brian. "We're not going anywhere. If you want to shoot me, go ahead. I don't give a damn."

"I know what happened in Florida. That you were about to kill yourself. But you didn't. You're here. We were watching, along with Simon. I sent a man to the cemetery to spook you, in the car, when you visited your father's grave, but you didn't back off. I'm not your enemy, Mr. Sagan. I'm an American intelligence agent, working for a unit known as the Magellan Billet. We're after Zachariah Simon and need your help."

Alle caught movement over Brian's shoulder.

Rócha appeared, holding a gun.

Her eyes went wide.

Brian saw her surprise and started to turn.

TOM SAW THE MAN AND IMMEDIATELY LUNGED toward Alle, his body covering hers, both of them pounding the floor.

Two pops echoed.

Brian's body lurched, his arms went skyward, his grip on the gun was lost and it clattered to the floor.

Another pop.

Blood seeped from Brian's lips. Then the body went limp and he collapsed into convulsions.

Tom rolled twice and reached for the gun on the floor, slipping his finger around the trigger. He swung his arm around and fired, the retort loud off the stone.

The bullet ricocheted and, instinctively, he covered his head.

When he looked up, the man at the end of the hall was gone.

And so was Alle.

———

ZACHARIAH KEPT WALKING, HEADING FOR WHERE the corridor intersected another. He heard shots and hoped that was the end of Brian Jamison. Béne Rowe surely had other people working for him, but the loss of his chief lieutenant would eliminate Rowe's most valuable eyes and ears in Austria. He'd read Abiram Sagan's note, which was explicit, but not as much as he'd hoped considering the Levite would be passing on all that he knew. Had Sagan changed it? After all, it was typewritten. How hard could it have been? Especially for a man accused of falsifying news stories.

His original plan was no more.

He now needed a few moments alone with Alle.

A loud bang, then more pops came from the catacombs.

One problem was surely gone.

Two more were about to be solved.

———

ALLE WATCHED AS BRIAN WAS SHOT THREE TIMES, HIS body finally ceasing all movement on the floor. Her father was trying to find Brian's gun and she used that moment to spring to her feet and race ahead, finding the passageway's end and turning a corner. She had no idea where she was headed, but it was in the direction her father had been taking them.

Brian's words still hung in her ears.

I'm an American intelligence agent.

What in the world?

A shot rang out from behind her, louder than the others. She slowed, but kept a brisk pace, her head constantly spinning, checking her flank. She spotted a stairway fifty feet ahead, the path well lit.

Another glance back.

More pops.

Her shoulders were grabbed from the front, her body spun.

The unexpected violation startled her and she was about to scream when a hand clamped over her mouth and she saw Zachariah's face.

———

TOM WAS PINNED DOWN, HUDDLED INSIDE ONE OF THE archways that framed an iron grille with a gate that separated the hall from bone rooms on each side. He was hugging the bars, keeping his body shielded, when he realized that the gate was not locked. He eased open the hinged section and rolled into the narrow room, his body now flush against a stack of blackened bones. He stared back, trying to spot whoever was firing at him.

Then he saw.

The bone rooms were not individual. The niches formed one long path, archways dividing them from the center passage. Lights illuminated the niches and the bones. He could actually escape the shooter, staying out of the corridor, the angle and pillars providing plenty of cover.

He crouched low and started to leave.

Another pop.

Bones a foot away shattered as a bullet slammed into the pile.

He dropped to the floor and lay flat.

Bad idea.

He told himself to calm down, breathe slower. Think. He still held the gun. His shot a moment ago, the first time in his life he'd ever fired a weapon, had been a message that he was armed. Strange that his first shot was here, among so many reminders of death, when it should have been two days ago. He crawled ahead across the gritty floor, paralleling the bones inches away. A musty, dirty smell filled his nostrils, which reminded him of Abiram's open coffin, but he kept moving, staying low to the ground.

He heard movement behind him.

He rolled onto his spine and stared back through the bars and arches.

A shadow grew in size.

Someone was approaching.

———

ZACHARIAH HELD ALLE TIGHT, HIS HAND OVER HER mouth. He could feel her shaking with fear.

He removed his hand.

"Are you all right?" he whispered, concern in his voice and eyes.

Her head bobbed. "I'm okay. Brian is back there. He was shot. Somebody is there with a gun."

"Listen to me, Alle. I need your help. Rócha will make sure your father is okay. No harm will come to him. But I need you to go with him. Find out what it is your father knows."

"He told you."

He shook his head. "He is holding back. There is no reason for him to be truthful with me. I would have no way to verify anything, and he knows that."

"Why would he lie?"

"Perhaps he feels an attachment or duty to his father. I have to know if he is being entirely candid."

"Brian is a government agent."

His heart shuddered.

Had he heard her correctly?

"He said he worked for U.S. intelligence."

How was that possible? But he contained his surprise and decided to use that fact. "That's exactly what I have been saying. The Americans would like nothing better than to stop me."

"Why?"

"I will explain later. Right now, find out for me what your father knows. Much is at stake here for us all."

"Why did you sell me out?"

"I wanted you to go with him. I thought it the only way to make sure you would not come with me."

A lie, but a good one.

He watched her eyes, searching for confirmation that she was still his.

"Okay," she said. "I can go with him and find out."

"I knew you could. You must know that I would never have allowed anything to happen to you. I took a great chance coming down here. Brian was a danger, but I had to make sure you were okay." He handed her his cell phone. "Take this. My home number is there in the memory. Call me when you learn something."

"Did you kill Brian?" she asked.

"Not me. Somebody else is here. That is why you and your father have to leave. Rócha is making that possible. We have enemies everywhere."

She did not know what to say.

He gently grasped both of her shoulders. "It is unfortunate that all this has happened, but much depends on you. Please, find out what we need to know."

CHAPTER FORTY

BÉNE HAD SEVERAL TIMES VISITED SANTIAGO DE Cuba, a city with half a million people. It was the island's second largest, behind Havana, which lay nine hundred kilometers to the west. Its deep bay made it invaluable, as from here Cuba imported and exported most of its goods. What he'd not known was its history relative to the Spanish. That had never been important, until today.

Tre explained that one of Spain's first conquistadores, Diego Velázquez de Cuéllar, founded the city in 1514 before he laid siege to the island. Cortez began his conquest of Mexico and de Soto his exploration of Florida from here. This was the center of Spanish power over Cuba, serving as the island's capital until 1589. More recently, the Battle of San Juan Hill happened not far away, which ended both the Spanish-American War and any European presence in Cuba forever.

"Castro proclaimed the victory of the Cuban revolution from this town's city hall balcony," Tre said.

They were climbing into a Range Rover that had been waiting at the airport. Béne had arranged for the vehicle through contacts he maintained for his export businesses.

"Columbus landed here on his first voyage in October 1492," Tre said. "He thought he was in Asia, on a new continent, so he searched for the Grand Khan. He had on board a man named Luis de Torres, who served as the ship's translator. He could speak Hebrew and some Arabic. Columbus sent de Torres and another man inland to find the Khan. Of course, all they found were half-naked natives, living simply. But de Torres did discover one thing." Tre paused. "The locals showed him how to roll leaves into what they called *tabacos*. They would light one end and draw a few drags. He watched as they took the fire-brands with them on hunting journeys, halting every hour or so for more drags. They were able to travel great distances thanks to those drags. We call them cigars today, and the leaves tobacco. De Torres could have been the first European to ever smoke. But within a hundred years, tobacco had spread through-out Europe."

Béne drove as they left the airport, heading for a small community west of town. Tre had told him the archive's location and a map had been waiting in the vehicle.

"De Torres never returned to Spain," Tre said. "He stayed in the New World and eventually settled here, in Cuba. He started a plantation and was the first European to cultivate tobacco. This island, more than Hispaniola, became the Spanish headquarters in the New World. So it makes sense that this is where the majority of documents from that time can be found."

Which probably saved them, Béne thought. As a socialist state, Cuba had been closed to most of the world since 1959. Only in the past few years had that changed.

"I've been told," Tre said, "that this archive is contained within a small museum about the Spanish time in Cuba."

"I despise Columbus." He was comfortable enough with Halliburton to express himself openly, at least on this topic.

"You're not alone. October 12, Columbus Day in America, is hardly celebrated anywhere else. In Mexico it's called the day of one race, *Raza,* with hardly a mention of Columbus. In Uruguay the natives commemorate it as their last day of freedom. Many other South and Central American nations feel the same. What happened in 1492 definitely changed the world, but it has created an era of unparalleled genocide, cruelty, and slavery."

They rode in silence for a while through kilometers of palm-lined cane fields. Béne thought about the information Simon had offered, which wasn't much. He'd not shared anything with Halliburton about the Austrian's existence. That was his alone to know. But what Tre had said about Luis de Torres, *a Hebrew translator,* stuck in his brain.

"Why was there a person speaking Hebrew on Columbus' ship?"

"Nobody knows, Béne. There are some who think Columbus was a Jew and that he was searching for some promised land where Jews lived in peace."

Which was what Simon believed. "Is that possible?"

Tre shrugged. "Who the hell knows? We know so little about Columbus that anything is possible. It's a fact that he brought no priests with him on the first voyage, which is odd in and of itself. Columbus was an enigma then, and remains so today. Who would have thought he found some lost Tainos gold mine? But maybe he did."

The highway led them into a small hamlet with

colonial-style buildings, a place where things seemed reused, mended, and recycled time and again. Three feed-and-supply stores catered to farmers, but there was also a tinsmith, tobacco shop, and what appeared to be a church. He parked the Range Rover near a cobbled square surrounded by more colonial-era buildings. The hot air reeked of ripe fruit and toiling humanity. Little breeze, just a trapped and boiling stew of conflicting smells. They'd passed their destination just down the street, a sign indicating MUSEO DE AMBIENTE HISTÓRICO CUBANO and that it was open until 4:00 P.M. He'd not come unprepared. A semiautomatic was tucked snugly beneath a thin jacket. Cuba, for all its supposed innocence, remained a hostile place, one where he'd learned to be cautious. Only a few people were in sight. A mangy-haired dog ambled over to investigate them. Some Cuban jazz leaked from one of the cafés.

He faced Tre. "You said this place was privately owned. By whom?"

"The Jews of Cuba."

That information piqued his interest.

"Surprised me, too," Tre said. "Once there were tens of thousands of Jews here. They came after Columbus. Then they fled here for Brazil in the 17th century because of the Inquisition. They came back after 1898, when the island gained its independence from Spain. Now only about 1,500 are left. Amazingly, Castro left them alone. Over the past decade they've made a name for themselves by preserving the island's history. Some of them are distant descendants from the *conversos* who immigrated here in the early 16th century with de Torres. They've spent a good deal of time and money gathering up documents and artifacts from that period and storing them away. Thank goodness they have a generous benefactor. Like with you and the Maroons."

He stepped away from the vehicle and wished for a cold drink. "I didn't know there were rich people in Cuba. The ones I deal with all claim poverty."

"This one's from overseas. A foundation. It's funded by a wealthy Austrian named Zachariah Simon."

CHAPTER FORTY-ONE

TOM LAY ON THE FLOOR AND WATCHED THE SHADOW approach. He decided to wait until whoever it was came close before firing. He angled the gun toward a set of bars in a niche twenty feet away. His right elbow brushed the bones stacked to his right and he instantly drew it away. Then he saw something on the wall to his left, four feet off the ground, inside the niche, hidden from view of the passageway.

A switch.

Steel conduit ran up the stonework, then paralleled where wall met ceiling. Offshoots from that conduit led to light fixtures that illuminated the niches. A quick scan and he saw this switch shut off every light in the niches from one end to the other.

He sprang to his feet and raked his right hand across the switch, plunging his side of the cavern into darkness. Light still spilled from niches across the center passageway, beyond the bars, but there was enough darkness for him to make an escape.

He stayed low and moved toward the end where he hoped another iron gate within an archway would be open and he could escape.

Two pops startled him.

But the rounds smacked into bones behind him.

His assailant was searching, but he'd managed to skip ahead.

He came to the end.

The iron gate within the arch opened. He carefully peered to his right, back down the semi-darkened main passage. No one was there. He wondered if his pursuer had entered the niches, just as he'd done. Not wanting to stay around and find out, he ran down the corridor, toward the exit Inna had told him was there.

He came to the base of a stairway and glanced back.

No one was following.

He climbed the risers two at a time and, at the top, turned left, racing down a short hall toward daylight.

Two darkened forms waited.

Inna and Alle.

"What happened?" Inna asked him.

"No time. We have to go."

Alle looked shaken, but he was, too.

They stepped out into an alleyway between two rows of buildings. He estimated they were somewhere east of the cathedral, its tall spire blocked by the rooflines.

"Who was there?" Inna asked.

"Uninvited guests."

Inna seemed to understand, nodding and saying, "Follow me."

ZACHARIAH CROUCHED DOWN AT THE TOP OF THE stairs, keeping watch on the doorway ten meters away, listening to Tom Sagan talk to another woman.

Rócha had joined him.

The exit door slammed shut.

Darkness and quiet returned.

They needed to leave. The shots could have been heard in the cathedral and he did not want to be around when anyone came to investigate. Thankfully, they'd garnered a few uninterrupted minutes that had turned productive. He could only hope Alle would do what he asked.

"Jamison dead?" he whispered.

"Yes. But there's something you need to know."

He listened as Rócha told him what Jamison had said before being shot, the same thing Alle had reported. He now wondered about Béne Rowe. Had everything and everybody been compromised?

But first, "Go get the body and clean up any mess."

He waited a few minutes before Rócha returned with Jamison slung across one shoulder. He led the way to the exit and carefully opened the inside latch. Daylight was fading into shadows.

"Wait here."

He stepped out and casually walked to where another street led away from the alley. A trash receptacle caught his gaze. Small, but large enough. He returned to the iron door and noticed no latch or lock on the outside. This was a one-way portal. Tom Sagan had thought ahead.

Again.

Which only reinforced the notion that Sagan had lied to him.

"I'm leaving. Dump the body in that container around that corner, then join me at the car."

———

ALLE FOUND HERSELF SHAKING. WAS IT FEAR? DOUBT? Confusion? She wasn't sure. The woman who'd introduced herself as Inna Tretyakova, apparently an acquaintance of her father's, had led them to a nearby

U-bahn station. They'd taken the subway across town to a residential area heavy with apartments. The St. Stephen's spire loomed in the darkening sky a mile or so away. A clock in the station had told her it was approaching 7:00 P.M.

Her father had said nothing on the train, speaking only briefly to Inna. The woman appeared to be in her forties, attractive, with blue eyes that had appraised her with a penetrating gaze. She'd introduced herself as an editor for *Der Kurier*, which she knew to be one of Vienna's daily newspapers.

She told herself to stay calm, but she could not rid her mind of the sight of Brian Jamison being shot. She'd never seen such a thing. He'd been a danger, a person she'd never accepted and never believed. He'd lied to her outside the cathedral about being alone. He spoke Hebrew, carried a gun—none of it made sense.

What was happening here?

She was a twenty-five-year-old graduate student with an interest in Columbus who wrote an article for a British periodical. One day she was in Seville wading through 500-year-old documents, the next she was in Austria involved with a man searching for the Temple treasure. Now she was on the run with her father, a man she deeply resented, acting as a spy.

Inna led them to a modest building and up to a third-floor apartment, not much bigger than the one Zachariah had provided her. This unit held Inna and her two children, both teenagers, whom she met. No husband, Inna explained, as they had divorced five years ago.

"You didn't mention that earlier," her father said.

"How was it important? You asked for my help and I gave it. Now tell me what happened back there."

"A man was killed."

Alle wanted to know, "What did you give Zachariah?"

"Do you have any idea the trauma you put me through?" her father asked. "I thought you were in danger. I watched while men—"

"That was real."

And she meant it. She could still feel their disgusting touches.

"I took a lot of chances for you," her father said.

"I was told you were about to kill yourself."

"A few more seconds and I would have never been a problem for you again."

"I'm not sorry for what I did. It had to be done. There's a lot at stake here."

"Enlighten me."

That she did not plan to do, especially in front of a stranger, whom she knew nothing about.

So she asked again, "What was it you found in Grandfather's grave?"

CHAPTER FORTY-TWO

Zachariah stepped from the car and told Rócha to wait behind the wheel. They'd driven out of central downtown to Vienna's western outskirts and Schönbrunn. Once the residence of the Hapsburg emperors, now the Baroque palace stood as a tourist attraction.

And a popular one.

He'd visited once himself, admiring some of the 1,400 rooms, particularly impressed by the Hall of Mirrors where, he'd been told, a six-year-old Mozart once performed. Its magnificent grand gallery was where delegates to the Congress of Vienna danced away the night in 1815, after carving up Napoleon's defeated empire. He admired that audacity.

The palace interior was closed for the day, but the gardens stayed open till dusk. Long promenades bisected rows of perfectly trimmed shrubs and a sea of late-winter flowers. An obelisk decorated the sky. Sculpted fountains gushed foamy water. He soaked in the careful mixture of color and style, allowing the ambience to soothe his raw nerves, as it had once surely done for emperors.

He hoped Alle Becket was doing as he asked. He'd already forwarded all calls from the phone at the estate to Rócha's cell phone, which he'd commandeered before leaving the car. When Alle called he'd be instantly available. What concerned him now was Brian Jamison's identity. So he'd made another call and arranged a meeting.

His contact within the Israeli embassy was an undersecretary who'd provided a wealth of valuable information. He was young, ambitious, and greedy. But sitting on the bench at the far end of the garden was a middle-aged woman. Tall, full-figured, with long black hair.

The Israeli ambassador to Austria.

She stood as he approached and said in Hebrew, "I thought it was time we spoke face-to-face."

He was alarmed and considered leaving.

"Relax, Zachariah. I'm a friend."

"Enlighten me." He kept to Hebrew.

She smiled. "Always so careful, aren't you? So prepared. Except for today."

They knew each other. Given his status as one of the wealthiest Jews in this part of the world it was understandable he'd be courted.

And this woman had done so.

She'd once been a teacher who joined the diplomatic service, first assigned to Central Asia. She'd taught at the National Defense College and served as the Knesset's political adviser, which surely brought her in contact with much of Israel's political elite. She'd been described as tough, blunt to the point of arrogant, and brilliant.

"In what way have I not been careful?" he asked.

"I know what you're doing. I've been watching."

Now he was concerned.

"Tell me, Zachariah, who do you think will soon emerge as our new prime minister?"

He caught her point. "Your name has never been mentioned."

She smiled. "Which is the way it should be. A front-runner today is a loser tomorrow."

He agreed, but remained on high alert.

"What you plan is audacious," she said. "Ingenious, too. And most of all, it could work. But it's what comes *after* that will really matter, isn't it?"

"And *you* are what comes after?"

"Israel is in need of another Iron Lady."

He smiled at the reference to Golda Meir, and the term used to describe her strength long before the Brits attached it to Margaret Thatcher. The first and only woman, so far, to be Israel's prime minister, she was called by many "the best man in government." Strong-willed, straight talking, her gray-bunned hairdo had lent her another title: grandmother of the Jewish people. He recalled his father and grandfather speaking of her with a deep reverence. She was one of twenty-four signatories on the Israeli declaration of independence in 1948. The next day war broke out and she fought like everyone else. She ordered the hunting down and killing of all the terrorists who massacred Jewish athletes during the 1972 Olympics. And she commanded Israel during the Yom Kippur War, making smart decisions that saved the state.

"Why are you telling me this?"

"As I said, you made a mistake earlier. The man you killed was an American intelligence agent. They're watching you, too."

"And why is that?"

She chuckled. "Okay, Zachariah. Be cautious. Watch every word. But know this. We're here, talking alone. If I were your enemy you could be under arrest. Instead I sent men to clean up your mess. The body you left in that trash receptacle? It's gone. I don't like the Americans. I don't like them in our business. I don't like having to cater to them."

Neither did he.

"Jamison was working with some of our people—off the record, unofficially. I have many friends, so I made sure those agents don't like Americans, either. Check it out. You'll find Jamison's body gone and no mention of his death anywhere in the press. The Americans themselves will not learn of it for several weeks. Take that as my show to you of good faith."

His thoughts were confused, a state he always tried hard to avoid. But he held his ground, kept his mouth shut, and listened.

"I'm returning home soon," she said. "To stand for election to the Knesset. From there, I will position myself to be prime minister. My support is growing by the day and, hopefully, will surge after you do what you have planned."

"How do you know what I plan?"

Her eyes narrowed. "Jamison learned quite a bit from Alle Becket. He's had a full day to interrogate her, as you well know. He reported that information to his superiors *before* you killed him."

"So you have contacts with the Americans?"

She nodded. "Excellent ones. From what Jamison knew and I suspected, it was easy to piece the rest together. I must confess, I wish I'd thought of it."

"And what of the Americans? Are they going to be a problem in a few weeks?"

She shrugged. "I'd say they are no longer a threat, and I will make sure that remains the case."

He caught the threat in her tone.

She could allow that to drop either way.

"Zachariah, once you accomplish your goal I want to be the one to take matters from there. It fits perfectly with what I have in mind. In that way, we will all have what *we* want."

"So I'm clear, what is it *we* want?"

"A strong, determined Israel that speaks with one, determined voice. An end to the Arab problem, with no concessions. And most of all, the world will not tell us how to exist."

He was still deeply suspicious. But there was no way, other than checking that trash bin, to verify her credibility.

"You're right," she told him. "The spark needed to reawaken Israel cannot come from any official process. That would never work. It has to be spontaneous and external, without any hint of politics. It has to be heartfelt, deep-set, and evoke an unconditional emotional response. When I finally understood what you have planned, I knew instantly that it was the right course."

"And if I succeed, will you carry through and do all that is required?"

Her understanding of what that entailed was a test, one she seemed to comprehend.

"Oh, yes, Zachariah. The Jews will remember the month of Av."

She did know.

"It is more than a coincidence," she said, "that our Second Temple was destroyed on the ninth day of the month of Av, 70 CE—the same day that Nebuchadnezzar's Babylonian soldiers destroyed the First Temple six centuries before. I've always thought that a sign."

He was curious, "And do you have allies who think as you do?"

That could be important.

"Just me, Zachariah. Do I have friends? In positions

of power? Many. But they know nothing. I will simply use them. Only you and I are part of this."

"Will you carry through on *all* that we require?"

He saw she understood.

"Rest easy, Zachariah. The Jews will have their Third Temple. That I promise you."

CHAPTER FORTY-THREE

Béne and Halliburton entered the museum, a detached building that appeared to have once been a two-storied house, the inside full of wood, marble floors, and frescoed walls. Moorish influences showed in the ornaments and lattice, a leafy courtyard visible beyond the windows. Displays filled the ground-floor rooms, one opening into another, cases filled with stones, fossils, photographs, books, and relics. Explanations were printed only in Spanish, which Béne had no trouble reading. A man of about fifty with a knotted face stood near one of the displays. Tre introduced himself and Béne, explaining that he was an academician from the University of the West Indies, come to see the document collection from the time of Spanish colonization. The man, who identified himself as the curator, offered a hand then explained that the document collection was private and permission would have to be obtained before they could examine it.

"From who?" Béne asked.

Tre's revelation that Zachariah Simon possessed a connection to this place had unnerved him. This wasn't Jamaica. He wasn't Béne Rowe here. He was just some foreigner, and he did not like that feeling of helplessness. True, he was armed, and would shoot his way back to the plane if need be, but he realized that could prove futile. Diplomacy was the smart play. Which in Cuba, meant bribery. Exactly why he'd brought cash.

"Tell me, friend," he said to the curator. "Are American dollars taken around here?"

"Oh, yes, *señor*. They are much appreciated."

For all their brash talk the Cuban government was partial to American money. He withdrew his money clip and peeled off five $100 bills. "Is it possible to obtain that permission? Fast?"

He laid the money on a nearby counter.

"*Sí, señor.* I will make a call to Havana."

———

TOM GLARED AT ALLE. SHE DESPISED HIM, THAT WAS clear, but he wanted answers. "You converted?"

"How did you know?"

"Abiram told me."

"In the note he wrote?"

He nodded.

She still seemed surprised. "What I did to you, I did for my religion."

"Being Jewish means living a lie?" He shook his head. "Your mother would have never approved of your conversion."

"My mother loved me. Always."

"Yet you had no problem lying to her. You converted before she died, but kept it to yourself."

That revelation surprised her, too. "How do you know that?"

He ignored her question. "You're a hypocrite. You tell me what a worthless father and husband I was, yet you're nothing but a liar yourself."

They stood in the living room alone, Inna's two children in their rooms. They should have gone outside to talk, but he felt safer out of sight, tucked inside one of the countless apartments that lined the street.

"Who is that woman in the kitchen?" Alle asked.

"A friend."

"You had lots of *friends*."

"Is that supposed to be an insult?"

"It's what it is. I saw the pain on Mother's face. I watched her cry. I saw her heart break. I wasn't a child."

She spoke of a reality he'd learned not to deny. "I was a bad person. I did bad things. But I never stopped loving your mother. I still love her."

"That's a joke."

He heard Michele's bitter tone in her rebuke, saw her anguish in Alle's eyes. He knew he bore a lot of responsibility for that anger. He hadn't taken Michele's advice and mended his strained relationship. Instead he'd wallowed in self-pity while his only child learned to hate him.

"Are you going to tell me what you found in Grandfather's grave?" she asked.

He decided to let her read it for herself. He found another copy of what he'd given Simon and handed it to her. She glanced up after reading, her youthful eyes full of questions. "He told you all about me."

He nodded. "Even old Abiram, at the end, had regrets."

"Is this what you gave Zachariah?"

The use of a first name was more a sign that this young woman was not to be trusted. "The same."

He'd retyped the original in Jacksonville, using the library's computer and printer to produce two copies. It had been easy to edit out the portions pertaining to where the golem slept, the rabbi's name, the coded directions, and all references to the key. He hadn't been sure what might happen in Austria, but he'd been ready.

"This says little to nothing," she said.

"So tell me. Was it all worth it?"

———

ALLE WASN'T SURE IF HER FATHER WAS LYING. HER grandfather had clearly left a message. There were references to the Temple treasure and a great secret a Levite had kept. But would he not have revealed that secret? Written all he knew? Explained everything? Was Zachariah right? Had the wording been changed?

"Aren't you concerned," her father asked, "that a man died back there?"

"He kidnapped me. Threatened to kill me more than once."

"He said he was an American agent."

"I was told he worked for a man named Béne Rowe."

"Who told you that?"

She decided not to answer.

"Zachariah again?" He shook his head. "Why do you think this man Brian let you go to Simon in the church? If he wanted to hurt you, he would have just done it himself."

"You heard him. Zachariah made a deal for my release."

"Do you pay attention to anything?"

She resented his condescending attitude, but could think of no good defense.

"I didn't get that sense from him at all," her father said. "That man, Brian, didn't want to hurt either of us. He was there to help."

Inna stepped from the kitchen and told them that she'd prepared some food. Her father seemed appreciative, but Alle could not care less. She still held the note.

"What are you going to do now?" she asked.

"Go back where I came from."

"Aren't you the least bit curious about any of this?"

"I came because I thought you were in trouble. I'll leave the saving of a religion to you."

"You really are worthless."

"And you are an insolent little bitch," Inna said to her.

Her spine stiffened.

"Your father came here thinking you in trouble. He did what he did to save you. Risked his life. And that's all you can say?"

"This is none of your business."

"It became my business when I helped get you out of that church."

"I don't know why you did that, nor do I care. I didn't ask for your help. *He* did."

The older woman shook her head. "I only hope my children never grow to resent me like this."

Brian had tried to sway her, that much she now realized. He'd also defended her father, made her feel bad about what she'd done. And all with questionable motives. Now, listening to another stranger defend him, was too much.

Zachariah would have to find another way.

"I'm leaving," she said.

———

TOM APPRECIATED INNA'S DEFENSE. HE SHOULD have said it himself, but could not bring himself to do it. He'd taken Alle's abuse for a long time, believing it his penance for all of the mistakes he'd made with her. Interesting how the world hated him for something he hadn't done—falsify a news story—yet almost no one knew a thing about his real error.

A mistake that was all his.

And so was the punishment.

He'd come to Alle's rescue because he had to. Now he knew the whole thing had been a ruse. A con. One his daughter had participated in, and she harbored no regrets.

He stared at the closed door where Alle had left.

"I'm so sorry," Inna said.

He shook his head. "It's my fault."

"There is a lot between you two."

"More than either of us realizes."

"She's going back to Zachariah Simon," Inna said. "He owns her mind."

"She took what you gave her."

He nodded. "It was meant for her."

Inna threw him a puzzled look.

"I retyped my father's note before I flew over here and removed the important parts. I didn't know what I was going to do here, but I wanted options. Every good reporter has to have options."

She smiled. "I remember that rule. I'm glad you do, too."

"I'm not dead yet."

And he meant it.

"So what are you really going to do?"

"Not what I told her."

CHAPTER FORTY-FOUR

ZACHARIAH WATCHED AS THE AMBASSADOR LEFT THE gardens at Schönbrunn. Dusk had arrived with 8:00 P.M., the sun waning, air cooling.

A most unexpected twist.

He would have Rócha check that trash bin.

But he already knew that she'd spoken the truth.

He cared little for politics. Nothing good, he'd ever seen, had come from that convoluted process. It was nothing but endless talk that led to debilitating compromise, all designed to gather popular support for another election. He wanted results, not votes. Action, not talk. Change, not status quo.

And secrecy had been his ally.

But not anymore.

At least one other thought the same way he did.

The phone vibrated in his pocket.

He found the unit and saw no number displayed. This was Rócha's, so he thought it best to answer.

"*Señor,* it is Mateo in Cuba."

He knew the name.

"It is Zachariah, Mateo. *Buenos tardes.*" He realized it was midafternoon in Cuba. He hadn't heard from his caretaker there in a long while.

"*Señor* Simon, we have problem."

He listened to the report of a black man named

Béne Rowe and a white man named Halliburton, there to view the archives. He was glad that the curator had followed directions. He was to be immediately informed of anyone who inquired about the archives. His grandfather had first found them, and his father had shielded them with a contribution that created a local museum. A way for the Jews of Cuba to establish themselves with something important, and it had worked.

"What do I do?" Mateo asked.

"Let them see what they want. I will call you back shortly."

———

ALLE LEFT THE APARTMENT BUILDING AND WALKED far enough away that she could be assured of being alone. Why couldn't her father have simply turned over whatever her grandfather had left? She hadn't asked for heroics. She hadn't asked for his involvement. This was about righting a wrong that had occurred thousands of years ago. Not repairing an irreparable relationship. Or him trying, for once in his sorry life, to do the right thing.

She was new to her religion, but not to the Jewish way of life. She'd watched her grandparents live that way and wanted to emulate their devotion. If she could also help restore what so many had held sacred for so long, then so much the better.

But she wondered.

Why had her grandfather not wanted the same? Why keep the Temple treasure secret? Why not tell her? Was it because of *those people* Zachariah had warned her about?

All she knew was that she could not deal with her father.

So she found the cell phone in her pocket and dialed the first number stored in its memory.

———

BÉNE DID NOT LIKE ANYTHING ABOUT THE SITUATION. Of course, he could not say a word to Halliburton since his apprehensions would generate questions he did not want to answer. The curator had returned from his phone call all smiles and led them to a windowless room lined with wooden shelves and plastic bins, each packed with journals, ledgers, and parchments. There was a loose order to the system, the containers identified by time and place. Tre had not been impressed with the preservation efforts, but seemed excited about the content.

"There are four bins loaded with 17th-century writings. That's the most I've ever seen in one place."

"Be quick and go through them."

"This could take hours."

"We don't have hours. Scan what you can."

"Something wrong, Béne?"

"Yeah, Tre. This is Cuba. So be quick."

———

TOM SAT IN THE KITCHEN AND CHEWED ON A PIECE of dark bread. Inna had prepared some stewed tomatoes and white rice that smelled great, but he had no appetite.

"I've written books the past few years," he told her. "Ghostwriting. Some fiction, some nonfiction. They've all been bestsellers. A few were number ones."

He was answering her question about what he'd done since the turmoil.

"I'm good at it, and the writers I worked for want me to be completely invisible."

She was nursing a cup of coffee and a plate of her food. "You were always good at what you did."

He liked this practical woman. So he decided to tell her the truth.

"I was set up, Inna. That story about Israeli extremists was planted. I was led to it, fed it, then ratted out. They faked the main sources and most of the information. They were good. I never suspected a thing. Everything was right on. Solid. I never saw it coming."

"Who did it?"

"Some group who does that sort of thing. Seems I pissed off both sides in the Middle East with my reporting. So, unbeknownst to each other, they each took me out."

"No way to prove what happened?"

He shook his head. "Like I said, they were good."

"I always knew there was an explanation. Thomas Sagan was no liar."

He appreciated her loyalty.

"No one stuck by you, Thomas?"

He thought of Robin Stubbs. She had. For a while.

"The evidence was overwhelming and I had no explanation other than *I didn't do it*. It was the perfect setup. Not a loose end to be found. I never knew who did it to me till over a year later."

He told her about that Saturday morning in the Barnes & Noble bookstore, the first time he'd ever spoken of that day to anyone.

"I'm so sorry," she said again.

"So am I."

"Your daughter is a problem."

He chuckled. "What gave you that impression?"

"She has no idea what she's doing, but thinks she knows it all."

"I was a lot like her when I was twenty-five. I was married by then and thought I could do no wrong."

"Why did you let her leave?"

"She'll be back."

He saw the curious look on Inna's face, which dissolved into understanding. "You think Simon sent her?"

"It's the only thing that makes sense. They spoke to each other in the church like old friends. She wanted to go with him, until he sold her out."

And he wondered if that had been part of the act, too.

"When Alle found you in the catacombs, was she running or walking?"

"Walking. Why?"

"She calm?"

Inna nodded.

"We were being shot at. She ran away. But then she just walks right up to you, a stranger, and waits for me?"

He saw she grasped his point.

"So what are you going to do?" she asked.

He reached for another piece of bread. "I have no choice." He then found a folded piece of paper in his pocket and handed it to her. "That's the full message I found in the grave."

She read.

"I did an Internet search. That part where it says, *The golem now protects our secret in a place long sacred to Jews.* And the name. Rabbi Berlinger. They connected with only one place in the world."

"Prague."

He was impressed.

"I know the tale of the golem," she said. "It's quite famous there. I've never heard of Berlinger, though."

"He was head of the congregation for several decades. He could have known Abiram and Saki, my mother's father, Marc Eden Cross. Berlinger is also still alive."

"Strange how you call your father only by his name."

"It's how I think of him. Distant. A stranger. Now all I can see is his decaying face. I misjudged that old man, Inna. We both kept too damn much to ourselves."

The room was quiet. Inna's two children had left, visiting at a neighbor's apartment. She'd already told him that he would spend the night here, on the sofa. Tomorrow they could retrieve his rental car. He was too fatigued to argue. Jet lag had caught up with him.

"This secret," he said in a near whisper. "It's time to expose it."

"If not you, then Simon seems intent on doing it."

"Which is all the more reason to find this Temple treasure first."

He thought of Brian Jamison. "Why would American intelligence be interested in this? He said he worked for something called the Magellan Billet. Can you find out what that is?"

She nodded. "I have contacts in the American embassy."

He was glad he'd called her. "There was a body in the catacombs. But something tells me it's long gone. Still, someone should take a look."

She nodded.

They sat for a few moments. He watched while she ate her tomatoes and rice.

"I'm going to Prague," he said. "And I'll take Alle with me."

"That could lead to big trouble."

"Probably so. But she's my daughter, Inna, and that's what I have to do."

Inna smiled, then reached over and squeezed his hand. "Thomas, you sell yourself short. You are far more of a father than either your daughter or you even realize."

CHAPTER FORTY-FIVE

ZACHARIAH LINGERED IN THE GARDENS AT SCHÖN-brunn, his mind racing. He imagined the tranquil spot as it had been two hundred years ago, when Napoleon's only son lived inside the palace. Or the Emperor Franz Joseph, who struggled here to hold the Austrian Empire together in the face of world war. Or 1918, when Charles I renounced his throne and left the palace for the last time, ending the monarchy.

But he cared nothing for Austrian history. For his people, this country had been nothing but an impediment. It had never cared for Jews, persecuting and slaughtering them throughout history by the tens of thousands. And though Austrians came to hate Hitler, it was not because he hated Jews. Few of the synagogues the Nazis razed had been rebuilt. Only a fraction of Jews who once lived here still remained. His family stayed, and weathered the storms. *Why*, he'd asked as a boy. *Because it is our home.*

The phone vibrated in his hand. This time the number displayed was familiar. His own.

Alle was calling.

He answered, "I hope you have good news."

He listened as she told him what had happened with her father. He asked her to read to him what she'd been shown and realized it was the same thing Sagan had already provided.

Now he was convinced.

"He's keeping the truth to himself. He showed you nothing new."

"Maybe that's all there is?"

"It cannot be. It is too incomplete."

But he realized that Sagan definitely suspected his daughter.

"Alle, your father most likely thinks you are there as a spy. But he is still your father. He won't reject you."

"What should I do?"

He wanted to ask her about Brian Jamison and what was said between them, but thought better. *Leave it alone.* Instead he told her, "Go back. Keep your eyes and ears open. You said it yourself—the Americans are now involved. Brian was an agent. We cannot allow them to find what we seek. This is for *us,* Alle."

He hoped the silence on the other end of the line meant she agreed with him.

"I'll try," she finally said. "Do you want to know where he is?"

"There's no need." He had something better than an address. "If you have the phone on, I can track it. But save its battery. Can you do that?"

"Of course."

"Then go back. And may good fortune be with you."

———

BÉNE STEPPED BACK INTO THE ROOM WHERE HALliburton was still shuffling through plastic bins, scanning parchments, examining brittle old ledgers, diaries, maps, and drawings.

"This stuff needs to be vacuum-sealed," Halliburton said. "It's falling apart."

Béne checked the door, having kept it open enough so he could hear if anything was happening back toward the front of the building. He'd been watching from the end of a short hall as the curator stepped outside and made a cell phone call. He could not approach any closer without being seen, so he'd heard nothing of what was said. But he had noticed the man return and lock the door. He'd checked his watch, which read a little after 2:00 P.M. Nowhere near closing time—so why lock the door? He wondered if his paranoia was justified, but ever since he'd learned who controlled this museum he'd harbored a bad feeling.

"Look at this."

Tre was holding an old volume, the binding decaying, its dried pages the color of dirt.

"This was bound in 1634. It's an account of life here on the island." Tre gently opened the book. "It's in Castilian, but I can read it."

He heard a chime from the front and crept back through the doorway and down the short hall. The curator was answering his cell phone and told the caller in Spanish to hold on.

The man stepped outside and closed the door.

Béne decided to risk it this time and made his way to a window, pressing his ear close.

————

ZACHARIAH SPOKE TO THE CURATOR OF THE CUBAN museum. He'd dealt with Brian Jamison, Tom Sagan, and Alle Becket. Now he was ready to deal with Béne Rowe.

"Are they still there?" he asked.

"They are looking in the private collection. Most interested in the oldest we have, from Columbus' time. But other materials are locked away, as you ordered. I have not mentioned those."

How the Jamaican had managed to find the archive he did not know, but the fact that he had done so only compounded his problem. Rowe had said on the phone that he was privy to some new information. Was this what he'd been speaking about? If so, the documents were of no value since the Simon family had long controlled them, the originals thought safe behind Cuban travel restrictions and overzealous socialists.

Time to end this problem.

"I want you to keep them there for a little longer. Be cordial. Friendly. Do nothing to upset them. Understand?"

"*Sí, señor* Simon. I can do that."

He ended the call and made his way back to the car, where Rócha waited. He slid into the passenger's seat and handed over the phone. "Rowe is at the archive in Cuba. The curator has called. Do you still have contacts with the Policía Nacional Revolucionaria?"

The PNR was Cuba's national police force.

Rócha nodded. "I've kept the payments current. They've always said, if there's anything we need, just ask."

"Ask. Then use GPS and track my phone. I want to know exactly where Alle Becket is in this city. I am not going to trust all that is at stake to the whim of some naïve girl."

BÉNE HEARD THE NAME.

Simon.

A chill gripped his spine.

This man wasn't calling for any approval from Havana. He was calling for marching orders. He employed hundreds just like this minion. Eyes and ears across Jamaica who made sure he was informed, money the fuel that kept that information highway flowing.

He fled the window and made his way back to the storage room.

"We need to leave," he said to Halliburton.

"I've barely scratched the surface. I need more time."

"We have to go, Tre."

"What's going on?"

"That curator is selling us out."

Tre's eyes widened. "How do you know that?"

"Like you said on the plane, I'm experienced in these kinds of things. We need to go."

"A few more minutes, Béne. For God's sake, there's real stuff here. I just found some references to Luis de Torres himself."

He caught the urgency and realized the importance. And he also recalled something else the curator had said. *But other materials are locked away, as you ordered.*

They'd come this far. A few more minutes may not hurt.

Then again, they could become a real problem.

———

TOM SAT ALONE IN THE DEN. INNA WAS IN HER BEDroom, making telephone calls, gathering information, doing what reporters did. Of course, not everything found was true or relevant—the tough job was sifting through the fat to find the meat. It had been a long time since he'd assembled a news story, but he hadn't forgotten how. The one that currently engulfed him was not atypical, and its layers were becoming clearer. The Levite. A key. A man named Berlinger. The golem. Temple treasure. Old Abiram.

And, most troubling of all, Alle.

How they all fit together remained to be seen.

He heard a door open and Inna appeared from down the hall. Her children seemed like good kids who loved and respected their mother. He envied and admired her.

"What happened to your husband?" he asked. "As I recall, your marriage was a good one."

"That's what I thought, too. But he had other ideas. He came home one day and said he was leaving. That was five years ago. We've barely seen him since."

"He doesn't visit the children?"

"They're not important to him."

Big mistake, he thought.

"How are they doing?" he asked.

"They seem not to care, but I know better. Children need their parents."

That they do.

"I found out," she said, "that the Magellan Billet is a covert division of the U.S. Justice Department. Twelve agents who work special assignments from the attorney general or the White House. It's headed by a woman named Stephanie Nelle. I was also able to find out that one of the twelve agents is a man named Brian Jamison."

"I need to know why they are interested in Zachariah Simon."

"I'm trying, but that may be difficult to learn. After all, Thomas, these people will not be admitting to anything."

"They might if they know their agent is dead."

"That's another problem. Nothing unusual was reported around the cathedral. No police activity. Certainly no body found."

He wasn't surprised. Just like eight years ago, he was on his own.

"I'm going to find that Temple treasure."

"Why do you feel the need? It's not your fight."

"It became mine when I read that note from the grave."

"You haven't been in a fight in a long time, have you?"

"No," he said, his voice in a whisper. "I haven't."

"And you want one."

He stared into her eyes, which seemed to grasp his pain. "I need one."

"It won't bring you redemption. What happened to you won't be undone."

Maybe not, but—

A knock came.

He knew who had returned.

Inna opened the door and invited Alle inside.

"Look," his daughter said to him. "I'm sorry for my attitude. I've had a tough few days. I know you have, too. This is important to me. It was important to Grandfather. I did what I thought was best. I understand why you're angry, I get it, but I want to be a part of this."

She was lying. But God help him, he was glad she'd returned.

She was all he had left in the world.

"I'm going to Prague tomorrow," he told her. "You can come with me."

She slowly nodded. "I can do that."

"Are you hungry?" Inna asked her.

"Some food would be good."

The two women retreated into the kitchen.

He sat alone.

What an incredible mess. He should leave her here. But he'd come this far and made sure she was okay. Better to keep her within his sights for as long as she chose to stay.

And forgive her for lying.

Like Inna said.

That's what fathers did.

CHAPTER FORTY-SIX

BÉNE READ HIS WATCH. NEARLY HALF AN HOUR HAD passed. He'd checked on the curator twice, the Cuban perched behind a desk, reading a book. Halliburton had gone through all four bins labeled 16TH and 17TH CENTURY, setting aside several items that appeared promising, now studying those in more detail. He'd noticed two other doors in the hallway—both locked—and wondered what they protected.

"Have you found anything?" he asked Tre.

"These are deed grants and colonial reports back to Spain. A couple of diaries, too. All of it is in bad shape. It can hardly be read."

He decided a dose of truth was in order. "Tre, you said this archive is controlled by Zachariah Simon. I know him. He's *bad bwai. Pyaka.*" He knew his friend spoke enough patois to understand. Bad man. Criminal. "We need to go."

Liars seemed to be everywhere. Felipe. Simon. The curator. He'd solved the first problem. The second remained to be seen. But the third he could handle right now. He reached beneath his jacket and found his gun.

Tre was surprised at its appearance. "What do we need that for?"

"I hope we don't. Stay here."

He retreated to the front of the house. The display room was quiet, the man still reading his book. He slipped the hand holding the gun into his pant pocket and casually walked over.

"Could you help us?" he asked in Spanish.

The curator smiled and rose from his chair. Béne allowed him to pass, then withdrew the gun and jammed its short barrel into the nape of the man's neck. He then wrapped his arm around the throat and squeezed tight.

"You're a liar," he said in Spanish. "You called Simon, not Havana. I heard you. What did he tell you?"

The man said nothing, only shook his head.

Tremors racked the man's body.

Béne increased the pressure of his forearm.

"I'll shoot you. Right now, right here. What did he tell you?" His thumb cocked the gun's hammer.

His captive clearly heard the click.

"He told me only to keep you here. Keep you here. Let you see what you want. Keep you here."

"You said the important things were locked away. Where?"

He heard the growl of engines outside.

With his grip and the gun remaining firmly in place, he dragged the man toward the windows. Two white Peugeots topped with blue lights, each marked PA-TRULLA, skidded to a stop down the street.

Three PNR officers emerged.

Keep you here.

Now he knew why.

They might escape out the back, but the chances of making it to the Range Rover and leaving, without attracting the police's attention, seemed slim. No. These three had to leave on their own.

"Listen to me, *señor*," he said to the curator. To make his point he pressed the gun tighter into the neck. "I will be right over there, just down that hall. I want you to send these police away. Tell them we left. We headed west, out of town, in a Mercedes coupe. Yellow-colored. You hear that?"

The man nodded.

"If you so much as twitch, I will shoot you dead, then them. If you say one word that hints at trouble, I will shoot you dead. *Comprende?*"

Another nod.

"And know this. If you do what I tell you, not only will you still be breathing with no holes in your body, but I'll double that $500 you took."

"*Sí. Sí.*"

He released his hold and backed away from the window, but not before catching a last glance as the three uniformed officers drew close to the front door. He shrank into the corridor and carefully peered around the edge.

The curator seemed to be grabbing hold of himself. Béne hoped the promise of more money would keep the lying bastard from doing anything stupid. He meant what he'd said. He'd kill them all, but preferred not to. To make his point, when the Cuban tossed a nervous glance his way he displayed the gun, aimed straight at him.

The locked front door's knob jiggled.

Then, a knock.

The curator answered, and the three officers entered. Each was armed with holstered guns. Interesting, since Béne could recall seeing many of the state police before, but none with weapons. He wondered how much the Simon was paying for this special service.

He kept his own weapon ready.

Behind him he caught movement and saw Tre appear

in the doorway. He quickly gestured with his hand for him to stay there and be quiet.

Halliburton nodded and disappeared back into the room.

He listened as the officers asked about two men, one black, the other white, from Jamaica, come to see the museum. The curator said they had been here, but they left suddenly. He tried to stop them, but they would not listen. They drove out of town, headed west in a yellow Mercedes, maybe ten minutes ago.

He liked that last part. Nice touch. That meant they were catchable.

The policemen, though, seemed not in a hurry to leave.

One sauntered around the displays.

Béne wasn't sure if the interest was genuine or feigned. Did he sense a lie? The other two remained near the front door. The curator stood silent, watching all three. The one officer approached dangerously close to the hallway. Béne shrank back, the gun pointed skyward, its barrel just below his nose, finger tight on the trigger. He could not risk a look. He held his breath, closed his eyes, and focused on the footfalls from the plank floor as the officer strolled the room.

"What is back down that way?" he heard one of them ask.

"Storage rooms. Nothing there. We get few visitors this time of year."

A few moments of silence passed.

More footfalls, toward him.

Then, away.

He exhaled and glanced around the corner's edge. All three policemen were at the front door. The curator was thanking them for coming, his voice calm.

They left.

He came back into view and hustled to the door, locking it. He stared out a window and saw the officers trotting to their cars. He heard engines rev and watched as they sped away. In an instant he pounced on the curator, slamming the man to the floor, stuffing the gun into an astonished face. Wide eyes stared back, the body beneath him frozen with fear.

"How long has the Simon owned this place?"

No answer.

"How long?" His voice was a shout.

"The family has paid for a long time. *Señor* Simon has been especially generous with us."

"Did he tell you to call the police?"

The man shook his head, though the gun stayed close. "No. No. No. He tell me only to keep you here."

Tre appeared from the hall. "Béne, my God, what are you doing—"

"Stay out of this." He kept his enraged eyes focused on the Cuban and cocked the gun.

"Béne," Tre yelled. "Are you nuts? Don't do this."

"This *mus mus* almost got us killed." He hated rats as bad as liars.

His gaze told the Cuban that his time was up. "You said to the Simon the important things were locked away. Where?"

"First door down the hall."

He wrenched the man to his feet and shoved him forward until they reached the door. "Open it."

The curator fumbled with keys in his pocket, hands shaking. He noticed that the wooden door opened inward and he needed a release, so he pounded his right foot into the door. Two more kicks and the jamb shattered, the hasp screws freeing themselves, the wooden slab banging open, revealing another windowless room.

Three plastic bins sat on a table.

"Check them out," he said to Halliburton. "Get what you want from here and back in the other room. We're leaving."

"We're stealing them?"

"No, Tre. I'll give them a credit card for collateral. Of course we're stealing them. Now get what you want."

Halliburton hustled into the room.

He dragged the curator back to the front.

"You're lucky," he said, "that you're a good liar since, one, those police believed you and, two, me shooting you would draw far too much attention."

"And three, *señor*."

Had he heard right? This fool was challenging him?

"You do not want to kill me in front of your *amigo*."

He resented the smug way the astute observation was delivered.

"Actually, my third reason would have been different. I want you to tell the Simon that he and I are going to have a serious conversation. Soon."

Then he swiped the butt of the gun across the man's head, sending him into unconsciousness.

CHAPTER FORTY-SEVEN

"1580 WAS THE YEAR. YES. THAT WAS IT, EXACTLY," SAKI said.

Tom listened. For a ten-year-old, there was nothing better than a good story and he loved the ones his grandfather told.

"It happened in Prague," the old man said. "Rabbi Loew was chief rabbi of the Jewish quarter. That meant he was in charge. Above his door, engraved in stone, was a lion with a grape to indicate his direct descent from King David himself."

"M. E.," his grandmother called out. "Don't fill the boy's head with tales."

Saki's name was Marc Eden Cross. Tom's great-grandmother's maiden name had been Eden, the label added to her only son's out of respect.

"Tommy here loves my stories," his grandfather said. "Don't you, boy?"

He nodded.

"He likes me to tell him about the world."

The old man was approaching eighty and Tom wondered how much longer he'd be around. Lately the concept of death had become all too real with the passing of two aunts.

"It all happened in Prague," Saki said again. "Another fanatical priest had decided that we Jews were *a threat. Christians feared us since kings relied on us. So, to increase their power, they had to destroy us. They used to say we killed Christian children and used their blood as part of our worship. Can you imagine such lies? Blood libel is what we call that now. But the lie worked. Every few years Christians would form mobs and slaughter Jews. Pogroms, that's what they're called, Tommy. Never forget that word. Pogroms. The Nazis instituted the greatest one of all."*

He told himself to never forget the word.

"Rabbi Loew knew he had to protect his people from danger and he found out how to do that in a dream. Ata bra golem dewuk hachomer w'tigzar zedim chewel torfe jisrael."

He knew some Hebrew and caught a few of the words.

"'You shall create a golem from clay, that the malicious anti-Semitic mob be destroyed.' That's what he dreamed. And that's what he did. He created a living body from clay using fire, water, air, and earth. The first three made the last one come alive."

Could that be true? How incredible.

"He made his creature real by inserting the shem. A small bit of parchment, upon which he'd written God's name, into the mouth. Then he said, 'Lord made a man from the clay of the Earth and breathed the breath of life into his mouth.' The golem rose to his feet. Rabbi Loew told the golem that his mission was to protect the Jews from persecution. His name would be Josef and he must obey the rabbi's commands no matter what may be asked."

Tom listened as his grandfather explained how Rabbi Loew would give the golem a plan every Friday and Josef would follow it for the next week, protecting the Jews. One Friday he forgot to provide direction *and the golem, with nothing to do, went on a rampage, wanting to demolish anything and everything. People were terrified until Rabbi Loew ordered him to stop. From that day on, he never forgot to provide weekly instruction. By 1593 threats to the Jews had lessened. Rabbi Loew decided it was time to send Josef from this world.*

"He told the golem to spend the night in the attic of the Old-New Synagogue in Prague. After midnight, the rabbi and two others climbed up and proceeded to do backward everything that had been done to create the creature. If they were at his feet then, they were at his head now. All the words were recited in reverse. When done, the golem was again a mass of clay, which was left there. From that day on it was forbidden for anyone to go into the loft of the Old-New Synagogue."

Tom sat on the sofa in Inna's apartment and thought about Saki. He'd loved that gentle soul. When he'd read Abiram's note and caught the reference to the golem, he'd immediately recalled that day long ago when he'd first heard the story.

And that's all it was.

A story.

As an adult, he'd written a puff piece for the LA *Times* about Prague and the legend. Golems were not a Czech concoction. They were first mentioned in ancient Egypt. Kabbalist texts spoke of them. The Bible even used the word. They were never associated with Prague until the 19th century. And nothing in any historical record connected the great Rabbi Judah Loew ben Bezalel, who lived in the 16th century, known as Rabbi Loew, with any golem. The story was first told in an obscure travel guide, reprinted in a popular book from 1858 on Jewish legends called *Sippurim*.

After that, the golem became a part of Czech lore. Novels and more books followed that incorporated the story, each incarnation making the tale even more fantastic.

"*This book is one of my favorites,*" Saki said to him. "*It's a novel published in 1915. I was a boy when I was given this copy. I've kept it ever since.*"

He stared at the thin volume, printed in another language.

"*Czech,*" Saki told him. "*It's called* The Golem *and was written by a man named Gustav Meyrink. A huge bestseller for its time. It's about magical Prague. Mystical things.*"

"*You can read this?*"

"*My mother was from there. She taught me Czech as a child.*"

While writing the piece he'd made a point to learn more about Meyrink's novel, which stoked the legend and eventually caused people from all over the world to visit Prague. The Iron Curtain halted those pilgrimages for decades, but the Velvet Revolution again allowed them. His story for the *Times* reported on how hundreds of thousands of Jews came each year in search.

The golem helps protect our secret in a place long sacred to Jews.

That's what Abiram had written. His grandfather, Abiram's father-in-law, had apparently used a fiction to shield a fact.

He held the key from the grave, with its strange markings.

What did it open?

Alle was asleep in one of the bedrooms. Inna's children had doubled up in the other. He and his daughter spoke little after Alle returned. She'd stayed quiet, calm, her customary anger suppressed. Which made him even more suspicious. Right now he was at least two steps ahead of Zachariah Simon, and he planned to stay that way.

At least until he solved this mystery.

And he'd decided to do just that.

All this talk of Levites, Temple treasures, and great secrets held for centuries. If there was something to find, then he was damn well going to find it. True, he would not be honoring what Abiram had wanted, but so what? He was in charge now. A man died earlier. He wondered how many more had died before him. He once reported problems, exposed wrongdoing. Informed people of what they needed to know. Keeping secrets was contrary to that mission. Surely Abiram knew that when he chose to pass down the duty.

He walked over and sat before Inna's computer. The apartment was wired with high-speed Internet— essential, he knew, for anyone in the newspaper business. When he'd first started in the business cyberspace had barely existed. Now it was indispensible. Certainly, writing novels had been made much easier with billions of websites available to surf. He'd never had to leave his house. He typed OLD-NEW SYNA-GOGUE into Google and selected from the 2,610,000 offerings, skimming the high points of a few.

The oldest building in Prague's Jewish quarter. The oldest extant synagogue in Europe. 700 years it had stood, virtually undisturbed. War had passed it by, and even Hitler had not razed it. When it was first built, there was already an Old Synagogue. So this one was labeled New. Then, in the 16th century, another was built and called the New Synagogue. Since the Old one still existed, someone came up with Old-New, and the name stuck. Both of the other buildings were razed in the early 20th century. But the Old-New Synagogue survived.

He found an exterior picture.

A simple oblong with a saddle roof and Gothic gables, facing east. Buttresses supported exterior walls
punctuated by narrow, pointed windows. Low an-
nexes surrounded its lower parts on three sides. It had
been completed in 1270, but renovations had occurred as recently as 2004.

He clicked around and found photos from other
angles, one showing the building's east side. The
loft seemed spacious, the roofline set at a high pitch.
Nineteen U-shaped iron bars extended from the east
side of the building, forming a path up to a loft
door. A caption informed him that the fire ladder
had been installed in 1880 to allow access to the
roof in an emergency, but the first rung was a good
fifteen feet off ground level. Another shot, a close-
up of the loft door at the top of the iron rungs,
showed a Star of David adorning its exterior. He
noticed the lock and the keyhole. Arched at the top,
flat at the bottom. The key from the grave sat on the
tabletop beside the computer.

He lifted it.

Could it fit? Possible.

Though jet-lagged, he was no longer tired. Sleep
was not coming tonight. He noted the time. 9:40 P.M.
He stood and walked to the door of the bedroom
where Alle had retreated and knocked. His daughter
apparently wasn't tired, either, as the door opened
quickly.

The lights were still on, and she was fully dressed.

"We're leaving," he said. "For Prague."

CHAPTER FORTY-EIGHT

BÉNE HEAVED A SIGH OF RELIEF AS THE PLANE ROSE from Santiago de Cuba's international airport. He'd been worried that when the curator awoke he'd alert the police, especially since he'd not left the other $500. He'd never mentioned that they'd flown in, but the airport still could have been staked out. No officers, though, had been anywhere in sight when they made it back, and they'd left unimpeded.

Tre had crammed two plastic bins with documents, some from both rooms, which they'd brought with them. The only repercussions from the theft would involve the Simon, and he wanted that to happen.

He owed him.

"Béne," Tre said. "Are you going to tell me what happened back there? You looked like you were going to kill that guy."

He needed his friend's help so he decided to say, "Simon and I have been working together on finding the mine."

"Which you've never mentioned."

"Why would I?" And he saw that his friend realized there was a line that need not be crossed. But he added, "Let's just say that I've come to learn he's not somebody you want to work with."

"Those police were there for us?"

He nodded. "Simon sent them. The curator called him. He didn't want us to leave Cuba alive."

The reality of the situation—the proximity of death—seemed to hit Halliburton. There'd been no time to explain while on the ground. They'd grabbed what they could and sped back to the airport, all the while keeping an eye on the rearview mirrors.

"Why would Simon kill us?"

"He wants the mine. He doesn't want me to know what he knows."

Tre had been thumbing through one volume ever since they were aboard. He'd seemed anxious to examine it.

"What is that?" he asked.

"Some sort of diary. A narrative."

Tre showed him the pages. The script was block style in thick black ink, justified on the right and left. Maybe twelve to fifteen lines per page.

"It's in great shape, considering how it's been stored," Tre said. "And it's written in Castilian."

"Is that important?"

"It could be."

All he wanted to know was, "Did we get what we came for?"

But Tre was reading.

He decided to leave him alone. The plane was still climbing, heading south toward Montego Bay, away from Cuba. The Simon's reach was far greater than he'd imagined, and his interest in the lost mine more intense than represented.

"Béne," Tre said. "Listen to this."

We find meaning of our mission in the sacred word. Numbers makes clear that "and with you bring your brother also, the tribe of Levi, the tribe of your father, that they may join you and minister to you while you and your sons with you are before the tent of the testimony. They shall keep guard over you and over the whole tent. They shall join you and keep guard over the tent of meeting for all the service of the tent, and no outsider shall come near you. And you shall keep guard over the sanctuary and over the altar, that there may never again be wrath on the people of Israel. And behold, I have taken your brothers the Levites from among the people of Israel. They are a gift to you, given to the Lord, to do the service of the tent of meeting." The Book of Jeremiah says even more. "As the host of heaven cannot be numbered, neither the sand of the sea measured. So will I multiply the seed of David My servant, and the Levites that minister unto Me."

Tre looked up from the page. "This came out of the locked room. It was written by a man named Yosef Ben Ha Levy Haivri—Joseph, the son of Levi the Hebrew. He says that in the beginning. He also says that his Christian name was Luis de Torres, one he was forced to take, but one he now rejects."

"Why is it significant?"

"There's more."

Though we are not born of the house of Levi, God has heard our pleas and chosen us. God is gracious and beneficent. God is compassionate. God protects the simple. I was born low and He saved me. My soul is at rest for God has been good to me. He delivered me from death, my eyes from tears, my feet from stumbling. I trust in God. Out of great suffering I spoke and said rashly, "All men are false." How can I repay God for all of His bounties to me? I will pay my vows in the presence of His people, in the midst of Jerusalem. I shall do my duty, as entrusted in me. Malachi said of the Levite, "The law of truth was in his mouth, and unrighteousness was not found in his lips." He walked with Me in peace and uprightness, and did turn many away from iniquity. O, Israel, trust in God. He is the help and shield. To those who shall assume this great duty, you shall be the Levite, as true as one born, for your task comes from God. To the Levite, trust in God. He is your help and shield.

Tre leaned across and showed him the pages, but Béne had already caught the one line that carried significance.

To those who shall assume this great duty, you shall be the Levite.

"De Torres wrote this for those who came after him. Instructions on what to do and why. Columbus told him, now he's telling his successor."

The great Admiral of the Ocean, the man falsely called Cristóbal Colón but who was born Christoval Arnoldo de Ysassi, never forgot from where he came. He was a most wise man who accepted his duty. He led his men on a great voyage and with God's help he succeeded where all believed he would fail. He told me before we sailed that we must accomplish our mission. I failed to realize then the importance of what he meant, but I do now. The whore Church and its Inquisition have decided to slaughter all who do not worship according to its dictates. They speak of God, but know nothing of His ways. They urge love and forgiveness, yet extend only pain and misery. Many have suffered much at their hands. Some were forced to renounce their faith, others fled. Still others were murdered on behalf of a false belief. May God forgive me, I was forced to convert, but I never succumbed in my heart. Now, here, in this new land, away from all that is evil about the ways of man I live in peace. The time for me is coming which will be neither day nor night. God will announce it for the day is His and also the night. He has appointed a watchman over his people all day and night. The Admiral has made me swear that a Levite who comes after our time shall one day enlighten us when the darkness turns to light. He chose me as the first and I shall select the next. Together we will accomplish our duty. God's great treasure is hidden away, now safe from all those who do it harm. Blessed is He who keeps his promise to Israel. For the Holy One, Blessed be He, calculated the end to do as He had promised Abraham our forefather. As it is said, "And He said to Abraham, 'Know well that your offspring shall be strangers in a land not theirs, and they shall be enslaved and oppressed, but I will execute judgment on the nation they shall serve and in the end they shall go free with great wealth.'" It is this promise that will stand. It is this promise that we shall keep. For not just a single person has arisen to destroy us, but in every generation people will arise against us to destroy us. And the Holy One, blessed be He, saves us from their hands.

Béne recalled what the Simon had told him about Columbus. That the Admiral converted to Christianity on threat of force, but remained a Jew at heart. He even knew his real name.

Christoval Arnoldo de Ysassi.

Of course he'd known that.

These documents were under his control.

"There's a lot more here, Béne. I'll need time to go through it."

"Start reading," he said. "I want to know every detail."

CHAPTER FORTY-NINE

TOM AND ALLE HUSTLED PAST THE GREAT ASTRO-nomical clock that adorned Prague's old town hall. Its gilded hands and orbs displayed the time, date, zodiac, and positions of the sun, moon, and planets in a confusing array. Best he could tell it was around 4:00 A.M., Friday, March 8.

Another day had passed with him still alive.

The first half of the drive from Vienna north had been two-laned through dense Czech forest and a string of quiet villages, then autobahn the remainder, traffic light even for the middle of the night. The historic old town square was deserted. He recalled from previous visits how its cobbles usually burst at the seams with people. The statue of Jan Haus remained prominent, the great religious reformer having been burned at the stake five hundred years ago. The Tyn Church still dominated one side, its spired twin towers lit to the night. Crisp air carried the last bit of winter's bite, and he was glad he'd brought a jacket.

A colorful array of buildings encircled the cobblestones, their windows dark, doors shut. The architecture and façades varied—Renaissance, Baroque, Rococo, Art Nouveau. He knew how Prague had escaped destruction during World War II, the country's leader summoned to Berlin by Hitler and told that either a document be signed requesting Germany to take the Czech people under the protection of the Reich or bombers would reduce the country's cities to ashes. President Emil Hacha, elderly and ill, had fainted at the threat. Once revived, he signed and, without resistance, Prague was occupied.

But the country paid a horrible price, especially its Jews.

Ninety percent died.

Stalin assumed control of the country after the war, and the city languished for decades behind the Iron Curtain.

But the old city survived.

Alle had said little on the four-hour ride. Neither had he. They both seemed satisfied just to be there, neither willing, as yet, to yield an inch. Before leaving Vienna he'd printed out a map of Prague's old town, including the nearby Jewish quarter, noting its major landmarks.

Legend proclaimed that Jews first came here after the destruction of their Second Temple in the 1st century. History records the 10th century as the start of their occupation. Jews called Prague *ir va'em b'Yisrael*. City and mother of Israel. As close to Jerusalem as one could get. Another myth proclaimed that angels brought stones for the synagogue from the destroyed Temple, on loan until another Temple rose from the mount. By the 13th century Jews had established their own town and were forbidden to live anywhere else, their movements restricted, their trades hampered. Eventually, they moved from one side of the Vltava River to the other, into an enclave bordering the old town, which was annexed into the city in 1851, renamed Josefov, becoming Prague's fifth quarter. Not much space. Only 100,000 square yards. A maze of streets, houses, yards, and passageways where, at its height, nearly 2,000 people lived.

And it flourished.

Establishing its own schools, forming a government, creating a culture. Forging an identity.

Which began to erode in 1848, when Jews were granted the same rights as all other Czech citizens, including the ability to live wherever they wanted.

The rich quickly vacated and the poor moved in, transforming the quarter into a ghetto. By the end of the 19th century a social, sanitary, and hygienic collapse led to a call for urban redevelopment. In the 1920s Art Nouveau façades and multistoried blocks of flats replaced the low-slung buildings—shops filling the ground floors, apartments the top. The low rampart wall with gates was razed, the streets now freely connecting with the rest of the city. Where the synagogues once towered over everything, now they were lost among high rooflines. Tom recalled the story he'd written, how sad the place had been to walk through. Only the six synagogues and town hall remained, all now more tourist attractions than places of worship.

And the cemetery.

That's what he remembered most.

Perhaps the saddest place he'd ever visited.

In Inna's apartment Alle had talked of her new religion and a duty she felt toward it. He wondered if she had any idea how Jews had suffered. Here, in Prague, twice through history they were expelled. Pogroms—that word Saki had burned into his memory—came more frequently. In the story he'd written he'd included what happened during Easter 1389, when Jewish youths supposedly tossed rocks at a priest carrying the Eucharist to a dying man. Christians were incensed, their hatred fueled by zealous clerics. Three thousand Jewish men, women, and children were slaughtered. Others committed suicide simply to avoid the atrocities. The quarter was plundered and burned. Even the synagogue was not immune, as marauders invaded and butchered people hiding inside their holiest place. For centuries after, their blood was left on the walls as a reminder.

Inside the Old-New Synagogue.

Whose exterior he now stared at.

Its austerity seemed intentional, allowing worshipers to concentrate on God without distraction. Its western and eastern façades faced differing streets, the eastern backing to a newer, tree-lined boulevard filled with trendy shops. The synagogue rested six feet below the newer boulevard, where street level had existed 700 years ago. Lights illuminated its walls, casting the rough stone in an eerie gray hue. They'd approached from the east, away from its main doors, where access to the attic loft could be seen. He counted the eighteen iron rungs leading up to the arched door with the Star of David. His right hand felt the key in his pocket. He still hadn't mentioned it to Alle.

"I have to climb up there," he said.

"There's no cover. If anyone drives by on this street, they'll see you."

He realized that. "I still have to do it."

"Why? What's up there?"

"You're not so up-to-speed on your new religion, are you? This is hallowed ground. The oldest synagogue still standing in Europe. Jews have been praying here for centuries."

"But what's up in the attic?"

"I don't know. I have to go see."

They'd walked from old town square to here seeing no one. But at 4:00 in the morning that was no surprise. No cars had passed, either, the chilly air devoid of sound, strange for a city of over a million people. Like in the photograph he'd studied earlier online, the first iron rung projected from the wall fifteen feet off the ground. One of the buttresses that supported the exterior wall rose adjacent to the rungs. An addition to the synagogue's lower level jutted out, topped with a tiled roof.

He walked down the sidewalk, six feet higher than the base of the synagogue, and used an iron railing that lined its edge to hoist himself onto the addition's roof. The clay tiles were slippery with moisture and he was careful as he worked his way close to the buttress. He wrapped his right arm around one side of the projecting wall and swung his body out, his left arm reaching for an iron rung, which loomed about eight inches beyond his grasp.

He realized what had to be done.

He steeled himself, grabbed a breath, and hoped for the best. A fifteen-foot fall to cold stone would leave a mark. He swung back around and released his grip, pivoting with his legs and leaping toward the rung. One hand locked onto the damp iron, then the other, his body swinging toward the synagogue wall, his feet breaking the impact.

He held tight.

He reached for the next hold and pulled himself up. One more and his feet found the bottom rung.

He turned back.

Alle watched him from the sidewalk, having retreated into the shadows beyond the wash of the nearest streetlamp.

He climbed.

One rung at a time.

Each was narrow in width, about sixteen inches, so he had to press his feet together and be careful on the slick metal. He told himself to keep a death grip on the rung above him. He stared up as he negotiated the makeshift ladder, trying to imagine who might have been the last person to make the climb.

He glanced back and saw nothing. Good. He was totally exposed. Hopefully, the key in his pocket would open the door at the top and he'd be inside, out of sight, before anyone appeared.

"The golem helps protect our secret in a place long sacred to Jews."

If that was true, then the creature was last seen in the loft above him. He realized it was all legend, but his grandfather had clearly used the story to conceal something important.

He found the top rung.

He was dangling forty feet in the air. A fall from here would kill him. He held on with his left hand, feet firmly planted, and found the key with his right. The lock definitely appeared to be the type that would accept a skeleton key.

He inserted the notched end.

But nothing turned.

He twisted harder. Left and right.

Still locked.

He readjusted the key inside the hole.

No success.

"You. Up there."

A male voice from below.

He glanced down.

Two young men stood on the cobbles at the bottom of the ladder.

Both toted guns in shoulder holsters.

ALLE SAW TWO MEN APPROACHING ON A NARROW COB-bled passage that separated the freestanding synagogue from a block of buildings. The alley connected the commercial avenue she was standing on with another street that ran deeper into the Jewish quarter. She'd been watching her father climb the iron rungs, her gaze darting occasionally to the passageway, vigilant to any passersby. Movement had caught her attention as two shadows appeared at the far end and hustled her way.

She retreated into a dark doorway for a closed shop and watched as her father reached into his pocket and found what looked like a key. He inserted it into the lock of the door to the loft and tried in vain to open it. The two shadows transformed into young men who stood at the base of the ladder, staring up. They did not appear to be police, each dressed in jeans and a dark jacket. Both armed. One of them yelled, "You. Up there."

Her father's head turned.

"Get down," the young man ordered. "Before you hurt yourself."

Her father did not move. But there was nowhere for him to go. The synagogue's roof was a steep gable impossible to negotiate and, apparently, the loft door was not to be opened.

The only thing to do was climb down.

Which her father did.

He made it to the bottom rung.

The two men stood below him.

"Stretch from the last one and drop. We'll get you."

He did as they instructed, falling to the pavement, their grasp breaking his fall. Then one of the men kicked her father's feet out from under him. The other shoved him to the pavement, wrestling one arm behind his back, a knee pressed tight to his spine.

"Stay still" came the order.

She needed to leave. Their attention was not on her. She could slip away and use the storefronts and recessed doorways for cover. The car was parked on the far side of the square, and her father carried the keys. But anywhere was better than here.

She crept backward, keeping her gaze locked on the men thirty feet away and six feet below her. The angle of the buildings would soon block her from their view.

She bumped into something.

Startled, she jolted back and whirled.

Another young man stood three feet away.

He, too, with a gun in a holster.

CHAPTER FIFTY

ZACHARIAH STOOD THIRTY METERS AWAY FROM where Tom Sagan and Alle Becket were being accosted by three men. He knew exactly who they were. Not the police, but a private patrol the local Jewish council employed to keep watch. And he knew why. Bigotry had not vanished.

Only about 1,500 Jews still practiced in Prague, sad for a place that had once been an epicenter for European Jewry. Kings and emperors had inflicted their damage, slowly and steadily, but the Nazis finished them off. Nearly 100,000 were exterminated. All that remained of a once thriving religious community was practically gone. He knew some of the local leaders and the challenges they faced. Almost weekly something was defaced. Though a stone wall enclosed the old cemetery, that had not prevented vandals from tossing dead animals over the top. Graffiti appeared regularly. The police did little to either stop or prosecute offenders. So the community had taken the task upon themselves. One of his foundations, geared to the preservation of Hebrew monuments worldwide, had contributed money to fund both cameras and people.

Rócha had tracked the phone he'd provided Alle to a Viennese residential neighborhood. He'd stationed a man there who reported that she and her father had abruptly left the residence and made their way to a car park not far from St. Stephen's Cathedral. He'd stayed the night in town and was able to quickly find the same highway north that Sagan and his daughter had taken, their man following and telephoning in reports. Eventually, they were able to catch up and ended here, in Prague at the Old-New Synagogue. He knew that the building was under video surveillance, the cameras concealed, monitored twenty-four hours a day. So it had not taken long for the citizen patrol to appear.

He and Rócha stood concealed at the entrance to one of the upscale boutiques lining Parizska Street. This one sold expensive porcelain. The whole place was an insult to his heritage. Once this boulevard had lain inside the quarter, the buildings lining both sides homes to Jews for centuries, all demolished at the beginning of the 20th century. Now it was Prague's most elegant way, home to Cartier, Prada, Louis Vuitton, and every other designer brand. More like Paris than Bohemia. Richly decorated shop windows lined the sidewalks on both sides of the boulevard. Balconies, gables, towers, and turrets rose overhead. The east façade of the Old-New Synagogue backed to Parizska, totally exposed. Tom Sagan had taken a foolish risk climbing to its loft.

But Alle had not escaped, either.

He watched as she was led down a short flight of stairs to where her father was being held.

Prague was informally divided into sections, formed directionally according to prominent monuments, the Vltava River bisecting the center. East was Zizkov, and an old quarter with little tourism and few attractions. West hosted Prague castle and suburbs where many locals lived. To the north sat more neighborhoods and the zoo. The south held its famous horse-racing course, which he'd visited several times. Old Town, at the center, was the showpiece, which included the once prominent Jewish quarter. New Town, nearby, with its bustling commercial center and department stores, was where students had demanded free elections in what came to be known as the Velvet Revolution.

A tiered government administered everything. The lord mayor and council were responsible for citywide public service, but ten administrative districts handled things locally. One of those ten oversaw the neighborhoods of the former Jewish quarter.

And he knew its mayor.

"You want me to follow them?" Rócha asked. "See where they go."

"No. There are cameras everywhere beyond the synagogue. You'll be spotted. I have a better idea."

———

BÉNE WAS TIRED. IT HAD BEEN A LONG DAY. HE AND Halliburton had landed in Montego Bay around 6:00 P.M., and the drive back southeast had taken two hours. Tre lived north of Kingston in Irish Town, named for coopers who came there in the 19th century and crafted wooden barrels for coffee transport. Béne's estate was farther north into the mountains, far away from the sights and sounds of Kingston.

The grandfather clock in the house's foyer banged out chimes for 10:30 P.M. He sat in his study, the veranda doors open to a brisk evening. Milder weather was one of the marvelous things about the mountains, as heat and humidity were generally confined to the lower elevations. He'd made it back in time to have dinner with his mother. The evening meal was something she always enjoyed, and he liked bringing her joy. He sat in the dark and munched on a bulla his chef had baked. He liked the flat, round cakes, sweetened with molasses and ginger. When he was little they were sold everywhere. Now, not so much.

During dinner his mind had stayed on Cuba and what they'd found.

So he'd asked his mother—

"Tell me about Martha Brae."

"We haven't discussed her since you were a boy."

"I'd like to hear the story again."

He'd listened as she told him about the Taino witch who once inhabited the banks of the Rio Matibereon. Spanish treasure hunters captured her, thinking she knew where the natives hid their gold.

"The island be so big, the dirty Spaniards could not imagine that gold was not somewhere here," his mother said.

So they tortured the witch until she relented and led them to the secret location. A cave beside the river.

"Was there an iron gate at this place?" he asked, recalling what Frank Clarke told him.

His mother shook her head. "Never heard that mentioned before with Martha Brae. No need for such things with her. What she did was disappear once they were inside the cave and that scared those Spanish. They started to leave, to run away, but they were all drowned. Martha Brae changed the course of the river and flooded the cave, sealing it forever. That river still bears her name and still flows the way she changed it."

But he knew the Martha Brae River was a long way

from the valley Tre Halliburton had discovered, and was more associated with the Cockpit Maroons of western Jamaica than the Windwards here in the east.

Not that the easterns didn't have legends.

"The golden table," he said to his mother. *"Where did it come from?"*

"You in some mood tonight. Lots of talk of stories. Duppies got you?"

He smiled. *"You could say that."*

She pointed her wrinkled finger at him. *"They be real, Béne. Duppies are all over. They guard the golden table."*

Another story from his childhood. A table made of gold, spotted from time to time at the bottom of certain rivers and lakes, glistening in the light.

"That be a bad one, Béne. Everybody who went in search of that table came to an end."

"Does the tale come from Maroon? Or Taino?"

"Not sure. Just a legend, Béne. Many people claim to see the golden table under the water. Too many, really."

He finished the bulla and reached for another.

A stiff wind molested the trees beyond the veranda.

He'd learned more over the past two days about Columbus' lost mine than he had the past two years.

And about Zachariah Simon.

He hoped his message had been delivered by the curator. He'd had enough of lies. He wondered what happened in Vienna. He'd heard nothing from Brian Jamison. But what did he care. The Americans were a pain in his ass. Maybe he was rid of them.

He ate his cake, listened to the darkness, and hoped duppies would come. He had questions for them, too.

A noise.

From the veranda.

A shadow appeared in the doorway, framed by the night.

He'd been waiting.

"About time you got here."

CHAPTER FIFTY-ONE

TOM WAS LED THROUGH A DESERTED STREET BEYOND the Old-New Synagogue. The narrow way was bordered by closed vendor stalls on one side and darkened shop windows on the other. A ten-foot-high stone wall backed the stalls and trees loomed above. He recalled the local geography and realized the old cemetery had begun to his left and continued on straight ahead. For 350 years Jews had been buried there, the few acres filling. The solution that allowed more graves was to bring in more soil and raise the level, eventually creating twelve mounded layers of sacred earth.

Alle walked beside him. Their captors were young men, anxious, no humor anywhere on their hard faces. He'd seen the same look many times before in the defenders of Sarajevo or on the streets of Mogadishu or on the West Bank. That determined resolve, fortified by youth. They knew fear, like anyone else, but it was simply ignored. Which explained why so many of them ended up dead. Too inexperienced to think before they acted. Too eager to please others. Two such persons had supposedly been the sources for the story that caused his demise. Ben Segev. An angry young Israeli. Quite convincing. And Mahmoud Azam. An equally angry Palestinian.

Both actors, hired to play a part.

Not real.

Unlike here.

He'd been yanked from the pavement and searched, his pockets emptied, Abiram's note, the map, the key, his passport, and his wallet taken. He wasn't sure if they'd searched Alle, as she'd been away from him when seized, but her shoulder bag was gone.

They turned a corner onto another street and kept walking.

The third man who'd been at the synagogue, the one who'd left with everything found during the body search, now returned and whispered something to the others.

A nod confirmed they understood.

They stopped at a door to one of the houses. A key opened the lock and they were led inside. The rooms were dark, but he spotted few furnishings, the air musty. Another door was opened and a light revealed a stairway down. One of the men with a gun motioned for them to descend.

"No," Alle said. "I'm not going down there."

In the penumbra of light he saw that none of the three appreciated her refusal. The one without a gun stepped forward.

"You come here and desecrate our synagogue. You trespass on our sacred site. You violate our laws. And you want to argue with us? You want to challenge us?"

"Call the police," Tom said, testing the water.

The young man laughed. "They don't care what happens here."

"Who is *they*?" he asked.

"The police. The lord mayor. The city council."

He knew anti-Semitism was on the rise in Europe.

That was another thing about the Internet, every day he could scan newspapers from around the world. He recalled reading more and more stories about bigotry.

"So what do you do with trespassers?" he asked.

"Last one we had, we beat the living hell out of him."

———

ALLE HEARD THE THREAT AND KNEW THIS WAS A BAD situation. They were alone, without help. They'd taken her shoulder bag that contained her passport and Zachariah's cell phone. The gun her father carried from the cathedral was tucked in the car, left there intentionally. She'd wondered why he hadn't brought it, but had not questioned him.

Her father did not seem scared. She was terrified. As much as in the car with Midnight. She could still see Brian Jamison bleeding, his body twitching in agony.

"Down the stairs," the man said again.

Little choice existed, so she led the way. At the bottom they stood inside a cellar, Romanesque arches of cut stone supporting a vaulted ceiling. Not a large room and nothing there except a wooden table with six chairs.

"Sit," one of the men ordered.

Her father slid out one of the chairs. "What now?"

"You wait," the man said.

———

TOM HAD BEEN IN TOUGH SITUATIONS BEFORE, ESPE-cially in the Middle East, when sources liked a little drama to go with their revelations. Most times it was only theater. One thing he'd learned was that terrorists, no matter the nationality, understood that their points would go unnoticed if no one reported them. The fear, which they so carefully cultivated, would have no effect without the targeted audience knowing it existed. That didn't mean they actually liked the press, just that they understood how to use it. Sometimes, to make the point that they were in charge, there were props like blindfolds, long car rides, and bravado that had to be endured. On his last story they'd staged the preparations for an attack, weapons and all.

What a show.

Academy Award caliber.

Once he'd been embedded within a Palestinian resistance group for six weeks. He'd seen and heard a lot, most of which he quickly realized had been for his benefit. Sure, he'd tried to understand them, but never had he shown either resentment or sympathy. Stay above the fray. And that was only possible with your mouth shut and ears open.

So he sat and waited for these young men to talk.

Another thing.

The younger they were, the looser the jaw.

He'd left the gun in the car on purpose on the off chance they'd run into the police. Carrying weapons around Europe could be a serious matter. Most likely it was against Czech law—which, he'd noticed, these men seemed not to care about.

"You're on your own, aren't you?" he asked them. "You police the quarter yourself because you have to."

"What do you care?" one of them asked.

"My parents were Jews."

"And what are you?"

"He decided he didn't want to be one of us," Alle said.

The man asking the questions threw her a strange

look. "*One of us?* Does one of us try to vandalize a synagogue?"

"We weren't vandalizing anything," Tom said. "And you know that."

He caught the appraising gaze. "You're in no position to be a smart-ass."

"And what is my position?"

"Not good," the young man said.

"Come now," a new voice said.

Older. Gravelly.

He and Alle turned to see an elderly man descending the stairs. He was short, Spartan-thin, with snow-white hair. His face was a maze of wrinkles, cheeks sunken, brow furrowed, one frail hand gripping the railing, the other holding the note, the map, and the key. Alle's bag draped his shoulder. He negotiated the risers one at a time, eyes down, careful with his movements.

The old man found the bottom and straightened himself.

"We must not be rude. Go now. Leave me."

The three young men stepped toward the stairs. One of them said, "You sure you do not want us to stay?"

"No. No. I will be fine. Go now. I want a chat with these two."

The three climbed the stairs and Tom heard the door upstairs close as they left.

A lively interest swept into the man's dark eyes as he gestured with what he held. "I am Rabbi Berlinger. I want to know where you obtained these items."

CHAPTER FIFTY-TWO

ZACHARIAH CHECKED HIS WATCH. 5:50 A.M. PRAGUE would soon be waking up.

He loved this city and felt a connection with its tumultuous past. Orthodox tradition was strong here. Many of Judaism's European precepts had been forged by wise rabbis living on the banks of the Vltana River. That was one reason he'd taken an interest in its preservation. The mayor for the local administrative district was an acquaintance, a diminutive man who'd made a point to tell him that if he ever needed anything to ask.

Today certainly qualified.

He'd first telephoned his estate in Austria and obtained the mayor's contact information. A second call to a house in Prague had not woken anyone, as the mayor had been quick to say that he rose each day at 5:00 A.M. After explaining the situation, Zachariah was told to meet at the Old-New Synagogue at six. Not a problem since he and Rócha had been standing less than thirty meters away from the building.

He now stood alone outside the synagogue's main door and watched the mayor approach, a thin soul with a thick mustache and sparse hair. Rócha remained on Parizska Street, out of sight of any surveillance cameras. He greeted the mayor in English and shook hands. He knew a little about him. Once a Christian, he converted early in life. He was Orthodox and pro-Israel, but not as harsh on the Prague central authorities as others before him had been. Far too conciliatory for Zachariah's taste but, thankfully, that's exactly what he needed at the moment.

The mayor withdrew a set of keys and opened the door. "I come here each morning to pray. One of the benefits of being in charge."

They entered through a Gothic portal adorned with intertwining grapevine reliefs. Twelve roots, one for each of the lost tribes. Lights came on in the vestibule and he spotted two strongboxes embedded in stone— used, he knew, centuries ago for the collection of special taxes on Jews.

He loved this building. Vienna's synagogue was impressive for its beauty. This one was spectacular in simplicity. Heavy octagonal pillars and vaults with five-section ribbing divided the rectangle into two naves. He knew there were five ribs overhead to prevent a cross from being formed by only four. The seat of the high rabbi was positioned at the east end along with the ark, iron bars and a drape protecting the Torah. An elevated platform surrounded by a wrought-iron grille consumed the center, the *almemor,* which accommodated a prayer easel. The walls and the center platform were lined with bench seats passed down, he'd been told, through generations. Not many, maybe seventy or so. Hanging from above was a red banner with a Star of David, a gift originally from Charles IV in 1358 as a sign of Jewish privilege. He'd always scoffed at such gestures, since history had proven none were sincere.

Little light leaked in from the twelve narrow windows high in the walls, the sun just beginning its rise.

"You were correct," the mayor said. "The night

patrol did find two people trying to enter the loft. It happens from time to time. People really believe there's a golem up there."

"Which you do nothing to discourage, since it brings visitors who spend money."

"Who am I to quell legends? That's not my job. Protecting all of this, that's my task. Unfortunately, it takes money to maintain things."

"Where are the two people now?"

The mayor raised one of his small fingers "That's the problem. They were not taken to the usual holding room in the community building. We normally question them first, then turn them over to the police, who promptly let them go. It's a big problem. But these two were diverted somewhere else."

He did not like what he was hearing.

"I am trying to learn that location. For some reason, no one in security knows."

"Do you come here every morning?"

The mayor nodded. "Most. Before it becomes a tourist attraction and not a house of prayer."

He envied that ability. "What is in the loft above us?"

"Nothing but rafters, insulation, and a roof. No golem, returned to clay, is waiting there."

"But the loft did, for centuries, serve as this building's *genizah*."

Every synagogue possessed a storeroom for old books and papers. The Talmud forbid the discarding of any writing that contained the name of God. Instead, those were held and buried every seventh year in a cemetery.

The mayor nodded. "Quite right. We kept everything up there since it was old anyway. The elements could not hurt them. But that stopped about forty years ago and the loft was emptied."

He wondered. Had something been stashed away before that? Forty years? That time frame would be consistent with Sagan's grandfather.

He heard the main door open then close, and watched as the mayor excused himself and returned to the vestibule. He was now convinced that Sagan had deceived him. He hoped Alle could learn something. He was still bothered by the meeting with the Israeli ambassador and the fact that both she and the Americans were interested in him. He'd sent Rócha back to the alley beyond St. Stephen's, and Brian Jamison's body was indeed gone. Not a word in the press about its discovery, either. The ambassador had said she would clean up the mess, and that she had.

The mayor returned as the outer door again opened, then closed.

"I've just been told that the two people caught earlier were taken to a house not far from here."

He noticed the look of concern on the man's face.

"What is it?" he asked.

"The Rabbi Berlinger was summoned. He is with them now."

TOM IMMEDIATELY CONNECTED THE DOTS. ABIRAM had mentioned this man specifically in his last message.

"He also gave me a name. Rabbi Berlinger."

"How old are you?" he asked, which he knew must sound rude, but he had to know.

"One hundred and two."

He would never have guessed. Maybe in his eighties, but nowhere near the century mark. "Life's been kind to you."

"Sometimes I think so. Other times not. I asked you a question. Please tell me where you obtained these items."

He saw that Alle was interested in that answer, too. But he wasn't ready to cooperate. "They were given to me. I was meant to have them."

This man would have seen the original writing, unedited, as that was all he'd had left in his pockets.

"I don't know any such thing," Berlinger said. "I only know that you have these items."

"M. E. Cross was my grandfather."

The old man studied him carefully. "I see him in your face. Your name is Sagan. I recall that your mother married a Sagan. Marc was your mother's father."

He nodded. "I called him Saki."

The rabbi sat, laying the items he held and Alle's bag on the table. "I must confess. I never thought I would hear of this subject again."

———

BÉNE STAYED SEATED AS THE SHADOW ENTERED HIS study. Outside, mountain winds continued to stir the night. He'd been waiting for Frank Clarke. A call made earlier had brought a promise that his friend would be at the estate before ten.

"You like the dark, Béne?"

Not a light burned in the room.

"Mother is asleep and the help is gone for the night. Just you and me, Frank."

He offered the plate of bullas, but the colonel waved him off. He lifted another one for himself before returning the platter to the side table.

"What have you found?" Frank asked. "I could hear it in your voice earlier."

"The mine is real. I know its location."

Tre had called after dinner to say that a quick survey of what they'd stolen from Cuba, along with the deed and other items found in the Jamaican archive, had led him to a spot. He'd checked the latest topographic maps the university had on file and confirmed that a cave did exist in the vicinity of where everything pointed.

"And where's that?" Clarke asked.

He did not have to see the face to know that he would be revealing something that was already known. Which he'd suspected all along.

"Why did you lie to me, Frank?"

"Because that mine must stay lost."

"That's not what you said in the cave. You told me to find it."

"I told you to find the Jews' wealth. If that still exists, then Maroons could make use of it. The mine? That's another matter."

The voice stayed in a near whisper, as if the words should not be spoken. But he had to know, "Why should the mine stay lost?"

"It's a sacred place. Maroons have so little left. Places like that are ours, Béne. They must be guarded."

"There's little left of Maroons, anymore, except stories. Why does it matter?"

Silence passed between them. He listened to the wind.

"The night was once our ally," Clarke said. "We made good use of it. Victory became ours, in part, because of the night."

More stories, Béne thought. Not reality.

During the last Maroon war, in 1795, 300 Maroons held out against 1,500 British troops. A truce came only after the Cuban hounds had been brought in to hunt them down. But when everyone assembled at Montego Bay to conclude a treaty nearly 600 Maroons were herded onto ships and deported to Nova Scotia. There they lived in the cold of Canada for two years, then were sent to Sierra Leone. Only 60 eventually returned to Jamaica.

Some victory.

"You still have not answered me," he said. "Why does this matter anymore?"

He watched the blackened form shift in the chair.

"There are things about us, Béne, you simply do not understand. Though you are of Maroon blood, you've been raised different. Poverty is rampant among us. Unemployment high. You live here, on this grand estate, in luxury. You drive whatever vehicle you desire. You never go hungry. You have money. You've always had money, Béne."

"You sound as though you resent that."

"I don't. It matters nothing to me. You're my friend. I've always liked you. But others feel differently. They take your money, take your favors. They smile, but never reveal what's in their hearts."

"That's not what you told me yesterday. You said no one cares what I am."

"I lied."

He did not like what he was hearing. He'd always felt a closeness with the Maroon community. Like family. He had precious little of that himself. Only his mother and a few cousins. He should marry, have children, build a family of his own. But he'd never met anyone with whom he might want to do that. Was it because of who and what he was? Hard to say. What he knew for sure was that no one was going to tell him what to do.

Not now.

Not ever.

"I'm going to the mine," he said.

"I feared this was what you wanted tonight."

"Will you come with me?"

"Do I have a choice?"

CHAPTER FIFTY-THREE

ZACHARIAH WANTED TO KNOW, "WHO IS RABBI BER-linger?"

"The former head of this community. One of the last alive who lived through the Holocaust."

"He survived the Nazis?"

The mayor nodded. "He was taken to Terezín, along with many others. He served on the governing council in the camp and tried to look after people."

The fortified town of Terezín had been a holding point from where tens of thousands of Czech Jews were transported east to death camps. Many, though, died there from squalid conditions.

"The rabbi is highly regarded," the mayor said. "No one questions him. If he asked to speak to these two intruders, then that's what would happen."

He also heard what was unspoken. This man's election depended on the support of such people. Though this man might be king, Berlinger was the kingmaker. But still, "I have to know why he is interested."

"Would you tell me *your* interest?"

"The man caught at the synagogue has something that belongs to me. I want it back."

"This must be something of great importance."

"It is to me."

He was choosing his words carefully.

Say enough, but not too much.

"I have sent someone to find out what is going on. How about until he returns you and I pray. Look there, in the east window, the morning sun can now be seen."

He glanced up the wall to the narrow slit that blazed with the day's first light. He realized that Jews for 700 years had watched that sight. Everything he was about to do, everything he'd planned, he did for them. 100,000 of his brethren had been exterminated during the war, the Czech president simply handing the country over to Hitler as a German protectorate. Immediately laws were implemented that forbid non-Aryan doctors from caring for the sick. Jews were forbidden from public parks, theaters, cinemas, libraries, sporting events, public baths, and swimming pools. They could not serve in public office and were forced to use only certain compartments at the rear of trains and none of the public facilities at stations. Shopping was allowed only at designated times. Curfew was 8:00 P.M. No telephones were permitted and none could change their residence without approval. The list of restrictions had been endless, all eventually leading to arrest and extermination.

But the Nazis had not razed the Jewish quarter.

The synagogues went untouched, including the Old-New. Even the cemetery had not been overly violated. The idea had been to transform everything into an elaborate open-air exhibit.

The Exotic Museum for an Extinct Race.

But that never came to be.

Russia liberated the country in 1945.

Coming to Prague always seemed to strengthen his resolve. Throughout history Jews had respected strong leadership, clear motives, and unflinching action. They appreciated decisiveness. And that was what he would provide. But the mayor was right. Time to pray. So he clasped his hands behind his back, bowed his head, and asked for God's help in all that he intended.

"There is one thing," the mayor quietly said.

He opened his eyes and stared down at the man, who was a third of a meter shorter.

"You asked about documents that were once stored in the loft. We do, as required, bury them from time to time. But we have developed a different way of accomplishing that obligation."

He waited for an explanation.

"Space in the old cemetery is gone, and no one really wants to dig there anyway. There are too many unmarked graves. So we have a crypt in which the writings are placed. They have been stored there since the war. It's a system that works. Our problem has been the upkeep of that crypt. Most expensive. Labor-intensive."

He caught the message.

"We fight every day," the mayor said, "to reclaim our property and restore the cemetery and the synagogues. We try to manage our lives, recall our heritage, restore the legacy. To do that, we encourage outside investment." He paused. "Whenever we can."

"I believe one of my foundations could make a suitable donation to assist with those costs."

The mayor nodded. "That is most generous of you."

"Of course, it would help if I could see this crypt, so as to gauge the appropriate amount of the contribution."

The head nodded again. "I think that would be entirely reasonable. We shall do that. Just after we pray."

TOM WATCHED THE OLD RABBI, LEERY OF EVERYTHING
that was happening. He had no idea if this man was
who he claimed to be. What he did know was that the
unedited message had been read, its contents now
known to a third party.

The smug messenger from Barnes & Noble came to
mind, along with his warning.

"You'll never know if it's the truth or us."

Like right now.

"When did you hear about any of this the first
time?" he asked Berlinger.

"Your grandfather came in the 1950s. His mother
was Czech. He and I became friends. Eventually, he
told me things. Not everything, but enough."

He watched Alle as she listened. He would prefer to
talk to this man in private but realized that was impossible.

"Marc was a fascinating person. He and I shared
many times together. He spoke our language, knew
our history, our problems. I never understood all that
he knew, only that it was important. I came to trust
him enough to do as he asked."

"Which was?"

The old man studied him through tired, oily eyes.

"A short while ago I was awoken from my sleep
and handed these things here on the table. The writing contained my name, so it was thought I should be
advised. I read it, then asked where it and the rest
came from. I was told that a man was caught trying
to enter the synagogue loft. Immediately I thought of
another time, and another man, who'd tried the same
thing.

"Get away from there," Berlinger yelled.

The man who supported himself on the iron rung

ladder attached to the Old-New Synagogue simply stared down and shook his head. "I've come to see the golem, and that I will."

Berlinger estimated the climber to be about his age, midfifties, but in better condition, the hair salt-and-pepper, the body lean, the face full of life. He spoke in Czech, but with the distinctive hint of an American, which he appeared to be.

"I mean it," he called out. "There's nothing up there. The story is foolishness. A tale. That's all."

"My, how you underestimate the power of Jehuda Leva ben Becalel."

He was impressed with the stranger's use of Rabbi Loew's proper name. Not many people came to Prague any longer, and of those that did none knew the great man's correct name. After the war the communists seized control and shut the borders. No one in or out. How this American had made it in he did not know. He watched as the intruder shoved open the iron door adorned with the Star of David. It had not been locked since long before the war. The man disappeared inside the loft, then his head popped from the open frame.

"Come on up. I need to speak with you."

He'd not climbed to the loft in a long while. It was where the old papers were kept, stored away until buried, as the Torah commanded. Someone had left a ladder propped against the synagogue's east wall, making it easy to reach the first iron rung. He decided to oblige the stranger and climbed to the door, entering the loft.

"Marc Cross," the man said, extending his hand.

"I am—"

"Rabbi Berlinger. I know. I came to talk with you. I was told you are a man who can be trusted."

"That's how we met," Berlinger said. "From there

Marc and I became the closest of friends, and remained that until the day he died. Unfortunately, I
saw little of him in the decades after, but we did cor-
respond. I would have gone to his funeral, but the
Soviets would not allow Jews to travel abroad."

Tom reached over and lifted the key from the table.
"This does not open the loft door."

"Of course it doesn't. The lock on that door is new,
placed there when the loft was reengineered and repaired a few years ago. We kept to the old style simply
for appearances. But there is nothing now up there of
any importance."

He caught what had gone unspoken.

"But there was at one time."

Berlinger nodded. "We kept the old papers there. But
those are now stored underground in the cemetery."
The rabbi stood. "I'll show you."

He wasn't ready to leave just yet and pointed to the
key. "There are markings on that. Do you know what
they mean?"

The old man nodded.

"You didn't even look at them."

"I don't have to, Mr. Sagan. I made the key and
placed those markings there. I know precisely what
they mean."

He was shocked.

"And the fact that you possess this precious key is
the only reason why you are not now in the custody
of the police."

CHAPTER FIFTY-FOUR

ZACHARIAH FOLLOWED THE MAYOR FROM INSIDE the Old-New Synagogue out onto a street identified as U Stareho Hrbitova, a short incline that led to a building he knew as the ceremonial hall. The neo-Romanesque structure had served, in times past, as a mortuary, erected for use by the local burial society. Now it was a museum on funerary customs and traditions. He knew the long tradition of the Prague Burial Society, formed in the mid-16th century, its job to ensure that the dead received a proper farewell.

He and the mayor had prayed for fifteen minutes. In his previous dealings with the man he'd never thought him all that devoted. More pragmatic and practical, as evidenced by the contribution he'd managed to extort simply for an opportunity to view where the old documents were now kept. Anything being there was a long shot, for sure, but he was genuinely curious. In Vienna there was no shortage of sacred earth, and books and papers were reverently buried in several Jewish cemeteries.

Here, things were vastly different.

An iron gate adjacent to the ceremonial house led to another walkway that entered the cemetery. A uniformed attendant manned the gate, which he was told was actually the exit for visitors, the cemetery entrance a block over. The mayor was not stopped as they passed through. Zachariah followed the man into one of the most sacred spots in the world. Across a mere 11,000 square meters, as many as 100,000 people were buried in the mounds of earth, beneath wild growths of thin grass, which explained the tombstones—12,000 of them, if he recalled correctly—pressed close together, set at odd angles as if from some earthquake.

Forbidden to bury their dead outside their district, for 350 years Jews had been laid to rest here. New land had been impossible to come by and the Torah forbid the moving of corpses, so the solution had been to bring in more soil and raise the level, one layer at a time, until the Talmudic injunction that graves be separated by at least six handbreadths of earth was satisfied. Eventually twelve layers, each nearly sixty centimeters deep, rose within the walls. Burials stopped in 1787, and he wondered how many *matsevahs* had disappeared, decayed, or been destroyed, how many people forgotten.

His gaze raked the surreal sight.

Ash trees cast everything in shadows. A simple look prevailed on the thick markers, the simplest straight or two-pitched, most with decorations and sculptures that referred to the deceased's name, family, marital status, and profession. He noticed the art—a tree of life, a menorah, grape clusters, animals. Some of the writing could be read, most could not. Here and there were four-sided tombs with high-fronted sides, each topped with a gable and a saddle roof, similar to his own father's grave in Austria. Cemeteries were holy, where the dead awaited resurrection. Which was why they could never be closed.

A graveled way lined with more thin grass wove a path through the headstones. No one else was inside the walls that encased the tight space. He noticed closed-circuit cameras at various points.

"Is there still vandalism?" he asked the mayor.

"Occasionally. The cameras have deterred intrusions. We appreciate your generosity in providing funds for them."

He acknowledged the comment with a nod.

"We bury the animals that are thrown over the wall in the far corner over there," the mayor said.

Once the dead touched sacred earth they could not leave it, no matter whether human or animal. He appreciated this community's adherence to Talmudic tradition. His own congregation, in Vienna, were not as strict. Progressive ideas had diluted what had once been a staunch Orthodox community. That was why he offered most of his prayers in a small synagogue on his estate.

"I had the attendant at the gate brought on duty early," the mayor said. "This site does not open for another two hours."

No one else was around. He liked the treatment he was receiving and realized it was all designed to open his checkbook. The mayor of this district had no clue why he was there, just that he was, and an opportunity like this could not be squandered.

The mayor stopped and pointed at a double set of metal doors in the far wall. "Beyond those doors is a ladder that leads down to an underground room, which was once used for tool storage. It has proven ideal as a place where paper can return to dust."

"You're not coming?"

The mayor shook his head. "I'll wait here. You have a look in private."

He sensed something with this man. Something he did not particularly like. But he knew Rócha was not far away, as he'd spotted him following them to the iron gate. So he made clear, "You do understand that I am not someone to be taken lightly."

"That is beyond question. You are an important man."

Before he could inquire further, the mayor turned and left. He almost called out to stop him but decided against it. Instead, he left the graveled path and wove his way through the *matsevahs* until he came to the outer wall. He realized that this portion ran parallel to U Stareho Hrbitova, the street they'd walked earlier. Ten feet above him another section of cemetery stretched beneath more ash trees, the earth supported by the wall. The double doors before him would lead beneath that section.

He opened them.

Rakes, shovels, and brooms were propped against one wall to his right. A metal ladder led down into a dark square in the stone floor.

He gazed down the chute.

A light burned below.

Apparently, he was expected.

He stepped onto the rungs but, before descending, he reclosed the double doors.

He climbed down, realizing that he was literally descending through time. Every sixty centimeters meant another layer of graves. When he reached the bottom he would stand where the burials had begun 700 years ago.

He glanced down beyond his feet and saw the ground approaching.

A few more rungs and he found stone.

He was perhaps seven to eight meters belowground. The lit room that stretched before him was about ten meters square, the ceiling not much above his head, the black earthen floor damp. Books and papers were stacked against the walls in haphazard piles, most nearly rotted away. The stale air was scented with decay and he wondered about the source.

Standing in the center of the room, beneath three bare bulbs that burned bright, was the same woman from Vienna who'd met him at Schönbrunn.

Israel's ambassador to Austria.

"You and I need to talk further," she said to him.

———

ALLE WAS LISTENING TO THE RABBI AND HER FATHER talk. Both men knew things she did not. Especially her father, who'd obviously withheld far more than he'd revealed.

Like the key, which resembled something that might open a pirate's chest, except that one end was adorned with three Stars of David. The other markings they were discussing were too small to be seen from her vantage point.

Hearing the story of how Berlinger and her great-grandfather had met moved her. She'd never known Marc Eden Cross or his wife, as both died long before she was born. Her grandmother had told her about them, and she'd seen photographs, but knew little except that Cross had been an archaeologist of some renown.

"What was my great-grandfather like?" she asked the rabbi.

The old man smiled at her. "A delightful man. You have his eyes. Did you know that?"

She shook her head. "I've never been told that before."

"Why are *you* here?" Berlinger asked her.

She decided to be coy. "My father brought me."

Berlinger faced her father. "If you are indeed the Levite, as the message says, then you know your duty."

"It's time for that duty to change."

She saw that the old man was puzzled.

"Such a strange choice in you," Berlinger said. "I sense anger. Resentment."

"I didn't make the choice. All I know is that my daughter and a man named Zachariah Simon are up to something. I don't know what and I only care about any of it because a man died yesterday for it."

"Yet you brought her here?"

"What better way to keep an eye on her?"

She resented his tone, but kept her words to herself. She was here to learn and arguing would not accomplish that goal.

Berlinger lifted the key. "I made this a long time ago. My contribution to Marc's endeavor."

"What was his endeavor?" she asked.

The rabbi appraised her with a stiff gaze. "He was the chosen one, called the Levite, to whom everything had been entrusted. But he lived at a time of great upheaval. The Nazis changed everything. They even searched for what he guarded."

"In what way?" her father asked.

"They wanted our Temple treasure. They thought it the ultimate prize in destroying our culture, as the Babylonians and the Romans had done."

"The Temple treasure has been gone for nearly two thousand years," her father said.

"But they'd heard the stories, too," Berlinger said. "As I had. That it survived. That it was hidden away. And only one person knew." The old man paused. "The Levite."

"Three days ago I would have said you were insane," her father said. "Now I can't do that. There is obviously something going on here."

Berlinger pointed to the note. "Your father was the Levite. He knew the secret, or at least as much of it as was revealed. Marc was a cautious man. Understandably. So, for the first time in hundreds of years, he changed everything about that secret. He had to, given the times."

She could only imagine what it had been like to be Jewish in Europe from 1933 to 1945. What horrors those people had experienced. Her grandfather had told her some, things his relatives had described to him. But here, standing before her, was a man who'd seen it firsthand.

"You said that you plan to change things," Berlinger whispered. "What kind of things?"

"I'm going to find that treasure."

"Why do such a thing?"

"Why the hell not?" Her father's voice rose, the anger clear. "Don't you think it's stayed hidden long enough?"

"Actually, I agree with you."

CHAPTER FIFTY-FIVE

BÉNE STEPPED FROM THE PICKUP TRUCK. HE'D driven from his estate west, then north into the mountains, entering St. Mary's Parish and the same valley he and Tre had visited yesterday, the site identified by the deed grant found in the Jamaican archives. The Flint River flowed nearby, as did a multitude of lesser tributaries dropping from the mountains toward the shore. Frank Clarke had followed him in another vehicle. He was agitated with his friend, irritated with more lies, hurt by how other Maroons might feel about him. He'd been good to those people, done more for them than anyone.

Yet they resented him.

He'd searched for the mine on their behalf, only now to be told that they've known of it all along.

Ahead, a vehicle was parked, beside which stood Tre Halliburton.

He and Clarke walked over and he said, "How far from here?"

"Maybe a ten-minute hike up that slope to the east."

A full moon cast the forest in a cold, pale light. Pink heat lightning flickered in the far-off clouds. He'd brought two flashlights and saw that Tre held one, too, along with something else.

He motioned toward the object.

"GPS locator," Tre said. "Unlike the Spanish, we don't have to grope in the dark. I have coordinates for the cave site."

"You really think this is it?"

"I do, Béne. Everything points this way."

He introduced Tre to Clarke and said, "He's Maroon, and already knows of this place."

He handed Frank a flashlight. Through the moonlight he caught the concern on his old friend's face.

"What else aren't you telling me?" Béne asked.

But there was no reply.

Instead Frank turned and headed into the trees.

ZACHARIAH STARED AT THE AMBASSADOR. "HOW DID you know I was in Prague?"

"Those friends of mine," she said in English. "Did you check on Jamison's body?"

"Of course. Impressive."

She nodded at his compliment. "The local mayor here is also a friend. After you contacted him earlier, I did as well."

"And how did you know I made contact?"

"That phone you carry. If you use it, the world will know."

"Which means you have friends in the Mossad."

"Among other places. But, like I said yesterday, they know nothing. This is between you and me."

"What do you want?"

"A private moment, and I thought this an excellent location."

"How did you know I would come here?"

"The lord mayor assured me that he would bring you."

He was uncomfortable with her presence. Yet there was nothing he could do but listen.

"I have to say," she said, "when I first reasoned out your plan I thought it preposterous. But, on reflection, I began to see that you are right. The Temple Mount is the perfect ignition point."

Since the 1967 Six-Day War Israel had controlled the city of Jerusalem. As a concession after the fighting, the Supreme Muslim Religious Council had been allowed to continue to police the thirty-five acres known as the Temple Mount. This was the place where God chose the Divine Presence to rest. From where the world expanded into its present form. Where dust was gathered to create the first man. Where Abraham bound Isaac. Jews around the world faced toward it when offering prayers. Solomon had built the First Temple there. The Second Temple rose from the same spot. So holy was the site that rabbinical law forbid Jews to walk there so as to avoid unintentionally stepping where the Holy of Holies once existed.

"You have never mentioned what my plan is," he said.

She grinned. "No, I have not."

Maybe it was good she'd come. He had a few questions of his own.

"God has never rescinded His command in Exodus that we build a sanctuary for Him," she said. "Muslim control of the Temple Mount is like a dagger in the side of every Jew, and they are not going anywhere."

He knew what Islam called the mount. *Noble Sanctuary.* The end point of Muhammad's journey to Jerusalem. The spot from where the prophet ascended into heaven. One of the oldest Islamic structures in the world, the Dome of the Rock, was there, facing

Mecca, built atop the spot where the Second Temple had formerly stood.

"We should never have ceded control," she said. "What did they say in 1967? *'If we try to keep it all, then there will never be any semblance of peace.'*"

"Yet we gave the mount away and still lived in fear. Arabs threatened to invade every day."

And they finally did. In 1973. The Yom Kippur War. Then, six years later, everything won during that conflict was given back at Camp David with the accords signed by Carter, Begin, and Sadat.

Damn Americans, interfering again.

He told her what he thought.

"We did learn one thing from those two wars," she said. "Keep the Arabs fighting among themselves, and they will never have time to fight their enemy."

Useless information, considering all that happened afterward. "I remember the day the Israeli flag flying atop the Dome of the Rock was lowered. My father cried. So did I. That was when I resolved to never concede anything to our enemies."

The ambassador knelt down, examining some of the rotting papers. "They lie here, in the dark, and slowly disappear. So sad."

But there was something more important. "Like the bodies encasing us."

She stood and faced him. "I want to hear more about your spark."

Enough. "I want to hear what you know."

———

TOM TRIED TO PROCESS WHAT BERLINGER HAD JUST said. "You agree with me?"

"Marc and I debated this point at length. He felt strongly that the secret should remain hidden. I thought

then it was time Jews were restored their sacred treasures. Why not? Christians, Muslims, Buddhists all
have theirs. Should not we also be allowed?"

He watched Alle, who was processing everything
that was being said. He decided to offer her the complete note. "Here's what your grandfather actually
wrote."

She accepted the paper and read.

"Why is their such tension between you two?" Berlinger asked.

"She hates me."

"Is that true?" the rabbi asked Alle.

She looked up from the page and asked him, "Why
did you trick me?"

"Your loyalty is to Simon."

"Who is Simon?" Berlinger asked.

And he told him.

"I know the man. He has been here several times.
His money is appreciated by some."

"But not you?"

"I am always cautious with men who offer money
freely."

"He's dangerous as hell," Tom said. "He's after the
Temple treasure. And so is the American government.
Any idea why?"

He saw that the information caught the old man by
surprise.

"Marc was afraid that, one day, the secret could no
longer be contained. His fears were centered on Germany and the Nazis. Mine were, too, but eventually I
feared the Soviets more. Neither of us, though,
thought of a threat from one of our own. Is Simon
after the treasure for all Jews?"

"That's exactly what he wants," Alle said. "He
agrees with you. It's time we have our sacred vessels
restored."

"But you don't concur," Berlinger said to Tom.

"That's the last thing Simon wants."

"Then what is he after?"

"My father," Alle said, "believes Zachariah is a danger. You may or may not know, but my father was once a newspaper reporter. He was fired for fabricating a story. So you better keep that in mind before you start listening to his tales."

He slammed his hands onto the table and sprang from the chair. "I've had enough of your smart mouth. You don't have a clue what happened with that story. I understand that you want to believe I'm a cheat and a fraud. That probably helps you keep on hating me. But you listen to me. I made enough mistakes with you as a father. Hate me for those, if you want. But don't hate me for something that I didn't do."

His gaze bore into her.

Alle stared back.

Berlinger gently laid a hand on his arm.

He faced the rabbi, who nodded slightly, indicating that he should retake his seat.

He did.

"We have to make some decisions," Berlinger said, his voice low. "Important decisions. Both of you, come with me."

CHAPTER FIFTY-SIX

BÉNE FOLLOWED TRE, WHO LAGGED BEHIND FRANK Clarke. None of them had switched on their flashlights. No need. Sharp rays of bright moonlight provided more than enough illumination. Tre was reading the GPS, but Frank plunged ahead without any electronic aid.

"He's headed straight for it," Tre said to him.

No surprise, considering the conversation he'd had with Clarke back at the estate. He'd never thought his old friend would deceive him in such a way. But that violation had made him cautious, so he'd come prepared, a semiautomatic tucked into a shoulder holster beneath his open shirt.

"Another fifty meters," Tre said.

A rush of falling water could be heard. They pushed through more foliage until they found a pool, water tumbling down from twenty meters above. A stream entered and exited the pool, disappearing into the black forest. He'd seen a thousand of these in the mountains around his estate. Water was not in short supply on Jamaica, and had always been one of its main draws.

Frank's flashlight clicked on and the beam cruised across the pool's surface, then up the waterfall. "There's a slit in the rock. Behind the water. A cave.

But it's a dead end. A false route that goes back to nothing."

"So why show it to us?" he asked.

The colonel lowered his light and turned. "It once led to the mine, but was sealed long ago. Maroons eventually laid traps there. A way to deter anyone who might come for a look."

"What are you saying, Frank?"

"That what you are about to see has cost men their lives."

He heard the unspoken part. *There's risk here.*

"I'm ready," he declared.

"That gun you're toting will do no good. You have to swim to get inside."

He stripped off his shirt, then removed the shoulder harness, handing both to Tre. He started to remove his pants and boots but Frank stopped him.

"You'll need those in there."

"So what do I do?" Béne asked.

"There's an opening about three meters down, below the waterfall. It's a shaft that leads up a few meters to a chamber that was part of the mine at the time of Columbus. Back then, you walked straight in through the slit behind the falls. Not anymore. That's why this place has never been found."

"How do you know about it?" Tre asked.

"It's part of my heritage."

"I'm going, too," Tre said to him.

"No. You're not," Béne said. "This is between Maroons."

———

ZACHARIAH WAITED FOR AN ANSWER TO HIS QUESTION.

"You want the Third Temple," the ambassador said. "Without the coming of the Messiah."

"It is my belief that the Messiah will return *if* we build the Third Temple."

"Most Jews believe that the Messiah must first come before we will have our Third Temple."

"They are wrong."

And he meant it. Nowhere had he ever read anything that convinced him that the Temple must await the Messiah. The first two were built without him. Why not the third? Certainly it would be preferable to have the Messiah. His arrival would herald the *Olam-ha-Ba*, the World to Come where all people would coexist peacefully. War would cease to exist. Jews would return from their exile to their home in Israel. No murder, robbery, or sin.

Which justified everything he was about to do.

"You also plan to start a war," she said. "Tell me, Zachariah, how will you return our Temple treasures to the mount?"

She did know.

"In a way that the Muslims cannot ignore."

"Your spark."

What better way to reawaken a sleeping Israel than to have the Jews' most venerated objects—lost for two thousand years—attacked on the Temple Mount. And the Arabs would react. They would regard any such act as a direct threat to their control. Every day they suppressed any semblance of a Jewish presence on the mount. For the Temple treasure to return after 2,000 years? That would be the greatest provocation of them all.

They would act.

And even the meekest of Israeli citizens would call for retaliation.

He could already hear commentators comparing the Babylonians to the Romans to the Arabs, each defiance a denial to Jews of their divine right to occupy the mount and build the Lord a sanctuary. Twice before destruction occurred with no consequences. *What about this time?* they would ask.

Israel possessed more than enough might to defend itself.

This singular act of sacrilege would resurrect its protective vigilance.

"A spark that will ignite a blazing fire," he said.

"That it will."

"And what will you do," he asked, "once all that happens?"

He truly wanted to know.

"A call in the Knesset for retaliation. The Temple Mount retaken. Every single Muslim expelled. When they resist, which they will, they will be shown that we are not weak."

"And the world? The Americans? They will not want any of that to happen."

"Then I will ask them, what did you do when your country was attacked by terrorists? You mounted an army and invaded Afghanistan. Eventually, you invaded Iraq. You defended what you believe to be important. That is all we will be doing and, in the end, we will have Israel, the mount, and our Third Temple. If you are right, the Messiah will then come and we will have global peace. I would say all that is worth the risk."

So would he.

As had his father and grandfather.

"How close are you to success?" she asked him.

"Closer than I have ever been before. The final piece of the puzzle is here, in Prague. Which I should have shortly."

She seemed pleased. "What can I do to help?"

"Nothing. I have to do this myself."

BÉNE DOVE INTO THE CHILLY WATER AND CLAWED his way down, following the light Frank Clarke held as he led the way. He should be cold but his blood ran hot. He felt like one of his ancestors, preparing to do battle with British redcoats, their weapons few, their determination great.

Clarke's light disappeared into a dark hole, the beam faded but was still there. With a light in one hand he followed and entered the same cavity, about two meters in diameter. He stared through the water and still saw Clarke's light toward the ceiling. His pants and boots were like anchors and he was reaching the limit of his breath, so he kicked toward the brightness, propelling himself upward, breaking the surface and sucking air.

Frank stood on a rocky ledge, pants dripping, staring down, holding his light. "It takes about all you have, doesn't it?"

That it did.

He laid his light on the rocks and leveraged himself from the water. His lungs stabilized. His nerves calmed, but remained on high alert.

Frank angled his beam around the chamber. He saw it was irregularly shaped, a few meters deep, the same in height, with one exit—beside which, carved into the rock, was a hooked X.

"The mark of the Spanish," Frank said. "Maybe made by the great Admiral of the Ocean, Columbus himself."

———

ALLE WALKED WITH HER FATHER AND BERLINGER. They'd left the underground room and house, emerging onto the street. The clock above what the rabbi noted as the Jewish town hall read nearly 9:00 A.M. People filled the cobbled streets, the quarter alive for another day. Vendors were beginning to open stalls that lined the cemetery wall, the iron gates leading inside to the graves now guarded by an attendant. She could hear a murmur of traffic and the growl of engines in the distance. The chill from earlier remained, though it dissipated rapidly beneath a brightening sun.

Her father's outburst had affected her.

She wondered about something he'd said.

"Don't hate me for something that I didn't do."

She'd called him a cheater and a fraud because of all that happened.

But what had he meant?

She should have asked, but could not bring herself to do it. She simply wanted to learn what she could and get away from him. She carried her shoulder bag once again with the cell phone inside. Her father harbored the note, the key, and the map.

Of Jamaica, she'd seen.

What did all this mean?

Berlinger led them to a turreted building identified by a placard as the ceremonial hall, built in 1908. Three-storied, neo-Romanesque style, fortresslike, with a turret rising from one side to a distinctive slate roof.

The rabbi stopped, then turned and faced them both. "From that balcony up there funeral orations were once delivered. This was the place where the dead were prepared for final resting. Now it's a museum."

Berlinger motioned to an exterior staircase. "Let us go inside."

CHAPTER FIFTY-SEVEN

BÉNE SWITCHED ON HIS LIGHT, GLAD HE'D BROUGHT waterproof cave lamps. And though his gun was outside, he'd not come unarmed. On the pretense of forcing more water from his pants he checked for the knife strapped to his right leg.

Still there.

The story of Martha Brae his mother reminded him of at dinner came to mind. How she led the Spanish into a cave to find gold, only to disappear and leave them to drown.

"The Tainos showed the Spanish this place," Frank said. "We have to follow that tunnel for a little way to see more."

He studied the chasm, its diameter about two meters. Clusters of black rock guarded the entrance. He'd noticed a moment ago, and now again—air rushed in and out from the tunnel, like breaths, in a rhythm.

"Columbus was stranded on Jamaica for a year," Frank said. "During that time there was a lot of contact among him, his men, and the Tainos. Once he was able to leave the island, he returned a few months later and bargained for six natives to help him with an expedition. They brought three crates into the jungle. Some say they were full of gold, but no one knows. Columbus left and the bodies of the six Tainos were found in the forest, all stabbed to death. The first to die for this place."

He said nothing.

"The Tainos returned and found the entrance behind the waterfall sealed by rock. The doings of the Spanish. The Spanish knew nothing of the second entrance we just used. So the Tainos were able to come back inside."

"What did they find?"

"I'll show you."

———

ZACHARIAH FOLLOWED THE AMBASSADOR UP THE ladder, back to ground level. He was invigorated discussing the possibilities. They'd both expressed regret that the precious relics might be harmed, but he'd made clear that their sacrifice was the price to be paid. Another menorah, more silver trumpets, and a second divine table could be made according to God's dictates. But the state of Israel—that was singular, a precious commodity, which could not be replaced.

They stepped back outside into the cool morning.

"Walk with me," she said. "I'd like to pay homage to the rabbi."

He knew to whom she referred.

They followed a graveled path through the markers to the far side, directly adjacent to the western wall. Still, no one else had, as yet, entered the cemetery. Traffic could be heard, but not seen. She stopped before one of the larger tombs, framed by Renaissance cartouches sunk deep into the ground. The side facing them was decorated with a motif of grapes and a lion. He knew who rested beneath the elaborate marker.

Rabbi Loew.

Chief rabbi of Prague in the late 16th century. Rector of the Talmudic school, teacher, author. An original thinker.

Like him.

"The most visited tomb in this cemetery," she said. "He was a great man."

He noticed the stones lined across the top and on every other available edge. Jews rarely brought flowers to graves, as stones were the traditional way of expressing respect. A custom that dated back to their nomadic ways in the desert when rock covered the dead to keep the animals at bay. These stones, though, were special. Many had scraps of paper beneath them, some affixed by rubber bands. Each contained a prayer or a wish left for the rabbi to act upon. He'd left one himself a few years ago.

His hope that one day he'd find the Temple treasure.

Which might soon come to be.

———

TOM ADMIRED THE CEREMONIAL HALL. FROM THE ARTICLE he'd written years ago, he was familiar with the Prague Burial Society. Membership was restricted to senior married men of unimpeachable repute who could provide for the sick and the dead. He'd toured the building then. The first floor had once been used for purification, the basement a mortuary, the second floor a meeting room. The walls were decorated with intricate murals, the floors a rich mosaic tile. This had been an important place. Now it was a museum.

He, Alle, and Berlinger stood among wood and glass cases that displayed funerary objects. Various paintings depicted the society's history and activities. A six-candled, polished brass chandelier burned bright.

"These objects were once used by the society," Berlinger said.

"They're not important," Alle said. "Why are we here?"

"Young lady, you may talk to your father in such a disrespectful manner. But not to me."

She seemed unfazed by the rebuke. "You're playing games with us."

"And you're not?"

"You *know* why we're here."

"I have to be sure."

"Of what?" she asked.

But Berlinger did not answer. Instead he reached for Tom's arm, leading him toward a set of display cases that fronted an outer wall. Three tall, arched windows with a Star of David design towered above the cases.

"You might find these interesting," Berlinger said to him.

They approached the displays, and Tom's eyes began to search inside.

"Out the windows. Look," the rabbi whispered.

Then the old man released his grip and turned back toward Alle.

"Come, my dear," Berlinger said. "I want to show you something in the next room."

Tom watched as they disappeared through an archway.

He turned to the window but discovered the glass in each was opaque. Only through small, transparent pockets here and there in the design could he see outside.

The view was of the cemetery, the tombstones, blooming trees, and emerging grass. All quiet except for movement on the far side. Near the wall. Two people. A woman.

And Zachariah Simon.

A touch to his shoulder startled him.

He whirled.

Berlinger stood a foot away.

"Would you like to hear what they are saying?"

ZACHARIAH STARED AT THE AMBASSADOR. TIME TO find out what was really going on. "No more games. What are you doing here in Prague? And do not tell me you came to simply talk."

"I would say it was good I came. You discovered that I truly do understand you." She paused. "And that I know what you are planning."

That was true.

"But you are right," she said. "I came to tell you that the Americans are more intent on stopping you than I realized. They have been watching you for nearly a decade. Were you aware of that?"

He shook his head.

"It is true. I have been able to divert them for a while, but eventually they will be back on your trail."

"And when will they discover that you are not their friend?"

She smiled. "After I become prime minister, when they will have no choice but to work with me. Hopefully, by then you will have changed the world."

What a thought.

"I wanted you to know this information," she said. "You have to be careful, Zachariah. Extremely careful. I can protect you only so far."

He caught the warning in her voice. "I am always careful."

"One can never be too careful."

He caught the smile on her lips.

He'd already plugged the leak within his inner circle. But he wondered. Had Béne Rowe sold him out to the United States? He'd been told Brian Jamison worked for Rowe. Twice, in Jamaica, Rowe had made Jamison available, touting his abilities. Rowe either was a party to the American lie or had been duped himself.

"And what of Thomas Sagan," she asked. "Is he proving helpful or a problem?"

This woman was informed.

"He has proven to be a problem."

"I assume you know he is a journalist who once covered the Middle East. I remember reading his stories. He was regarded as one of the best in the region. Not a favorite, though, of those in positions of power. He took both sides to task."

"How do you know so much about Sagan?"

"Because, Zachariah, I know who destroyed him eight years ago."

"Destroyed?"

She nodded. "See, there are things that you do not know. The supposedly fabricated story that brought about Sagan's downfall? I read it yesterday for the first time. It dealt with Israeli and Palestinian extremists. Explosive information, detrimental to both sides. And all false. Sagan was set up. The sources he quoted were actors, the information fed to him, all designed to end his career. Like the subject of the story itself, a bit extreme, but the tactic worked."

"There are people with that capability?"

"Certainly. Their services are for sale and they are not ideologues. They work for any and all sides."

Unlike himself.

"Do what you have to with Sagan," she said. "Handle the problem. I am on my way back to Israel. I came here to meet with you one last time. You and I shall never speak again. You know that once you have accomplished your objective, you cannot be a part of what happens after. You are David to my Solomon."

From Chronicles. King David had wanted to honor the Lord with a permanent monument to take the place of a roving tabernacle. He possessed ample slaves from his many war victories, along with gold and silver, and planned to build the greatest temple then known. But God told him that he'd spent his life in violence. He was a man of blood. So the privilege of erecting the temple would pass to his son, Solomon.

"You are a man of blood," she said to him.

He considered that a compliment. "Which is necessary."

"As it was to David. So finish this last battle, start your war, and allow Israel to reap the reward."

———

TOM STARED AT THE MONITOR. BERLINGER STOOD beside him. They'd descended to the basement of the ceremonial hall. What had once been a mortuary was now some sort of security center. A bank of eight LCD screens hung from one wall, fed by cameras located throughout the Jewish quarter. Berlinger had explained that this was where they kept an eye on things. He saw that the Old-New Synagogue was monitored in two views. Easy to see how his presence had been so quickly detected.

I know who destroyed him.

That's what the woman had said.

No one else occupied the windowless room. Berlinger had excused the man on duty when they'd entered. Alle had been taken to the Old-New Synagogue for prayers.

"She went willingly," the rabbi said. "Though I gave her little choice. I thought it better that only you see this."

He wanted to flee the building and confront the woman. She was the first person, other than the man in Barnes & Noble, who'd ever uttered those words.

He stared at Berlinger.

Who clearly knew more than he was saying.

"You believe me, don't you?" he said. "You know who I am."

The rabbi nodded. "That is right. You are indeed the Levite. But you are in grave danger."

CHAPTER FIFTY-EIGHT

BÉNE FOLLOWED FRANK CLARKE AS THEY NEGOTI-
ated the ever-tightening tunnel. Thankfully, he'd
never been claustrophobic. He actually felt comfortable within closed spaces, away from a world that
demanded he act like one person, but be another. Nobody watched him here. Or judged him. He was just
himself.

"You told me the Tainos cared nothing for gold,"
he said. "So why have a mine?"

"I said that they didn't *value* gold. For them, it was
decoration. So when the Spanish asked about the
mine, it meant little to reveal its location. It was much
later that this place became special."

Frank kept walking, the dry, rocky floor brittle beneath their wet boots. Luckily the route was a straight
line with no offshoots. No evidence of bats or any
other creature could be seen or smelled, the unique
entrance ensuring that the cave stayed pristine.

He spotted something ahead, just beyond the reach
of Clarke's light.

They came closer and stopped.

A grille of stalactites barred the passage, the rock
thick and black, like metal.

"The iron grille?" he asked.

Frank nodded. "A little fact creeps into every legend."

He recalled what else he'd been told. "And men have died getting this far?"

"That they have."

"What killed them?"

"Curiosity."

They wedged their way between the rock. Another tunnel stretched on the opposite side. He heard a rush of water and they found a swift moving underground stream. His light revealed a blue-green tint to the surging flow.

"We have to jump," Frank said.

Not more than two meters, which they both easily negotiated. On the other side the tunnel ended at a spacious chamber formed from two massive slabs, one the roof, the other the floor. The walls were brick-shaped stones, their surface worked smooth, their rise about five meters. Carvings and pictographs dotted the whitish surfaces.

Too many to count.

"It's amazing," Frank said. "The Tainos knew nothing of metal smelting. All of their tools were stone, bone, or wood. Yet they were able to create this."

Béne noticed another level that extended out from the far wall, up maybe two meters. He shone his light and spotted more ancient art.

Then he saw the bones, all shapes and sizes, scattered on the floor against the far wall. And what looked like a canoe.

"The Tainos came here to escape the Spanish. Instead of being slaves they waited here, in the dark, to die. That's what makes this place so special." Frank stepped to a rocky ledge that extended from the wall like a half table. Two lamps were there and Béne watched as both were lit. "Burns castor oil. Odorless. Which is good here. The Tainos knew of it, too.

They were much smarter than the Spanish ever thought."

The mention of castor oil made him think of his mother, and how she'd make him swallow the black, smelly, evil-tasting liquid every year, just before he returned to school. A purging ritual that most Jamaican schoolchildren endured, one he came to despise. He knew that the Tainos and Maroons used the oil to ease pain and swelling, but the only use he'd ever found for the stuff was as a lubricant for tractors.

Their lamps revealed the chamber in all its glory.

"This is where Columbus came," Frank said, "after he murdered the six warriors. Why he killed them, no one knows. He left the island after that and never returned. But hundreds of other Spaniards did come. Eventually, they enslaved and slaughtered the Tainos." Clarke pointed upward. "On the second level, there, in offshoots, are gold veins. The ore is still there."

"And you've done nothing with it?"

"This place is more sacred than gold."

He remembered what Tre had told him. "And the Jews? Did they store their wealth here, too?"

Two men appeared from the portal leading out.

Both wet, dressed only in swim trunks.

Béne's heart thumped with a pang of fear that he quickly quelled with anger.

"I'm sorry," Frank said in a cold, calculating monotone. "The colonels overruled me. These men are from a group in Spanish Town. Yesterday they came and asked if anyone had heard or seen anything in the mountains the past few days. They say their don is missing and you were the last one to meet with him."

"Why didn't they come and ask me?"

"'Cause we knows the answer," one of the black forms said. "*Da posses seh* you to pay."

He wasn't interested in what some gang had decreed. He was more concerned with Frank Clarke's betrayal.

"*Mi nuh like di vides, man,*" he said to his friend in patois.

He meant it, too. Lots of bad vibes here.

Frank stared at him. "*Mi nuh like, either. But dis your worry, Béne.*"

The colonel turned to leave.

"*If yu a deestant smadi, mi wi gi yu a cotch.*"

He knew Clarke understood him. "If you were a decent man, you'd stay a little while."

"That's the thing, Béne. I don't feel so decent."

And Clarke left through the portal.

"*I wuk o soon done,*" one of the men said to him. "*We gon kill you.*"

No more patois. He'd used it to disarm these two. "I'm going to give you a chance to leave here and we'll forget this happened. That way you'll stay alive. If you don't, I'm going to kill you both."

One of them laughed. "*You nut dat good, Béne. A no lie. You gon die.*"

He'd not had a fight in a long while, but that did not mean he'd forgotten how. He grew up in Spanish Town among some of the roughest gangs in the Caribbean and learned early on that to be a Rowe meant to be tough. Challenges came from all quarters, each pretender wanting to be the one who took Béne Rowe down. None had ever succeeded.

The two men flanked him. Neither was armed. Apparently they intended to kill him with their bare hands.

He almost smiled.

Apparently, the idea had been to lure him here using Frank Clarke. He wondered how much the gang had paid for that service, since little in Jamaica was free.

He studied the men. Both were tall and broad. Surely

strong. But he wondered how tested they were. British redcoats had been the best-trained, best-equipped soldiers in the world. But a group of runaway slaves with little more than spears, knifes, and a few muskets brought them to their knees.

This was his world.

His time.

And nobody was going to take that from him.

He pivoted, grabbed the nearest lantern by its handle, and hurled it at the man to his left. The projectile was deflected with a bat to the ground. It only broke the glass receptacle and spread the oil, which burst into flames, the fireball driving the one man back. He seized the moment to yank his trouser leg up and free the blade from its sheath.

A diving knife, used when he snorkeled. He kept the thick blade sharp, one edge serrated.

As the one man rounded the flames, he advanced on the other, faking right, then thrusting left, grabbing the man's arm and whirling the body around. As he did the hand with the knife rushed up and, with one swipe, he opened the throat.

He shoved the man aside.

He heard the gurgle of breath and saw blood spurt out. The man reached for the wound, but there was nothing he could do. The body dropped to the ground, twitching in agony.

The other man pounced, but Béne was ready.

The knife swished upward again and a second throat was slit.

Shock filled his assailant's eyes.

He watched as death immediately grabbed hold and the body collapsed.

Enough of this.

Frank Clarke was now his concern.

Movement in the darkness beyond the exit caught

his gaze. He leaped to one side of the portal, knife ready. Reinforcements?

Someone entered the chamber.

A man.

He lunged and slammed the body to the rock wall, bringing the knife up, its leading edge pressed to flesh, ready to cut.

Tre Halliburton stared at him, eyes wide with terror.

He exhaled and relaxed his grip. "I told you to stay outside."

Tre aimed a finger at the doorway. "He told me to come."

Béne's gaze darted to the man who stood there.

Frank Clarke.

CHAPTER FIFTY-NINE

TOM'S PATIENCE HAD RUN OUT. "EXPLAIN YOURSELF, old man. And fast."

"Is what that woman said about you true?"

He nodded. "I was set up. Taken down."

"Your daughter does not know?"

"It wouldn't matter to her. My mistakes there were my own. And as you've seen, probably irreversible."

"I had a son like that, too."

He caught the past tense.

"He died before I had the chance to make amends. I've always regretted that."

Not his concern. What mattered was the woman. Barely a hundred yards away. Who could clear his name. His gaze darted to the monitor.

"You can't do it," Berlinger said, seemingly reading his mind.

"The hell I can't."

"If you confront them, the quest will end."

"What makes you so sure?"

"Because it can't continue without my assistance. I won't give that if you leave this room."

"I don't give a damn about this quest. My life was destroyed. Everything I worked for was taken from me. I was about to blow my brains out a few days ago because of that. I want my reputation back."

"It's not that simple. You are the grandson of Marc Eden Cross. He knew this day would come. He told me many times to be ready. You have to fulfill what he started."

"For what?"

"For us."

He knew what he meant.

"I'm not a Jew any longer."

"If that were the case, then why did you come to Prague? You climbed to the synagogue's loft, just as your grandfather did. You know, in your heart, that you have to do this. You're the only one who can."

"Do what?"

"Find the Temple treasure. Give it back to all of us."

But in his mind he heard the words the woman on the screen had said. *"So finish this last battle, start your war, and allow Israel to reap the reward."* "What *is* Simon going to do?"

"I don't know, but it's clear that it will not be good."

"Go to the authorities."

"And tell them what? There's a treasure? Lost for two thousand years? Zachariah Simon wants it?" Berlinger shook his head. "No one would listen."

He pointed to the screens. "You have a video."

"No, I don't. Nothing was recorded."

"Why not?"

"This is not about involving the authorities. This is about you. Only the Levite can complete this journey. I will tell what I know only to the Levite. I promised Marc that would be my duty, and I will not violate that pledge."

"Then tell me what it is and I'll go to the authorities."

"If what that woman said is true, about you being ruined, who would believe you? You have no proof."

He was right. If the woman and Simon were in a conspiracy, neither was going to admit it. He'd have no source, no information, no corroboration. Nothing. Just like eight years ago.

Simon and the woman were now leaving the cemetery.

This may be his only chance.

The hell with it.

He rushed from the room.

———

ALLE FINISHED HER PRAYERS.

She'd been escorted by an older woman the rabbi had brought to her. Clearly, Berlinger had wanted to speak to her father outside her presence. If she was going to have any chance of learning anything, she would have to give them some slack. Already she'd been able to read her grandfather's complete message. But she'd pressed her father hard in front of Berlinger.

Maybe too hard.

And Jamaica.

That locale seemed important.

Why else include a fifty-plus-year-old road map?

The Old-New Synagogue was about to open for the day, the vestibule busy with attendants preparing themselves. She stood in the main hall, drawn to a set of seats that abutted the east wall, right of the tabernacle. One was adorned with a raised back, higher than the others, topped by a Star of David.

"The chief rabbi's place," the older woman told her.

But a chain barred anyone from sitting.

"It has long been reserved only for Rabbi Loew. No one else sits there. He was a man greatly respected and we honor him by preserving his seat."

"How long has he been gone?"

"Four hundred years."

"And no one has sat there?"

"Only during the war. The Nazis learned of our honor. So they all sat in the seat. As many as could be. Their way of providing an insult. Of course, that was before they started killing us."

She did not know what to say.

"My parents died during the war," the woman said. "Shot by Germans not far from here."

She wondered if this woman was Berlinger's way of sending her a message. She'd resented being shuttled away. Treated as a child.

"I'm sorry for your loss," she said. "I'm going back to the ceremonial hall."

"The rabbi asked us to stay here until he sent for us."

"No, that's not right. I'm sure he asked you to *keep* me here until he sent for us. I'm going back."

She headed for the vestibule.

The older woman nipped her heels.

"Please, my dear, stay."

She stopped and turned back, wondering at the urgency. So she decided to make clear, "This does not concern you."

And she left.

———

ZACHARIAH WALKED WITH THE AMBASSADOR BACK toward the same iron gate where he'd entered, adjacent to the ceremonial hall. He noticed that the mayor was gone and that a group of visitors had finally entered the cemetery from the opposite end.

"They come here from all over the world," the ambassador said. "This is as close to Israel as many of them will ever get."

"But it is not Israel."

"Few understand the pressures faced in the Holy Land," she said. "Unless you live there every day and know the fear that comes from being surrounded by enemies, how could you? We fought that fear for thousands of years. Now the people may have finally succumbed to it. You and I know what a mistake that is."

"My father tried to warn them decades ago. We gave away too much then, and received too little in return."

"Jerusalem has been invaded more than any other city on earth. Egypt, Assyria, Babylon, Syria, Greece, Rome, Persia, Muslims, Crusaders, Turks, the British, Palestinians, and now, finally, the Jews. I don't plan to give it back."

"I shall parade the treasures to the mount without warning," he said. "The more public the display, the better. To make that happen, I may need some of your help."

He knew what would happen. Jews would see the return of their treasures as a sign. The menorah, the divine table, and the silver trumpets had returned. Thousands would come. In the past large crowds had been routinely turned away. But this was different. Muslims, too, would see a sign. The presence of the Jewish treasures would be taken as a challenge to their presence, something they had defended for centuries with violence and blood.

This time would be no different.

Or so he hoped.

"I am afraid not, Zachariah," she said. "For that you are on your own. As I said, you and I will not speak again."

No matter.

Until yesterday, he'd planned on accomplishing his goal without any help.

He'd stick to that plan.

They stood before the ceremonial hall, part of which jutted into the cemetery grounds, shaded by ash trees. More people were entering from the far side, admiring the graves, some offering stones to markers in remembrance. They all wore yarmulkes, which he knew were given to them with their admission tickets.

"Our heads should be covered, too," he said.

"Not to worry, Zachariah. The dead will forgive us."

———————

TOM LEFT THE SECURITY ROOM AND FOUND A DOOR that led outside.

But it was locked, no way to open it without a key.

He rushed to the interior stairway and leaped the short risers two at a time up to the first floor where visitors were entering the exhibits, showing their tickets to one of the female attendants.

This was too much.

Here he was in the Czech Republic, eight years after the fact, about to be confronted with someone who knew the truth.

He told himself to calm down. Think. Be rational.

Calmly, he left the stairs and excused himself past the visitors and out the door to the exterior staircase. The landing was enclosed on three sides, periodic openings offering views down to the cemetery. Through one of those he spied Simon and the woman, standing on a graveled path among the graves, talking. He watched them from the safety of his perch, no way for them to see him. To his left the stairway right-angled to ground level, the view open to a street that led down a short incline, past the vendor stalls, to the Old-New Synagogue.

He spotted Alle.

Fifty yards away.

Marching toward the hall.

———

ALLE IGNORED THE VENDOR STALLS TO HER LEFT, busy with tourists, and concentrated on the iron gate fifty yards away. More people were negotiating the exterior staircase for the ceremonial hall, heading up to the exhibits on the first and second floors, where she had been an hour ago.

Berlinger's rebuke still stung.

As did her grandfather's.

In the final years of his life she'd been there for him, pleasing him beyond measure with her conversion. He'd never thought his grandchild would practice his faith. He'd resigned himself to the fact that since his son had abandoned the religion, all would be abandoned.

"But you, my dear, are so special. You chose on your own to become what your birthright entitled you to be. It must be God's will."

They'd many times talked of life and the Jews, in the abstract, him responding to her questions.

"I may not agree with your mother's beliefs," he told her. *"But I respect them. As much as I wanted my son to be a Jew I understand how she would want you to be a Christian. So I would never violate that."*

And he never had.

But in the end, he still hadn't thought her worthy.

Or at least her new religion had not.

The Levite must be male and I failed to find anyone capable. So I took the secret entrusted to the grave.

She kept walking up the street, stepping around several tour groups. *She* was worthy. *She* could be the Levite. And do a better job than her father, who seemed not to care about anyone or anything. And where was he? Still inside the ceremonial hall? Her gaze focused ahead and she spotted two people beyond the iron gate, up another inclined path.

A man and a woman.

One was a stranger.

The other was Zachariah.

Here?

———

ZACHARIAH SPOTTED ALLE.

Too late for a retreat.

She'd clearly seen him.

"Time to deal with her," the ambassador said.

And he watched as the woman walked away, back toward the cemetery's main entrance.

He headed for the iron gate and the exit.

———

TOM WATCHED AS SIMON LEFT THE CEMETERY GROUNDS, walking down the street toward Alle.

The woman.

That's who he wanted.

From his vantage point he saw her follow a path through the graves, going against the grain of tourists entering in a steady pace.

He turned back toward Alle. Simon approached her, grasped her arm, and they headed away from the ceremonial hall, on the street that led back toward the house where they'd been held.

More visitors were climbing the stairs around him.

He quickly descended and rushed toward a glass-enclosed placard that detailed the quarter. He located the cemetery and saw that the entrance point was a block over.

Where the woman was headed.

A quick glance and he saw Alle and Simon, their backs to him, still moving away.

If he hurried, he could catch his one chance to right the wrong.

CHAPTER SIXTY

BÉNE RAISED THE BLOODIED KNIFE TO FRANK CLARKE. "I should slit your lying throat, too."

"Don't you find it odd, Béne, how you so detest lying, but don't mind doing it to your own mother?"

Not what he expected Frank to say.

"And the point?"

"Only that you did exactly what I knew you'd do."

Not a hint of fear laced Clarke's words. In the light from the remaining lamp and the glow of the dimming fire from the broken one, he saw no concern in the hard eyes.

"The gang came," Frank said, "offered money, and some of the colonels took it. When you called earlier and told me that you had found the mine, I had to report that information."

"No, you didn't."

"I'm Maroon, Béne. I take my oath of allegiance to my brothers in a serious way. Is their don dead?"

"He's scum. My dogs hunted him down."

"You killed both of them?" Tre asked, pointing at the bleeding bodies.

He raised the knife. "They got what they deserved, too." He turned to Frank. "And why shouldn't I kill you?"

"This had to happen. You know that, Béne."

The voice never rose above a whisper.

"And what will the colonels say when I emerge from this cave?"

"That you're a man to be feared."

He liked that. "And there will be debts to be paid. By them."

And he meant it.

"Why did you come back?" he asked Clarke.

"You need to see why this place was special to the Spanish." Frank pointed to the upper portion of the chamber. "We have to climb up there."

"Lead the way."

He was going to keep this man in his sights and he wasn't about to discard the knife. Halliburton was still shaken by the corpses.

"Forget them," he told Tre.

"It's not easy."

"Welcome to my world."

He motioned for them to follow Frank up rough boulders that acted as a makeshift stairway to the next level. There he spotted three exits from the chamber, each a dark yawn in the rock wall.

"Which one?" Béne asked Clarke.

"You choose."

He assumed it was some sort of test, but he was not in the mood. "You do it. We'll get there faster."

"You tell me all the time that you're Maroon. That you're part of us. Time to start acting like one."

He resented the implications.

"They call you B'rer Anansi," Frank said to him.

"Who does?"

He hated the mythical reference. Anansi was often depicted as a short, small man or, worse, a spider with human qualities whose most notable characteristic was greed. He survived by cunning and a glibness of speech. Béne's mother used to tell him how the slaves told tales of Anansi.

"I don't think they mean to insult you," Frank said. "It's just their way of describing you. Anansi, for all his faults, is loved. We've told his stories ever since being brought here."

He wasn't interested in what others thought. Not anymore. He was here, finally, in the lost mine. "Which tunnel?"

"I know," Tre said.

He faced his friend.

"I read in the journal we found in Cuba, the one from Luis de Torres, how this place was chosen as the *cripta.*"

"A vault?"

Tre nodded. "A hiding place. Columbus himself came, inspected, and chose it. They hid something away here. Something of great value, or at least that's what de Torres wrote."

"Like crates of gold from Panama?" he asked.

Tre shook his head. "I don't know. He talked of this mine and three paths. He wrote that to know where to go is to know where you are from. Then he rattled off a list of things. *'The number of vessels for the altar of burnt offerings, the altar of incense, and the Ark. The number of sections for the blessing. The number of times the word holy is repeated in the invocation of God. And the percent the Holy of Holies occupied in the First and Second Temples, per God's command.'"*

None of which meant anything to him.

"You have to be Jewish to know the answers," Tre said. "I looked them up. There were three vessels for each altar. Three times the word *holy* is repeated. And one-third, 33 percent, is the amount of space the Holy of Holies occupied. That was the Jews' most sacred spot in the world." Tre pointed to the third opening. "That's the way."

Clarke nodded.

"What's down there?" Béne asked.

"Something that is not Maroon or Taino." Frank approached the doorway and shone his light inside. "Maroons discovered this cave long after the last Taino died. We respected them. So we protected this."

Béne wondered who Clarke was speaking to. Him? Or the ancestors? If duppies did in fact exist, this would be their home.

Frank led the way into the cavern, its walls the same coarse stone. He wondered about gold veins since he'd seen little evidence of any mining. He asked Clarke about them.

"In the other tunnels there are offshoots that lead to crevices. In some the Tainos found gold. Not much ore, but enough to attract the Spanish."

The duct meandered in a straight line, the air becoming progressively more stale. Béne felt light-headed. "Why is it hard to breathe?"

"That sound you heard when we entered from the pool, like the earth sucking lungfuls of air, then exhaling? It creates a suction. More bad air here than good, which was why the Tainos chose this place to die."

Not comforting, and he saw Tre was likewise concerned. But with his eyes he said to his friend, *You chose to come.* And he could understand why. For an academician this was the ultimate experience—a chance to see firsthand something history could only talk about.

His head began to hurt.

But he said nothing.

"The Tainos knew religion," Frank said, "in every way the Spanish did. They just didn't think themselves superior to everyone. They respected their world and one another. Their mistake was thinking white men felt the same way."

They'd walked maybe fifty meters, as best he could estimate. And they'd risen slightly. Their three lights revealed only a few meters ahead, the darkness around them absolute. No moisture anywhere, which was unusual for Jamaica's caves, which were generally saturated from underground lakes and rivers.

Then he saw something.

In the first wash of Frank's light.

Ten meters before them.

A wooden door, the planks warped and misshapen, blackened from time. No hinges lined any side. Instead the rectangle simply fit into an opening carved from the stone. Chunks of rock and boulders lay scattered on the tunnel floor, nearly blocking the way.

Béne stepped forward, intent on climbing over the debris and seeing what was there.

Frank grabbed his sweaty arm. "You sure you want to go in there?"

"Try and stop me."

CHAPTER SIXTY-ONE

"WHAT ARE YOU DOING HERE?" ALLE ASKED ZACHA-riah. "I thought you wanted me to handle this."

Her anger toward Berlinger and her father was now spilling over. Did anyone think her capable of anything?

"I am here because it is necessary. I've learned more about the Americans. They are definitely trying to stop us."

"Why would they care about finding Jewish religious objects?"

They stopped walking, not far from the house where she and her father had been taken. The street here was not as crowded with visitors.

"Alle, American foreign policy has long included active intervention in everything associated with Israel. They provide billions in aid and military support, and think that entitles them to tell us what to do. Our current situation is directly their fault. I am assuming that obtaining our Temple treasures works into their plans in some way."

She would ordinarily think him paranoid, but Brian Jamison had been real.

"Who was the woman you were talking to?"

"Someone providing me information on the Americans. What have you learned?"

"That my grandfather told my father a lot more than we thought."

She told him what the message from the grave actually said, as best she could remember. "Berlinger and my father are in the ceremonial hall."

She pointed to the building fifty yards away, around a slight bend in the street.

"How long have they been in there?"

"An hour."

"I was in the cemetery, behind the hall. Was there any mention of seeing me?"

She shook her head. "They told me little. I was dismissed to the synagogue for prayers."

She heard a hum and watched as Zachariah found a cell phone in his pocket.

"It is Rócha."

He answered, listened for a moment, then said, "Keep me posted."

He ended the call.

"Your father is on the move."

———

TOM TROTTED DOWN THE STREET TOWARD THE OLD-New Synagogue. From the map on the placard he knew he had to round the block, circling the cemetery's outer wall and an array of buildings. The woman he sought was exiting from the entrance to the cemetery and, if he hurried, he could catch her.

He'd slipped away from the ceremonial hall without Simon or Alle seeing him. They'd disappeared around a bend in the street that led away from him. He was moving as fast as he could without drawing attention. At the end of the street, he turned right and passed more souvenir shops. Sidewalks here were less congested, so he ran.

Who was this woman? How could she possibly know what had happened to him? At first, he'd tried to tell people that he'd been manipulated. But the effort had been futile. He was saying exactly what they expected to hear and, without proof, he sounded even more guilty.

Which had surely been the idea.

That was when he disappeared, went silent, stopped defending himself. Newspapers and television shows across the country filleted him. His silence only added to their furor, but he came to discover it had been the right response.

Especially after that visit in Barnes & Noble.

He kept moving, turning another corner, now headed back parallel to the cemetery wall up an inclined street toward the Pinkas Synagogue, which sat at the cemetery entrance. Buses lined the curb, people streaming toward a concrete ramp that led down to the original street level. Signs indicated the cemetery's entrance was there.

He spotted the woman.

Coming up the incline, against the wave of visitors, making her way to the sidewalk.

He slowed his pace.

Stay calm.

Don't blow this.

She turned away from him and walked up the sidewalk, paralleling a wrought-iron fence that guarded the synagogue. The street to his left was one-way, but a busy boulevard could be seen at its end, past the synagogue, maybe a hundred feet away.

Then he saw the car.

A black Mercedes coupe, parked at the curb, engine running, wisps of exhaust evaporating from its tailpipe.

He quickened his steps.

The woman approached the car.

A man emerged from the passenger's side—young, short-haired, dark suit—who opened the rear door.

The woman was ten feet away from entering.

"Stop," he called out.

And he ran the last thirty feet toward her. Dark Suit spotted him, and he saw the man reach beneath his jacket.

The woman whirled.

Tom came close, then stopped.

Dark Suit advanced toward him, but the woman grabbed her protector's arm.

"No need," she said. "I've been expecting him."

ZACHARIAH DECIDED TO PLACE SOME DISTANCE BE-tween him and Alle and the ceremonial hall. He was unsure where Tom Sagan had gone, and the last thing he needed was to be spotted. He wondered if Sagan had seen him in the cemetery. Alle had finally provided him with some useful information, telling him more of what Sagan had learned from his father. Rabbi Berlinger now seemed a player in this game.

His mind reeled, processing all the new information.

At least he now knew.

This place, long held sacred by Jews around the world, was a part of the quest. But how? And Jamaica seemed an important locale, too. The curator from the museum in Cuba had called to say that Rowe and his companion had fled before the police arrived, no way to stop them.

"He said you and he will talk soon."

That would not be a friendly conversation. He'd thought himself through with Rowe. But that might not be the case. Abiram Sagan had included a road map of Jamaica for a reason.

His phone vibrated.

He found the unit and saw it was Rócha.

"Where are you?" he asked, answering.

"Sagan left the hall and ran around the block. He's confronting some woman at the moment who has a bodyguard."

"Describe her."

He already knew who, but he had to be sure.

Which answered another question. Sagan had seen him. And maybe even heard, considering the bombshell she revealed about the ex-journalist.

"I had to be careful so he wouldn't spot me," Rócha said. "But I'm where I can see them now."

"Let me know what happens."

He ended the call.

"What is it?" Alle asked.

He'd not masked his concern.

"A problem."

———

TOM STARED AT THE WOMAN AND ASKED, "WHO ARE you?"

"That's unimportant."

"Like hell. You know what happened to me."

She turned to Dark Suit. "Wait in the car."

The man climbed back into the passenger's side. She shut the rear door.

"You said you were expecting me. How," he asked, a plea in his voice.

"You heard me in the cemetery?"

He nodded.

"The rabbi said he would make sure you did."

"Berlinger is in on this?"

"Just offering some assistance."

"Who are you," he asked again.

"I am a Jew who believes strongly in who we are. I want you to believe, too."

He could not care less about that. "They stole my life. I deserve to know who did that and why."

"It was done because you did your job. You know that. They sent an emissary to tell you."

This woman knew everything.

He stepped closer.

"I wouldn't do that," she said, motioning to the car. "He's watching you through the mirror."

His gaze darted past her and he saw the man's watchful face in the exterior mirror. He stared back at her. "You're working with Simon?"

"Mr. Sagan, at present, you are in no position to barter. But you could be. As I said, I am someone who has great respect for our beliefs. You are the Levite. The chosen successor. The only one who can find our Temple treasure."

All of which Simon would have known.

"I don't care about any of that. I want my life back."

She opened the car's rear door and climbed inside. Before closing it, she looked out and said, "Find the treasure. Then we will talk about your life."

She closed the door.

And the car sped away.

CHAPTER SIXTY-TWO

BÉNE AVOIDED THE DEBRIS, CLIMBING ACROSS THE boulders and finding the wooden slab. He aimed his light past the doorway into another chamber, this one smaller than the previous. No smooth walls. No art. Just a harsh cavity in the rock that extended about twenty meters back and half that tall. He stepped inside. Frank and Tre followed him.

Their lights dissolved the darkness.

He spotted what appeared to be an altar of some sort, fashioned of rock and situated against one wall. Nothing rested on top. To its right was a low rectangle of rough stone, maybe half a meter high and two meters long. A taller slab projected upward at one end.

"It looks like a grave," Tre said.

They walked closer, loose gravel crunching beneath their feet. Their lights brought the scene into clear focus. Béne now saw that the end slab was a tombstone. He recognized the two letters atop the marker.

פ נ

"Here lies," he said. "It's Hebrew. I've seen this on a lot of other graves."

All of the remaining writing was likewise in Hebrew.

Tre bent down and examined it closely.

"What is a Jewish grave doing here?" Béne asked Clarke.

"I wondered that, too," Frank said. "So a few years ago I photographed the marker and had the words translated. It says, '*Christoval Arnoldo de Ysassi, Pursuer of Dreams, Speaker of Truth in His Heart, Honored Man, May His Soul Be Bound Up in the Bond of Everlasting Life.*'"

Tre stood. "It's the grave of Christopher Columbus. De Torres wrote that Columbus' real name was Christoval Arnoldo de Ysassi. This is where he's buried."

Béne recalled what Tre had told him on the plane about Columbus' grave. "You said yesterday that the widow of Columbus' son brought the body to the New World."

"She did. First to Santiago, then the remains were moved to Cuba. There's a lot of controversy over who is buried in Santiago now, or whether the bones are in Cuba or Spain. Now we know that she brought them here, to the island the family controlled. Which makes the most sense."

"I've always wondered who this is," Clarke said. "We had no idea who the man might be. We knew him to be Hebrew, but that's all. So we left the grave alone. If others knew this was Columbus, they would have destroyed it."

"Damn right," Béne said. "He was a thief and murderer."

"This is an important historical find," Tre said. "It's never been proven where Columbus is buried. Nobody knew. Now we do."

"Who cares?" Béne said. "Let him rot here." He turned to Frank. "Is this all?"

"Look around. What else do you see?"

He scanned the chamber with his light.

And saw niches carved into the far wall.

He stepped over and examined the closest one with the flashlight and saw bones. Each of the others was likewise filled with a body.

"Our greatest Maroon leaders," Frank said. "That one to your left is Grandy Nanny herself. Laid to rest here in 1758."

"I thought her grave was in Moore Town, on the windward side, Portland Parish?"

"At first, then she was brought here by the Scientists." Frank pointed. "The bones you just examined are Cudjoe's."

He was shocked.

Cudjoe had been a great Maroon chief in Grandy Nanny's time, her brother, who fought the British, too. But he made a disastrous peace, one that forever changed the Maroon way of life, and began their downfall.

Even so, he was revered.

"He lived to be an old man," Béne said.

Frank came close. "Some say he was over eighty when he died."

Béne rattled off a quick count and saw fourteen niches cut into the rock.

"Johnny, Cuffee, Quaco, Apong, Clash, Thomboy. All leaders from long ago," Frank said. "Special people, laid here in this place of honor. We thought the person buried here had to be important, at least to the Jews, so we decided to make use of this place, too. That has always been the Maroon way. Little was ours, all was shared. Here, our special people could rest quietly."

Béne did not know what to say.

This was totally unexpected.

He motioned to a rum bottle in one of the niches.

"For the duppies," Frank said. "The spirits like their drink. We replenish it every once in a while so they're never without."

He knew the custom. His father's grave outside Kingston was similarly stocked.

"There's more," Frank said. "But, as with all things Maroon, it is a tale told only among a select few. Mainly Scientists, who considered this room sacred."

Béne had never cared for Maroon healers, who'd taken the odd name of Scientist. Too much mysticism for him, too few results.

"Is that why there's an altar?" he asked.

Frank nodded. "The Scientists once conducted rituals here. Private things that only they could see."

"Not anymore?" he asked.

"Not in a long while. And there's a reason for that."

"You keep a lot of secrets," he said to Frank.

"As I've told you many times, some things are better left unsaid . . . until the right moment."

"So tell me your tale."

Frank explained about a time when there were four other objects in the chamber. A golden candlestick, about a meter high, with seven branches. A table, less than a meter long and half that high, with golden crowns bordering the top and a ring at each corner. And two trumpets, made of silver, each about a meter long, inlaid with gold.

"Are you sure of those?" Tre asked.

"I never saw them myself, but I talked to others who say they did."

"Those are the most sacred objects in Judaism. They came from the Second Temple, when Jerusalem was sacked by the Romans. People have searched for those for 2,000 years. And they were here? In Jamaica?"

"They had been placed with the Hebrew grave. I was told that they were magnificent in workmanship."

"And no Maroon ever tried to sell them?" Tre asked.

Frank shook his head. "The spirits are important to us. They roam the forests and can either protect or harm. Never would we offend them by taking something from a grave. Instead, we protected those objects and made this place special."

Béne faced Tre. "What does all this mean?"

"That a lot of history books are going to be rewritten."

But Béne was more concerned with something else. "What happened to those objects?"

"The Scientists returned here one day and the treasures were gone. Only colonels and Scientists knew of this location. They concluded that the duppies took them away. After that, this place was no longer used for worship."

"When was this?" Béne asked.

"Sixty years ago."

Béne shook his head. Another dead end. "Is that it? People wanted me killed to protect this?"

"These graves are important. They are our past. And for a Maroon, the past is all we have. Even the Hebrew grave is important. It is clearly from long ago. The Jews helped us when no one else would. So we honored the Hebrew, as one of us. His treasure was also honored."

"And now it's gone."

But he wondered. Were those objects what Zachariah Simon was really after? He'd talked about finding Columbus' grave and the mine, but it made more sense that Simon would be after a treasure. Apparently this place had indeed been a gold mine, but for a different style of gold.

Which did not exist anymore.

He shook his head and headed back for the cave's exit.

Tre and Frank followed.

None of them said a word.

CHAPTER SIXTY-THREE

Tom watched as the Mercedes merged into traffic and turned the corner, disappearing. The woman, whoever the hell she was, knew everything. And his salvation depended on finding the Temple treasure. How was that possible? Why would that be possible?

A hand touched his shoulder, startling him.

He turned.

Berlinger stared back and said, "She's gone."

"Who is she?" he demanded. "She said you knew she was here."

The old man shook his head. "I did. But she did not identify herself, nor did I ask."

"But you did what she wanted. You made sure I heard what she had to say."

"I saw no harm in that."

"Rabbi, this is important to me. What the hell is going on here?"

"I have to show you something and tell you a few things. Important things."

"Where's Alle?"

"I don't know."

"Your cameras can't find her?"

"I'm sure they can. But this we have to do alone."

"You have no idea what I've gone through. No idea what happened to me."

He was exasperated.

And angry.

"Come," Berlinger said. "Walk with me and I'll tell you a story."

"My father passed this on to me," Marc Cross said to Berlinger.

He listened as his friend explained.

"The first Levite was Luis de Torres, who was given the task by Columbus. The duty has been passed for five hundred years from one to the next, and all has been fine until recently."

The Second World War had been over nearly ten years, but its remnants remained. Nobody knew, as yet, how many millions of Jews had been slaughtered. Six million was the number most widely bantered. Here, in Prague, the pogrom's effects were clear. A hundred thousand were taken, only a handful returned.

"It's our Temple treasures," Marc said. "The sacred objects. That's the secret we hold. Columbus took them to the New World. His voyage was financed by Jews of the Spanish court. Ferdinand and Isabella were useless. They lacked either the vision or the money to explore. Columbus possessed the vision, and the Sephardi Jews of Spain provided the money. Of course, they'd all been forced to convert in order to stay in Spain, and Columbus too was a converso."

He'd never heard such a thing. "Columbus was a Jew?"

Marc nodded. "And remained one all of his life. He sailed to the New World hoping that he would find a place where we could live in peace. A prevalent theory of the time said that Jews in the Far East lived free, without persecution. He, of course, thought he was sailing to Asia. That's why he brought de Torres with him. A Hebrew translator. Someone who could speak to the people he found."

This was amazing.

"The Sephardi Jews had long protected the Temple treasure. It was brought to them in the 7th century. But in 1492, Spain became a dangerous place. All of the Jews had either been expelled or converted. The Inquisition was rooting out the faintest hint of false Christianity. To even be suspected of being Jewish meant death, and thousands were executed. So they tasked Columbus with a special mission. Take the Temple treasure with him. When he found those Asian Jews, have them protect it."

"But there were no Jews waiting for him."

Marc shook his head. "And when he finally realized that, at the end of his fourth voyage, he hid the treasure in his New World. Luis de Torres was there and assumed the duty of guardian, calling himself the Levite. I am his successor."

"You know where our precious objects rest?"

"That I do. To reveal this to anyone is a violation of my duty, but what happened during the war changes things. I need your help, good friend. This is something I cannot do alone. You are the most honest man I know."

He smiled at the compliment. "I would say the same about you."

Marc reached out and grasped his shoulder. "When I first came here and climbed to the loft, and you followed, I knew then that you were a man I could trust. The world has changed and this duty that I have been given must change, too."

"He told me where the treasure was located," Berlinger said to Tom. "We were standing not far from where you and I are right now, though these streets looked much different in 1954."

Tom imagined that was true. The Nazis would have left a mark, then the Soviets made it worse.

"Our synagogues were in ruins," the rabbi said. "The Germans had gutted the interiors, using the buildings for storage. Nothing had been repaired. The Soviets hated us as much as the Germans did, and they killed us, too. Only slower, over a longer period of time."

They stood at a street corner, down from the town hall, everything busy with morning activity. Most were tour groups, here for the day.

"They come from all over," Berlinger said. "I've often wondered, what do they take away from the experience?"

"That to be Jewish is dangerous."

"It can be. But I would be nothing else. Your daughter said you are no longer one of us. Is that true?"

"I renounced twenty years ago and was baptized Christian. My way of pleasing a new wife."

Berlinger lightly pounded his chest. "But in here, what are you?"

"Nothing. Nothing at all."

And he meant it.

"Then why are you in Prague?"

"I came because I thought my daughter was in trouble. I've since discovered that is not the case. She's a liar. Naïve, as hell, but still a liar. She doesn't need my help."

"I think she does. Zachariah Simon is dangerous."

"How did you know the connection?"

"They are together, right now. I watched as you left the hall. I watched her, too. I've never cared for Simon."

He could see that this 102-year-old man had lost

none of his edge. "What did you do for my grand-father?"

Berlinger smiled. "Now, that's a story I will never forget."

"It's in Jamaica," Marc told him. "That's where Columbus hid the treasure. In a mine the natives showed him. He blocked its entrance, left the island and the New World, and never returned. He was dead two years later."

"Have you seen our treasures?" Berlinger asked.

"I've touched them. Held them. Hauled them from one location to another. I changed the place. It had to be done. De Torres left coded instructions on how to find the mine. They are impossible to now decipher. Every landmark that existed in his time is gone. So I've changed those instructions."

"How did you move them? Are not the menorah, the divine table, and the trumpets heavy?"

"They are, but I had some help. My wife and a few others, more good men I can trust. We floated them out of the cave where they rested, down a river to another cave. There I found my own golem to help protect our treasures. A remarkable creature. I know you think that golems are not real. But I tell you, they are."

He sensed something. A foreboding. "What is it, old friend?"

"This may be the last time you and I speak face-to-face."

He hated to hear that.

"The Cold War is heating up. Travel into Eastern Europe will become next to impossible. My duty is done. I've protected the treasure the best I can, placed it where it should be safe."

"I made the box, as you asked."

Marc had specified the size, about thirty centimeters square, modeled after the treasury containers nearly every synagogue possessed. Usually they were made of iron and held important documents, or money, or sacred utensils. This one was of silver. No decoration adorned its exterior, the emphasis on the safety the container provided to its contents rather than appearance. An internal lock sealed the lid. He found the key in his pocket and handed it over. His friend examined it.

"Lovely. The Stars of David on the end are well crafted."

"There's engraving."

He watched as Marc brought the brass close to his eyes and studied the stem.

פב X

"Po nikbar," Marc said, interpreting the two Hebrew letters. "Here lies. That it does. And you did a good job on the hooked X."

His friend had specifically requested the symbol.

"These markings will ensure this is the correct key," Marc told him. "If anyone ever appears here with this, you decide if they are worthy, then show them the box. If it never happens during your lifetime, choose someone to carry on the duty."

They stood at the base of the east wall of the Old-New Synagogue, the iron rungs above them leading up to the loft.

"I changed everything," Marc said. "But I tried to stay with the tradition. Place the box up there, in the loft, where it will be safe, among the old papers." Cross paused. "Where your golem can look after them."

He smiled, then nodded, acknowledging his duty.

"Before leaving Prague that last time," Berlinger said, "Marc placed something in the box and locked it. I stored it in the loft. Your grandfather told me nothing else. He said it was better that way. The box stayed in the loft for thirty years, until finally removed during a renovation. Luckily, I was still here to ensure its safety."

"You never looked inside?"

Berlinger shook his head. "Marc took the key with him."

Tom rubbed his tired eyes and tried to make sense of what he was hearing.

"This was once a central point in the Jewish quarter," Berlinger said, motioning to their surroundings. "Now it's just another part of Prague. Everything we built is nearly gone. Only memories remain, and most of those are too painful for any of us to recall. Your grandfather was one of the finest men I ever knew. He trusted me with a duty. It was my task to pass that duty on to someone else, and I have made a choice for when that happens."

"But now I'm here."

The rabbi nodded. "So I will pass what I know to you. I want you to know that if there had been a way for me to find the treasure, I would have. We deserve to have it back. That was the one thing Marc and I disagreed on, but I was in no position to argue with him. He was the chosen one, not me. Now the choice *is* mine. I should like to see those objects once again in a temple."

"I'll find them." He removed the key from his pocket. "Where's the box this opens?"

Berlinger pointed right.

"Not far."

CHAPTER SIXTY-FOUR

TOM WALKED WITH BERLINGER AWAY FROM THE OLD-New Synagogue following a street labeled Malselova. Shops and cafés, busy with people, huddled close to the cobbled lane. He knew what building sat just around the bend. The Maisel Synagogue, built by Mordecai Maisel in 1591. He'd visited it several times while writing his article on Prague. Maisel had been a wealthy Jew who ingratiated himself with Emperor Rudolph II, becoming a trusted adviser and eventually securing a special permit that allowed the building's construction. For over a century it was the largest and most lavish structure in the quarter. But it burned in the fires of 1689, rebuilt in the late 19th century then completely restored, he recalled, in 1995. Services were no longer conducted inside. Now it held a permanent exhibition dedicated to the history of Czech's Jews.

They entered the vestibule and Tom admired the stylish vaulting and the stained-glass windows. The towering walls were a warm shade of yellow. People milled back and forth, admiring display cases filled with silver objects. Little sound could be heard, besides their footsteps. Berlinger nodded to a woman behind the ticket counter and they were waved through.

"This was where the Nazis brought the artifacts

stolen from all the synagogues," the rabbi whispered. "They were to be displayed as part of their museum to our extinct race. Those precious objects were piled into this building and several more. I saw them myself. A terrible sight."

They wandered into the nave, beneath unusual chandeliers, their bright lights inverted, pointing downward. Above him, a second floor was visible past a balustrade that lined the nave on two sides, broken by archways that each displayed a shiny menorah.

"Those artifacts are now gone, returned from where they came. We could not find the home for some, so they stayed here. Eventually, we decided this would be the best place to exhibit our heritage. A museum not to an extinct race, but to one that is still quite alive."

He caught the pride in the old warrior's voice.

"You and your daughter," Berlinger said. "Is there any way to salvage that relationship?"

"Probably not. I had a chance, long ago, and I let it go."

"What she said about you, faking a news article. I looked into that. You were once a respected journalist."

The word *once* stung. "Still am, and that woman knows the truth."

"I know, and if you could prove that you were not a fraud?"

"Then things would change."

"I don't know any more than I told you. She was most mysterious, but also most persuasive."

"What do you know?"

"Only that with most things in life, there is more to the story."

His spine stiffened. "Why would you say that?"

"And I suspect there is but one person you care to be vindicated with."

He noticed that his question had gone ignored, so he decided to return the favor.

"During the war," Berlinger said. "I was forced to do things that no decent man should ever be forced to do. I headed the council at Terezín. We had to decide life and death every day. Thousands perished, many because of the decisions we made. Only time has brought what happened there into focus."

Memories seemed to have captured the old man's attention.

"My own son. May God rest his soul."

He stood silent.

"I have to tell you something," the rabbi said. "In the war, many were sent to camps. Before I was sent, something happened. Marc and I talked of it. May I share it with you?"

They kicked down the farmhouse door.

Berlinger stood back as two men and Erik, his fifteen-year-old son, rushed inside, dragging the house's sole occupant out into the night. Summer had brought warmth, and the man was barely dressed. He was called Yiri, a Czech whom Berlinger knew from before the war. A simple, quiet man who'd made a huge mistake.

"What do you want?" Yiri said. "Why are you here?"

He was shoved to his knees.

"I have done nothing. I work my fields. I bother no one. Why are you here? I told the Nazis nothing."

Berlinger caught the last part. "You speak to Nazis?"

They were all armed, even Erik who'd learned to handle a pistol with great skill. So far, all four had avoided detention, escaping into the forest and resist-

ing. He wished more Jews could join them, but their number was dwindling by the day.

Yiri's head shook. "No. No. I talk to no Nazis. I tell them nothing about the Jews in the forest.".

Which was why they'd come. A family had escaped Prague and managed to hide in the woods outside of town. Yiri had been supplying them with food, a good thing, what should be expected from a countryman. But when the family's money ran out, Yiri had turned them in for the reward. He wasn't alone. Others had done the same.

"Please. Please. I had no choice. They would have killed me. I had no choice. I helped that family for many weeks."

"Until they couldn't pay you anymore," one of the men spit out.

Berlinger saw the hatred in his compatriots' eyes. Even Erik's were filled with disgust. He'd never seen that in his boy before. But the war was changing them all.

"What do you want me to do? You Jews have no chance. There's nothing that can be done. You have to—"

A shot echoed in the night.

Yiri's head exploded, then his body smacked the ground.

Erik lowered his gun.

"Yashar Koyach," one of the men said, and the others joined in slapping Erik on the back.

May your strength increase.

What was said after reading from the Torah.

Now it had become a salutation for murder.

———

"WE HAD NOT COME TO KILL THE MAN," BERLINGER said. "Or at least that's what I thought. To do that would be no different than what the Germans were doing to us."

"So why did you go there?"

"To hold him accountable, yes. But not to murder him."

He considered that a bit naïve, given the circumstances.

"I was sent to Terezín shortly after that," Berlinger said. "My son escaped that fate. He became part of the resistance and fought the Germans for another year, until they finally killed him. He and I never spoke to each other after that night. He was proud of what he'd done, and I was ashamed. A division came between us, one that I regret to this day."

"And what has time taught you?"

"That I was a fool. That man deserved to die. But I had yet to witness the horror of Terezín, and all that came after. I had yet to see how barren men's souls can be. I had yet to realize how much I could come to hate."

"It's been only eight years for me and little is in focus. All I can say is that the past few days have changed everything."

"For the better?"

"That remains to be seen."

"Marc would have liked you."

"I only knew him for a short while as a boy."

"He had a spirit about him. So adventurous. He was a good Jew, though not devoutly. Maybe it was the world in which he lived. I know my own beliefs were strained to the breaking point. Or maybe it was his profession. An archaeologist studies the past almost to the exclusion of the present. Maybe that clouded his mind. Still, he was a good man who did his duty."

"As the Levite?"

Berlinger nodded. "I would have so liked to have seen our lost treasures. What sights they would have been."

"You might get that chance. Saki changed the rules of this game. That means it's okay to do that. So I'm going to change them again."

"Are you not simply going to end the game?"

He stood silent for a moment, realizing the implications. Five hundred years this secret had stayed hidden.

"That's exactly what I'm going to do."

Berlinger walked toward one of the display cases, this one containing a pair of silver candlesticks, a Kiddush cup, an elaborate silver spice box, and another rectangular container, about a foot square. No decoration adorned its silver exterior. An internal lock sealed the lid. Just as Berlinger had described.

He found the key in his pocket.

"That," the rabbi said, "opens the lock. I shall have the box removed and taken to one of the side rooms, where you can examine it in private."

The old man extended his hand and they shook.

"My duty is done," Berlinger said. "The rest I leave to you. I wish you success and will pray for your soul."

And the rabbi walked away.

CHAPTER SIXTY-FIVE

Zachariah kept Alle close, the two of them just outside the quarter at a busy restaurant called Kolkovna. He'd decided a strategic retreat was in order until he could ascertain exactly what was happening. Rócha was following Sagan and had reported that he and Berlinger had entered the Maisel Synagogue. With no choice, Rócha had entered, too, careful to stay back as Sagan knew his face. Berlinger had directed Sagan to a silver box, which had been removed from its display case and taken to another room. Berlinger was gone, but Sagan was there with the box. Rócha was still in the synagogue—Sagan behind a closed door.

"What's happening?" Alle asked him.

"I wish I knew. Your father is doing something. For a man who wanted to die, he is most active."

"For a long time, he was good at his job."

"I'm surprised to hear you say that. He was caught fabricating a story."

"I know that. I just attacked him a little while ago with that fact. But that doesn't mean that everything he did was a lie. I remember reading his stuff when I was in high school. He was on television all the time. I hated him for what he did to me and my mother, but he seemed to be a good reporter. His job actually meant everything to him. More so than his family."

"When I checked his background I learned that he was respected in the Middle East. People feared him. He left a lasting impression on many in power there. I would imagine they were glad to see him fall."

"Which only shows that he did his job. At least until he was caught with that last story."

"For the first time, you sound like a daughter."

"I don't mean to be that. Our relationship is gone. I hate that we even involved him. It was better when we never spoke, never saw each other."

"There's a part of you that doesn't mean that."

"Luckily, it's way down deep. The main part of me says to stay away from him."

He could see she needed reassurance, so he laid a hand on hers. "I appreciate everything you have done. Your assistance has been invaluable."

His mind had been working, deciding on the next move. Sadly, the value of this young woman had depreciated to the point of nothing. Shortly, he would deal with her. Rócha had Sagan under surveillance. So there seemed only one avenue left for him. He knew nothing about Rabbi Berlinger but, from everything he'd heard for the past few hours, that man was part of whatever was happening.

They needed to speak.

But how to approach him?

Then it came to him.

One more performance should do it.

———

HE KNOCKED ON THE DOOR, SOFT AND RESPECTFUL. No sense of urgency.

He'd found the house a few blocks over from the Jewish quarter, on a lovely side street with multistoried flats. This one was brick-fronted with flower boxes adorning the upper windows. Little traffic could be heard from the boulevards beyond, the residential block near the river. It had taken only one call to his estate and a few minutes of Internet research to learn the address for Rabbi Berlinger.

An old man answered the door. Dry-cracked lips, silvery stubble on his chin, patches of wiry white hair. Zachariah introduced himself and asked if they might speak. He was invited inside. The rooms were neat, clean, and simply furnished. The air smelled of coffee and peppermint. Dingy windows allowed little light and no noise to enter. His host offered him an opportunity to sit. He declined.

"I'd rather come to the point," Zachariah said. "You've been manipulating Tom Sagan since he arrived this morning. I want to know what it is you told him."

"Perhaps, in your world, you are accustomed to having your way. But here, in mine, you are nothing."

The words came in a calm, clear voice.

"I understand you are a man to be respected, perhaps even a sage, but I have not the time or patience to extend any courtesies today. Please, tell me what I want to know."

"Where is Sagan's daughter?" Berlinger asked.

"That's none of your business."

"You made it my business when you came here."

"She's waiting for me to return. I told her this was between you and me. I must learn what it is Sagan has been told. I know you provided him a silver box. What is inside?"

"You seem to have a problem. You know so much, yet it is so little."

Zachariah withdrew a gun from beneath his jacket and pointed it at the rabbi.

"You think that will persuade me?" Berlinger asked. "I have had guns pointed at me before. None made me do what I did not want to do."

"Do you really want me as your enemy?"

The rabbi shrugged. "I have had worse."

"I can cause you and your family harm."

"I have no family. I outlived them all. This community is my family. I derive all of my strength and sustenance from it."

"Like another rabbi from the past?"

"I would never presume to compare myself to Rabbi Loew. He was a great man who left a lasting impression on all of us."

"I can harm this community. Or I can help it."

"Ah, now we come to the point. The gun is for show, it is your money that you think will buy answers." Berlinger shook his head. "For a man of your experience and age, you have much to learn. Your money means nothing to me. But perhaps if you were to answer a few questions, I might be persuaded to trade information. What will you do with our Temple treasures?"

Now he knew for sure. Sagan and this old man had seen and heard him in the cemetery.

The rabbi seemed to read his mind.

"The cameras," Berlinger said, "which we bought with your donations. They have many uses. So what is it you will do with our sacred objects?"

"More than you can ever imagine."

"Start a war?"

More of what had been spoken of with the ambassador.

"If need be," he said.

"It is amazing how the world changes. Once it was the Germans who threatened us. Then the communists.

Now the single greatest threat comes from one of our own."

"That is right, old man. We are our own worst enemy. We have allowed the world to corral us into a corner, and if people start to slaughter us again few will rise to our defense. They never have, in all our history. Sure, there is talk of the past horrors and pledges of support, but what did the world do last time? Nothing at all. They let us die. Israel is our only defender. That state must exist and remain strong."

A polite wave of the hand dismissed his point. "You have little idea what will make Israel strong. But it is clear that you have your own vile intentions relative to how to do that."

"And what would you do?" he asked Berlinger. "How would you protect us?"

"The way we always have, by working together, watching over one another, praying to God."

"That got us slaughtered once."

"You are a fool."

Silence passed between them for a few moments.

"The daughter is in great danger, isn't she?"

"As you have already determined, she means nothing to me."

"Yet she thinks otherwise." Berlinger shook his head. "Naïveté. The greatest sin of youth. Which most times is accompanied by arrogance."

"She is not your concern."

"I lost a son long ago to the same two maladies. Unfortunately, I learned later that he was right, which only compounded my regrets."

"So you, of all people, should want to see us strong."

"That I do. We simply disagree on the method."

"Where is Sagan going from here?"

Berlinger shrugged and aimed a blunt finger. "That I will never tell you."

He decided to try another tack. "Think about what it would mean for our treasures to be restored. The Third Temple built. Would that not make you proud? Would you not marvel that you had a hand in that?"

"What Jew would not?"

"Imagine the Temple standing again, built as the Book of Chronicles commands. Can you not see the great embroidered curtain hanging on the western wall, concealing the entrance to the Holy of Holies. Finally, after so many centuries we would have our sacred spot returned. The divine table, the menorah, the silver trumpets, all back where they belong. If only we had our ark, too."

"How many will have to die for that to happen?" Berlinger asked. "The Muslims control the Temple Mount. They will not relinquish it without a bloody fight. They will never allow any Third Temple, and the mount is the only place it can be built."

"Then they will die."

"In a war we cannot win."

More weak talk. He was sick to death with weakness. No one seemed to possess the courage to do what had to be done. Not the politicians, the generals, or the people.

Only him.

"Tom Sagan is the Levite," Berlinger said. "He has been selected by the method prescribed. Only he can find our treasures."

"By Columbus? You can't be serious. How did that man come to possess such power?"

"When the treasures were entrusted to him and he took them to the New World."

"You know a great deal."

"He was given a duty, which he performed. He was one of us."

"And how would you know that?"

"In his day only Jews were experts in cartography, a skill Columbus excelled in. Jews were the ones who perfected nautical instruments and astronomical tables. Jewish pilots were in high demand. The notes Columbus wrote in his books, that have survived, show a deep appreciation for the Old Testament. I saw some of those myself in Spain. He dated a marginal note 1481, then gave the Jewish equivalent of 5241. That, in and of itself, is conclusive enough for me."

And Zachariah knew why.

No one, other than a Jew, would have bothered adding the required 3,760 years to the Christian calendar.

"I've seen the portrait of him in the Uffizi Gallery in Florence," Berlinger said. "It is the only one crafted by someone who might have actually seen him alive. To me his features are clearly Semitic."

Nothing he did not already know. He'd studied the same image.

"We financed his first voyage," Berlinger said. "History notes that. For those Sephardi Jews, Columbus' dreams were their salvation. They truly believed that they could live in peace in Asia, that they could escape the Inquisition. Columbus sailed to the New World mainly to find a new home for them."

"Unfortunately he didn't live long enough to achieve that goal. His family, though, did provide us a home in Jamaica for 150 years."

"Which is why we must respect all that he did, and all that was done after. How that task is accomplished from this point forward is now in Tom Sagan's hands. You and I cannot affect that."

The old man sat straight-backed and stiff-legged,

hands resting on the arms. This icon had lived a long time.

But Zachariah had heard enough.

He stood. "I see I am wasting my time. You will tell me nothing."

Berlinger remained seated.

He leveled the gun.

The old man raised a hand. "Might I say a prayer before I die?"

He shot the rabbi in the chest.

Only a soft pop from the sound-suppressed pistol disturbed the silence.

Berlinger gasped for breath then his eyes glazed over, his head drooping to one shoulder. The mouth opened and a trickle of blood oozed down the chin.

He checked for a pulse and found none.

"The time for prayer is over, old man."

CHAPTER SIXTY-SIX

TOM INSERTED THE KEY INTO THE SILVER BOX AND turned the lock. Whatever was inside had been placed there by his grandfather. He felt a connection to the man, one he'd never experienced before. Now he was the last link in an unbroken chain that stretched back to the time of Columbus. Hard to believe, but it was true. He thought about all of the other men who'd assumed this duty, what they might have thought. Most of them probably had little to do except pass the information on to the next in line. Saki, though, was different. And he could understand why his grandfather had been paranoid. There'd been pogroms in the past, Jews had suffered and died, but never on the scale they endured from 1939 to 1945.

An unprecedented time called for unprecedented actions.

He was alone inside a room off the nave in the Maisel Synagogue. An older woman had opened the glass display case and removed the silver box, never saying a word. She'd laid it on a wooden table and left, closing the door behind her. His thoughts flew back to the room at the cemetery and Abiram's coffin, lying on a similar wooden table.

A lot had gone unsaid between the two of them.

Now there were no more opportunities to right any wrongs.

True, as Berlinger had said, time had brought everything into focus, but it was not an image he wanted to see. Even worse, it seemed the same mistake he had made twenty years ago was being repeated by his own daughter toward him.

He flushed those troubling thoughts from his brain and opened the lid.

Inside was a black leather bag, identical to the one from Abiram's grave that had held the key. He pressed the outside with his finger and felt something hard beneath.

He lifted out the bag and opened the top.

What came out was spherical, about four inches wide, and looked like a large pocket watch with a brass face.

But it wasn't.

Instead it was an assemblage of five interlocking disks, one above the other, held together by a central pin. On top were pointers that could be rotated and lined with symbols that appeared on the disks. He noticed the lettering. Some was Hebrew, some Arabic and Spanish. It weighed maybe half a pound and seemed of solid brass. No tarnish marred its exterior, and the disks freely turned.

He knew what this was.

An astrolabe.

Used for navigation.

Nothing else was inside the box.

No explanations, no messages—zero to explain what he was supposed to do next.

"Okay, Saki," he whispered.

He laid the astrolabe down and found Abiram's note and the Jamaican road map, laying both on the table. He added the key from the lock.

All of the pieces of the puzzle.

He opened the map and pressed its folds flat, careful not to tear the brittle paper. He saw again the ink additions to the map, numbers scattered around the island. He made a quick count. Maybe a hundred written in faded blue ink.

He lifted the astrolabe and tried to remember anything he knew about the device. Used for navigation, but how he had no idea. Across the rim of the outer disk were symbols laid out at intervals. A pointer, notched like a ruler, stretched from one edge to the other and connected symbols from opposite sides. All of the writing was either Hebrew or Spanish. He knew no Spanish and only a smattering of Hebrew.

He turned it over.

The back side was a grid of rows encircling the disk, five in total, everything in Hebrew. One row he recognized.

Numbers.

As a child Abiram had insisted he study Hebrew. Unlike many languages, numerals were formed using letters, and he recalled the number combinations. He recognized 10, 8, 62, 73, and most of the others. Another pointer stretched from one end to the other. He rotated the disks, which spun easily on their central axis. His gaze drifted to Abiram's message and the main point Saki had explained.

$$3. \ 74. \ 5. \ 86. \ 19.$$

He searched the astrolabe and found 3, amazed that he could still translate. He twisted the pointer and lined one end with the symbol for 3. At the opposite end was Hebrew for 74.

Not a coincidence.

The second number from Saki's message was 5. He

twisted the pointer and found the symbol for 5. The opposite side rested at 86.

One left, which seemed the whole point. The first two were there simply to confirm, *Yeah, you're on the right track*.

He searched the grid for 19 and found what he thought was correct.

The opposite number was 56.

He immediately surveyed the map, looking for 56. He found it east of the center of the island, south of a town called Richmond, adjacent to the Flint River. Small print on the map, just beside the inked number, noted that the area was called Falcon Ridge. He searched the remainder of the map. The number 56 appeared nowhere else.

He smiled.

Ingenious.

Absolutely no way existed for anyone to know which of the hundred or so numbers was relevant without the sequence and the astrolabe.

He gathered up the map, note, key, astrolabe, and the black leather bag large enough to hold them all.

He left the building and walked back toward the Old-New Synagogue. He debated trying to find Alle. But how was that possible? And what was the point? She'd made her choice. He'd done all he could for her, but she was Simon's now, and he only hoped that she'd be okay. He could go to the police, but what would he say? He'd sound like a crazed nut, and he doubted Berlinger would back him up.

"My duty is done. The rest I leave to you."

The only thing for him to do was leave.

He glanced around one last time. The clusters of buildings that at first seemed protective in their famil-iarity were now cold and unappealing. His stay had been short, but memorable. Like his parents' home, there were a lot of ghosts here, too. But he wondered.

What waited ahead, in Jamaica, at Falcon Ridge?

There seemed only one way to find out.

But his heart sank in disappointment.

"Take care, Alle," he whispered.

And he walked away.

CHAPTER SIXTY-SEVEN

ZACHARIAH WALKED BACK TO THE RESTAURANT where Alle was waiting. He'd locked both doors that had led out of Berlinger's house before leaving and would be long gone before the body was discovered. He'd had no choice but to kill the old man: He knew far too much and could definitely link him to the ambassador.

Prayer?

That had never been enough and never would be. Force, or at least its threat, was what offered real security. Jews had never possessed enough force. Only once, at the time of the Second Temple, had they risen in revolt and ousted the Romans, but that victory had been short-lived. The empire returned and crushed them. In modern times the state of Israel had enjoyed more success. Twice invasions were tried, and twice the invaders were defeated. But Israel's will to fight had waned. The thoughts of rabbis were heeded over the advice of generals. There was no room in this world for any more Rabbi Berlingers.

He found the restaurant and saw Alle. Noontime was approaching, and the tables were beginning to fill. An aroma of dumplings and roast duck enticed him, but there was no time for lunch.

"Did you learn anything?" she asked.

He wondered if she truly believed that he would share with her whatever he may have discovered, but he showed no irritation and simply shook his head.

"He is a stubborn old man. He told me about your father, but nothing we did not already know."

His phone vibrated.

He found the unit and saw that it was Rócha.

"Sagan is on the move. Back to his car, I think."

He stood from the table and motioned for Alle to follow.

"We're coming your way."

"Avoid the old square. He'll be there shortly."

He ended the call.

"Your father is leaving. That means we are, too."

He'd not lied to Berlinger. This young woman meant nothing to him any longer, but he would not be as quick as before to kill her. He'd keep her close until he was certain she was of no further use. With Tom Sagan on the move to who-knew-where, that time had not yet arrived.

So he smiled and led her away.

———

ALLE WAS UNSURE ABOUT WHAT WAS HAPPENING, only that her father seemed to be leaving Prague. He'd apparently decided to press on without her, but what choice did he have? He had no way of finding her. And she was glad. She preferred being with Zachariah. She had a purpose here. Felt a part. Like she had with her grandparents.

They were making their way back toward where she and her father had left their car, worming through traffic and thick streams of pedestrians.

"We followed you from Vienna," Zachariah said as they walked, "and parked nearby. Illegally, so I hope the car is still there."

He motioned left.

"We have to avoid the town square. This route will take us where we want to go, away from there."

They kept moving.

Interesting how her father leaving actually bothered her. Like another slap in the face. A rejection. For all he knew, she was looking for him.

Yet he'd decided to leave.

"Does my father know that I'm with you?" she asked.

Zachariah nodded. "The rabbi told me that he saw us earlier, together on the street."

Which explained some.

"Where's he going?"

"That's what we have to find out. I am assuming he will head to an airport. I am hoping it will be the one in Prague."

————

TOM DROVE WEST SIX MILES OUT OF TOWN TO Prague's Ruzyne airport. He left the car with the rental agency and found the British Airways ticket counter, thinking that might be his best bet to get to Jamaica. There was a flight leaving for London in two hours with seats still available. After a two-and-a-half-hour layover, another flight would take him to Kingston. The ticket price was outrageous but he could not have cared less. He paid with his credit card and obtained a day pass for the airline's lounge.

Before settling down inside to wait, he bought a few toiletries. He should call Inna and see what she may have discovered, but what did it matter anymore? Everything he needed to know was here, inside the black leather bag. He looked like crap. He needed a shower and a shave, just like in the old days while on the hunt. Thankfully, appearances mattered little to a print reporter. The byline. That's what counted. And where the story was positioned. Front page, above the fold, the Boardwalk and Park Place of the newspaper business, and he'd owned that real estate.

But those days were gone.

Never to return?

He thought of the woman in the car. *Find the treasure. Then we will talk.*

Was it possible?

He was actually tired, but he'd sleep on the plane. Once in Jamaica he'd rent a car and head to Falcon Ridge. A lot was at stake here. For himself and for others.

A war?

Was that Simon's intent?

Something came to mind he read once while in the Middle East.

From the sacred *Midrash Tanchuma*.

As the navel is set in the centre of the human body, so is the land of Israel the navel of the world . . .

People believed that to the point of fanaticism.

Plenty enough to start a war.

———

ZACHARIAH WAITED WITH ALLE IN THE BAGGAGE claim area. They'd made it to the car, where Rócha had been behind the wheel with the engine running, watching from across the street as Sagan found his car and climbed inside. They'd followed him out of town, his destination immediately obvious.

The airport.

So he called Vienna and told the charter service to fly the jet to Prague. The flight time was less than an hour. All he needed to know was Sagan's destination.

Which Rócha had left to find out.

He spotted his man on the down escalator and watched as he walked over. He caught Alle's apprehension.

"Not to worry," he told her. "I spoke to him. He will not bother you again."

Rócha approached.

"It cost me €500 but the ticket agent told me Sagan booked the three o'clock flight to London, then on to Kingston, Jamaica. I have the flight times."

Jamaica.

Why was he not surprised?

Rócha faced Alle. "I want to say I'm sorry for what happened in Vienna. I took things too far. I was only trying to do my job."

He watched as Alle accepted the apology. He'd told Rócha what to do in the event that she was back with them and was pleased that his man had followed directions.

She seemed more at ease already.

"Our jet will be here soon," he said.

"Sagan went through Customs, then security," Rócha said. "He's gone, waiting for his flight."

Zachariah's mind was on a greater problem.

Sagan would beat them to Jamaica. They'd have to refuel at least once, probably twice. Even with a layover, Sagan would arrive first. Which meant he had to have someone there, on the ground, ready and waiting.

And there was only one candidate.

"I have to make a call," he said.

CHAPTER SIXTY-EIGHT

BÉNE WAS AT HIS ESTATE, THE LONG NIGHT OVER, THE Jamaican morning barely beginning. Halliburton had returned home, too, and Frank Clarke was back in Charles Town. He'd changed out of his wet clothes, now outside at the kennel, where his dogs waited. They were glad to see him, Big Nanny especially. He petted them all and accepted their affection.

He thought about Grandy Nanny herself.

She'd managed to escape not long after arriving in Jamaica and took her five brothers with her. One set of siblings came east and became the Windward Maroons. Nanny and the others traveled west and became the Leewards. She built Nanny Town, clearing 600 acres of raw forest. She fought the British and, while her brothers and most Maroons sought peace, she merely signed a truce. Legend said that immediately afterward she asked the British to shoot her. They obliged, but Nanny spun around, then straightened up, walking to a British officer and returning the bullets that had been fired her way. She pointed toward the sky and told him, "Only one can kill me."

He smiled. That was the thing about legends.

You wanted to believe them.

He stared out at the mountains, packed with a profusion of lush vegetation, a sea of green, the morning sun casting the thick slopes in a purple glow.

What beauty.

He gathered the dogs and opened the gate. The animals fled the kennel, stretching their legs, readying themselves for a hunt.

He was still bothered by the attempt on his life.

Being born Maroon was an initiation into a secret society. His mother taught him as a child *"never tell more than half of what you know. That's not lying,"* she would add. *"That's smart."* His father had been more practical. Hammering into him more of Maroon culture. Secrets shared become secrets betrayed. *"Go to your grave,"* his father said, *"with your secrets."*

That was how he justified not telling his mother about his life. A betrayal? Sure. Was he a hypocrite? Probably. He resented Frank Clarke keeping things from him, but his friend had been right in the cave. He'd done the same toward his mother.

And the colonels?

Those men he resented.

That was the thing about Maroons. They'd never been able to stick together. Grandy Nanny herself led 300 of her people from the west to the east in what was known as the Grand Trek. Her goal was to reunite the two Maroon factions into one, then attack the British with a full force. But her brother, Cudjoe, who headed the east, refused. He wanted peace. So she retreated to the Leeward side and resumed the fight. And though she eventually made a truce, she never made peace.

Smart lady.

The dogs seemed anxious.

Two of them tangled.

He yelled and halted their dispute.

Both retreated, and he petted each, letting them know that everything was okay.

Maroons were taught early in life to not speak of their ways. Any knowledge dispensed should come in small increments. Trust was fragile. To reveal all of what you knew made yourself vulnerable to betrayal. Speaking freely of "Maroon things" ran the risk of incurring the ancestors' wrath.

Best to say nothing.

That was what he'd been taught. Frank Clarke, too.

So why was he bothered by Frank's withholding?

Simple. He was not an outsider.

He *was* Maroon.

Frank's statement that he was not trusted by the others—that hurt him. Who the hell were they to judge?

And to decide to kill him?

"Ungrateful bastards," he whispered.

What to do now. The mine was nothing and, according to Frank, no one knew what had happened to the gold and silver objects.

Then again, he had no way of knowing if any of that was true.

Always guard your knowledge.

Was Frank Clarke still protecting?

The dogs continued darting in all directions, always circling back to where he stood. Clouds had rolled in off the peaks, the sky the color of ashes.

His phone rang.

The display read UNKNOWN.

He decided to answer.

"Zachariah Simon," the voice said.

He steadied himself.

"I understand you want to talk to me."

"Actually, I'd like to kill you."

And he meant it.

"I did what I had to do. The same you would have done. We're both successful men, Béne. To remain that way, we make hard decisions. Just like you did when you pointed the Americans my way."

Interesting. Simon had become informed. "I had no choice."

"I doubt that. But it doesn't matter. Jamison is dead. It is just you and me now, Béne."

Which explained why he'd heard nothing more from Brian. He hoped the Americans were out of his life for good. "What do you want?"

"Let us call it even between us."

"Would there be a point to that?"

"There's a man named Thomas Sagan on his way to Kingston."

"The man from Florida?"

"That's right. He's flying in late tonight, your time. I am on the way, but I will not arrive before he does. I need you to follow him and see where he goes."

"And why would I do that?"

"He will lead you to the location of a great treasure. I lied to you, Béne. I am not after Columbus' grave or even the lost gold mine. Whether or not there were crates of gold from Panama hidden somewhere on the island, who cares? I want something far more valuable that does exist. Four objects. The Jews' Temple treasure."

Now he was interested. Simon was telling him things he knew to be true. "This man, Sagan, knows where that treasure is?"

"I think so."

But Frank had made clear that the objects were moved. Did this man Sagan know their *current* location?

He decided to hold that nugget and discuss it with Sagan.

"Since you already know about Sagan," Simon said, "find his photo on the Internet, then find him. He will be on a British Airways flight from London that arrives around eleven tonight, your time. He may have with him a small black bag. What is inside is important."

"Why call me?"

"Because you want another shot at me."

That he did. Like Grandy Nanny and the British there might be a truce, but no peace would pass between them.

"Do this," Simon said, "and you will get that chance, because you will have something I want."

But Béne knew something else.

Thomas Sagan was Simon's enemy.

And that he liked.

"There is one other point," Simon said. "Something for you to consider before you act. I have a piece of the puzzle that Sagan does not. Without it, you will find nothing. I need to be there, with Sagan, and I will provide that piece for us all."

He chuckled. "Always an angle."

"It is the way of the world."

"I'll have a man waiting for you at the airport with a car," he said. "In the meantime, I'll find Thomas Sagan."

CHAPTER SIXTY-NINE

TOM ACCEPTED HIS PASSPORT BACK FROM THE woman behind the counter. He'd traveled all over the Caribbean and Central America as a reporter, but never to Jamaica. His trip had started with an hour flight from Prague to London, then another nine and a half hours east across the Atlantic. To his body it was after four o'clock in the morning tomorrow. Here, it was 11:15 P.M.

The transatlantic flight had not been packed, so he was able to stretch out and sleep. For the first time in a few days he'd relaxed, safe thirty thousand feet in the air. He'd even eaten a meal. Not much, as he'd never cared for airplane food, but enough.

The tropical air was thicker and warmer than Prague's. More like Florida. Like home. Funny he would think that way. He hadn't considered the concept of home for a long time.

He headed for the rental car counters, which placards said were in the Ground Transportation Hall. Construction was evident everywhere, the terminal undergoing renovations. The gate they'd arrived at appeared new, as did the concourse. Few vendors were open this late, but a fair number of passengers came and went.

He should be jet-lagged, but he wasn't. He'd never

suffered much from that malady, adrenaline both then and now an effective countermeasure. He spotted the Hertz counter, which was lit and manned.

Two men suddenly appeared beside him.

"Need a ride?" one of them asked, an eager look on his face.

He shook his head. "No thanks."

"Come on, man," the other one said. "We can take you wherever you need. Quickie quick. Low cost. No problem."

He kept walking.

They stayed with him.

"We have good car," the first one said. "Fast. You like."

"I said no thanks."

The man to his left hopped in front of him. The other dropped in behind. The one in front reached beneath his shirt and produced a gun, which he nestled close to Tom's belly.

"I think you do come."

He now realized the seriousness of the situation. The black leather bag was tucked into his back pocket. He wore the jacket from Europe, but had left the gun in the Czech Republic. The bag was freed from his pocket.

He turned.

The man behind him carried a gun, too.

"Now, now, be cool. You in Jamaica now."

They herded him away from the rental car counters toward the exit doors. Outside, he raked the night with his eyes trying to spot any police or security.

He saw none.

People flowed in and out of the terminal. Cars came and went. The two men kept him close. One hid his weapon and led the way, the other kept his tucked close to Tom's midsection, shielded from view.

A pickup truck waited at the curb.

The driver's door opened and a man stepped out. He was short, black, and trim, his hair cut close, the face clean-shaven. He wore a light-colored shirt, open to a colored T-shirt beneath, and cotton trousers. No jewelry adorned his hands, arms, or neck. From the way the men reacted at his presence, this one was in charge. A smile formed on his lips and revealed pearly white teeth.

"I'm Béne Rowe."

A hand was extended for him to shake.

He did not accept the offer.

"I understand that we have a mutual enemy. Zachariah Simon."

No sense being coy. "That we do."

"Then shake my hand and help me stick it to that sorry, no-good SOB."

———

BÉNE SHOOK THOMAS SAGAN'S HAND AND SAW APprehension in the man's eyes. Good. He *should* be cautious.

His man handed him a black leather bag, just as Simon had predicted. Inside he examined an assortment of odd things, including a circular brass object with Spanish and Hebrew on its face.

"What is this?" he asked.

"An astrolabe."

"I assume you know how to use it."

Sagan shrugged. "Not really."

He pointed a finger at his guest. "Playing stupid with me?"

"Just like you're doing with me."

He flicked a hand and dismissed his two men. He

assumed Sagan was going nowhere without the black bag. He needed this man to trust him so he handed over everything. "You're not a prisoner. Leave. Go. But if you want to stay, I'll help you. Simon tried to kill me. I owe him. If helping you hurts him, then you have my help."

"How did you know I'd be here?"

"Simon told me. He knew exactly where you'd be." He saw the concern on the other man's face.

"I've been honest," he said to Sagan. "I have no reason to lie. He told me that you know where the Jews' great treasure is hidden on this island. I know some about that."

"And what is it you know?"

TOM WAS MAKING DECISIONS, THE KIND HE ONCE made in the field when sources appeared out of nowhere. You had to judge words, actions, and make a call. Sometimes you were right, others times not so lucky.

Like in Israel, eight years ago.

Not now, he told himself.

Focus.

He knew Falcon Ridge was located somewhere northwest of Kingston, in the mountains, toward the center of the island. Once there, he had no idea what to look for, and Simon knowing he was here was of great concern.

How was that possible?

His parents and his ex-wife were dead. His daughter was gone. All he had left was the woman in the car.

Find the treasure. Then we will talk.

But he needed help.

And though this congenial black man of obvious

power had said he was free to leave, he doubted that was the case.

Take a chance.

He asked, "Do you know a place called Falcon Ridge?"

Rowe nodded. "It's not far from my estate."

An estate? Of course. What else?

"That's where we have to go."

CHAPTER SEVENTY

ZACHARIAH BUCKLED HIS SEAT BELT AND WATCHED as Alle and Rócha did the same. The long flight across the Atlantic was about over. They'd stopped only once for fuel, in Lisbon, then flown directly here to Kingston. His watch read 12:25 A.M., local time, March 9th. Saturday.

Another day had passed.

Both Alle and Rócha had slept on the trip. He'd dozed in and out, his mind unable to relax. It excited him to know there were Israelis in authority waiting for him to act. Finally, after decades of concession and complacency something might be accomplished. His father and grandfather would be proud. He was about to succeed where they each had failed. But that all depended on Béne Rowe's cooperation.

Sagan should already be on the ground, which meant Rowe was with him, probably trying to learn all that he could. He hoped his ploy about another piece of the puzzle would at least give Rowe some pause. He was betting Rowe would limit those involved. Doubtful that he'd want any of his men trying to take advantage. Sure, Rowe had made clear that somebody would be waiting at the airport to meet them, but he'd never said where they would be taken.

So he wondered.

Could the odds be evened?

Alle stood from her seat and made her way to the lavatory. The pilot had just advised that they would be landing shortly. He waited until the door was shut then motioned for Rócha to leave his seat and come closer. In a low voice he explained what he wanted done.

Rócha nodded.

The answer clear.

Yes, of course.

———

TOM SAT IN THE PICKUP'S PASSENGER SEAT AND ASKED, "How do you know Simon?"

"I read about you on the Internet. A big-time reporter who found some trouble."

Not an answer to his question. "Don't believe everything you read online. Big mistake."

Rowe chuckled. "You should read what they say about me there. Shocking. Disgraceful stuff."

But he wondered how far off the mark that slander might be.

And already he began to question the wisdom of his actions.

They were leaving the airport on a black highway, the road smooth and straight, traffic nearly nonexistent. A full moon brightened the midnight sky.

"How do you know Simon?" he asked again.

"We met a year ago. He wanted help finding a lost mine and I offered it."

"And Brian Jamison? You know him, too."

"Did you meet Brian?"

"He was an American agent, working for the Justice Department. My daughter was told he worked for you."

"That was a lie."

"He's dead."

"So I've been told."

"I'd say Jamison leaned on you. Judging by your entourage, I'd also say that you know your way around the local criminal justice system. What did Jamison want? Simon?"

"What else. He made me help, and I did what he wanted."

"Did you have him killed in Vienna?"

Rowe shook his head. "Simon took him down. All his doing."

"I assume Jamison never said why the Americans were interested in Simon?"

"He wasn't the talkative type. He liked to give orders."

"Like you?"

Rowe laughed. "You really were once a good reporter."

"I still am."

And he meant it.

"The Simon said he has information that you don't. That's why I'm supposed to hold you up until he gets here."

"And you don't believe him?"

"Not a man known for telling the truth."

"He knows nothing."

"Then it's good for me that I took a chance on you."

He wasn't so sure if the reverse were true. "How far to Falcon Ridge?"

"In a straight line, maybe fifty kilometers. Unfortunately, roads here don't go so straight. I'd say two hours to get there. What are we looking for?"

"A cave."

"Jamaica has thousands of those."

"Is there one at Falcon Ridge?"

Rowe reached for a phone. "Let's find out."

Tom watched as the man dialed a number, waited while the party answered, then listened as Rowe explained what he wanted to someone named Tre.

Rowe then ended the call.

"Calling and driving is dangerous," Tom said.

"That's what I hear. But lots of things are dangerous. Like getting into a truck with a stranger."

"As if I need reminding."

Rowe grinned. "I like you. Smart guy. I heard what you did to the Simon in Florida."

He asked what he wanted to know. "Who was on the phone?"

"A friend of mine who knows about caves. He'll call back and let us know what's at Falcon Ridge."

"Why are you so interested in the Jews' Temple treasure?" he asked Rowe.

"I wasn't, until a few hours ago. You realize Simon is coming to Jamaica."

He nodded. "I do now. He's probably bringing my daughter with him."

"Your daughter? Still with him? I bet that's quite a story."

"You could say that. How will we know when Simon arrives?"

"No problem. I have people waiting to welcome him."

———

ZACHARIAH SLIPPED HIS PASSPORT BACK INTO HIS pocket and walked with Alle out of the building. The hangar sat away from Kingston's main terminal, used by private planes, his charter now among the many parked on the tarmac. Rócha had deplaned first and disappeared.

A warm blanket of humid air soaked him.

"How are we going to get around?" Alle asked.

"I do not think that is going to be a problem."

He pointed at two black men strutting their way, chests inflated like dogs eager for a fight. The area where they'd exited the hangar was secluded, near a small parking lot with few cars. Weak bulbs splashed pale yellow light onto dark pavement. Palm trees lining the edges rustled in a light breeze. The two men wore jeans and khaki shirts stained with moisture. They approached and stopped a few meters away.

"Mr. Rowe sent us to fetch you," one of them said, the face beaming with hospitality.

"How kind."

They followed their hosts into the parking lot, where one of the men motioned to a light-colored sedan.

"You not going to make any trouble, are you?" one of them asked.

"Why would I?"

Alle seemed concerned, but he allayed her fears with a slight shake of his head.

A shadow lunged from the trees.

He heard a crack, then the man to his left spilled facedown to the asphalt. The other man reacted to the assault, a hand plunging into his pant pocket, surely for a weapon, but the shadow leaped forward.

"Now, sir," Zachariah said. "I need you to keep your hands where we can see them."

Rócha held a gun to the man's head.

"Are you carrying a phone?"

"Sure, man."

"Do you know how to contact Béne?"

The head nodded.

"He wanted you to call once you had us in the car?"

Another nod.

"And he would tell you then where to bring us?"

A third confirmation.

"Remove the phone, slowly, and make the call. Tell him you have us. Keep to English. No patois. I want to clearly understand what you say and what he says to you. Any problem and you are dead."

He saw a hesitation in complying, and Rócha jammed the gun farther into the man's temple.

The phone was found and dialed.

Zachariah stepped close and angled the unit so he could hear. The man's chest was thin, arms hairless, and he reeked of coppery sweat.

Three rings and Béne Rowe's voice answered.

"We have 'em," was the report.

"All good?"

"No problems."

"Bring them to Falcon Ridge. It's on the map, in St. Ann Parish. Come up A3, then west at Mahoe Hill. Get here fast."

"We on our way," the man told Rowe.

The call ended.

"You did good," Zachariah said.

He motioned for Alle to enter the car.

He walked around to the passenger's side.

Rócha used the moment to slip the hand holding the gun around the man's neck. His arms locked, right hand came up, and the head was jerked to one side, snapping another neck.

He entered the car as Rócha dragged the body into the trees.

"What's happening out there?" Alle asked.

Rócha returned and retrieved the other body.

"We just prevented Mr. Rowe from harming us," he told her.

"You killed them?"

"Not at all. Just unconscious. That will give us time to leave. But, remember, Alle, those men are gangsters. They would have hurt us."

Rócha returned with the keys to the car, two weapons, and two cell phones, which he handed over.

Zachariah said, "Now let us see if we can maintain our luck."

Rócha drove with Alle in the backseat.

Her questions and fears were no longer relevant.

If all went right, by dawn she'd be dead.

———

BÉNE CLICKED OFF THE CELL PHONE AND STARED across the truck at Thomas Sagan.

"Simon is here. I have him."

"And you just told your people to bring him to Falcon Ridge."

"I want him there. I plan to deal with him. You have your priority and I have mine."

"And if Simon is one step ahead of you?"

He chuckled. "That happens all the time, but I'm real good at catching up. Not to worry. We'll beat the Simon there by a good hour. Plenty of time to look around and be ready."

His phone rang again.

Halliburton.

"There's a cave at Falcon Ridge. A big one called Darby's Hole. It's sealed off. The geological society categorizes it as ultra-hazardous. Three people have died in there over the past fifty years. The society's website says to stay out."

"That's all I needed to know."

"You going in there, Béne?"

"You're out of the loop on this one. Okay?"

He hoped his friend understood.

"Do you know what you're doing?" Tre asked.

"Not really. But I'm doing it anyway."

He ended the call.

"What's your interest in all this?" Sagan asked him.

"I've been asking myself that question all day. Now it's just a matter of pride. What's yours?"

Sagan shrugged. "Seems to be my assigned job."

"You were about to kill yourself in Florida. What changed for you?"

He saw that Sagan was surprised he knew that.

"I had a spy in Simon's camp. He kept me better informed than Jamison. Simon needed you. He went after you. Your daughter lied to you. Yeah, man, I know the story. At least up to a point. Now here you are. This is more than a job. Much more. This is damn personal for you."

"Your father alive?"

Strange question. "Been dead a long time."

"Mine was to me, too, then he really died. I disappointed him."

Now he could understand. "But not this time?"

"Something like that."

"I know some of the story of the Jews' treasure here. Maybe stuff you don't know."

And he told Sagan about the cave, Columbus' grave, and the four objects that had been there, now gone.

"That cave where I went is not at Falcon Ridge. It's a mile or so away."

"Is there a river?"

He nodded. "Runs from one to the other."

"Then we're in the right place. My grandfather took those four objects out of there and moved them to Falcon Ridge."

"So they could still be here?"

"We'll soon find out."

"How do you know I won't kill you and keep them for myself?"

"I don't. But, to be honest with you, Mr. Rowe, I don't really give a damn. Like you said, I was ready to die a few days ago."

He was liking this man more and more. "Call me Béne. No one calls me mister. And not to worry, Thomas—"

"I'm Tom. Almost nobody calls me Thomas."

"Then not to worry, Tom, you're in good hands with me."

CHAPTER SEVENTY-ONE

ALLE SAT IN THE REAR SEAT AND WONDERED WHAT was happening. She'd felt safer with Zachariah in Prague, but did not have the same feeling here. Rócha still turned her stomach, his apology not nearly enough, and it had taken all she had to ride on the plane with him.

Thoughts of the Temple treasure filled her brain.

Her family had kept a secret for a long time. One that traced its roots straight back to Christopher Columbus. Now here they were, in Jamaica, where the Columbus family had ruled for 150 years. They'd kept the Inquisition out, creating a safe haven for Jews in the New World. Was it possible that the menorah, the divine table, and the silver trumpets still existed?

Zachariah certainly thought so.

She'd heard what Béne Rowe had said on the phone.

Falcon Ridge.

That was the place.

Where, apparently, her father was headed.

Still, she was apprehensive, her body coated in a cold sweat. Outside was dark but a full moon cast an eerie light, mummifying the world. They'd stopped at a convenience store and obtained a Jamaican road map, one showing that their destination was less than an hour ahead, paved roads most of the way. In the store Zachariah had also bought three flashlights and given her one, assuring her things were under control.

But she wondered.

Brian Jamison had claimed that he worked for Béne Rowe, then later changed that to being an American agent. Which was the truth? Zachariah had told her from the beginning that there would be people who would try to stop them. That was the nature of the prize they sought. Which was exactly why it had been hidden away for nearly two thousand years.

Would it be found tonight?

What a thought.

Almost enough to ease her fears.

———

TOM STEPPED FROM THE TRUCK. THE TROPICAL NIGHT was clear and bright. They were parked at the top of a ridge, where a graveled parish road began its descent to a forested valley. Miles away, to the far north, shafts of silver moonlight shimmered off the sea.

"This is Falcon Ridge," Rowe said. "Good thing for you I came prepared."

Rowe reached into the pickup's bed and found two flashlights. He handed over one, which Tom switched on. He saw that the truck bed was loaded with tools.

"I brought things," Rowe said. "Just in case. I own a coffee plantation not far from here."

"And what else do you do?"

"If you mean am I a criminal, no, I'm not. But I do have people who work for me who can cause a lot of harm. Lucky for you none of them is here tonight. This is between you, me, and the Simon."

"And what makes you think he's going to play by your rules?"

"He won't. But we're ahead of him, so let's stay that way."

Rowe snapped open a metal container and removed a shoulder holster and gun, which he donned.

The sight unnerved him, but was not unexpected.

"For Simon," Rowe said.

———

BÉNE LED THE WAY INTO THE TREES. TRE HAD TOLD him where the cave called Darby's Hole was located. Not far. Down a precipitous ridge to the valley floor, where a tributary of the Flint River raced toward the sea.

He could hear the rushing water.

His eyes were adjusted to the dark, his ears attuned to the jungle whispers around him.

Which made him nervous.

He sensed they were not alone.

He stopped and signaled for Sagan to stand still.

In the sky overhead he watched the muted flutter of bats. A few insects made their presence known. The gun he'd brought was nestled close to his chest in the holster. His right hand gently caressed the weapon. Reassuring to know it was there. Still, he could not shake the feeling they were not alone.

All of the land for kilometers in every direction belonged to Maroons, part of what had been ceded to them two hundred years ago by the British. It had remained forest, unpopulated, controlled by the local Maroon council.

He motioned and they continued to clamber down, the ground slippery with pebbles and mud. He switched on his light and tried to locate the water cascade. The river was just below them, maybe ten meters wide, the flow extra swift.

They reached the wooded bank.

He plunged the light beneath the clear, blue-green water and saw that the stream was shallow, less than a meter deep. Typical of Jamaica's many waterways.

Sagan activated his light and scanned right and left. "There."

He saw that, fifty meters away, the river swung. At the bend rose a vertical cliff with a crack across its face, the jagged slit signaling a cave.

"That must be it," he said. "We can follow the bank and get there."

A long, low wail disturbed the night.

Its tone changed several times, but continued unabated for nearly a minute.

That sound he knew.

An *abeng*. Made from a cow's horn. By blowing into holes and working the thumb, notes could be produced. He'd learned to play as a child. Maroons in the 17th and 18th centuries used the horns to communicate. A trained ear could decipher the notes, extracting messages that could be passed over long distances. It was one of several advantages they'd managed over the enemy. The British found the mournful sound terrifying, since it usually signaled death. But what did it mean tonight? He'd never heard one blown outside of a staged celebration.

"What is that?" Sagan asked.

The wail stopped.

Another started.

Much farther off.

His concern became fear.

Maroons were here.

TOM FOLLOWED ROWE AS THEY PARALLELED THE river. Tangled foliage blocked their way, the going slow. Dried twigs and leaves crackled underfoot. They finally made it to a point close to where the cave opened. Their lights scanned the black yawn across the river and he saw something strange.

A dam.

Fashioned of cemented rock, the rough joints thick. It rose two feet from the water and blocked the cave's entrance, keeping water out.

"We'll need to walk through the river to get there," Rowe said as he slipped the gun from the holster and stepped into the swift-moving flow, which rose waist-high.

He followed.

Cold water sent a chill through him that actually felt good considering the amount of sweat that covered his body. The riverbed was smooth stones in varying sizes that challenged his rubber-soled shoes and made footing tricky. Twice he almost lost his balance. If he fell and allowed the current to take him, he'd be gone in a matter of seconds. Luckily, the water ran shallow.

Rowe made it to the dam, hopped on top, and re-holstered the gun.

Tom did the same.

They both shone their lights on the other side, into the cave opening. Some water leaked through the dam and trickled inside, down a flat, smooth, chute-like incline about ten feet wide.

"This river once flowed into there," he said.

"And someone dammed it up."

A sign was posted adjacent to the entrance labeling the cave Darby's Hole. The warning made clear NO ADMITTANCE. Unchecked water flows, unexplored

and unmarked passages, dangerous pits, and unpre-
dictable surges were listed as reasons.

"That's comforting," he said.

But Rowe had turned from the placard, studying
the trees on the river's far bank.

No more wails had been heard.

"What aren't you telling me?" he asked Rowe.

"Let's go inside."

CHAPTER SEVENTY-TWO

ZACHARIAH CHECKED THE MAP. THEY'D FOUND THE highway marked A3, just as Rowe had instructed, then sped north through a series of dark towns. Just past one named Noland the road began to climb into the Blue Mountains. A bright moon sheathed the landscape in a wondrous, divine light and he wondered if its presence was a sign.

"Mahoe Hill is only a few more kilometers," he told Rócha. "There we go west."

Falcon Ridge was on the map, with an elevation of 130 meters noted.

"You okay back there," he said to Alle.

"I'm fine."

His head spun a little from the twists and turns in the road. He'd never been fond of mountain drives. "I think we are only a few hours away from finding what we are after."

He wanted to reassure her, calm any fears she may have. The violence at the airport had been necessary, but he'd told Rócha to keep it discreet.

And that he had.

He wondered if Berlinger's body had been found. Nothing linked him to the rabbi's house, and he'd been careful inside to stand and to touch nothing. He'd opened the door through his jacket and wiped the knob clean. He'd seen no one, and nothing had occurred that would alert anyone.

Now to finish this matter.

Where they were headed seemed isolated.

Exactly what he needed.

———

TOM HOPPED OFF THE DAM ONTO SLICK ROCK. HE kept his light angled down, watching each step through the steady flow of inch-deep water that seeped from the makeshift dam into the cave. Both the warning sign and Rowe's evasiveness unnerved him. He'd never been inside a cave before, much less one advertised as dangerous with a man who was clearly not telling him everything. Yet here he was, in the middle of Jamaica, doing just that.

Rowe entered first, his halogen light casting a bright cone ahead. They were standing on a ledge, twenty feet wide, the roof thirty feet or more overhead. The rock beneath their feet extended ahead another twenty feet then stopped, water pouring over the side, splashing somewhere below. Rowe crept to the edge, but the thought of what might be on the other side unnerved Tom. Heights were not a favorite of his, and the swift-moving water and polished floor made footing chancy at best. One slip and there was no telling what waited in the blackness beyond.

Rowe stopped at the edge and shone his light into the abyss.

Tom saw a rocky cavern extending out and up, the far wall a good fifty feet away. Vertical strata of sandy-colored limestone soared upward to form a rough dome. The cave was like a chute that funneled water in, then down, the cascade's roar loud but not deafening.

"It drops a long way," Rowe said. "There are steps the water follows. The next one is three meters beneath us."

He crept closer to the edge and peered over. His light revealed the next level down, maybe ten feet below, which jutted out to another black edge where water disappeared over the side.

"Do you have any idea what we're supposed to do here?" Rowe asked.

He shook his head. "Not a clue."

A loud smack could be heard over the falling water. Then another.

They stared at each other.

The sound came from outside.

They both doused their lights and walked cautiously back to the exit. Outside, atop the dam, stood a man. Tall and thin. Swinging the outline of what appeared to be a sledgehammer, smacking the stones with full force.

"Stop that," Rowe yelled.

The man's head glanced up, then he lashed down with another blow.

Rowe unsnapped his holster and removed the gun. He pointed the weapon toward the blackened figure.

"I said stop."

The man swung one more time.

Rowe fired.

But his target had disappeared over the side into the river.

The dam burst open, water and rock exploding toward them. Twenty feet separated them from the calamity, which bought maybe three seconds. Alarm sent Tom darting left, away from the entrance, hoping that he could move out of the onslaught's path.

Rowe was not as quick.

The water, which before had been a few inches deep, was now a raging flood, full of projectiles, pouring into the cave.

Tom yelled, but it was too late.

Rowe was swept off his feet and disappeared in the darkness.

———

ZACHARIAH EMERGED FROM THE CAR. RÓCHA HAD parked a few meters away from a pickup truck that sat just off a narrow graveled road. They were high on a bluff overlooking dark forest, the Caribbean a few kilometers to the north.

Falcon Ridge.

He inspected the truck's bed. Full of tools. Rowe had come prepared. But for what? Rócha and Alle were now out of the car, Rócha checking the cliff edge, staring down. Water rushed below.

He heard a shout.

Then another.

And a gunshot.

"It came from down there," Rócha said.

———

BÉNE REALIZED HE WAS IN TROUBLE. EVERYTHING blurred into one whirling spiral. The swift current surged him toward the edge and there was nothing he could use to stop himself. He knew the drop on the other side was about three meters, and he hoped there was enough water down there to cushion his fall. Otherwise, bones were going to break.

He plunged over the side.

He tried to right himself and land on his feet, but gravity's pull on both him and the water was relentless.

He hit the next ledge with his boots, rebounded, then slammed to the rock. Water battered his body. He gasped for breath and bit his tongue, tasting blood. The flow was deeper here, maybe half a meter, the current fast, but not overpowering. He was planted on his soles, body not moving. Splashes around him signaled rock from the dam raining from above. He still held the light in his right hand.

More splashes.

He had to move.

He turned and spotted a ledge extending from the vertical wall, where the water from above was diverted, creating a waterfall within a waterfall.

Cover.

Not much, but maybe enough.

He leaped toward it and pressed his body close, water pouring down only a few centimeters away.

More thuds came as boulders from the dam kept falling.

———

TOM COULD NOT GO AFTER ROWE. TOO MUCH DEBRIS was sweeping in from the collapsed dam, the largest chunks wobbling to a halt just past the opening, most of the others vanishing over the edge.

Why had somebody deliberately burst the barrier?

The flow continued in a brisk current, the water now knee-high, but the debris had lessened. He risked walking ahead, the larger rocks making good handholds. He made his way to one side of the cavern and pressed himself close to the wall, keeping his flashlight aimed at his feet, watching every step.

He crept ahead and found the edge.

He pointed his light into the darkness.

"Béne," he called out. "You there?"

ZACHARIAH HEARD BÉNE ROWE'S NAME ECHO FROM across the river. He spotted faint trails of a flashlight streaking inside the cave.

"They are in there," he said.

In the moonlight he saw that a rock dam had once blocked the cave entrance but a gash now existed, water pouring through into the cave.

"We can walk across," Rócha said.

And he saw that was correct. Their lights revealed the river to be waist-deep.

"Your father is in there," he told Alle.

"That must be where his grandfather told him to go."

He believed the same thing.

Or at least he hoped that was the case.

———

BÉNE HEARD HIS NAME CALLED OUT.

"I'm here," he yelled back. "Any more rock coming?"

"I think it's all down there now," Sagan said. "You okay?"

"I didn't break anything."

He stepped out from under his protection and moved right, toward the cavern wall. He figured the closer to the side, the better. Then he saw something. His light revealed notches that stretched upward, at regular intervals. Like a ladder.

"Sagan," he yelled.

He saw the light above, but not the man. Then a face peered down close to the wall. "There's a way down. See it there." He pointed his light. "Come on. Let's keep going."

"Somebody just tried to kill us."

"I know. But they didn't, so let's keep going."

"What if they come back?"

"Actually, I hope they do. It'll save me the trouble of finding them."

CHAPTER SEVENTY-THREE

ZACHARIAH HOPPED ONTO THE DAM AND EXAMINED the gash. Alle and Rócha climbed up with him. None of their flashlights burned. He'd ordered them extinguished after they entered the river. He did not want to alert Rowe or Sagan that he was here.

Water rushed toward the cave.

Rócha slipped off and stepped past where the water flowed, reaching for something. In the moonlight he saw it was a tool, and heavy.

A sledgehammer.

Had someone opened the dam?

Rowe? Sagan? Someone else?

Both he and Rócha were armed, their guns kept above the water on the trek over. Now his was again secure in his back pocket.

"What is it?" Alle whispered.

"I don't know. But we are about to find out."

———

TOM USED THE NOTCHES IN THE WALL AND LOWERED himself to the next level. Some were natural, others clearly hewn from the rock. He found Béne standing in thigh-high water.

He motioned with his light. "You lost your gun."

The shoulder holster was empty.

"That's okay. I've rarely needed one."

Béne pulled his wet pant leg up and he saw a sheathed knife strapped to his leg. "This has always worked better for me."

He decided to risk a look over the side, hoping there would be more notches for climbing. With a padding movement, setting his feet down cautiously with each step, he eased toward the edge. Sure enough, there were more notches, the next level about eight feet below.

"I don't suppose your friend who knows caves told you what's down there?" he asked Rowe.

"Nope. And you didn't think this was going to be easy, did you?"

———

ZACHARIAH CAUGHT A WASH OF LIGHT IN THE DARKness beyond a rock ledge. He heard nothing except the roar of falling water. More lights continued to dance in the blackness. He crouched low, as did Rócha and Alle, and they used large rocks scattered here and there to work their way to the end of a ledge.

Two figures stood below.

Béne Rowe and Tom Sagan. At the edge of the next level, doing the same thing he was doing. Checking out what was below.

He signaled to Rócha, and a gun appeared.

"What are you doing?" Alle whispered.

He ignored her.

Rócha maneuvered through the dark, closer to the edge, planting his feet in the water. They'd get only one chance. It had to count. He was pleased to see that his man understood that, too.

Rócha leveled the weapon.

The shot was about twenty meters, but Sagan's and Rowe's lights made for easy targets.

Two pulls of the trigger and—

"No," Alle yelled. "Stop."

And her flashlight sprang on.

———

TOM HEARD SOMEONE YELL, THEN A LIGHT BLAZED from above.

He whirled and saw an illuminated man crouched at the ledge's end, aiming a gun their way.

Rowe saw it, too, and leaped over the side.

A shot banged.

———

ALLE HAD POINTED HER LIGHT AT RÓCHA, HOPING to blind him.

And she had.

He'd been caught off guard, one arm rising to shield his pupils at the same time he fired.

"What are you doing?" she said in a loud voice.

Zachariah backhanded her across the face, sending her down into the water. She rolled and kept her balance, planting her feet, then tried to stand.

"You stupid child," he spit out.

Had she heard right? Never had he spoken to her in such a way, and never had he struck her. She still held her flashlight, which Zachariah yanked from her grip.

"I never wanted my father killed," she said.

"Why do you think we are here? Your father and Rowe threaten all that we do. Millions of Jews have been slaughtered through time. Do you have any idea how many died defending the First and Second

Temples? What are two more deaths? They mean nothing. Your father is in our way."

In the wash of her light she saw fury on his face.

"You're insane," she said.

He lunged for her. "Since you feel the need to protect your father, then be with him."

She tried to shrink back and avoid his grasp, but he grabbed her hair and wrenched her head downward, tripping her legs out from under her. She hit the swift-moving water and tried to stand. But he helped her along with a kick, the flow too fast, her body too close to the end.

She screamed.

And dropped over the edge.

―――――

TOM HAD AVOIDED THE SHOT FROM ABOVE THANKS TO a light that blinded the shooter momentarily, the fired round ricocheting off the cavern walls. By the time the shooter recovered, he'd pushed himself through the rushing water, light off, back toward the cavern wall. He kept his focus above, eyes mated to the darkness, but the man had disappeared.

A stab of light suddenly appeared, bouncing across the roof.

He could hear shouting but couldn't make out what was being said, the words lost in the trills and gurgles of the falling water.

More movement above.

Then a scream jolted his nerves.

Female.

Could it be?

A body came over the edge and splashed into the waist-high water. Whoever it was came up, gasped for breath, and tried to stand.

"Dad."

The word tore at his heart.

Alle.

He lunged toward her, wrapping his arms around her body, intent on stabilizing them both. Then he saw two forms above, one holding a flashlight aimed down.

"It is all over," Simon called out.

The other man raised a weapon.

With Alle in his grip, one hand still holding his unlit flashlight, he dropped them into the water, out of the beam's glare.

Simon adjusted, trying to relocate the targets.

But the current sent them over the side.

———

ZACHARIAH STARED DOWN, AMAZED.

"He took them both over," he said to Rócha.

But he wondered. What did Tom Sagan know now that he didn't? Water raced past his legs. He used the light and scanned the cavern wall.

And saw niches. Leading down.

Rócha saw them, too, and moved closer with his light.

"So let us see what it is you know," he whispered.

CHAPTER SEVENTY-FOUR

BÉNE HAD WILLINGLY LEAPED OVER THE SIDE, KNOW-ing that the next level was less than three meters below. His impact was broken by more water about a meter deep. He'd heard a gunshot, the sound within the rocky confines like an explosion. Had Zachariah Simon arrived? Or was it the same person who'd destroyed the dam?

The *abeng* he'd first heard was the question, the return wail the answer. But why had the Maroons staked out this cave?

And why flood it?

He wondered about the extra depth of water on this level, much more than above, and the answer to his question came as he sloshed his way ahead. The rock angled upward, transforming this step into a rough bowl that first had to fill before any liquid continued its downward assault.

Thank goodness.

The deeper the better.

He switched on his light, which he still held, and saw that the ledge was about ten meters wide. He glanced over its end and saw that the next one below was close, maybe two meters down, shorter and thinner, too, water quickly disappearing over its edge into more blackness.

He heard a scream from behind.

He whirled and saw lights reflecting off the ceiling in a chaotic dance. A splash, then a dark clump spilled from above and plopped into the pool two meters away.

He aimed his light and saw Sagan holding a woman.

"You can stand," he yelled.

Sagan released his grip and steadied himself. The woman—young, small-boned, maybe in her twenties with long dark hair—swiped water from her eyes. Both of them grabbed breaths.

He kept his light angled away so as not to blind them. "You okay?"

Sagan nodded his head, sucking deep breaths of the dank air. "Simon is here."

His nerves came alert and his head stared up. What happened to his men at the airport? Nothing good, he assumed. He caught the faint glow of light on the far cavern wall.

And knew what was happening.

Simon was climbing down.

Sagan stood. "He's not alone."

"His name is Rócha," the woman said.

"Béne, this is my daughter, Alle."

"The son of a bitch shoved me over the side," she said. "He tried to kill me."

Béne heard the shock in her voice.

"But you saved my life," she said to Sagan. "Why did you do that? You jumped in and grabbed me. You went over the side first. You could have been killed."

"I'm just glad there was water here," Sagan said.

"We have to go," Béne said. "I know Rócha. He's trouble. And they're both coming this way."

He angled his light down and crept toward the edge. "It's a short drop. Do it fast."

They all three hopped down, the water now only ankle-deep.

Quickly he found the next edge and aimed his light. A series of short steps made a steep descent.

Then he noticed something.

A glow from below.

"What is that?" Sagan whispered, apparently seeing it, too.

"I don't know, but it's the only way to go."

The men behind them were armed. They weren't. Their only choice was to use the darkness to their advantage.

He switched off his light.

"Down," he breathed.

ZACHARIAH SAW A LIGHT BELOW, FLICKING ON AND off. Somebody was on the move, careful how long they betrayed their location.

Rowe? Sagan?

He and Rócha had utilized the rock ladder for the first change of levels, but now they simply hopped down each ledge. This cave was a natural chute that channeled groundwater, one level at a time, into the earth like a massive fountain. Before the dam had been destroyed rain would have been all that seeped inside. Now water poured with a pealing rumble, and he wondered where it led.

The light below had stopped strobing.

Were they armed?

Knowing Rowe, the answer was yes.

Unfortunately, he had to use the same trick, switching his flashlight on and off, since there was no way to see anything in the void.

But then he noticed something in the depths.

Light.

And constant.

What was that?

They kept descending.

———

TOM HOPPED OFF THE LAST LEDGE AND STARED AT the amazing sight.

They'd made it to the bottom.

He estimated they were more than a hundred yards underground, the gushing torrent launching off into a dark, misty void in the far rock wall. The cavern that rose around them stretched at least a hundred feet high and that much wide. White stalactites dropped from the ceiling. Ten torches, projecting from the wall thirty feet up, illuminated the space, their fires spangling the darkness, trails of sparks popping skyward like comets. More climbing niches etched into the wall stretched below each torch, which explained how they were lit.

But by who?

And why?

No more darkness provided cover.

Nowhere to hide.

"What is this?" Alle asked.

He noticed that the water from above had lost nearly all of its strength, sapped by the many levels of varying lengths and depth. Several of the steps had been angled, forming pools that further arrested the flow. Here, at the bottom, the final remnants poured off the last ledge in a transparent sheet that stretched thirty feet wide and eight feet tall, pooling into a lake. To their right, the lake spilled over a rocky ledge and cascaded a few feet down to the river, which had the effect of keeping the lake level constant. A moldy smell of wet earth filled his nostrils. On the far side was another slit in the rock, large enough to walk through, a narrow ledge before it. There was no way to get to that ledge without crossing the lake. They stood on the only dry patch in the oblong-shaped cavern, the rock coated with a green, sandy patina.

A man appeared on the ledge above them.

Black-skinned, thin, older, with short hair.

Rowe seemed to know him.

BÉNE STARED AT FRANK CLARKE.

"We have our eyes and ears, too, Béne. Just like you. We watch those who bear watching."

Apparently so. Maroons had always done that. In the war years they'd cultivated spies in every plantation and town, people who would keep them informed as to what the British were planning.

"Then you know," he said, "there's somebody else coming this way."

"Do you have 'em?" Frank called out.

A moment later Béne saw Simon, Rócha, and two Maroons, armed with *machets,* on the next ledge up. They hopped down. Two handguns and flashlights were handed over to Frank.

"I see you survived," Simon said to Sagan's daughter.

"Go to hell," she spat out.

Simon seemed unfazed by her rebuke. He simply turned to Clarke and asked, "And who are you?"

"We are the keepers of this place."

"And what is this?" Sagan asked.

"Sixty years ago," Frank said, "we were asked by a friend to hold something of great value. He was a special man, someone who understood Maroons in a deep way. He was also a Jew. There is a deep connection between Maroon and Jew, always has been."

No one said anything.

"Yankipong is our supreme being. Our god," Frank said. "Maroons were handpicked by Yankipong to serve as a conduit of His divine power. We have always thought of ourselves as chosen."

"Like the Israelites," Simon said. "Chosen by God. Singled out for divine favor."

Frank nodded. "We noticed the similarity long ago. Maroons were able to overcome what others deemed hopeless. Jews have done the same. We'd already found the treasure the man who came here spoke of, but when he told us how sacred it was, we regretted our violation of it. That's another thing about Maroons. We're respectful of others' ways."

"You found the Temple treasure?" Simon asked.

Frank nodded. "Long ago. It was brought here for safekeeping in the time of the Spanish, by Columbus himself."

"You told me those objects disappeared," Béne said to Clarke.

"Another lie. I was hoping you'd let this go. I thought maybe the attempt on your life would stop you. But here you are. You couldn't have found this place on your own, so I assume one of these outsiders is the Levite."

That word Béne knew.

"I am that person," Simon said.

"Liar," Alle yelled. "You're nothing."

Simon faced Clarke. "I have come for the treasure."

"Then you'll know how to find it."

Béne kept silent. What was the colonel up to?

Frank stepped to the lake's edge. The water was shallow, no more than a third of a meter deep, its surface smooth as a mirror, like an infinity pool at one of his resorts. It was shaped as a rough oblong, about thirty meters wide, stretching the entire cavern.

"Leave," Frank called out.

The two Maroons with *machets* climbed up the rocky ledges, disappearing toward the surface.

"This is a private matter," Frank said.

But Béne was worried. Even though Frank still held the two guns and the flashlights lay on the ground, Rócha could make a move.

"If you think attacking me will solve anything," Frank said, "be warned. Only the Levite can go from here. I know nothing. But I do need to show you something."

Frank tossed one of the guns he held into the lake.

It sank to the shallow bottom.

Béne had already noticed stones scattered beneath the surface, and now realized that in between them was mud. Frank lifted a rock, about the size of a melon, and dropped it into the lake. A splash, then the water cleared and the rock met bottom, settling beside the gun. Bubbles oozed to the surface. Then the rock sank, sucking the gun down into the mud with it.

"At the time of the Maroon wars," Frank said, "British soldiers were brought here for questioning. One of 'em was tossed into the lake and the others watched as he sank in the mud. After that, answers to our questions came easy."

"The person who came here," Sagan said. "The one who told you about the treasure. Was it Marc Eden Cross?"

Frank nodded. "I'm told he was a remarkable man. The colonels at the time had great respect for him. He asked for our help with a great duty imposed on him, and we provided it. This place was changed . . . for him."

CHAPTER SEVENTY-FIVE

ALLE WAS WET, SORE, AND PISSED. AT SIMON. AT HER-self. She'd been an idiot, allowing her anger, her whims, and her fantasies to be exploited.

"Who are you?" she blurted out to the older man who'd tossed the gun in the water.

"My name is Frank Clarke. I'm colonel of the local Maroons. This land is ours by treaty. That means I'm in charge. Who are you?"

"Alle Becket."

"That man," her father said, "who came here sixty years ago. That was my grandfather, Marc Eden Cross. Her great-grandfather. He told you the truth. He was fulfilling a special duty given to him."

"I am told he spent a lot of time in Jamaica and came to know Maroons in ways outsiders rarely do. We offered him this place as sanctuary and he accepted." Clarke pointed to the lake. "This pit filled with mud long ago. It's a thick soupy mixture. You see the many stones scattered beneath the water. Some have numbers etched into them. Cross did that himself. His addition to this place. This water, this mud has served Maroons for centuries. Now it serves the Jews. It is for the Levite to take the next step."

Alle was unsure what the man meant.

As, apparently, were the others.

"You saw how the gun rested on the bottom. The mud will support weight, so long as it's not disturbed. The stones beneath the surface with no numbers rest on solid rock and will never sink. The others, with numbers, float on mud. The only way to the ledge on the far side is to step on the right stones."

"And what prevents us from floating across?" Zachariah asked.

"It's too shallow to do without a raft, and there's none here. If anyone tries to cross this lake, except through the prescribed method, they die. That was our promise to the Levite. Three have tried over the past sixty years. Their bodies are in the mud. None has attempted it in a long time."

"This is nuts," she said.

"It is what your great-grandfather wanted. He created this challenge."

"How do we know that?" she asked.

Clarke shrugged. "You have only my word. But he told us that another Levite would arrive one day and know exactly how to get across."

"And what's over there?" Rowe asked.

She wanted to know that, too.

"What the Levite seeks."

She saw that Simon was thinking. In Prague she'd told him everything she could remember about the message her grandfather left in his grave. Including five numbers: 3, 74, 5, 86, 19.

Her father also knew those numbers.

"I know the way," Simon said. "I accept the challenge."

Clarke stepped away from the lake's edge and casually motioned with the second gun. "Your success will tell us if you're the Levite."

ZACHARIAH WAS SURE HE WAS RIGHT.

The five numbers Alle had told him had to be the way. 3, 74, 5, 86, 19.

He'd noticed something about them while thinking on the plane. The first three together, 374, were the number of years the First Temple had stood until the Babylonians razed it. The second three, 586, the number of years the Second Temple had stood until the Romans wreaked havoc.

That was not coincidental.

Cross had obviously picked his numbers with care.

The last number—19?

He had no idea.

But he was certain they led the way across the lake.

Why else include them?

And there was something else Cross had done.

"Remember the message from Abiram Sagan," he said. "*The golem helps protect our secret in a place long sacred to Jews*. A golem is a living body, created from raw earth, using fire, water, and air. Exactly what we have here. This lake is a golem."

"Why flood it?" Sagan asked Clarke.

"It stays wet from rainwater and serves its purpose but, for this challenge, a bit more depth was required. Once I learned Béne was coming here, I ordered the dam be opened. We built it. If you fail here tonight, we will rebuild it and await the true Levite."

"Why do this?" Rowe asked Clarke. "Seems like a lot of trouble for outsiders."

"As I told you before, Béne, you really don't understand us. Maroons were always outsiders, brought here in chains. We fled to the mountains to be free. The Jews were no different from us. They were never accepted, either. Many of us remember what they did for Maroons during the two wars. I am told that this was our way of repaying them."

Zachariah had heard enough. He pointed at Rócha. "You go. I'll direct the path."

He saw the apprehension in his man's eyes.

"Not to worry," he said. "I know what I am doing."

"Then go yourself," Sagan said.

"And leave you here? I do not think so."

He hoped that once he conquered the challenge this Frank Clarke would have no choice but to acknowledge he was the Levite, entitled to what awaited on the lake's far side. Maybe then Clarke would deal with Rowe, Alle, and Sagan for him.

He faced Rócha. "You will be fine. I know the way."

Rócha nodded his acceptance, then stepped to the rock edge. Torches shed a blood-red luster over the water. Half a dozen stones, all devoid of numbers, lay scattered across the bottom, about a meter apart, extending out five meters. Rócha plunged his foot through the shin-high water and stepped on the nearest one, nodding his head that it was solid. He then worked his way out into the lake, sloshing through the water, following more stones with no numbers.

Then stopped.

"Ahead are five stones," Rócha called out. "They are numbered 9, 35, 72, 3, 24."

Zachariah nearly smiled. He was right. "The one with the three is safe," he called out.

He watched as Rócha tested the stone and saw that he'd chosen correctly.

Now he knew.

Another series of blanks, then a second cluster of numbered stones. The one with 74, as he thought, proved solid. Two more times, and 5 and 86 offered safe passage. Rócha was now about twenty meters from the far ledge, calling out the next sequence of numbered stones. Zachariah told him 19 was the safe play.

And he was right.

Except that Rócha was still not at the ledge.

Ten meters of water remained.

"There's a final sequence of stones," Rócha called out. "Twenty of them numbered. The others are blank, but there's no way to reach them."

A final sequence?

But the message only provided five numbers.

"Can you make it to the ledge?" he called out.

Rócha shook his head. "No way. Too far."

He glanced over at Tom Sagan, who appraised him with a cool glare. He'd said nothing about being the Levite when Clarke spoke up, allowing only Alle to challenge him. The son of a bitch. There was something more, something Sagan had not allowed his daughter to learn. And he'd stayed silent to see if he was right.

Rócha had no idea that the next choice would be a guess. Only Sagan would know that, and the former reporter surely could not care less if Rócha died. In fact, he was probably counting on it.

"Tell me the numbers you see," he yelled across the water.

Rócha rattled off twenty.

"Thirty-four," he said.

Rócha did not hesitate. Why would he? Every other choice had been right.

His man stepped toward the stone, planted one foot, then the next. And began to sink.

Panic immediately grabbed hold. Arms went into the air searching for balance. He tried to leap away and find another stone, but the mud around his feet was too strong.

Rócha began to sink.

As the others realized what they were watching, Zachariah elbowed Frank Clarke in the gut.

The older man reeled forward, the breath leaving his lungs.

Rowe surged his way.

But Zachariah wrenched the gun from Clarke's grasp and aimed it straight at his adversary.

"Back off, Béne," he ordered. "I will shoot you dead."

Rowe stopped his advance.

He motioned with the gun for Sagan and Alle to join Rowe and for all of them to step back. Clarke, too. He wanted them where he could see them.

"Mr. Simon, help me," Rócha screamed. "Send one of them. They can get this far and pull me out."

But he could not risk it. Not now. He had the situation under control and planned to keep it that way. Besides, he had a better way to get across.

Rócha sank fast, nothing to stop him, the mud now chest-high.

Clarke straightened himself up.

"Mr. Simon, help me," Rócha screamed.

"You just going to let him die?" Sagan asked.

"That's exactly what I'm going to do."

"You really are a monster," Alle said.

"A warrior. On a mission. Something you could not possibly understand."

"Somebody. Please," Rócha yelled.

"Stay still," Sagan called out.

But that was surely easier said than done.

Too late.

Rócha disappeared.

Ripples disturbed the mirrored surface, which

quickly receded, leaving no trace that anyone had ever been there. Everything assumed a strange quality of unreality.

"You are clearly not the Levite," Clarke said.

Zachariah aimed the gun at Sagan. "You know the sixth number."

No response.

"And you would never tell me. So your daughter will make the next trip across."

"Like hell I will," Alle said.

He cocked the gun, aimed, and fired.

CHAPTER SEVENTY-SIX

TOM CRINGED AS THE SHOT EXPLODED.

But Simon had readjusted his aim and fired at Alle's feet, the bullet careening off the rock.

She'd leaped away in terror.

"The next bullet will not miss," Simon said.

And Tom had no reason to doubt that. None of them meant a damn thing to him. Only what was on the other side of the lake. That's what mattered and he'd do whatever was necessary to get there.

"Go," Simon ordered Alle. "Into the water."

She shook her head.

"I'll go," Tom said. "I'll do it. You're right, I know the way."

Simon chuckled. "Which is exactly why she is going. I haven't forgotten how we met. For all I know, you will go out there and finish what I interrupted at your father's house. No. To be sure you will tell the truth, she will go."

"I'll do it—"

"She goes," Simon yelled, "or I kill her and Béne can take her place."

Tom stared at his daughter and, with no choice, said, "Do it."

Her questioning look challenged the wisdom of that move.

"You're going to have to trust me," he said.

He spied no anger or resentment in her eyes.

Only fear.

And it tore his heart.

He stepped close to her. "The first stone is number 3."

She did not move.

"We can do this. Together."

She steeled herself and faced the challenge. Then she nodded, acknowledging the futility in arguing. He watched as she entered the water, only about a foot deep, on blank stones, settling her feet. He could see the first assemblage of numbered stones and was pleased when she found the one marked 3.

Which supported her, as it had Rócha.

Simon stepped back, keeping the gun ready to deal with anyone who made a move on him. He caught Rowe's gaze and read what his dark eyes telegraphed. Simon could not shoot all three of them before one of them got to him. But he shook his head and threw him a look that said, *Not yet.* Neither Rowe nor the other man, Clarke, knew what he'd been privy to. His grandfather had left a specific message. Time to see if it he was interpreting it correctly. The five numbers had led to the sixth, through the astrolabe. But that did not mean the sixth number, which had located this cave on the map, also provided safe passage across. A safety valve could have been built in. Like when different passwords were used for different accounts.

But something told him he was right.

Or at least he hoped so.

His daughter's life depended on it.

———

ALLE'S LEGS SHOOK WITH FEAR.

She'd been afraid before, but never like this.

Her father called off the five numbers and she worked her way across the shallow pond, toward the far ledge. Rócha had paved the way this far. Now she stood on the stone labeled 19, where Rócha had waited for the sixth number.

Her breathing went shallow.

A good twenty feet of mud was between her and solid ground. She glanced down and counted nineteen stones with numbers affixed to them, another ten or so blank. The twentieth, once labeled 34, was gone, taking Rócha into the mud with it.

Not that his death bothered her.

It was her own that mattered.

"Call out the numbers you see," her father said.

———

TOM LISTENED AS ALLE PROVIDED A LIST.

As she did, he glanced at Rowe and saw that the Jamaican understood.

Be ready.

Soon.

———

BÉNE WONDERED IF SAGAN ACTUALLY KNEW THE sixth number. He'd clearly encouraged his daughter to go. But what choice had he been given? Simon would have killed her. Frank Clarke stood beside him, saying nothing. Simon was watching both them and the woman on the lake. If she made it across, Simon would shoot them all. That was a given. He'd know everything at that point.

Then why not act now?

Frank seemed to read his mind.

"Not yet," the colonel whispered.

ALLE'S KNEES SHOOK AND SHE WILLED THEM TO STOP.
Did her father know the way across? Here she was, trusting someone whom she'd spent the last ten years of her life despising. But what did she know? Look how wrong about Zachariah Simon she'd been.

Shame clouded her thoughts, but did nothing to alleviate the terror sweeping through her.

One wrong step and she was dead.

———

TOM GLANCED AT SIMON AND SAID, "JUST SO WE'RE clear. You're not the Levite. I am."

"That is not possible," Simon said to him. "You are not even a Jew. By your own admission."

He ignored the insult, concentrating instead on Alle's recitation of numbers. She hadn't reported a stone with 56 on its face, which was the sixth number the astrolabe had revealed. But she had noted that there were two stones marked 5 and 6 among the nineteen.

And he knew.

That was the fail-safe.

Saki had split the last number into two.

It's the only thing that made sense and, if nothing else, from everything he'd seen or ever been told, Marc Eden Cross always made sense.

He cast his gaze back across the lake.

"Five and six. Use both of them. I'm assuming you're going to need them to cross the distance."

———

"I SEE THEM," ALLE SAID. "FIVE IS FIRST, THEN SOME blanks. Six is closer to the ledge."

"That's the way," her father called out.

"And if you're wrong?" she asked.

"I'm not."

She liked the definitive way he'd answered but wondered if that was for her benefit or Simon's.

She stood petrified, willing her right foot to come out of the water, but anxiety held it in place. She was safe here. Why go any farther?

Go back.

No way.

Simon would shoot her before she made it halfway across.

———

BÉNE WAS READY TO CHARGE.

Of course, he may well get shot before he made it to the Simon, but he was going to try.

Frank slowly shook his head.

And in the eyes of his old friend, he saw why he had to stay still.

At least for a little while longer.

This must resolve itself.

We cannot interfere.

He'd resented being considered not Maroon. Angered by colonels who regarded him as a threat. Frank had told him that he did not understand Maroon ways.

Time to show that he did.

So he held his ground and waited.

Hoping that he wasn't making a mistake.

———

ZACHARIAH KNEW THAT IF SAGAN WAS RIGHT AND Alle made it across, that was the time to kill all three men, then Alle, and find the treasure. If the two who'd left earlier were still around at ground level, he'd use the darkness and avoid them, returning tomorrow with a contingent of his own.

That was the thing about having money.

It could buy a multitude of things.

Including results.

———

ALLE STEELED HERSELF.

Five.

Then six.

The stone labeled 5 waited three feet away. A full stride, but she could make it. She lifted her right leg, pivoted forward, and nearly lost her balance. Her arms immediately extended, her lungs tightened, and she fought hard not to fall.

Her right foot settled back down beside her left.

She stabilized herself.

"What happened?" her father called out.

"Just scared to death. The shallow water makes this tricky."

"Take your time," he said to her.

"But not too much," Simon added.

"Go screw yourself," she yelled, keeping her head and eyes focused on the stones beneath the water.

In one quick stride she lifted her right foot, swung out, and resettled it into the water, the sole of her wet shoe resting on the 5 stone.

Which held.

She transferred herself over.

If 5 worked, why not 6?

This time with no hesitation she stepped onto the 6 stone.

Solid.

Three more feet and she was on the ledge.

Relief and joy swept through her.

She turned back just in time to see Béne Rowe rushing toward Simon.

CHAPTER SEVENTY-SEVEN

Béne was ready.

The woman was safe.

And Simon's attention was momentarily on her success.

He lunged.

Simon reacted by swinging the gun, but Béne's right leg arched upward and snapped Simon's arm, the grip on the gun releasing, the weapon clattering away.

Simon froze.

Béne smiled. *"Yu tan deh a crab up yuself, sittin o do yu."*

He saw that the Simon did not understand patois. "It's a saying of ours. 'If you keep on scratching yourself, something is going to happen to you.' "

He lunged forward and grabbed the lying bastard with one hand, swinging his right fist hard into the stomach. He released his hold and allowed Simon to stagger back.

He readied himself for another blow.

Simon recovered and tried to land a fist of his own.

Béne dodged, then landed an uppercut to the jaw. He was twenty-three years younger than this man, with a lifetime of experience in facing down opponents.

He righted Simon, who was woozy and breathing hard.

He wrapped his right arm around the neck, tightened, and began to choke the life away. Simon's muscles tried to counter but, as oxygen lessened, so did his resistance.

Béne lifted Simon off the ground, stepped to the lake's edge, and dropped him over the side.

———

ZACHARIAH HAD NEVER FELT THE PRESSURE OF strong muscles encircling his throat, arms immovable, a vise tightening. He could neither breathe, nor call out. Even worse, Rowe was dropping him into the water.

And not on stones.

His feet found mud.

For a few seconds he held, then his body sank, the mud consuming him. He searched for something to hold on to. Nothing. He tried to arrest the panic rushing through him and recalled what Clarke had said, what Sagan had advised Rócha.

Stand still.

If the mud was unmolested it would support weight.

He told himself to stop moving. He'd sunk to just about his knees, but the rigidity worked. He stabilized.

No more sinking.

Rowe, Sagan, and Clark stood on the bank and watched him, all three within an arm's grasp.

He was at their mercy.

———

TOM WAS UNCONCERNED ABOUT SIMON.

He wanted to get to Alle.

So he grabbed one of the flashlights lying on the ground, stepped into the water, and worked his way across the pond, following the prescribed path to the ledge on the far side.

Alle waited, watching what was happening a hundred feet away with Simon.

He hopped out of the water.

They both stared across.

"I appreciate you being right," she said to him.

"Thanks for trusting me."

"I didn't have a whole lot of choice."

"That's not our problem anymore," he said to her, motioning to the far side. "Time for you and me to see what your grandfather spent his life protecting."

She nodded, but he could read her thoughts. She'd trusted Simon, believed in him, done his bidding. All for nothing. In the end, he tossed her away as meaningless.

He touched her shoulder. "Everyone makes those kind of mistakes. Don't sweat it."

"I was an idiot. Look what I did to you."

No anger. No resentment. Just a daughter speaking to her father.

He switched on the light. "That's history. Let's do this."

He led the way into the crack, which opened to a narrow corridor that wound a path through a natural fissure cut at tall, odd angles. Absolute blackness consumed them. If not for the flashlight, they would not have been able to see their fingers touching their noses.

The treasures Saki had secreted here were created 2,500 years ago according to directions provided from God. The Ark of the Covenant was long gone, destroyed when the Babylonians torched the First

Temple. Or at least that's what most historians believed. But the golden menorah, the divine table, and the silver trumpets could still exist. He knew about the Arch of Titus, on the summit of the Sacred Way in the Forum, upon which was a relief showing the menorah and trumpets being paraded through Rome in 71 CE. The Israeli government had asked and the Italians obliged, forbidding anyone from passing through the arch. The last dignitaries to have formally walked under it were Mussolini and Hitler. Tour guides actually allowed visiting Jews to spit on the walls. He'd written a story about that, long ago. He recalled how every Jew he interviewed spoke with reverence about the Temple treasure.

On one thing Simon had been right.

Finding it would mean something significant.

They kept walking, the flashlight illuminating the rocky floor ahead. No moisture here. Dry as a desert. The brittle sand crunching with every step.

Ahead, the corridor ended.

———

BÉNE STOOD SILENT AND WATCHED ZACHARIAH Simon standing perfectly still, not a muscle moving.

"What are you going to do?" Frank asked him.

"So-so cross deh pon mi from him."

He felt more comfortable speaking with Simon not being able to understand.

"A wa you a say?"

A good question. He'd told Frank that there'd been nothing but trouble from Simon. Now his adversary, who'd lied to him from the start and tried to kill him in Cuba, was helpless. All he had to do was jostle the mud and the man would sink to his death.

But that was too damn easy.

"You were testing me," he said to Frank. "And testing Sagan."

"We promised that only the Levite would make it across, according to the instructions. I had to make sure that happened. I had to trust the quest. I was sure this man"—Frank pointed at Simon—"was not the Levite, but I had to know that the other one was."

"Maroons want to trust, don't they?"

"For all the fighting we were, at heart, a peaceful people who simply wanted to exist. Even when we made peace, we trusted that the British would be fair."

"But they weren't."

"Which was to their detriment, not ours. They lost more than we did. History will always remember their lies."

He saw the point.

"What happened here today was important for the Jews," Frank said. "I'm glad we could play a part in it."

"What's back there?"

Frank shook his head. "I don't know."

"I didn't come here for any treasure." He pointed at Simon in the water. "I came for him."

"And he's yours."

Béne extended a hand, which Simon grabbed.

He pulled his nemesis onto the bank.

"That's right," he said. "He's mine."

———

TOM STARED AT THE OPENING, A JAGGED SLIT NOT much taller than him, where the dry passage ended at a choke point. He shone the light and saw more sandy floor on the other side.

He approached, Alle behind him, and they entered.

A quick survey with the light revealed a room about twenty feet deep and that much wide, with an uncomfortably low ceiling. In the flashlight's beam during the sweep he'd spotted a glitter where the light reflected back toward them.

Once satisfied that the chamber was no threat, he aimed the beam and counted three stone pedestals. Rocks, about three feet high, their tops and bottoms chiseled flat, stood upright. To his left, atop the first, was the seven-branched menorah, its golden hue dulled only slightly. Next the divine table, the golden patina brighter, its jewels twinkling like stars. Two silver trumpets lay on the third dais, their silver exteriors dotted with more gold, the rest tarnished black but still intact.

The Temple treasure.

Here.

Found.

"It's real," she said.

That it was.

He imagined all those who'd died protecting it. Thousands were slaughtered when the Romans sacked Jerusalem. After that, only cleverness had assured that the treasure survived. For two thousand years it had stayed hidden, safe from the world, safe from the Zachariah Simon. It even made it across the Atlantic, on a voyage whose chances of success had been deemed minimal.

Yet here it was.

And his family.

The secret they'd kept for at least two generations, and who knows how many before that.

Now that duty had passed.

To him.

He heard Alle utter a prayer. Had there been a religious bone in his body, he'd have joined her. But all he could think about was the past eight years.

His life. Its ruin.

And what the woman in Prague had said.

Find the treasure. Then we will talk.

CHAPTER SEVENTY-EIGHT

BÉNE TOOK STOCK OF THE TWO WOMEN WHO STOOD on his veranda. One was petite, in her early sixties, dark hair streaked with waves of silver. She was dressed in a stylish blouse and skirt, low-heeled pumps, and introduced herself as Stephanie Nelle, head of the Magellan Billet, United States Justice Department.

"Brian Jamison worked for me," she said. "So let's not play games with each other. Okay?"

He'd smiled at her forwardness, confident that the rules, which once favored her, had changed completely.

The other woman was taller, stouter, a few years younger, and similarly dressed. She introduced herself as the Israeli ambassador to Austria.

"You're a long way from home," he said to her.

"We came to see you," the ambassador said.

He offered both women drinks, but they refused. He poured himself some fresh-squeezed lemonade, one of his favorites, sweetened with honey from bees kept here on the estate. A fickle March sun tried to break through in patches from rising afternoon clouds. Rain was coming, but not for a few hours. A little over twelve hours had passed since he'd emerged from Darby's Hole.

"What happened last night?" Nelle asked.

He sipped his lemonade and listened in the distance.

He heard the dogs.

Barking.

He'd opened the pens over an hour ago, his pets grateful for the release. Big Nanny led and he'd watched them disappear into the familiar territory of the high forest.

Their wail was slow and steady.

Businesslike.

As with the Maroons' *abeng,* he'd learned the meanings of their call.

"Last night?" he asked, referring to the question. "I slept well."

Nelle shook her head. "I told you we didn't have time for games."

"Zachariah Simon landed here a little after midnight," the ambassador said. "He came with one of his employees, a man named Rócha, and Alle Becket. Tom Sagan arrived about an hour before. Two bodies were found at the Kingston airport this morning. Men who, I am told, work for you."

He'd been troubled to learn of their deaths. He'd told them to be on guard, to expect Simon to be trouble. Unfortunately, the personalities that came into his employ were often too confident and too inexperienced, which sometimes proved a deadly combination. One of the men was married, with children. He'd pay the widow a visit tomorrow and make sure, financially, she'd be okay.

"You have a remarkable amount of information for two people who don't live here. How does any of it relate to me?"

Trucks headed off in the distance for one of the far pastures, where his prized horses grazed. He'd been

told a few days ago that the coffee beans were blooming, and it looked like a good year ahead.

"Quit the act," Nelle said. "Simon killed Brian
Jamison. For all we know, you okayed that."

"Me? I liked Brian."

The Justice Department woman never broke a
smile. "Yeah, I'm sure you did. But did you think
we'd forget about you?"

He said nothing.

"I was there," Nelle said, "when Brian's body was
fished out of a trash bin. He was a good man. A good
agent. Dead, because of you."

"Me? You sent him here to pressure me. I cooperated with you. The Simon was the problem for Brian."

"Mr. Rowe," the ambassador said. "I had to cover
up Agent Jamison's death. I, too, was there when his
body was found. I do not like that he had to die.
This entire operation gyrated out of control. I am
told that there is quite a file on you. More than
enough charges to bring you down."

He sipped more of his cold drink. "This is Jamaica.
If I have done something wrong, then take it to the
authorities." He bore his gaze into her. "Otherwise,
keep threats to yourself."

"If I had my way," Nelle said, "I'd handle you myself."

He chuckled. "Why so much hostility? I don't
bother you." He pointed at the other woman. "I
don't bother you."

The ambassador said, "Mr. Rowe. Most likely,
sometime in the next year, I may become prime minister of Israel. I realize that is not important to you,
but Zachariah Simon is important to us."

He shook his head. "That's a bad man. A lying
man."

The ambassador nodded in agreement. "We have

been watching Simon for many years. He's been in and out of this area on more than one occasion. Up until recently his activities were deemed only . . . misguided. But that may no longer be the case. A good man, a rabbi named Berlinger, was found shot to death in Prague a few hours ago. Simon, or someone working for him, probably killed him. Unfortunately, that rabbi was one of only five people that we know of who may have the answers we seek. You're one of the four still left alive."

He knew the other three. Sagan. His daughter. And Simon.

But what about Frank Clarke? These women apparently knew nothing of him. Which was fitting. As the Maroons of old, he'd disappeared back into the forest. "What is it you want to know?"

"Where's Simon?" Nelle said to him.

He leaned on the veranda's rail. Its wood had come from the nearby forest, the trees felled centuries ago by slaves.

His ancestors.

Some of whom became Maroons.

The dogs continued to bark in the distance.

The sound comforted him.

As did the fact that neither of these women had a clue about Falcon Ridge or Darby's Hole. If they did, they'd be there, not here. He'd dispatched men to stake out the cave since leaving hours ago. No one had returned.

Di innocent an di fool could pass fi twin.

He told himself to be neither.

Instead, be in charge.

"Simon can no longer help you."

Nelle started to speak, but the ambassador grabbed her arm and said, "Zachariah Simon is a dangerous fanatic. He wanted to start a war. Thousands would have died because of him. But we may have stopped all that. For all his insanity, though, he sought something of great value to Jews. A sacred treasure that we thought lost, but may be found. Four objects. Do you know where they are?"

He shook his head. Which was the truth. He'd never crossed the stones to follow Sagan and his daughter. Instead he'd yanked Simon from the mud then climbed back to ground level, bringing his prisoner here, to the estate, where he'd been locked away. Sagan and his daughter had emerged from the cave and left with Frank, neither saying a word. What they may have found was not something he cared to know. Time for him to start acting like a Maroon. These women were *obroni*—outsiders—not worthy of the knowledge he possessed. Silence was the Maroon way.

"I truly don't know."

He caught a shift in the dogs' wail. A deepening, the rhythm lengthening, and knew what that meant.

"But you do know where Simon is," Nelle said.

"The last I saw, he was running."

"You are going to kill me?" Simon asked.

"Not me." He pointed to the dogs. "They do it for me."

The look was the same he'd seen from the drug don four days ago.

He enjoyed more of his lemonade and caught the scent of cooking pork. A wild hog, killed earlier, roasting for later.

There'd be some good jerk to eat tonight.

Hopefully, his mother would make yams.

He thought of Grandy Nanny, knowing now that the woman was no legend. She was real. It was said that she held special power over wild hogs and could call the animals to her.

"Three hundred years ago my ancestors were brought here in chains and sold as slaves. We worked the fields. Mine were Coromantees from the Gold Coast. Eventually, we rebelled. Many fled to the hills. We fought the British and won our freedom. I am Maroon."

"And the point of that genealogical lesson?" Nelle asked.

He caught a pause in the dogs' bay and counted the seconds. One. Two. Three. He kept counting till eight, when the sound began again.

Big Nanny had found her prey.

What a leader.

He drank the remainder of his lemonade.

Life was good.

He knew there were secrets to be kept. Like Darby's Hole. The underground lake. Numbered stones. And what lay on the other side.

He heard a scream.

Distant. Faint. But unmistakable.

Both women heard it, too.

Then the dogs.

Not barking.

Howling.

He had no idea where they'd cornered Zachariah Simon, only that they had. Of course, like the don a few days ago, if Simon had not resisted they would not have harmed him.

But this time the prey had resisted.

"The point of the family lesson?" he said. "Not one, really. Only that I'm proud of from where I came."

Silence from the distance.

No dogs could be heard.

And he knew why.

His dogs always ate what they killed.

"I don't think Mr. Rowe can help us any longer," the ambassador said.

Smart lady.

He saw that the other woman from the Justice Department also knew that to be true.

"No," Nelle said. "It's all over, isn't it?"

He said nothing.

But she spoke the truth.

Zachariah Simon was gone.

CHAPTER SEVENTY-NINE

IT HAS BEEN SIX YEARS SINCE THE GREAT ADMIRAL DIED. I find myself praying for his soul even more than I pray for my own. Life on this island is difficult, but rewarding. My decision to stay instead of returning to Spain has proven wise. Before I leave this life and meet my Lord, my God, I wish to record the truth. This world is far too crowded with lies. My own existence has, in many ways, been a lie. The admiral's was the same. As I was a learned man of letters, capable of writing, before he left for Spain the last time he told me the truth. I shall not bore the reader with many details, as the admiral would have disapproved of their revelation. But a quick survey seems in order, especially at this moment when I begin to face the end of my own life.

The name Colón was long common in the Balearic Islands. The man who would later call himself Cristobal Colón was born in Genova, on the island of Majorca, near Palma. Later, when necessary to conceal his true origin, the admiral chose Genoa for his birth, leaving the constant impression that he meant the city in Italy. The Admiral was Catalonian. Never did he speak or write Italian. His father was known as Juan, a landowner of means on Majorca. The family were conversos of long standing. Outwardly,

Juan Colón named his eldest son after himself, but within his heart and inside the confines of his home he called him by his true name. Christoval Arnoldo de Ysassi. There was another son, younger, Bartolome, who remained close to his elder brother all of his life. On Majorca, the admiral called himself Juan. Only when he traveled to Spain to secure the moneys needed for his great voyage did he become Cristoforo Colombo, from Italy, called Cristobal Colón by the Spanish. Throughout his life the admiral never forgot his birthplace. On Majorca there is a sanctuary known as San Salvador, a hill of great beauty and peace, so he named the first island he discovered in his New World after that spot.

In his youth Marjorcan farmers were oppressed by excessive levies and harsh treatment. They eventually rose in arms and revolted, the brothers Juan and Bartolome actively participating. The King of Naples eventually suppressed the revolt. His father lost all of his lands and many were slaughtered. The two brothers fled the island. Juan took to the sea, operating a pirate ship from Marseilles, fighting the King of Aragon's attempt to take Barcelona. He then joined with the Portuguese in their war with Spain and its Catholic queen, Isabella. During a battle against Venetian vessels in the employ of Aragon, Juan attacked and set them on fire. His own ship was lost but, despite being wounded by gunfire, he managed to swim ashore. The bullet from that wound stayed inside him all of his life. A reminder of a time when he openly fought authority.

Never again would Juan be a pirate. He migrated to Portugal and became a merchant, sailing the cold waters above Europe. He married the daughter of the governor of the Madeira Islands and moved there to administer the estate left by his father-in-law. There a son, Diego, was born. Later, another son, Fernando, was born to a Catalonian mistress. Both sons would always be close to their father.

In 1481, while living in the Madeira Islands, he met Alonso Sanchez de Huelva, a mariner and merchant, who regularly sailed among the Canary Islands, Madeira, and England. On one voyage a storm blew his ship off course where it encountered unfavorable winds and currents, dragging it far to the southwest. Finally, land was sighted, an island, upon which lived small, hairless, brown natives who worshiped de Huelva and his crew as gods. After a short stay de Huelva left and sailed east, landing on Porto Santo Island in Madeira. There Juan Colón listened to de Huelva speak of what he found and became fascinated by the possibility that de Huelva had found India and Asia. De Huelva provided him with a chart of the waters he'd sailed. He studied that chart for several years, and became so certain of what he would eventually discover, it was as if he held the key to the box in which it was locked.

He returned to Spain and approached the Catholic monarchs, Ferdinand and Isabella, for ships. He could not reveal himself as Juan Colón, the Majorcan rebel and pirate who had fought against them, so he invented Cristoforo Colombo, from Genoa, Italy, assuming the identity of a dead seaman and wool merchant he once met in the Madeiras. The deception worked and no one ever learned the truth. Even when enemies stripped him of all that he had rightfully earned, he remained to the Spanish Don Cristobal Colón. Only now, after death has long claimed the admiral and the Queen Isabella, and as it is soon to come for me, can the truth be revealed. It is my hope that this account survives and that others will know *what I have known. Life here is harsh, but I have come to admire the natives in a way that makes me appreciate their simple way of life. Here I can be Yosef Ben Ha Levy Haivri—Joseph, the son of Levi the Hebrew. As with the admiral and his persona of Colombo, mine as Luis de Torres has served me well. But I have not used that name in six years. Here, it matters not whether you be Jew or Christian, only that you be a good man. That I have tried to be. I have performed the duty imposed on me and will ensure that the task passes to my eldest son, born to me from a wife I took from among the native women. She has made my time here more pleasant than I could have hoped it would be. I have taught her about God and urged her to believe but, learning from the wicked ones from whom I fled, never have I forced her to accept that which she could not embrace in her heart.*

Béne stopped reading and glanced up at Tre Halliburton.

"I found that in the documents we took from Cuba," Tre said. "That's my translation of what he wrote. Explains a lot, doesn't it?"

He knew little about Columbus.

"The story generally told," Tre said, "starts with Columbus being born in Italy. His father was Domingo, his mother Susanna. Interestingly, a lot of the accounts say that his father was a wool merchant, as was this Colombo whose identity he assumed. Most historians say he took to the sea at an early age, ended up in Portugal, couldn't get King Juan the Second interested in a voyage, so he went to Spain in 1485, spending seven years waiting for Ferdinand and Isabella to say yes. Whether he ever met Alonso Sanchez de Huelva, nobody knows."

"Is that true about de Huelva? Did he find America?"

Tre shrugged. "Some say he did. Most think the story was made up by Columbus' enemies to discredit his accomplishments. But who the hell knows? Unfortunately, Columbus wrote virtually nothing about himself during his lifetime. And the things he did record usually conflicted with one another. Now we know why. He didn't want anyone to know where he came from."

Halliburton had driven north from Kingston to the estate. The hog that had been roasting since this morning was about ready to eat. The two women—one from the Justice Department, the other an ambassador—had been gone for hours. One of his men had made sure that they drove straight to the Kingston airport and left.

"What are you going to do with all of this?" he asked Tre.

He had to know.

"Like I have a choice?"

He smiled. His friend understood. Everything must remain private. "It's better that way."

Tre shook his head. "Who'd believe me anyway?"

The dogs were back in their pens, their bellies full from the hunt. He doubted much remained of Zachariah Simon, and whatever might still be there would soon be consumed by scavengers.

"What happened to de Torres?" he asked.

"History records nothing. He faded away after Columbus' last voyage. Not a word, until now. Apparently, he lived on Cuba until at least 1510 and fathered a son."

A sadness filled his gut. How terrible to live such an extraordinary life—yet not to be remembered. Maybe, if only for Luis de Torres, the truth should be told?

But he knew that could not be.

"What did you find in the cave?" Tre asked.

"Enough to know that the legend is no more."

"The Maroons have control of whatever it is, don't they?"

They sat on the veranda, the evening air cool and dry. One of his men near the corral signaled that the hog was ready. Good. He was hungry.

He stood. "Time to eat."

"Come on, Béne. Give me something. What did you find?"

He thought about the question. The past few days had certainly been hectic, but also enlightening. Myths had been revealed as fact. Maroons thought to be legend had been proven real. Justice had been meted out to men who'd shown no respect for anyone, or anything, save themselves. And along the way, Brian Jamison died.

He'd not cared at the time, but regretted that now.

So what had he found?

He stared at Tre and told him the truth.

"Myself."

CHAPTER EIGHTY

TOM OPENED THE DOOR.

Two women stood outside his house. One was the same from Prague, in the car, who'd met with Simon, and the other introduced herself as Stephanie Nelle, United States Justice Department. A little over twenty-four hours had elapsed since he and Alle had emerged from Darby's Hole and left Jamaica for Orlando. He'd wondered when the woman from Prague would appear and was shocked to learn that she was the Israeli ambassador to Austria.

He invited them inside.

"We tried yesterday to speak with Béne Rowe, but he told us nothing," Nelle said. "We think Simon is dead. He hasn't been seen or heard from since landing in Jamaica. Neither has his man, Rócha."

He decided to offer nothing except, "They killed Brian Jamison. I was there when it happened."

Nelle nodded. "We know. That means only you and your daughter can now provide us answers."

"Did you find the Temple treasures?" the ambassador asked.

He nodded.

Her eyes went alive with anticipation. "They exist?"

He nodded again.

"Then I owe you that explanation," she said.

That she did.

"I can publicly refute all that happened to you eight years ago. Some of the people who assisted in setting you up still exist within positions of power. Others we know about. You were not the only one they destroyed. But you were the first. They manufactured that story about Israeli settlers and Palestinians and created the sources. They fed it to you and your editors, then watched it all unravel. They were a team who became quite good at what they did. But that is not our way, Mr. Sagan. What they did to you was wrong."

"And you waited eight years to tell me that?"

"I was not aware myself of what happened until your involvement in this matter became clear."

"But others knew?"

She nodded. "They did, and their silence is shameful."

He was not prepared to cut her any slack. "What did you do, play Simon in Prague?"

The ambassador nodded. "That was my assignment. To lead him on. Keep him moving forward. We wanted him to find that treasure. But of course, we didn't want any violence associated with it."

"Did Rabbi Berlinger know about you?"

She nodded. "I spoke to him. He understood the urgency and agreed to spur you along. He made sure you were listening when I spoke to Simon in the cemetery. That is why I twisted the conversation your way. I wanted you to know of my presence and what I knew about you."

He recalled what she'd said when he confronted her on the street in Prague. *"I've been expecting him."*

"You and Berlinger knew I'd go straight to you."

"That was the idea. To keep you moving forward."

"So you used me, too."

"In a manner of speaking. But so much was at stake.

As you heard, he wanted to start a war, and would have. Thousands would have died."

"Which only involved me because you made it so."

"What you may not know," the ambassador said, "is that Rabbi Berlinger is dead. We think Simon killed him before leaving Prague."

He was sorry to hear about the old man's death. "You said you *think* Simon is dead? Is he?"

"Most likely," Nelle said, "Rowe had him killed. But we'll never know. All we know is he's gone."

"And I did manipulate Simon," the ambassador said again. "I did this for our government, which came and specifically asked for my help. If Simon had been successful in his quest Israel could have been irrevocably harmed. If that meant I had to use you, then so be it."

He was not interested in her justifications. "You understand that the Sephardi Jews who hid away the Temple treasure trusted its safety only to the Levite. Not to the state of Israel."

"Those objects belong to every Jew. We will make sure they receive them, and not the war Simon wanted to start. As I said, we don't need violence to incite a sense of security. There is a better way. It's time for the violence to end."

On that he agreed. He pointed at Nelle. "And I assume she's here to stamp the U.S. government's seal of approval on me telling you everything I know."

"Something like that. You were set up, Mr. Sagan. A terrible thing. They ruined your career. That can be fixed."

"And what if I don't want it fixed?"

The question seemed to surprise them both.

"You lost everything," the ambassador said.

He nodded. "That's the point. It's gone. Never to be reclaimed. My parents will never know. My ex-wife will never know. The people who called themselves my friends? I don't give a rat's ass if they know. It's gone."

He was shocked at himself, but the realization had become crystal clear in the cave while staring at the Temple treasure. What's past is past. There was no undoing it. All that mattered was what lay ahead.

"A strange attitude from a man who took the beating you took," Nelle said. "Your Pulitzer Prize could be restored. Your credibility regained. You wouldn't have to ghostwrite novels anymore."

He shrugged. "It's not so bad. Pays good, and there's no pressure."

"So what are you going to do?" the ambassador asked.

After he and Alle had recrossed the lake and climbed from the cave, the Maroon, Frank Clarke, had waited for them. They'd watched as Béne Rowe and two other men led Simon across the river and back up to the road.

"What happens to this place now?" he asked Clarke.

"We will rebuild the dam and guard it, as we have. You are the Levite, so this is always yours. When that duty passes to the next, then we shall respect that person. What do you plan to do?"

He hadn't answered Clarke because he truly did not know.

And he could not answer the woman now staring at him, either. So he simply said, "I'll let you know what I decide."

"You understand," the ambassador said, "that no one will ever know the truth about you, unless you work with us."

Her threat infuriated him, but anger was also a thing of the past. "You see, that's the thing. It only matters that one person knows the truth." He paused. "And you just told her."

Alle stepped from the kitchen, where he'd sent her on seeing who his visitors were. He hadn't known how far they would go with their comments, but he'd hoped.

"My father didn't lie, did he?" she asked.

Neither woman said a word.

But their silence was more than enough of an answer.

They seemed to sense that the conversation was over and both headed for the door.

Before leaving, the ambassador turned back and said, "Be kind to us, Mr. Sagan. Think what those treasures would mean."

Her plea did not impress him. "And you think about what almost happened, because of them."

Tom and Alle stepped from the car and entered the cemetery outside Mount Dora. They'd driven from Orlando just after the two women left his house. The day was late, nearly five o'clock, the burial ground empty. A late-winter sun warmed chilly March air. Together they walked to his parents' graves. For the first time in a long while he did not feel like he was intruding.

He stared at the two *matsevahs*.

"You did good on his marker," he told her.

"I'm sorry," she said.

He faced her.

"I'm so sorry for everything I ever did to you."

Her words shook him.

"I was a fool," she said. "I thought you were self-ish. That you cared nothing for me or Mother. I thought you were a fraud. A cheat. An adulterer. I thought everything bad I could about you. And I was wrong."

They'd said little since leaving Jamaica, and nothing after the women left the house. What was there to say? That was the thing about the truth. It silenced everything to the contrary.

"I lied to Mother," she said. "You were right in Vienna. I'm a hypocrite. I knew how she felt about Judaism. How you converted for her. But I did it anyway, then lied right to her face, up until the day she died."

He understood her agony.

"What's worse," she said, "my converting made what you did in leaving the Temple so unnecessary. The thing Mother didn't want to happen, did. All the battles between you and your father came to nothing. He died before either of you could resolve anything. And it's all my fault."

She sobbed and he allowed her to release the pain.

"I wasn't the best husband or father," he said. "I was selfish. I *was* an adulterer. A liar. I made a ton of mistakes. And I could have patched things with Abiram, and you, but I didn't. It's not all your fault."

"You saved my life in Jamaica. You dove into the water after me. You got me across the lake. You kept Simon from killing me."

"As I recall, you saved mine, too." She'd told him how she'd aimed a light in Rócha's face and yelled.

"You're not a lying reporter."

Her statement carried the tone of a declaration.

"You're a journalist. A Pulitzer Prize winner. You deserve all that you earned. Did you mean what you said to them? You don't want anyone to know the truth about you?"

"It's not important anymore that people know that. You know. That's all I care about."

He meant every word.

"And what about the Temple treasure?" she asked.

"Only you and I know what's in that cave and how to get it. True, there are other ways across that lake. But it's sat safe for sixty years, and I think the Maroons will keep it safe for sixty more. How about you and I decide what to do when things calm down."

She nodded through her tears.

"We'll be the Levite," he said. "Together."

His grandfather had involved Berlinger, now he would include Alle. He'd already decided to make peace with his religion. He was born a Jew to Jewish parents, and a Jew he would always be.

He'd already spoken to Inna and told her what happened. There'd be a story at some point about Zachariah Simon, his plans, and the dangers of fanaticism. Whether the Temple treasure would be included remained to be seen. He'd write the story himself and give it to her. She hadn't liked that idea, insisting that his byline appear. But he was a ghostwriter, and that he would remain. In the end, she'd understood and respected his wish. He liked Inna. Maybe he'd visit her again one day.

Interesting.

He'd finally started thinking about the future again.

"How about this," he said to Alle. "We both made a ton of mistakes, let's call it even and start over."

More tears streamed down her cheeks. "I'd really like that."

He extended his hand. "Tom Sagan."

She managed a smile and accepted his handshake. "Alle Beck—"

She caught herself.

"Alle Sagan."

He shook her hand. "Nice to meet you, Alle Sagan."

One last thing to do.

He turned to the graves and bent down.

For two decades he'd built a barrier to protect his emotions, one he'd thought insurmountable. The last five days had showed him the foolishness of his ways. In the end what mattered was family. And all he had left was Alle. He now had a second chance with her. But none existed with the man lying beneath his feet. For twenty years he'd called him Abiram, old man, anything and everything except what he deserved. So much bad had passed between them but, in the end, he'd been loved. And trusted. Of that there was no doubt.

He was going to be all right.

That much he now knew.

Alle stood behind him and laid a hand on his shoulder. He caressed the marker's smooth granite and hoped that maybe, just maybe, his words could be heard.

"I love you, Dad."

WRITER'S NOTE

THIS NOVEL TOOK ELIZABETH AND ME ON INTRIGU-
ing journeys, one to Jamaica, another to Prague. Vienna and Mount Dora, Florida, were locales visited
in the past.

Now it's time to separate fact from fiction.

Columbus was indeed marooned on Jamaica for
over a year (prologue, chapter 7) and made use of a
lunar eclipse to trick the Taino natives into supplying
his crew with food (chapter 35). Eighty-seven men
sailed with Columbus on his first voyage in 1492, and
not a single priest was among them. But a Hebrew
translator, Luis de Torres, was part of that first contingent. De Torres' background as a *converso,* provided in chapter 17, is accurate, as is the fact that he
stayed in the New World and was probably the first
European to sample tobacco. His involvement as a
Levite with the Temple treasure is my addition—but
the notion that the first words that Europeans spoke
in the New World may have been Hebrew is entirely
possible (chapter 17).

The legend of a lost Jamaican gold mine connected
to Columbus is one often repeated. *Jewish Pirates of
the Caribbean,* by Edward Kritzler, deals with this
intriguing myth. The coded information quoted in
chapter 35 (which supposedly leads to the mine)

came from documents cited in Kritzler's book. The story of the Cohen brothers, a deed to 420 acres of land, the lawsuit between the brothers, and Abraham Cohen's swindling of Charles II (chapters 10, 19, and 20) is also from Kritzler's book. The *Santa María,* Columbus' flagship, did run aground in December 1492 off the coast of Haiti. The ship was lost, but its cargo was salvaged and brought ashore. Three mysterious crates being included within that cache was my invention. Crates from Panama loaded with gold and hidden by Columbus in 1504 during his year marooned on Jamaica (chapter 7) are noted in several historical accounts, but whether they actually existed is hard to say. For an interesting prequel to *The Columbus Affair,* check out my short story "The Admiral's Mark."

The Taino (chapter 28) presence on Jamaica, 7,000 years before the Europeans, is true, as is the fact that by 1650 they were wiped out. Calling them Arawaks is incorrect, though their language is known by that term. Gold was not precious to the Tainos (chapter 28), but whether they possessed a mine shown to Columbus, nobody knows. Little remains today of the Tainos except for some artifacts, their caves, and legends (chapter 24).

The Maroons are a fascinating group of people. Their history and sociology are accurately portrayed (chapters 3, 19, 24), and their propensity for secrets is real (chapter 68). How slaves made it to the New World (chapter 28) is accurately related, as is the fact that Jamaica, situated at the end of the trade route, received the toughest of the lot (chapter 19). Charles Town exists, as does the Maroon museum there (chapters 24 and 25). Grandy Nanny is a part of both Maroon and Jamaican history. How she looked, who she was, and whether she even actually lived are matters of debate (chapters 3, 68). An image of her currently appears on the Jamaican $500 note, known locally as a "Nanny." *Abengs* (chapter 71) were used by Maroons to communicate over long distances, their wail terrifying British soldiers. Maroon war tactics, as described throughout, were implemented to great success. Duppies (chapter 28) are a part of Jamaican folklore. The tales Béne's mother tells about Martha Brae and the golden table (chapter 50) are still told. Both the Tainos and Maroons sometimes buried their dead in caves, but the crypt in chapter 62 is wholly imaginary. Interestingly, there are many striking similarities between Maroon religious beliefs and Judaism (chapter 74).

Cuban bloodhounds were imported from Spain, then brought to Jamaica by the British to combat the Maroons (chapter 3). The *chasseurs* are accurately described (chapter 10), as is the damage the hounds could inflict.

The locales for this story were particularly noteworthy. All are accurately described. Jamaica is spectacular, its Blue Mountains worth a visit (chapter 3). Thousands of caves dot the island and the ones used herein are hybrids of several (chapters 56, 58, 72–77). A good source from which to learn more is *Jamaica Underground,* by Alan Fincham. Mount Dora (chapter 17) truly does have the look of New England, and Lake County is aptly named (chapter 23). St. Stephen's Cathedral in Vienna has catacombs and bone rooms (chapters 34, 36, 37, 39, 41). The gardens at Schönbrunn palace (chapter 42) and the Stadttempel synagogue (chapter 8) are most impressive. Blue Mountain Coffee is regarded as one of the finest in the world (chapters 10, 30) and its regulation by the Jamaican government is accurately depicted, but any involvement by the Rowe family was my invention.

Prague is spectacular (chapters 49–51), its Jewish quarter solemn. The Old-New Synagogue (chapters 47, 49, 59) is faithfully described, including the iron rungs outside that lead up to its loft. Cameras do indeed keep watch throughout. The ceremonial hall, burial society, and Maisel Synagogue (chapters 56, 57, and 64) are there. The Old Cemetery is particularly moving, but an underground room for the disposal of sacred texts is my invention (chapter 54). Kolkovna (chapter 65) is a restaurant just outside the old quarter. Parizska Street is as depicted (chapter 50), crowded with expensive shops, bordering the Old-New Synagogue. Rabbi Loew lived in Prague (chapter 47) and remains a revered hero, his grave is the most visited site in the Old Cemetery (chapter 57). His seat in the Old-New Synagogue stays chained (chapter 59). The legend of the golem is one often told in Prague, but it's erroneously associated with Rabbi Loew (chapter 47). The tale was created as described in chapter 47. Many, though, still believe that the golem rests in the synagogue's loft.

Terezín (chapter 53) was a place of horror. The account of what happened to Prague's Jews, from 1939 to 1945, is accurate (chapter 53). Only Rabbi Berlinger's presence there is my invention.

Drug dons, unfortunately, thrive in Jamaica (chapters 3, 7). Their popularity with the people exists, as does the government's inability to combat them. Spanish Town can be an intense place (chapter 14). Jewish cemeteries (chapter 13) are found all across Jamaica, but mine is imaginary (chapters 3, 7). Throughout, Jewish burial customs are accurately depicted (chapter 22).

The Jewish presence on Jamaica, which began at the time of Columbus, is historic fact (chapter 7). Columbus' daughter-in-law did in fact secure the island from Ferdinand and wrestle away religious control (chapter 7). The Inquisition was kept off Jamaica for 150 years. When the Spanish finally returned in 1650, the Jews there sided with the English and helped expel them. Cromwell did in fact make a deal with them, promising and delivering tolerance (chapter 7). Eventually, Jamaica's Jews helped build the island's economy. Their commercial dealings with Maroons are real, as is the curious opposition by the emancipated blacks to Jewish equality (chapter 24). Eventually, the Jewish presence on Jamaica dissipated. Today only a few remain, the oldest congregation in the Western Hemisphere still worshiping in Kingston. On Cuba, Jews lived during Columbus' time and today (chapters 38, 40). When the Spanish finally fled Jamaica in 1655 they buried both their wealth and their records, thinking they would soon return (chapter 18). That, of course, never happened, and both were lost. The presence of a records repository on Cuba was my invention. The Jamaican archives in Spanish Town is real.

The hooked X, introduced in chapter 10, was actually a symbol found in Minnesota in 1898. What it is, nobody knows. But it is true that a hooked X is contained within some images of Columbus' strange signature (chapter 15), identical to the symbol found in Minnesota. *The Hooked X,* by Scott Wolter, is a good source of information on this mystery.

The astrolabe (chapter 66), as described, is my invention, but is based on one from the British Museum, fashioned by a 14th-century Hebrew craftsman. The pitcher is the symbol for a Levite (chapter 7) and can be found on some graves. The biblical history of the Levites, as detailed in chapter 13, is accurate.

What happened to the First and Second Temple is historic fact (chapter 8). Amazingly, just as described in chapter 42, both were destroyed on the same day, 656 years apart. The Temple treasure is indeed gone, its journey from Jerusalem to Rome to Constantinople documented (chapters 8, 29). Where it went after that, nobody knows. The Arch of Titus exists and visually confirms the treasure's temporary presence in Rome (chapter 77). An excellent resource on this subject is *God's Gold* by Sean Kingsley.

The history of Sephardi Jews is a matter of record (chapter 29, 31). Only my addition of their involvement with the Temple treasure is fictional (chapter 63). But their financing of Columbus' first voyage is factual. All of what Alle Becket says in chapter 31 can be substantiated. Luis de Santangel lived, as did the other financiers mentioned. De Santangel's close relationship with Ferdinand is fact. And not only do de Santangel's account books (chapter 31) exist, but those who have studied them state that they corroborate the fact that de Santangel advanced moneys for Columbus' first voyage.

The Temple Mount, with its history and politics, is accurately related (chapter 55). Jerusalem is, indeed, the world's most besieged city (chapter 59). A hope for a Third Temple still remains alive in Israel, with or without the Messiah.

At the heart of this story is an assumption: that Christopher Columbus was a Jew. Many have postulated the premise, none more convincingly than Simon Wiesenthal in *Sails of Hope*. Thousands of Sephardi Jews became *conversos* to escape persecution. Whether Columbus himself or his parents made that choice is unclear. What is clear is that virtually nothing is known of Columbus. Accounts as to his birth date, birthplace, upbringing, parentage, education, and life radically conflict. No known portrait of him exists. Both the chart he used for navigation (chapter 8) and his original journal, *Diario de a bordo, Outward Log,* are gone (chapter 15). The so-called *Journal of Columbus,* cited by nearly everyone as an authentic depiction of his voyages, is an unreliable thirdhand account produced decades later. The Spanish government's refusal to allow any independent search of its archives for either the chart or the original journal (chapter 8) only compounds the mystery.

Even Columbus' grave site is a matter of intense argument (chapter 38). My placing it in Jamaica is, of course, fictional (chapter 62). But all that Alle Becket writes in chapter 15 and all that Rabbi Berlinger says about him in chapter 65 is true. That Columbus sailed before midnight on August 2, 1492, and that all Jews had to be gone from Spain by August 3, are facts (chapter 9). Columbus' possible real name—Christoval Arnoldo de Ysassi—is more speculation. So is the tale, told in chapter 79, of Juan Colón from Majorca. That account is not mine, but was presented as a lecture in 1966 to explain why the Catholic Church had turned a deaf ear to all suggestions that Columbus be made a saint. Interestingly, with regard to Alonso Sanchez de Huelva (chapter 79), there is a great debate as to whether he, not Columbus, was the first European to find the New World. One line of thought says his exploits were lies promulgated by Columbus' enemies to discredit the Admiral's accomplishments. Another insists de Huelva never existed. A third says that de Huelva found the New World, but Spain's Catholic monarchs kept the discovery secret until Alexander

VI, a Spaniard, was elected pope in 1492. Then they seized on Columbus' request for ships and allowed him to rediscover what they already knew existed.

As with so much else on this subject, the truth will never be known.

For 500 years historians have pondered the question: Who was Christopher Columbus?

The answer truly is another question.

Who do you want him to be?

Read on for

The Admiral's Mark
A Short Story
by
Steve Berry

Published by Ballantine Books

Eight Years Ago

Cotton Malone hated funerals. The only thing worse was a wedding. Both events involved an expected display of emotion, and both sparked memories better left forgotten. He'd attended only a handful of either since leaving the navy six years before and working full-time for the Justice Department. Today's funeral was further complicated by the fact that he hadn't particularly liked the man in the coffin.

Scott Brown had been married to Ginger, his wife, Pam's, sister. Scott had never held a real job, was always pitching some risky venture to investors, most of the schemes borderline illegal. Two years ago Malone had to intercede with Texas authorities and smooth over one that involved a few hundred thousand dollars and a lot of angry ranchers. Luckily, Scott still had the money and its return made everything go away.

This time things had turned out different.

Scott Brown was dead.

Killed in a diving accident off the coast of Haiti. What he was doing there was anybody's guess. Haitian officials could not have cared less. They fished him from the Caribbean, labeled the death accidental, and shipped him home for burial.

One less problem they had to worry about.

One more for Malone.

"You have to go to Haiti," his wife said to him. "Ginger is devastated."

Pam's sister was two years younger, ten years less

mature, and liked the bad boys. Scott was her third
husband. Of the crop, he was probably the cream,
which wasn't saying much. Handsome, he'd been a
talkative soul, never met a stranger, which had certainly helped with his cons. His problem came from
not knowing, to quote the song, "when to hold 'em,
when to fold 'em, and when to walk away." He just
couldn't resist the lure of an easy buck. Thankfully,
there were no children of the union, and Ginger
worked a solid job that paid the bills.

"And why do I have to go to Haiti?" he asked.

"Scott drowned. Case closed."

A report had accompanied the body. It explained
everything the locals knew—which wasn't much—
and was signed by a police inspector in Cap-Haïtien.

"Scott called Ginger a day before he died. He
sounded like he was in trouble. He said people were
after him."

"He's a pathological liar, and he was always in
trouble."

He spotted the look on her face. The one that said,
*You can argue all you want, but you're going down
there to see what happened.* So he decided to try, "I'm
off for the next week. I thought you wanted me home
to spend more time with you and Gary?"

His son was eight and growing up fast. First the navy
had kept him away, now it was his job with the Magellan Billet. He'd missed most of Gary's childhood, a sore
spot between him and Pam.

Their marriage was in trouble. And they both knew it.

"I want you to do this," she said, her voice calm.
"It'll help Ginger get over him."

"What am I looking for?"

"How would I know? You're the secret agent. Find
out what happened to him."

There was no sense arguing any further. When Pam made up her mind, that was it.

The graveside service was ending, the few who'd attended paying their respects to Ginger.

"I should check out their apartment," he said.

The Browns lived on Atlanta's south side.

"I doubt your sister has been totally honest about what her husband was involved in. She knows how we feel."

Pam handed him a key from her purse. "I've lived with an agent long enough to know the drill. Go, while everyone is at our house after the funeral."

He was beginning to wonder how much planning she'd invested in this.

"I love my sister," she said. "But she's blind when it comes to men. There's no telling what's going on."

———

HE FOUND THE APARTMENT COMPLEX JUST OFF THE interstate, one of hundreds that dotted the Atlanta metropolitan area. No gate barred access and the parking lot was devoid of cars, most of the residents at work on a Tuesday afternoon. The Browns lived on the second floor, and he used the key to gain access. Inside was spotless, everything in its place. Ginger, like her sister, appreciated order. Interesting how she waived that rule when it came to her love life. He'd visited here only a couple of times, as usually the Browns came to the Malone house on the other side of town.

He wasn't sure what he was looking for, but found a checkbook in a drawer, the account only in Ginger's name, with $4,200 on deposit. A savings book showed another $14,000. Good to know that his sister-in-law kept some money under her control.

A stack of mail caught his attention.

Then someone knocked on the door.

Which startled him.

Another knock.

He hadn't locked the knob after he'd entered. Why would he? Nobody was around. Family and friends were at the funeral.

The knob began to turn.

He retreated to the bedroom and slid under the bed. A frilly dust ruffle draped down on three sides and provided cover. He wasn't sure why hiding was necessary, but something didn't ring right.

"Is anyone home?" a male voice said.

A moment of silence.

"Check the rooms."

A gap of about half an inch provided a line of sight past the dust ruffle out into the bedroom. He pressed his cheek into the carpet and watched as two feet stepped to the bedroom door, hesitated a moment, then walked to the bathroom and closet, checking both.

"No one is here," another male voice said.

A burglary?

"They are still at the funeral, so we have some time. Make a search."

If so, apparently not an ordinary one.

He heard drawers open, items shuffled about.

"No need to look any further," the first voice said. "Here is what we want."

He gently raised the dust ruffle enough so that he could see more than shoes.

Past the bedroom doorway he spotted two men. One was maybe fifty, pale, with salt-and-pepper hair and a matching beard. The other man was younger, black-haired, dark-complexioned. The older man was holding the stack of mail. He tossed the letters aside and kept one, removing what was inside a large brown envelope.

The older man shook his head. "Seems Herr Brown led us on a diversion. This is nothing."

"But the wife read it."

"It would mean nothing to her."

He watched as the letter was replaced in the envelope and tossed back on the table.

"There is no need to linger," the older man said. "Unfortunately, Herr Brown managed to get ahead of us. The answers we seek are not here, but we had to come for a look."

They both left, gently closing the door behind them.

He slid from beneath the bed and rushed to the window, watching as the two men exited the building toward a dark blue Honda.

They climbed inside and started to leave.

He darted to the table, grabbed the envelope, then raced downstairs, slowing his pace to a normal gait as he came to the bottom and walked toward his car.

The Honda was turning a corner, heading toward the exit gate.

He jumped into his own vehicle and followed.

———

HE SWITCHED OFF THE CAR ENGINE AND WATCHED as the two men parked the Honda. They'd driven from the apartment complex, found Interstate 85, then headed south to Fayette County and a small private airport. He'd first thought their destination to be Hartsfield-Jackson International, which could have proven a problem. Thankfully, they'd avoided Atlanta's main terminal. Several single-engine craft and two luxury turboprops waited near a large hangar. His targets entered a metal-sided administration building, stayed a couple of minutes, then climbed aboard one of the turboprops. A few minutes later engines whined and the plane taxied to the runway.

He'd opted not to confront them.

Instead, he should be able to learn what he needed without drawing any unnecessary attention. Before leaving the car he grabbed the envelope from the apartment, which displayed a handwritten return address for the Hotel Creole, Cap-Haïtien, Haiti. He slid out a single sheet of unfolded paper and studied what was there.

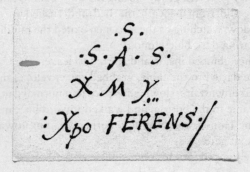

He had no idea what the combination of letters meant.

He tossed the envelope on the passenger's seat and stepped from the car. Inside the building he displayed his Justice Department badge. "Who were the two men who left in the plane just now?"

The person on duty, a short stump of a man, seemed not to want to answer.

"We can do this here, or back in Atlanta in a more formal setting. Your choice."

Magellan Billet headquarters was located in Atlanta. Its head, Stephanie Nelle, had insisted on that as a condition of her employment, wanting the unit away from Washington and the Department of Justice, both physically and symbolically. Which worked. The Billet had developed a reputation for independence, utilized on the most sensitive of investigations, both domestic and international. Twelve agents worked under Stephanie's exclusive control, selected by her and specially trained. Of course he was bluffing, since none of this had anything to do with Billet business. Still, something out of the ordinary was definitely happening.

"Older guy is Zachariah Simon. He showed an Austrian passport. The other guy was—"

He watched as the man tried to remember.

"Rócha. Yeah, that was it. Rócha."

"He have another name."

The guy shrugged. "Can't remember. Didn't know I had to. They flew in on a charter, paid their fees, bought some gas, and left."

"And that car outside?"

"Mine. They rented it."

"When did they get here?"

"A few hours ago."

"You get their passports?"

He knew the rules. Small airports like this were required to maintain copies of entry documents for Customs.

"Yeah, I got 'em."

"I need them." Now for what he really wanted to know. "Where are they headed?"

"These guys in trouble?"

"If they are, here's the problem. They're gone, and you're still here."

He hoped the message was clear.

"The charter pilot filed a flight plan for Cap-Haïtien."

CAP-HAÏTIEN WAS A TOWN OF 180,000 PEOPLE ON
Haiti's north coast. Its architecture reminded Malone
of New Orleans, the same gingerbread-style houses
lining its narrow streets, the same French feel throughout, though its overwhelming poverty spoiled any
further comparisons. Streets, where they existed, suffered potholes and puddles, their gutters trickling
with stinking sewage. Hundreds of tin-roofed shacks
crumbling in the heat dominated bare mountain
slopes. Two hundred years ago the harbor would
have been filled with merchant ships, here to load coffee and sugar from French planters. Now the bay
loomed empty save for a few small boats, its waters
ruined by pollution. A strong odor of decay filled the
humid afternoon air. Yesterday, after what had happened in the Browns' apartment and at the airport
south of Atlanta, he'd questioned his sister-in-law
about the envelope.

"*What were you doing in my apartment?*" Ginger
asked.

"*I sent him,*" Pam said. "*I gave him my key and
told him to look around.*"

"*What for?*"

"*Your husband's dead. Don't you want to know
what happened?*"

"*Of course, but—*"

"*Do you have any idea what this means?*" he asked
her, showing her the sheet from the envelope.

Ginger shook her head. "*It came from Haiti a day
or so after Scott died. He told me on the phone he
sent me something. But he didn't tell me what it
means.*"

"*And you never mentioned this envelope to me,*"
Pam said, with an irritation that he'd come to know.

"I didn't think it was important. Come on, Scott drowned."

"But he said someone was after him," Pam said.

"I know. But I have to confess, I didn't believe him."

Pam had continued to reprimand Ginger for not telling anyone about the letter, but all that brought was tears. For safety, she'd insisted Ginger stay at their house, though he doubted there'd be any more visits.

Whatever was going to happen, would happen here, in Haiti.

Before leaving Cap-Haïtien's airport, he located the private hangars and learned that the plane from Atlanta was there. Inside, $50 U.S. bought him the name of the hotel where Zachariah Simon and Rócha were staying. Hotel Creole. The same one noted on the envelope Scott had sent. He could start with the police, or with the charter boat Scott had used, or with the two men who'd come to Atlanta. He decided that the charter boat seemed the best bet, so he bartered for a cab into the congested mess of central downtown.

Haiti filled the west half of an island Columbus discovered in 1492, which he named Hispaniola. Populated first by native Tainos, then the Spanish, then by slaves brought to work the cane fields, the island fell under the control of the French in 1697. Forty thousand colonists lorded over 500,000 Africans. By 1790 it was one of the richest places on earth—France's number one revenue source—thanks to immense profits from sugar, coffee, and indigo. It was also one of the most picturesque, with dense tropical forests, sparkling clear water, and towering mountains. Palm-shaded châteaus filled with Parisian furnishings were common. Its Code Noir established rigid social rules, making it one of the world's most efficient slave colonies. Eventually, though, freed mulattos, offspring of colonists, and female slaves combined forces with thousands of other slaves and expelled the French, establishing the only nation ever born of a black revolt.

Then the turmoil started.

After two hundred years Haiti was now the poorest nation in the Western Hemisphere, its forests gone, waters ruined, poverty an accepted way of life. He'd read an article recently about how the cruise ships had stopped coming—simply because passengers complained at how depressing the place could be.

The cabdriver dropped him at the waterfront, where crumbling docks jutted from a narrow mud beach. Tin-roofed wooden sheds stood at their base, a small crane at the end of one. A pale green sea, splashed with shades of blue, stretched to the horizon. Soft white waves lapped the shore. From the police report he knew the name of the owner who'd taken Scott out, and found him after asking around.

The boat was a twenty-footer, with a small cabin forward and a cluttered deck aft. The man moving about on board was short, thin, and walked with a hitch in his left knee. He had a broad nose, tense jaw, and dark eyes, his black hair cut close.

"*Bonsoir*. Are you Yann Dubois?"

The man glanced up at him with a faint smile. "You want to dive?"

"Looks like a calm day. Can you take me out?"

He saw that he'd now attracted interest. Here was money to be made, and Dubois seemed ready to accommodate.

"Sure, I take you out. You have card?"

He shook his head. "Not on me. But I'm U.S. Navy certified. I can handle it."

He assumed that requirements like diving certifications were not much of a problem in Haiti.

Dubois smiled. "U.S. Navy. That's good, mon. Where you want to go?"

"Same place the guy drowned last week."

Dubois' pleasant attitude vanished. "You police? Here to bother me more? I don't want that."

"No police. A relative. The man who died was my brother-in-law. I need to find out what happened."

"He drown. That what happened. Not my fault."

"I didn't say it was. I just want to see where it happened. Have a look around. I'll pay double your usual rate."

He watched as Dubois considered the offer, but the outcome was never in doubt.

"Let's go, mon."

———

MALONE DONNED THE AIR TANK AND BUOYANCY vest, fastening the belt around his waist and adjusting the shoulder straps. Not the newest of equipment, but it appeared in reasonable shape. The trip out from shore had been short, the stern engulfed in a boiling exhaust from overheating engines. They were anchored no more than three hundred yards from the beach, dark smudges in the turquoise water indicating a reef below. A wet wind blew steady from the west. He kept time with the deck's jerking pitch, glad to know that his sea legs had not left him.

The navy had taught him how to dive ten years ago. He liked it but, unlike his father who'd been a submariner, he hadn't wanted a career underwater. The sky appealed to him, so he learned to fly fighter jets. Ultimately, he was steered toward the law, where he found a home first as a JAG officer, now in the Justice Department.

"We go down thirty feet," Dubois said as he adjusted his own harness. "Lots of current. Watch yourself. I show you where it happened."

"Did you fish him out?"

"Yeah, mon. He not come up, so I go down."

"Why didn't you go down with him?"

Dubois eyed him with irritation. "'Cause Scotty say he don't want me down there."

None of which had been detailed in the police report. But the whole thing was more overview than report. Few details, even fewer conclusions. Just a simple statement of "diving accident."

"Scotty?" he said. "You and him buddies?"

Dubois eyed him again with a cool stare. "I like him. He okay."

Then Dubois rolled over the side into the water.

Malone followed.

A gray reef shark immediately greeted him. The air from his tank carried a dank, oily aftertaste, probably from a bad compressor. He hadn't been underwater in five years, but he quickly acclimated himself, listening to the burbling sound of his exhaled breath.

Dubois led the way to the bottom.

He checked the depth gauge snaking from his regulator.

Twenty-five feet.

Shallow enough to have no decompression worries.

He stared around in the aquamarine sea and noticed only a few tropicals here and there, some wrasses and an angel, but nothing like the numbers one would expect. He knew Haiti's reefs had been decimated by overfishing and sedimentation. Most of the trees on the island were gone—cut down for fuel and shelter with few replantings—allowing rainwater to cascade from the mountains unimpeded, carrying along tons of mud that ended up on the seafloor. Not enough reef fish also meant fewer to keep the coral clean of algae. So the twisted limestone hulks loomed mostly lifeless, everything stained dark green.

Dubois motioned to a formation fifty feet away and indicated that Malone should lead the way.

He swam toward it.

A loud rasp from the regulator accompanied each of his breaths. He was trying to ignore the foul-tasting air and hoped nothing was toxic.

They came to a coral formation, this one, too, devoid of polyps. A few fish were gorging on the algae. The shark had drifted off. The water was warm and comforting, almost too much so, and he cautioned himself to stay alert. Rays of bright sunshine, fractured by the surface, danced to a quick beat. Dubois had been right. A steady current in their face made the going difficult.

They arrived at the limestone hulk, which rose ten feet toward the surface, stretching out many more yards toward the open sea. A darker hue in the water a few hundred feet away signaled greater depths, and he assumed that was where the shallow reef ended.

Dubois pointed to an opening in the rock, where chunks had fallen away to reveal a crack that spread for twenty feet. A small, cavelike opening led into the crevice. Dubois motioned with his hands, indicating that a storm had caused the damage.

Malone swam close and peered inside. He saw what appeared to be wood timbers on the bottom, encrusted with barnacles and algae. Other shapes lay embedded in the sand, thick with encrustation.

A wreck of some sort. Old, too. Hidden beneath this rock mound for a long time. He motioned—*Is this all?*—and Dubois nodded. He decided he'd seen enough. He'd need to return for a closer inspection, but first more information was called for.

He motioned for them to surface.

They drifted away from the limestone wall.

Scott had apparently found a shipwreck. But there were probably thousands of those in these waters, as Cap-Haïtien had been a bustling seaport. French, Spanish, British, and Portuguese ships had plied these waters, along with buccaneers. Probably hard even to count the number of ships that met the bottom.

What made this one so special?

He exhaled and turned his attention toward the surface, watching as the bubbles drifted upward.

His next breath drew nothing.

What?

He tried again, sucking harder.

No air came through the regulator.

He reached for the pressure gauge, which read zero.

He whirled around, searching for Dubois, who was only a few feet away watching through his mask. The tiny bit of air in his lungs was about gone, no way to ditch his weight belt and make it twenty-five feet up before he blacked out. He slashed his right hand across his throat, the universal sign for no air, and kicked toward Dubois.

The Haitian handed over his regulator.

Malone drew a deep breath.

Then another.

Two more were required before his nerves stabilized.

He shared the air, then watched as Dubois reached around him. He felt something being turned, then noticed the air gauge move from zero to more than 2,000 pounds.

The son of a bitch had turned the valve off at the tank.

He replaced his regulator in his mouth, and Dubois motioned for them to surface. They made it to the boat and Malone climbed aboard first, quickly releasing his weight belt and dropping the tank to the deck. Dubois came up and, before he could do a thing, Malone pounced, slamming the Haitian to the deck. Dubois remained still—as if he'd expected an attack—calmly releasing his own belt and freeing himself from the harness.

"What in the hell just happened?" Malone yelled.

Dubois stood. "Scotty not drown. He be killed. Just like I show you."

It was true, he'd never felt his air valve being closed. Never seen it coming. If Dubois hadn't been there, he'd be dead.

"That's what I tell police."

"He was down there alone. Who the hell killed him?"

"The other man."

"The police report said nothing about another man."

"I tell them. They don't want to hear. I know something wrong with that policeman. Something wrong with all of them here."

Which was one reason why United Nations peacekeepers were all over the country. Corruption had long been a way of Haitian life.

"I don't mean to kill you," Dubois said. "But I want you to know truth. You said Scotty your relative. So you need to know. The other man kill Scotty."

"Was he on this boat?"

Dubois shook his head. "He come in another, anchor over there." He pointed east. "Not far away. Diver go down. I don't think much. Lots of divers around here every day. Next thing I know he comes up and boat leaves. But Scotty never comes up. So I go down."

"You get a look at the other guy?"

Dubois nodded. "Good one."

Playing a hunch, he stepped over to his travel bag and found the copies of the two passports he'd obtained in Atlanta. He showed them to Dubois.

"That's him," Dubois said, pointing at Rócha.

"Sure?"

"Real sure."

Murder changed everything.

"Scotty was good to me," Dubois said. "I bring him here several times. He pay me good, always nice to me. He come to my house and eat with my wife and children. I like him."

That had been Scott. A liar. A thief. But a friendly soul.

"What was Scott after?"

"He tell me he find *Santa María.*"

That shocked him.

He knew the tale.

On his first voyage Columbus anchored somewhere in these waters. But on Christmas Day, 1492, his flagship, the *Santa María,* lodged on a reef. With no way to free the keel, the ship was dismantled, its timbers and cargo hauled ashore and used to construct a settlement. Three weeks later Columbus sailed away in the *Niña,* leaving 39 of his crew behind in what he called La Navidad, the first settlement of Western Europeans in the New World. He charged those men with exploring the island and finding gold. But when he returned in November 1493 with 17 ships and 1,200 men on his second voyage, La Navidad lay in ashes. All 39 crew members were dead, slaughtered by the Tainos. What remained of the *Santa María* settled on the sea bottom and had been sought by archaeologists for decades.

And Scott had found it?

"He tell me it is there," Dubois said. "In that rock. He dive several times. Always alone. Until last time."

"You could have just told me this. You didn't have to try to kill me."

"You look like man who can handle things. Not like Scotty."

He caught something in the man's voice. "You don't like what happened to him?"

Dubois shook his head. "He not deserve that. But there be nothing I can do. Police have the power here."

He'd heard enough. "Take me back to shore."

"You going after man in picture?"

"What do you think?"

"I think you need help. That man is here, in Cap-Haïtien. I know where. I have car. You need to get around. I owe that man." Dubois paused. "For Scotty."

———

HE FOUND THE HOTEL CREOLE JUST OFF THE PLACE d'Armes, near the Cathedral Notre-Dame, a striking Victorian building, its entrance separated from the street by a leafy courtyard, an iron gate manned by security. When he appeared, bag in hand, saying he was there to check in, he was welcomed inside. Dubois had driven him from the docks. This was the hotel the man at the airport had said Simon and Rócha were staying at, the same one noted on the envelope sent to Ginger by Scott, the same one Dubois had identified, too. He was still leery of his new ally, but he'd many times enlisted aid from locals. All part of the job. So were deceit and betrayal, so he stayed on guard. In his favor was the fact that Simon and Rócha had no idea he existed, and he planned to use that anonymity to his advantage.

The hotel's lobby seemed straight out of the 18th century, with a vaulted ceiling and lots of stone and wood that opened to an inner courtyard. Behind the front desk he noticed numbered slots on a wall, one for each room. Not something one saw much anymore. So he decided to try an old trick. He approached and said he wanted to leave a message for Zachariah Simon. He pretended to scribble something on a pad, folded the page over several times, then handed it to the clerk, along with a $10 bill. The man smiled, thanked him, then turned and inserted the note in a slot marked 25.

"And I'd like a room."

He tossed his bag on the bed.

His room was on the third floor, spacious, clean, the design minimalist with little furniture. Thankfully, the doors were also antiques, fitted with simple tumbler locks and no dead bolts. He left the room and descended to the second floor, finding the door marked 25.

He listened outside, heard nothing, then knocked.

Another try.

No answer.

He found the small diamond pick he kept in his wallet and tripped the tumblers in less than five seconds, a handy trick learned during his first few months on the job with the Justice Department.

The room inside was similar to his own. Two travel

bags lay against one wall. He gave each a quick inspection and saw nothing that caught his attention. What did interest him were the papers on the desk. One was a report on Scott Brown, a background investigation that was surprisingly detailed. He scanned the paragraphs and learned things about his brother-in-law that he'd never known: where he'd been born and raised, the number of aliases he used, the multiple Social Security numbers associated with his several identities, and a bank account in the Cayman Islands with nearly $600,000 on deposit. From all he knew the Browns lived paycheck-to-paycheck—hers. Typical of Scott, though, to squirrel away money and never tell his wife. Most likely the stash was either seed money for the next con or living expenses between marriages.

One thing, though, became clear. The two men who occupied this room were intently interested in Scott.

Unfortunately, Herr Brown managed to get ahead of us. The answers are not here.

That's what the older man, Simon, had said in Atlanta.

Something else caught his eye.

A printed catalog for a local auction to be held at another hotel, La Villa St-Louis, tonight. He thumbed through. Mostly antiques. Some jewelry. Furniture. All from an estate being liquidated. Contrary to popular misconception, there was wealth in Haiti.

He noticed blue ink on one of the pages.

Numbers. 5,000. 7,000. 10,000.

Above the writing was an item for sale.

Small volume (215 x 130mm), 62 leaves with hand printing in dark ink, another 12 blank. Fine original leather over wood binding. Significant soiling and browning, occasional spotting and staining. Dutch vellum, gilt edges, extremities rubbed. Provenance still in question, but verified to mid- to early-16th-century origin.

A color photo displayed the book. He'd seen many like it before. Books were a love of his. He collected them by the hundreds, all encased in plastic sheaths, lined on metal shelves in his basement back in Atlanta. Pam hated them, as they took up a lot of room, not to mention the money he spent on them. But he was a hopeless bibliophile. A dream that he allowed himself to sometimes enjoy was to one day own a rare-book shop.

He wondered what it was about this book that was so interesting.

The brochure noted that the auction began at 6:00 P.M. His watch read a little after two. He decided that his anonymity could be stretched a little further, so he'd be there to see what happened.

He left the room, relocked the door, and made his way downstairs to the lobby. He needed to find Dubois. His ally had said he'd wait outside the main gates, on the street. People streamed back and forth through the hotel from the courtyard, two restaurants, and a bar that was doing a brisk business for the middle of the afternoon. He turned for the main doors and was immediately flanked by a man on either side. Both were young, clean-shaven, with short hair, dressed casually, their shirttails out.

"Mr. Malone," one of them said.

So much for being anonymous. He said nothing and waited for them to make the next move.

"You need to come with us."

He stopped walking. "I hope you have a better reason than that."

"Like I said. You *need* to come with us."

He could take them both. No problem. So he held his ground. "I don't need to do anything."

The other man reached into his back pocket and produced a leather wallet. He opened it and displayed an identification.

One he'd seen before.

HaMossad leModi'in uleTafkidim Meyuchadim.

Institute for Intelligence and Operations.

Israeli.

"What's the Mossad's interest in Haiti?" he asked.

"We need to talk. But not here."

———

HE STEPPED FROM THE CAR, THE TWO AGENTS ALSO exiting. He'd ridden with them a few miles outside of Cap-Haïtien to a spot he'd read about but never visited.

Sans-Souci Palace.

Henri Christophe, or King Henri I as he'd labeled himself—tall, strong, smart, and unruly—built it in the early part of the 19th century, part of his plan to show Europe and America the power of the black race. Eventually, scattered around the island, were six châteaus, eight palaces, and the massive *citadelle*, but none compared to Sans-Souci. An earthquake toppled much of the building in 1842, the ruins never rebuilt. Once the equivalent of Versailles, with fifty rooms, a Baroque staircase, and stepped gardens, home to a grandiloquent court of dukes and duchesses, centuries of neglect had allowed nature to again take control. But though gutted by flames, roofless, exposed to tropical wind and rain, the shell seemed in harmony with its surroundings.

He followed his minders toward the ruin across a carpet of green grass. He recalled that *sans souci* translated to "without care," which did not accurately describe the current state of his emotions. Though the Israelis were allies, he'd never liked dealing with them. The fact that they were here, watching him, and he hadn't known, made things worse.

What in the world had Scott involved himself in?

A man waited for him at the base of the crumbling château. Interesting that Christophe had built the palace to advance African supremacy, but everything here screamed European monarchal prestige. Few other people were around, odd considering that this one of the region's main attractions.

"Mr. Malone, I appreciate your coming here," the man said. He was mid-fifties, thin, fit, with a full head of brown hair. He, too, was dressed casually, and was clearly in charge. The two young men from the hotel withdrew to a discreet distance, keeping an eye on things, but not close enough to hear.

"You have a name?"

The man smiled. "Matt Schwartz."

"And why is Israeli intelligence here in Haiti, watching me?"

"You're a man to be watched. Quite a reputation. An agent with the famed Magellan Billet. One of Stephanie Nelle's hand-chosen twelve. In fact, from what I've been told, you're her prized agent, the one she sends on the toughest jobs."

"You can't believe everything my publicist says."

Schwartz chuckled. "No, you can't. What were you doing in Zachariah Simon's room?"

"My mistake. Went into the wrong one. That hotel is like a maze."

"I was hoping you might offer something more creative."

"And why would I do that?"

"Professional courtesy?"

Now he smiled. "Why don't you tell me why you're here?"

"Simon is someone we've kept an eye on for a while. You know anything about him?"

He shook his head.

"Billionaire. Lives in Austria. His family is a big supporter of Israel. They survived the Holocaust, even prospered after the war. His father and grandfather helped form our state. But this third generation is not nearly as benevolent. In fact, Zachariah Simon is a problem."

"Terrorism?"

Schwartz shook his head. "If so, not the garden variety."

He wasn't getting much more than what a department summary might reveal, available to anyone with even a minor security clearance. This man was doing his job, keeping things close, offering just enough so his listener might reciprocate. So he offered, "I'm not here on official business."

"Really? You just decided to take a little trip down to Haiti?"

"My brother-in-law, Scott Brown, drowned here last week. I came to find out what happened."

"Scott Brown." Schwartz shook his head. "*That* man was a problem, too."

———

MALONE WAS TAKEN ABACK BY THE COMMENT. NOW he wondered if the Israelis had been part of what had happened, so he asked, "What did Scott do?"

"He nearly wrecked a year's worth of effort. He was working some sort of con on Simon. But he had no idea who he was dealing with."

Now he was getting angry. "So you let them kill him?"

"We didn't let anything happen. It just did. Our surveillance on Simon is loose. We can't spook him. He has no idea we're watching. I want to keep it that way."

"But you knew Scott was in danger?"

"With his background we figured he could take care of himself."

"You figured wrong."

Schwartz caught the message, but seemed undeterred. "You know the rules of this game."

Yes, he did. But that didn't mean he either liked or approved of them. One day, maybe, he'd get out, and then he could play by his own rules.

"My brother-in-law took a lot of chances. But he never played for keeps. His marks were the nonviolent type. *He* didn't know the rules of this game."

"But he took something Simon wants back."

Herr Brown managed to get ahead of us.

"Unfortunately, we don't know what that is."

"And you want me to find out?"

"We were hoping you might help."

He was still pissed about the cavalier attitude toward Scott's death. He may not have liked Scott Brown, but the man was Ginger's husband and she was family, and that counted for something.

And another reality hit home.

Seemed not only Scott had stumbled into a mess. So had he.

"I'm leaving," he said.

"Not until I say you can."

"I don't work for you."

"But if you're not going to cooperate, you're going to leave this island. I can't risk any more interference."

He'd already assessed the situation and concluded that the two young men who'd brought him were all the army Schwartz had, at least here. Only a handful of others wandered through the ruins, none raising any alarm. He assumed Schwartz was armed, so the first play was obvious.

He shook his head and grinned. "You don't give up, do you?"

Schwartz pointed both palms skyward, shrugged, and said, "It's my nature."

"Look," he said, casually stepping closer, as if he wanted to say something in private, "I'll leave—"

His right arm swung out and clamped Schwartz's neck in a vise as he brought the man toward him. The move caught his opponent off guard, and he was able to reach beneath the hanging shirttail and find the gun he knew was there. With weapon in hand he kneed Schwartz in the groin, doubling the man over.

An elbow to the nape of the neck sent the Israeli to the ground.

He whirled and caught the other two problems reaching for their own weapons. He fired at both, sending them scattering for cover among the crumbling stones.

He darted right, seeking refuge behind a standing column. Making his escape would require a sprint of fifty yards, back down the grassy path to the parking lot. Schwartz was still on the ground, barely moving, the other two agents somewhere to his left. The next patch of safety lay twenty feet away. He leaped, hit the ground, and rolled toward it.

Bullets came his way, but missed.

He sprang to his feet behind a clump of stone infested with lichens and caught sight of Twittily Dee and Dittily Doo trying to make their way to Schwartz. He used that moment of distraction to race ahead and hop a waist-high stone wall that separated the grassy path from the rocks beyond. Crouching low, he kept heading forward until he turned a bend and was out of the line of fire. He leaped back over the wall, onto the grass, and raced to the parking lot.

Now what?

The car he'd come in waited to his right.

No way were the keys in it, but he checked to be sure.

Three more cars were there and he checked those too.

No keys, either.

He'd have to keep moving.

The growl of an engine could be heard from the steep switchback road that led back to the highway.

A vehicle appeared around the last bend.

One he recognized.

Dubois.

The engine rattled and strained, but sounded to him like a fine orchestra. His ally wheeled to a stop. He jumped into the passenger's side and said, "Good timing."

"I follow from hotel. They don't look like good men."

"They're not. Let's get out of here."

Then something occurred to him.

"Wait."

He popped open the door, stood, and fired one round into the Israeli's car, flattening a rear tire.

———

THEY DROVE BACK TOWARD CAP-HAÏTIEN, THE TIRES wobbling, the wretched road more holes than pavement. No one had followed, and Dubois decided to take them to his house.

"Scotty come there a lot. He like it."

The dwelling was another shanty, tin-sided, tin-roofed, a few hundred square feet. It sat among a cluster of several hundred, east of town, not far from the airport, the rough land succumbing to weeds. Goats milled around in the front and on the sides, and a group of children played. The stench was over-powering, but he'd become accustomed to the pall. Then again, who was he to judge? Dubois seemed like a hardworking, decent man who'd genuinely liked Scott Brown. Life was tough here, but he was making the best of it.

Besides, he owed him one.

Two of the children rushed over. The boy maybe nine or ten, the girl a bit younger. Both hugged Dubois.

"These be mine. Violine is my precious girl, but Alain is future man of house."

Malone nodded to them both.

"This be Cotton Malone. He was close to Scotty," Dubois told them.

"Are you a secret agent, too?" Alain asked.

He threw Dubois a curious look.

"Scotty told them he be an agent for the Americans. Worked for the Billet."

He decided not to burst anyone's bubble. "I think it's called the Magellan Billet."

"That's what Scotty say. Very secret thing."

"Scotty say anything else?"

Dubois shook his head. "Only that he be here on a mission. He need help. I give it, like I do with you."

The children ran back to their friends. A woman appeared in the shanty's door. She was thin, long-haired, with bright eyes and a fresh face.

"This be Elise. My wife."

Malone shook the woman's hand, and she threw him a warm smile.

"You were Scotty's relative?" she asked.

He nodded. "He was married to my wife's sister."

"We liked him a lot. He was a good man."

Her English was cleaner than Dubois' and carried no accent, each syllable perfectly pronounced.

"Elise teaches school," her husband said with pride in his voice. "She be real good at that."

The auction would begin in three hours. In the meantime he'd decided to talk with Stephanie Nelle. Though this trip hadn't started off as Magellan Billet business, things had changed. His boss had to know about the Israelis.

"I need to make a call," he said. "I'll step out over there where I can talk in private."

"Take your time," Dubois said. "Elise make the food. We eat."

He nodded at the hospitality and found the phone in his pocket. It was state-of-the-art, Magellan Billet–issue, satellite-rated. The smallest unit on the market, produced solely for U.S. intelligence. But he wondered how long it would be before everyone's phone was similarly capable.

Stephanie was in her office and answered the call.

"I thought you were on vacation," she said.

"So did I."

He told her what had happened, omitting nothing.

"Schwartz is right," she said. "Zachariah Simon is a fanatic who just recently crept onto our radar. We're not sure what he's after, but we passed what we had along to the Israelis and they became awfully interested."

He knew his boss. "So you ran a full check?"

"Of course. Simon is wealthy, reclusive, a religious zealot. But he keeps his fingerprints off everything. He also openly stays out of politics and never talks to the press."

"In other words he's careful."

"Too much so, in my opinion."

"What's he doing in Haiti?"

"An excellent question. I'm sorry about what happened to your brother-in-law, but he was in way over his head."

"That much is obvious. What isn't is why the Mossad wants us out of the way."

"I'd like to know what they're up to."

He'd thought she might, and he had a way to find out. "I can do that, but I'll need some help from your end. I want to go to the auction and buy that book. Simon wants it. My guess is the Israelis are interested, too. If nothing else, it's our ante into the game."

"I agree. Do it. I'll set up a line of credit. But, Cotton, keep the price reasonable. Okay?"

"Don't I always?"

———

HE WALKED BACK TOWARD THE HOUSE AND COULD hear people all around him, some within their own dwellings, others out in the bright afternoon. Inside, he discovered that Elise Dubois was making rice and beans, along with a soup of potatoes, tomatoes, and meat, all simmering on a small electric stove. The house contained four rooms, sparsely furnished, everything clean and orderly.

He sat at the table with Dubois and the two children.

"What do you do?" his host asked.

He decided again not to burst Scott's bubble. "I work with the same people Scott does."

"You're a secret agent?" Violine said, the young girl's face alight with anticipation.

"Not like Scotty. He was higher up than me. But I do work for the same people."

"Scotty taught us things," Alain said. "Secret-agent things."

The boy pushed back from the table and rushed from the room.

"They get excited," Dubois said. "We not meet people like Scotty all the time."

Elise brought the meal to the table.

Dubois squeezed his wife's arm with affection. "She good teacher and good cook."

Alain returned with some papers, which he eagerly displayed.

"Mr. Malone has no time for that," the boy's mother said. "Sit and eat your food."

Malone smiled. "He's fine."

Alain pointed. "Can you read the messages?"

The three pieces of paper were all blank.

He shook his head. "Why don't you read them for me."

"It's easy."

The boy jumped up on his chair and held one of the blank sheets to the overhead light. Slowly, brown letters appeared on the paper.

HELLO ALAIN.

Then he knew. Lemon juice. Reacting to the heat of the bulb. "That is an old spy trick. Scotty should not have revealed that to you."

"It's a secret?" Violine asked.

"You use it, too?" Alain said as he hopped down. "Scotty said secret agents use this all the time."

"He was right. We do. All the time. But you can't tell anyone."

"Scotty was a good man," Elise said. "He spent a lot of time with the children. We were so sad when he died."

He saw that she meant it. Obviously, Scott had forged an ally in Dubois and ~~his~~ family, cementing that with the right words, said at the right time, coupled, most likely, with a liberal sprinkling of money. The Magellan Billet? Interesting Scott had used that as his cover. What kind of con had his brother-in-law been working?

He doubted these people knew.

So he kept his mouth shut and allowed them to continue to think the best.

———

MALONE ENTERED LA VILLA ST-LOUIS, THE HOTEL located outside Cap-Haïtien, on the coast, inside a stunning building with Spanish and French influences. More upscale than where he was staying, its lush grounds fenced and guarded. The auction was held in a paneled hall that could accommodate a few hundred comfortably. He estimated that fewer than seventy-five were there, many already seated and awaiting the first item. To his right and near the front sat Zachariah Simon. The other man, Rócha, was not in sight. Malone grabbed a chair to the left of the center podium, at the end of an aisle of eight seats.

A copy of the day's *International Herald Tribune* lay on the next chair. To make himself less conspicuous, he grabbed the paper and scanned the front page, noticing an article about a *Los Angeles Times* reporter whose name he knew. Tom Sagan. Caught falsifying a story from the Middle East. Interesting. After an internal investigation, the *Times* had fired Sagan and apologized for the scandal. Too bad. He'd never thought Sagan the type to lie. His eyes drifted from the newspaper, keeping a watch on what was happening.

More people drifted in.

The auction began and four items were sold, three paintings and a beautiful piece of mahogany furniture, all from the same estate being liquidated. According to the catalog the 16th-century book would be the fifth offering, and it was brought in by a white-gloved attendant, who laid it before the auctioneer.

Bids were called for. Simon wasted no time.

"Five thousand."

Malone waited to see if anyone else planned to make a bid. Seeing none, he offered his own.

"Six thousand."

The auctioneer's eyes raked the crowd and waited.

"Seven thousand" came Simon's reply.

"Eight," Malone quickly added.

"Ten."

A new voice.

From behind.

He turned to see Matt Schwartz, standing, his arm raised to identify himself.

Simon spotted the newcomer, too, then said, "Twelve."

Malone decided to see how bad the Austrian, and the Israelis, wanted the book. "Fifty thousand."

Auctioneers were usually noted for their poker faces, but he'd clearly caught this one off guard. The surprise showed, but was quickly suppressed before he asked, "Any more bids?"

"Seventy-five thousand," Schwartz said.

"One hundred thousand," Simon countered.

Apparently they both wanted the book. *Okay, let's make it really interesting.* "One hundred fifty thousand."

Silence.

Neither Schwartz nor Simon countered.

The auctioneer waited thirty seconds before asking for any further bids.

No reply.

"Sold."

———

MALONE ACCEPTED THE BOOK, NESTLED SAFELY INside a clear plastic bag, wrapped in brown paper. The $150,000 had been transferred into the auction company's account, thanks to an online account he'd accessed with the password Stephanie had provided.

She was going to kill him.

He'd just dropped a chunk of public money on a questionable purchase.

But at least he had everyone's attention.

He exited the hall and, before leaving the hotel, detoured to the bathroom. There he entered one of the stalls, carefully opened the package, and passed the plastic-encased book beneath the divider. A hand grabbed the offering, then another book appeared—a French novel bought before arriving—which Malone stuffed into the brown wrapping. He left the stall and the bathroom. Dubois would wait five minutes then do the same, heading home with their prize.

He knew it would not be long and, just as he exited the hotel and followed a lighted path toward the street, someone called out.

"You paid far too much for that."

He stopped and turned. "And you are?"

"The man you outbid. Zachariah Simon."

The older man stepped closer but offered no hand to shake. Good. He'd prefer to wring the SOB's neck.

Simon motioned to the package. "What's your interest?"

He shrugged. "I collect books."

"Why that one?"

"You already know the answer to that question."

"Yet why do I feel that you do not? Which is interesting."

"Enlighten me."

Simon pointed out beyond the palms, toward the ocean and an ever-darkening sky. "Not far from here was the first place Europeans settled in their New World."

"La Navidad."

"Ah, I see you are not wholly ignorant. Thirty-nine men left by Columbus to search for gold and make a colony. But none survived a year. Slaughtered by the Tainos for their cruelty toward the natives."

"A rare victory for the good guys."

Being a bibliophile also meant he was a reader. He'd read plenty about Columbus and the century after his discovery. Cultures that had existed for many millennia were violently extinguished—hundreds of thousands died—all in the name of religion and fueled by greed.

"Who are you?" Simon asked.

"Harold Earl Malone. But everyone calls me Cotton."

"Interesting nickname. How did you—"

"Long story." He motioned with the package. "Why did you want this?"

"What do you know of Christopher Columbus?"

A strange answer to his question. "In 1492 he sailed the ocean blue?"

Simon grimaced. "I am not particularly fond of humor. From your accent, I would say you are from the American South."

"Georgia boy. Born and raised."

"That line you quoted," Simon said. "It is from a poem written to commemorate Columbus Day, which for some reason Americans feel the need to celebrate."

"I think it's just an excuse to take a day off from work."

"That actually might be correct, but the poem is fiction. Nearly nothing in it is true. Yet it has been used for decades as a teaching tool."

"You don't sound like a Columbus fan."

"We know nothing of Christopher Columbus."

This man clearly wanted to talk, which bothered Malone. He'd expected more action. And where were the Israelis? Nearby? He hoped so. For once he was counting on them.

"His birthplace, his parents, where he was raised, educated. His early life. All of that is unknown," Simon said. "We don't even know what Columbus looks like. Every portrait that exists was painted long after he was dead by people who never saw him. If you read many books on him, as I have, you would see that every account conflicts with the others. Columbus himself only added to the mystery, as he barely spoke of himself during his lifetime and the few mentions he did make were not consistent."

"Maybe he had a reason to keep things confused."

"That he did, Herr Malone. Truly, he did. But that reason is not important to our present situation. What is relevant is the book."

He decided to stop playing games. "Why did you kill Scott Brown?"

"I suspected there was a connection. I appreciate your directness, so I will answer your question. Mr. Brown stole from me."

"And what did he steal?"

"The book you bought. I had it in my possession, then Mr. Brown decided to take it, collecting the finder's fee offered by its owner for its return."

"So you stole it first?"

"The way of the world, as I am sure you understand. I had employed Herr Brown's services as an intermediary, to secure the book, but he decided on another course."

"Not out of character."

"Indeed. But fatal this time."

"So you killed him. Or, should I say, your associate killed him."

"There are consequences to risks taken. I was aware of Herr Brown's past. I do not do business with people I do not know. But I thought the fee being paid to him for his services would be enough. Sadly, I was wrong."

"He had a wife."

"Then she should thank me. Being married to someone so inherently dishonest could not have been pleasant."

He agreed, but Ginger had loved the idiot. And this arrogant ass's indifference was, like Schwartz's earlier, pissing him off.

"I have spent the better part of my adult life studying Christopher Columbus," Simon said. "I consider myself well versed in his peculiarities—"

"And the purpose of such a seemingly worthwhile endeavor?"

He saw Simon did not appreciate the rebuke. "Again, not something that is relevant to our current dealings."

Simon stepped to the edge of the walk, near one of the low-voltage lights, and bent down. Malone watched as something was drawn in the soft sand.

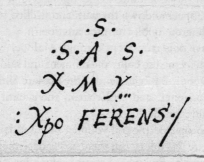

The same strange letter combination from Scott's letter to Ginger.

"This is the mark of the Admiral," Simon said. "The way Columbus would sometimes sign his name. Odd, wouldn't you say?"

To say the least.

Simon stood. "Interesting that the man would not use his given, Christian name."

He wondered why that would matter.

"Instead he sketches out these letters. To this day, no one knows what he meant by it. There are many interpretations, none of them persuasive. Some say it's a combination of Greek and Latin. Others say Hebrew. One thing we do know: He wished his heirs, after his death, to continue to use this triangular arrangement of letters as *their* signature."

"What does this have to do with anything?"

"Everything. The book you bought contains the mark of the Admiral. Open your package and I will show you."

That he could not do, since the book was long gone.

Simon stared at him. "Your trick in the bathroom fooled no one."

He wasn't going to be bluffed that easily.

Simon raised a hand and gestured. The man called Rócha appeared down the path and walked their way.

Holding the book from the auction.

A wave of alarm swept through Malone.

Simon seemed to enjoy the moment and said, "I have Yann Dubois." Rócha handed the book to Simon. "He is my prisoner, and will remain there until you do something for me."

Simon opened the old volume. "By and large these words are worthless. But there is one page that is not." He seemed to find what he was looking for. "Here."

Malone saw a smooth cut at the edge nearest the binding, where a page had been surgically removed.

"On this missing folio was the mark of the Admiral and a message from Columbus. When I first found the book I saw it, but was not afforded the opportunity to translate the page. The writing is in Old Castilian, a language that only a few today can adequately understand. Unfortunately, Herr Brown knew all that. I wondered why he returned the book. Now I know. He removed the most important page, pocketed the reward money from the owner, then wanted to sell the page back to me."

"But you don't buy from people who steal from you."

"Sends the wrong message. Don't you agree?"

Malone gestured at Rócha. "So your lapdog killed Scott."

"As he will Yann Dubois if you do not bring me that page."

"What if I don't have it?"

"I am betting you do. I suspected that Brown was not working alone. Your appearance here seems to confirm that."

"If that is true, why would I buy the book?"

"I don't know. But I am sure that you and Herr Brown are connected. Bring me that page."

Interesting, this man who thought himself so careful made mistakes, too. But things were happening too fast for the right prep work. He was improvising, snatching Dubois the fastest way to generate a reaction.

"Tomorrow, Herr Malone. Bring me the page and Dubois will be unharmed. I have no argument with him. But, if not, then he will never be seen again."

He thought of Elise and the two children. No way he could allow that to happen, so he asked, "Where and when?"

"I assume you want a public place. One with limited access. Preferably one way in and out."

"I see you've done this before."

Simon smiled. "More of that delightful southern America wit."

"It's a gift."

Simon pointed south. "The Citadelle Laferrière."

He knew the spot, had seen it from the air earlier before his flight landed. The fortress sat atop a mountain, built by Henri Christophe two hundred years ago.

"Ten A.M.," Simon said. "That should give you plenty of time."

No point arguing. He had no choice.

"*Bitte*, Herr Malone," Simon said.

The two men started to walk off.

"Oh," Simon said. "I nearly forgot."

Something was tossed his way, which he caught.

Keys.

"To Herr Dubois' vehicle. I assume you will need it to make your way around. He, of course, will not be using it."

Simon and Rócha left.

Now he had a big problem.

————

MALONE STEPPED FROM THE CAR. HIS WATCH READ
8:30 P.M. He'd managed to find Yann Dubois' house,
recalling the route from earlier. The door to the shanty
opened and Elise appeared, surely expecting her husband.

Instead all she saw was the stranger who'd shared
their dinner.

He stepped to the lighted doorway.

She spotted the concern on his face.

Her eyes watered, but no tears came. "Yann is in
trouble?"

He nodded. "The same men who killed Scotty have
him."

"And what do you plan to do about it?"

Interesting that she made no mention of police or
anyone in authority. Only what *he* planned to do.
He assumed people here had long ago abandoned
any trust in government.

"I'll get him back."

"How can you promise such a thing?"

He couldn't, but she did not need to hear that.

"You are the real secret agent, aren't you?"

He nodded.

"Scotty was a joyful man. Much like a child. He
showed the children many tricks, winning their favor.
But he was not what he wanted us to believe."

"And you said nothing?"

"Why? He was harmless. In him, I sensed only op-
portunism. In you, I see resolve. You may actually be
able to get my Yann back."

This was an intuitive woman.

"I need to stay here tonight."

She sensed his reason, and he saw the realization in her eyes. "Will they come here? After us?"

Matt Schwartz's gun was nestled beneath his shirt.

"I doubt it. But to be sure, I'd like to stay."

MALONE STARED UP AT THE CITADELLE LAFERRIÈRE. The night had passed uneventfully and he'd managed a few hours of light rest, remaining alert. He'd driven Dubois' car fifteen miles south of town, into the mountains, to Bonnet de l'Évêque—the Bishop's Miter—which rose 3,000 feet into a clear morning sky. A twisting road led to a parking lot just below the impressive fortress.

A cobblestoned track wound from the lot upward and could be either walked or ridden on horseback. He was thirty minutes early for the 10:00 rendezvous. No need to come any sooner, since he assumed that was precisely what Simon had done. Instead, he was counting on something else as his fail-safe.

He stopped and studied a placard that told him about the locale, long designated a UNESCO World Heritage Site. Walls 130 feet high, 20 feet thick. *Built to outlast the ages.* No foundation, instead the gray grim stones rested only on rock, the heights held together by a mortar of limestone, molasses, and cow's blood. Two and a half acres of enclosed space, once home to several thousand soldiers and enough food and water to sustain five thousand people for a year. Henri Christophe intended the fortress to be his last redoubt. If the French returned and invaded the north coast, he and his people would have burned Cap-

Haïtien and the surrounding land, then retreated to the mountains and used the few passes as choke points, surviving at any cost, the idea to never again be slaves. Of course the French never returned, but the *citadelle* became a symbol of their will to fight for freedom, and it remained Haiti's most revered monument. Unfortunately, that pride was marred by the fact that Christophe used 20,000 slave laborers to build it, many of whom died in the process.

He began his walk upward to the entrance.

He knew what had happened here in March 1811.

Faced with a revolt, come to extinguish Haiti's first monarchy, Christophe, instead of fighting, killed himself inside the Sans-Souci Palace with a silver bullet fired into his heart. His wife and children dragged the body up the mountain to the *citadelle*, where it was flung into a vat of quicklime, depriving the mob of its prize.

His climb lasted about twenty minutes.

Sheer cliffs protected on three sides, the only entrance subject to unimpeded cannon fire from above. He stepped through the gates, still on their hinges, and wondered if the legend that Christophe, to test the mettle of his men, marched a company over the tower's parapet was true.

And the other tale.

How the king had buried gold somewhere within the walls.

The ramps and steps loomed dim and damp. He exited the cool interior into a sunny courtyard. Most of the building roofs were gone, save a few that were red-tiled. Amazing that a man who could not read or write, who'd worked as a dishwasher and waiter, could create something so impressive.

Settled in slavery, liberated in agony.

That was Haiti.

The unimpeded view for miles was of green slopes and rolling mountains. Terraces defined the fortress, creating several levels from which an attack could be repelled. Cannon were everywhere, some still on their carriages, most strewn about. Nearly four hundred of them, that was what the placard below had said. And a million cannonballs, stacked in pyramids, still awaited use. He spotted the mound in the center—solidified lime—where Christophe's body had been dumped, and where it remained.

Then he saw Simon.

To the right of the mound.

Maybe another fifty people milled about, admiring the grandeur left to crumble. Schwartz's gun rested in Malone's back pocket, shielded by his shirttail. The morning was warm and humid, his brow damp with sweat. He'd never been much of a gambler for money, not liking the house odds, but it seemed every day as a Magellan Billet agent was a gamble. Of late, he'd found himself tiring of the risks. Like now. Yann Dubois' life depended on the bluff he was about to make, and the ante he hoped would come.

He stepped over to Simon and said, "I have it."

"Show me."

"Get real. If you want it, show me Dubois."

A tour group appeared from within one of the buildings, the guide spouting something in English about how people said Henri Christophe would magically fly from the Sans-Souci Palace to the *citadelle* and his spirit was still seen roaming at night, looking for his soldiers. About ten formed the group, and they ambled closer to the lime pit. Simon seemed to resent the intrusion and drifted away. He followed, keeping an eye on what surrounded him.

"Herr Malone," Simon said. "Do not take me for a fool. Herr Brown made that mistake. I would hope you learned from his error."

"I have the page and, you're right, the mark of the Admiral is there. I recognized it last night when you drew it. I don't give a damn about that. I just want Dubois and the $600,000 in the Cayman Islands."

Simon's face lit with recognition. "Did Herr Brown cheat you?"

One of the advantages of an eidetic memory was the ability to recall exact details. Malone had been born with the gift, which had come in handy when he was a lawyer—and came in even handier in his current line of work.

"Account number 569328-78-9432. Bank of the Cayman Islands. I have a definite interest in that money."

He'd thought about it last night and concluded that using what he'd learned from Simon's own background check might work.

And it apparently had.

"I am aware of those funds," Simon said, "and I have no claim to them. They are yours. I just want that missing page."

"Then you're wasting time."

Simon seemed to know what was expected of him and pointed.

Malone turned to see Dubois standing a hundred feet away, across the courtyard, the man called Rócha beside him. Though he saw no gun, he knew Rócha was armed.

Okay, nearly all of the players were here.

He started toward Dubois.

"First, the page," Simon called out.

He turned back. "After I make sure he's okay."

He held his ground, making clear that the point was non-negotiable. Simon hesitated, then nodded his consent.

He turned and kept walking.

If he'd read this right, Zachariah Simon was not a man prone to public displays. That was why he had Rócha. Not that Simon wasn't a danger—it was only that the most direct threat lay in front of him, not behind.

His hand slipped into his back pocket and found the gun.

He leveled the weapon and fired at Rócha.

But his target had leaped to the left.

Dubois fled to the right. Hopefully, he'd get the hell out of here.

Malone huddled behind the limestone mound, taking refuge with Henri Christophe.

He turned back.

Simon had not moved.

People were scattering.

A few screaming.

A gunshot cracked and a bullet ricocheted off the stone a foot away from his face.

Rócha retaliating.

He'd seen no guards when he entered, but he assumed a place like this had to employ security. Gunshots and mayhem would draw attention.

So he needed to act fast.

He decided to draw Simon in. The Austrian continued to stand his ground, confident that Malone would not shoot him and that Rócha had the situation under control.

He whirled the gun, but before he could fire the earth around Simon erupted in explosive puffs. Three. Four. Five. Which finally caused a reaction as

Simon realized someone other than Malone had him in their sights.

The shots came without a retort, which meant a sound-suppressed weapon was on the ramparts above them.

Simon fled to the safety of a nearby building.

Malone smiled.

The Israelis.

Finally.

He'd assumed they were watching. No contact had come last night, but that had not meant they were gone. He knew they would not risk exposure, using him to achieve whatever they were after. Since they were here he assumed they knew Simon possessed the book. But they would also know that a page was missing, and they would have to wonder.

Did the Americans have it?

His gaze raked the deserted courtyard, but he saw neither Rócha nor Simon. Above him all was quiet, too. He needed to leave. But where was Dubois?

He dropped the arm with the gun to his side and shielded the weapon with his thigh as he hustled out of the sunlight, back into the fortress. He heard people chattering in different languages, their voices raised and excited, all of them surely headed for the exit.

He made his way there and saw people racing down the cobbled path toward the parking lot. A quick glance behind and he saw no one else. So he followed, keeping a watch on his back until he rounded the first bend. High above the gate, on the parapet, he caught sight of Matt Schwartz.

A wave from the Israeli said, *You're welcome*.

He returned the gesture.

He knew the drill. The Israelis had flushed Simon

out, but they would not risk anything more. Instead, they'd watch from their perch as everyone left. The lack of security or any law enforcement told him something else—the Haitian government had cooperated.

Diplomacy.

Ain't it grand?

He found the parking lot and still saw nothing of Simon or Rócha. He had to go back and find Dubois. But in the distance, still on the parapet high above the *citadelle*, Schwartz was gesturing for him to leave.

Why?

Then it occurred to him.

He walked over, opened the driver's door, and slipped behind the wheel of the car.

Dubois' face appeared in the rearview mirror, up from his hiding place.

"I see my car and wait for you."

"You okay?"

His friend nodded. "I good. Get going."

He agreed.

———

MALONE DROVE STRAIGHT TO WHERE ELISE DUBOIS taught school to let her know everything was okay. She was glad to see her husband unharmed and thanked Malone with a hug and kiss.

"I knew you would do it."

He appreciated her confidence, since he hadn't been so sure. The problem now was the Israelis, as they would want payback. But just as with Simon, he had no missing page to offer them. He decided to leave Haiti and report back to Pam, Ginger, and Stephanie Nelle. At least he knew how and why Scott had died.

He also had the account number for the $600,000 on deposit in the Cayman Islands, which the Magellan Billet could easily obtain. Ginger deserved that money, and he'd make sure she received it.

They left the school and stopped by the Hotel Creole, where Malone learned that Simon had checked out earlier. Most likely, the Austrian was now headed to the airport, unsure of what had happened at the *citadelle* but glad to be away. He grabbed his bag from the room on the third floor and left, riding with Dubois to the docks and his boat. Along the way, he called and secured a seat on a flight out of Cap-Haïtien to Miami that left in six hours. From there he'd shuttle home to Atlanta.

"Sorry about getting you into all that danger," he told Dubois.

"I get myself into it. I want to help you."

"Fortunately, it's all over, and I appreciate what you did."

He sat on the aft deck, beneath a canvas canopy, out of the sun. Most of the other boats were gone, out earning a day's wage. He hadn't really noticed much about the boat on the first trip, except for its struggling engine.

"You need a mechanic," he said to Dubois.

"That be me. It makes a lot of noise and smoke, but works. Always has. Scotty help with that. He give me money for parts."

And he would, too, when Dubois dropped him at the airport.

The least he could do.

"He buy me GPS."

"Scott did?"

Dubois nodded. "He say we need it. He use it some, then leave it with me."

He stepped into the forward cabin. Above the wheel, mounted to the old timbers, was a new GPS, wires snaking a path to a power source.

He wanted to know. "What did Scott do with it?"

"That's how he found *Santa María.*"

"But you don't know if that wreck is Columbus' flagship."

And nobody ever would. Most likely, Scott intended to use his find to work another con on somebody.

"He mark the site with GPS numbers. That's how I know where it is. He tell me that was secret-agent stuff. But I never believe he is an agent. Just a man who treat me good."

His mind swirled. Everything fit into place, except one thing. The paper Scott sent to Ginger. That had been bothering him for the past two days. Why do it? And why would Simon think it important enough to fly to Atlanta for a look?

Then it hit him.

How simple.

So simple that it had almost eluded him.

He stepped to the aft deck and found the brown envelope in his bag. He removed the page with the Admiral's mark written across its face and brought it back inside the forward cabin. He switched on the overhead bulb and held the sheet close as the filament heated.

Slowly, brown numbers materialized.

Dubois watched carefully and realized. "He use lemon juice."

Malone smiled. "That he did. Actually, not a bad way to send a message, if you don't know it's there."

"I know those," Dubois said. "They be for the wreck site."

"Fire up the engine. I want to go back down."

MALONE KICKED HIS FINS AND SWAM TOWARD THE massive hulk of rock with the crack and crevice. He'd come down alone, Dubois staying up top with Schwartz's gun, keeping a lookout. No other boats had been around, and he wanted to keep it that way. The current today was weaker, but the same shark remained on patrol fifty yards away. The GPS numbers Scott had secretly sent to Ginger had led them straight back here.

He approached the opening and eased himself inside.

He examined the timbers in the sand and could see that they'd been hewn, man-made, now petrified by centuries in the water. A few other artifacts lay scattered. What looked like a cup, some nails, belt buckles. This was clearly a shipwreck. Whether it belonged to Christopher Columbus remained to be seen.

He fanned the sand and stirred up the bottom, revealing what lay a few inches beneath. The storm rose, then settled quickly, the warm water retaining its crystal clarity. A niche caught his eye, but he knew better than to stick his hand there. Some eel might decide a few fingers would make a great lunch.

Another niche to his right seemed more inviting.

Shallow, no more than a foot or so deep, the entire interior visible.

He fanned its sand.

And saw something.

Glass.

A little more stirring revealed more glass.

He reached down and freed the object.

A Coke bottle, the top stuffed with a cork and sealed with wax. Inside was a rolled piece of dirt-brown paper, similar in size and color to the other pages of the book he'd bought at the auction. A wax-sealed plastic bag provided an additional measure of protection.

He'd found the hiding place.

Risky as hell to leave it underwater, but Scott had never been noted for caution.

———

MALONE STEPPED FROM THE CAR AT CAP-HAÏTIEN'S main airport terminal. Dubois had driven him from the docks, and they'd made it here in plenty of time for his flight.

He shook his friend's hand and thanked him again.

"No problem, mon. I glad you come. We solve everything."

Not quite everything, but enough.

He handed Dubois $500. "Fix that engine, okay?"

"Ah, mon. This be too much. Way too much."

"It's all I have or I'd give you more."

They said their goodbyes and he entered the terminal, checking in for his flight.

Matt Schwartz waited for him just before the security checkpoint.

"I didn't think you'd let me leave without saying goodbye," he told the Israeli.

"Did you find the page?"

He nodded.

"I thought you might. We wondered why you went back out on the boat."

"What happened to Simon?"

"Went straight to the airport and is long gone."

"Probably thinking that I had help in the *citadelle*."

"That was the idea. Can I have the page?"

"I assume you're not going to let me leave with it?"

"Payment for the favor I did you with Dubois."

He reached into his back pocket and removed the curled page, still in its plastic bag. He'd broken the bottle to free it. The sheet was filled with nineteen lines of writing in faded black ink, along with the mark of the Admiral, just as Simon had described.

"Can we at least be provided with a copy?" he asked.

"I don't suppose you would take my word that none of this is important to anything related to America."

"It's not my nature."

"Then that copy you made on the way here should alleviate all of your government's fears."

He assumed Schwartz knew they'd stopped at the hotel on the way to the airport.

He handed the page over and said, "Any idea what this is? I speak several languages, but I can't read it. Simon said it was Old Castilian."

The Israeli shrugged. "Our people will translate it, as I'm sure will yours."

"Simon killed a man for it."

"I know. Which makes us all wonder. But people higher up than me will deal with this now."

He understood. "Being at the bottom of the pile does come with disadvantages."

Schwartz smiled. "I like you, Malone. Maybe we'll see each other again."

"Maybe so."

The Israeli gestured with the bag. "Something tells me we've not seen, or heard, the last of Zachariah Simon."

He agreed.

"All we can hope," Schwartz said, "is that next time he's someone else's problem."

"You got that right."

And he headed for home.

Read on for an excerpt from

The King's Deception
by
Steve Berry

Published by Ballantine Books

COTTON MALONE STEPPED UP TO THE CUSTOMS
window at Heathrow Airport and presented two
passports—his own and his son, Gary's. Positioned
between himself and the glass-enclosed counter,
however, stood a problem.

Fifteen-year-old Ian Dunne.

"This one doesn't have a passport," he told the attendant, then explained who he was and what he was
doing. A brief call to somebody led to verbal approval
for Ian to re-enter the country, which didn't surprise
Malone. He assumed that since the Central Intelligence Agency wanted the boy here, they'd make the
necessary arrangements with the British.

He was tired from the long flight, though he'd
caught a few hours of sleep. His knee still hurt from
the kick Ian had delivered in Atlanta, before trying to
flee from that airport. Luckily, his own fifteen-year-
old, Gary, had been quick to tackle the little Scot before he escaped the concourse.

Favors for friends.

Always a problem.

This one for his former boss Stephanie Nelle at the
Magellan Billet.

"You're headed that way," Stephanie said, her voice
tinny but still commanding over the phone.

"And how does anyone know that?"

"It's the CIA, Cotton. Langley called me directly. Somehow, they were aware that you're in Georgia. All they want is for you to escort the boy back to London and hand him over to the Metropolitan Police. Then you and Gary can head to Copenhagen. In return, they've purchased first-class tickets all the way home to Denmark."

Not bad. His own tickets were coach.

"Seems like a simple request," she said.

Four days ago he'd flown to Georgia for two reasons. The State Bar of Georgia required twelve hours of continuing legal education from all of its licensed lawyers. Though he'd retired from the Navy and the Magellan Billet, he still kept his law license active, which meant he had to satisfy the annual education mandate. Last year he'd attended a sanctioned event in Brussels, a three-day meeting on multinational property rights. This year he'd chosen a seminar in Atlanta on international law. Not the most exciting way to spend two days, but he'd worked too hard for that degree to simply allow it to lapse.

The second reason was personal.

Gary had asked to spend the Thanksgiving holiday with him. School was out for the week and his ex-wife, Pam, thought an overseas trip a good idea. He'd wondered why she was so reticent, and found out last week when Pam had called his bookshop in Copenhagen.

"Gary's angry," she said. *"He's asking a lot of questions."*

"Ones you don't want to answer?"

"Ones I'm going to have a tough time answering."

Which was an understatement. Six months ago she'd revealed a harsh truth during another call from Atlanta to Denmark. Gary was not his natural son. Instead, Gary was the product of an affair some sixteen years past. For Malone, the news had been both crushing and disturbing. He could only imagine what it had been for Gary.

"Neither one of us were saints back then, Cotton."

She liked to remind him of that—as if somehow he'd forgotten that their marriage ultimately ended because of mutual lapses. He'd been foolish enough to think all of those demons had been dealt with last year during the divorce.

Now she'd sprung something new on him.

"Anything else you've not told me?"

"Gary wants to know about his birth father."

"So would I."

She'd told him nothing about the man, and refused his requests for information.

"He has no involvement here," she said. "He's a total stranger to all of us. Just like the women you were with have nothing to do with this, either. I don't want to open that door. Ever."

"Why did you tell Gary about this? We agreed to do that together, when the time was right."

That decision had been made back in October, when Pam was in Copenhagen with Gary.

"I know. I know. My mistake."

But not out of character. She liked to be in control. Of everything. Only she wasn't in control here. Nobody was, actually.

"He hates me," she said. "I see it in his eyes."

"You turned the boy's life upside down."

"He told me today that he might want to live with you."

He had to say, "You know I would never take advantage of this."

"I know that. This is my fault. Not yours. He's so angry. Maybe a week with you would help ease some of that."

He'd come to realize that he didn't love Gary one drop less because he carried no Malone genes. But he'd be lying to himself if he said he wasn't bothered by the fact. Six months had passed and the truth still hurt. Why? He wasn't sure. He'd not been faithful to Pam while in the Navy. He was young and stupid and got caught. She supposedly forgave him, but now he knew that she'd had an affair of her own. Would she have strayed if he hadn't?

He doubted it. Not her nature.

So he wasn't blameless for the current mess.

He and Pam had been divorced for more than a year, but only back in October had they made their peace. Time and circumstances had a way of making that happen.

Now this.

One boy in his charge was angry and confused.

The other seemed to be a delinquent.

"Ian Dunne was born in Scotland," Stephanie said. *"Father is unknown. Mother abandoned him early. He was sent to London to live with an aunt, who wasn't much of a parent. He drifted in and out of her home, finally running away. He has an extensive arrest record—petty theft, trespassing, loitering, that kind of thing."*

"And why is the CIA involved?"

"One of their people was shoved, or jumped, into the path of an oncoming underground train about a month ago. Dunne was there, in Oxford Circus. Witnesses say he might even have stolen something from the dead man."

"Is he a suspect?"

"Just a person of interest they want to talk to."

Not good, but also not his concern. In a few minutes his favor for Stephanie Nelle would be over, then he and Gary would catch their connecting flight to

Copenhagen and enjoy the week, depending, of course, on how many uncomfortable questions his son might want answered. The problem was the Denmark flight departed not from Heathrow, but from Gatwick, London's other major airport, an hour's ride east. Their departure was several hours away, so it wasn't a problem. He would just need to convert some dollars to pounds and hire a taxi.

They left Customs and claimed their luggage.

Both he and Gary had packed light.

"The police going to take me?" Ian asked.

"That's what I'm told."

Gary appeared bothered. "What will happen to him?"

Malone shrugged. "Hard to say."

And it was. Especially with the CIA involved.

He shouldered his bag and led both boys out of the baggage area.

"Can I have my things?" Ian asked.

When Ian had been turned over to him in Atlanta, he'd been given a plastic bag that contained a Swiss Army knife with all the assorted attachments, a pewter necklace with a religious medal attached, a pocket mace container, some silver shears, and two paperback books with their covers missing. *Ivanhoe* and *Le Morte d'Arthur*. Their brown edges were water stained, the bindings veined with thick white creases. Both were thirty-plus-year-old printings. Stamped on the title page was ANY OLD BOOKS, with an address in Piccadilly Circus, London. Malone employed a similar branding of inventory, his simply announcing COTTON MALONE, BOOKSELLER, HØJBRO PLADS, COPENHAGEN. The items in the plastic bag all belonged to Ian. They'd been seized by Customs when they took him into custody at Miami International, after he tried to enter the country illegally.

"That's up to the police," he said. "My orders are to hand you and the bag over to them."

He'd stuffed the bundle inside his travel bag, where it would stay until the police assumed custody. He half expected Ian to bolt, so he remained on guard. Ahead he spied two men, both in dark suits walking their way. The one on the right, short and stocky with auburn hair, introduced himself as Inspector Norse.

He extended a hand, which Malone shook.

"This is Inspector Devene. We're with the Met. We were told you'd be accompanying the boy. We're here to give you a lift to Gatwick and take charge of Master Dunne."

"I appreciate the ride. Wasn't looking forward to an expensive taxi."

"Least we can do. Our car is just outside. One of the privileges of being the police—we can park where we want."

The man threw Malone a grin.

They started for the exit.

Malone noticed Inspector Devene take up a position behind Ian. Smart move, he thought.

"You responsible for getting him into the country with no passport?"

Norse nodded. "We are, along with some others working with us. I think you know about them."

That he did.

They stepped out of the terminal into brisk morning air. A bank of thick clouds tinted the sky a depressing shade of pewter. A blue Mercedes sedan sat by the curb. Norse opened the rear door and motioned for Gary to climb in first, then Ian and Malone.

The inspector stood outside until they were all in, then closed the door. Norse rode in the front passenger's seat, while Devene drove. They sped out of Heathrow and found the M4 motorway. Malone knew the route, London being a familiar locale. Years ago he'd spent a lot of time in England on assignments. He'd also been detached here for a year by the navy. Traffic progressively thickened as they made their way east toward the city.

"Would it be all right if we made one stop before we head for Gatwick?" Norse asked him.

"No problem. We have time before the plane leaves. The least we can do for a free ride."

Malone watched Ian as the boy gazed out the window. He couldn't help but wonder what would happen to him. Stephanie's assessment had not been a good one. A street kid, no family, completely on his own. Whereas Gary was dark-haired with a swarthy complexion, Ian was blond, fair-skinned. He seemed like a good kid dealt a bad hand. But at least he was young, and youth offered chances, and chances led to possibilities. Such a contrast to Gary, who lived a more conventional, secure life. The thought of Gary on the streets, loose, with no one, tore at his heart.

Warm air blasted the car's interior and the engine droned as they chugged through traffic.

Malone's eyes surrendered to jet lag.

When he woke, he glanced at his watch and realized he'd been out about fifteen minutes. He willed himself to alertness. Gary and Ian were still sitting quietly. The sky had darkened. A storm was approaching the city. He studied the car's interior, noticing for the first time that there was no radio or communications equipment. Also, the carpets were immaculate, the upholstery in pristine condition. Certainly not like any police car he'd ever ridden in.

He then examined Norse.

The man's brown hair was cut below the ears. Not shaggy, but thick. He was clean-shaven and a bit overweight. He was dressed appropriately, suit and tie, but it was the left earlobe that drew his attention. Pierced. No earring was present, but the puncture was clear.

"I was wondering, Inspector. Might I see your identification? I should have asked at the airport."

Norse did not answer him. The question aroused Ian's attention, who studied Malone with a curious look.

"Did you hear me, Norse? I'd like to see your identification."

"Just enjoy the ride, Malone."

He didn't like the curt tone so he reached for the front seat and pulled himself forward, intending to make his point clearer.

The barrel of a gun came around the head rest and greeted him.

"This enough identification?" Norse asked.

"Actually, I was hoping for a picture ID." He motioned to the weapon. "When did the Metropolitan Police start issuing Glocks?"

No reply.

"Who are you?"

The gun waved at Ian. "His keeper."

Ian reached across Gary and wrenched the chrome handle up and down, but the door would not open.

"Great things, child locks," said Norse. "Keeps the wee ones from slipping away."

Malone said, "Son, you want to tell me what's going on?"

Ian said nothing.

"These men have apparently gone to a lot of trouble to make your acquaintance."

"Sit back, Malone," Norse said. "This is none of your concern."

He reclined in the seat. "On that we agree."

Except his own son was in the car, too.

Norse kept his head turned back toward them, his gaze and the gun glued on Malone.

The car continued through morning congestion.

He absorbed what was whirling past outside, recalling what he could about the geography of north London. He realized the bridge they'd just crossed was for Regent's Canal, a corridor-like waterway that wound a snaking path through the city, eventually spilling into the Thames. Stately trees lined the four-laned promenade. Traffic was heavy, but not congested. He spotted the famous Lord's cricket ground. He knew that the fictional Baker Street of Sherlock Holmes lay a few blocks over. Little Venice wasn't far away.

They crossed the canal again and he glanced down at the brightly painted house boats along the waterway. Longboats dotted the canal, no more than three meters high, designed to fit under the tight bridges that spanned the canal. Rows and rows of Georgian houses and flats lined the street, fronted with tall trees less their leaves.

Devene turned the Mercedes off the boulevard onto a side lane. More houses rolled past on either side. The scene was not unlike Atlanta, where his own house had once sat. Three more turns and they entered a courtyard enclosed on three sides by high hedges. The Mercedes stopped outside a mews constructed of pastel-colored stones.

Norse exited. Devene also climbed out.

Both rear doors were released from the outside.

"Get out," Norse said.

Malone stood on cobblestones outlined by emerald lichens. Gary and Ian emerged on the other side.

Ian tried to bolt.

Norse slammed the boy hard into the car.

"Don't," Malone called out. "Do as he says. You too, Gary."

Norse shoved the gun into Ian's neck. "Stay still." The man's body pinned Ian to the car. "Where's the flash drive?"

"What drive?" Malone asked.

"Shut him up," Norse called out.

Devene jammed a fist into Malone's gut.

"Dad," Gary called out.

He doubled over and tried to regain his breath, motioning to Gary that he was okay.

"The flash drive," Norse said again. "Where is it?"

Malone rose, arms hugging his stomach. Devene drew back to swing again, but Malone jammed his knee into the man's groin, then smacked Devene's jaw with his right fist.

He was retired and jet-lagged, but he wasn't helpless.

He whirled in time to see Norse aim the gun his way. The retort from a single shot came the instant after Malone lunged for the pavement, the bullet finding the hedges behind him. He stared up into the Mercedes' passenger compartment and saw Norse through the partially open doors. He sprang to his feet, pivoted off the hood, and rammed his legs through the car's interior into the far-side door.

The panel flew out and smashed into Norse, sending the phony inspector reeling backward into the mews.

He propelled himself through the open door.

Ian was running from the courtyard, toward the street.

His gaze met Gary's.

"Go with him," he called out. "Get out of here."

He was tackled from behind.

His forehead slapped wet stone and pain shuddered

through him. He'd thought Devene was out of commission. A mistake. An arm wrapped around his throat and he tried to release the stranglehold grip. His prone position gave him little room to maneuver, and Devene was hinging his spine at an unnatural angle.

The buildings around him winked in and out.

Blood trickled down his forehead and into his eye.

The last thing he saw before blackness enveloped him was Ian and Gary, disappearing around a corner.